"A riveting, honest, and incisive novel about love, lust, and the complications of youth."

—Daisy Alpert Florin, author of *My Last Innocent Year*

"A compelling story about chasing true happiness while trying to do no harm. I found myself reading this novel late into the night, thinking about the characters as if they were my own friends."

—Adrienne Celt, author of *End of the World House*

JUST WANT YOU HERE

A NOVEL

JUST WANT YOU HERE

MEREDITH TURITS

Little
a

Published by Little A, New York

www.apub.com

Amazon, the Amazon logo, and Little A are trademarks of Amazon.com, Inc., or its affiliates.

ISBN-13: 9781662523991 (hardcover)
ISBN-13: 9781662524004 (paperback)
ISBN-13: 9781662524011 (digital)

Cover design by Emily Mahon
Cover image: © Uwe Krejci, © flas100, © Boris Zhitkov / Getty

Printed in the United States of America

First edition

For my parents, for everything, forever

MORGAN

ARI

When Morgan closes the bedroom door behind him, Ari knows it's over. It's been over for a while, he's argued. And maybe he is right.

Still, it doesn't soften the blow. Ari leans forward on the tattered green couch, drops her head between her knees. Her hair falls in front of her eyes like a blackout curtain. The blood rushing to her brain until the pressure makes her sick. She would ask herself how they got to this place, but there's no point. They've arrived—and, soon, Morgan will depart without her. It's like nothing that happened before matters. It's like a decade has gone up in smoke.

We need to figure out who we are on our own. You have to see it, too, he'd said, barely able to make eye contact with her. *No,* Ari had replied, she did not. He'd seemed to be parroting a self-help book, the kind he would never read. She had simply stared at him, mouth agape—she couldn't believe he had the balls to even sit her at the kitchen table, float the idea. That's never been Morgan. He's constantly needed her to push him down the road, give him the map in the first place. *We can leave New York. I can give you time or space. We can go to couples' therapy. Anything,* she'd bargained. He'd shaken his head. *Ari, I love you. But it all just feels so stuck.*

After the longest ten minutes, Morgan pads gently out of the bedroom, easing open the moaning door. Despite everything, he's checking on her. His short, black-coffee hair is sticking up in the back, mussed like he's just woken up. He looks shattered, too.

"Sorry," he says as he returns to her, a gruffness that doesn't fit him. It's clear he doesn't know what he's apologizing for. Ruining her life, getting on with his? "I just . . ."

He joins her on the couch, but he can't possibly sit farther away.

"Ari," he says. He palms his knees, spreads his broad shoulders until she hears his back crack. "Please."

Her throat closes as she swallows dry. What can she do but stare at the ground? She can't face him, and, looking around the apartment, a rain-drenched Saturday evening in early May, she sees only the life they've shared for ten years. There are no *his things* and *her things*. This couch they pooled meager savings to buy off Craigslist, the pictures they chose to frame of the places they visited together. The forks, the sheets, the dish detergent. Everything they have is just one thing. They are just one thing.

Except now, Morgan sees himself in a life outside the one he's so precisely, joyfully built with Ari—living on his own, keeping the minutiae of his days to himself, anxiously waiting outside a fussy cocktail bar for a first date, standing at the altar with a woman whose face he hasn't seen yet. Betting there's something out there for him that'll make this all worth it, a risk Ari can't possibly fathom. The idea that he spent months turning over these rich, alternative lives while he was in bed beside her makes her feel like she has to spit blood.

"Ari," Morgan says again.

For as much as she's still pleading with him to change his mind, she's also aware they have stagnated. Gotten *stuck*. When he said it felt like they'd *lost steam* and he was *not sure how to find it again*, she'd hated to hear it, mostly because she knew it was true. It's why she's here, crying on a couch, twisting an engagement ring around her finger without a wedding band beside it.

"Morgan," she says. Carefully. She feels like she has only a few times left to say his name, has to ration them.

"I don't know what to say," he says.

"Then don't say anything."

"That's exactly the problem."

He puts on a bright-red windbreaker and threadbare Hartford Whalers hat, tells Ari he'll pick up Thai food, as if nothing has changed.

∼

With empty take-out containers littering the particleboard coffee table, they spend three silent hours watching a TV series. Too many episodes remain for them to finish it together now. At eleven thirty, Morgan gets up to put his beer cans in the sink. He sighs, looks back at Ari with a chilling combination of affection and death. She never imagined he could make a face she'd never seen. Next, Morgan braces himself on the counter, slowly breathes out. The muscles beneath his white undershirt shift. How well Ari knows his form: the way it's changed, grown stronger, become the body of an adult. She can still see the way he looked years ago—a man with a lither body running toward the high school field with a lacrosse stick in his hand. A boy, really. She, too, was lighter, longer, leaner. A girl.

Still in front of the television, Ari fixates on the screen saver. The photo slideshow tells the story of their life together: under the weeping willows in Savannah, where Morgan's mom sent them to celebrate their engagement; scorching days at Jones Beach over the years, since they couldn't afford to go anywhere for real; even their grainy senior-prom photo, in all its low-resolution glory. Who has that kind of history? Who is willing to let it go?

"I'll take the couch," Morgan says, returning to Ari. His wide hazel eyes look exhausted, face pale. He apologizes he has nowhere else to stay for now.

She shakes her head. "I will." She can't remember the last time they slept in separate beds.

Through the door to the small bathroom, Ari can hear Morgan pee, run his electric toothbrush, fumble in the medicine cabinet for his contact-lens solution. Mundanity that doesn't have shape or meaning to anyone but her: sounds of a life in progress. Ari wonders what she'll miss most. Morgan's companionship, or the way his heartbeat sounds when her head rests against his chest? Maybe these whispers of little habits.

Morgan leaves the bedroom door cracked, a sliver of light from his bedside lamp slipping through. The apartment is quieter than New York has ever been. Nothing's ever unsettled her this way. She wants the sounds that keep her up at night—the blare of car horns, shrill wail of ambulances. Morgan's gentle wheeze in her ear.

"You can sleep in here," he calls. "It's not like we hate each other."

Crawling into bed beside him is the only thing Ari wants. She says nothing, turns over and buries her head in the cushions, waits until he switches off his light, then silently cries so hard she's not sure she'll ever breathe again.

~

Morgan is usually the first one up, yet Ari wakes early and sits at the small table that juts awkwardly into the middle of their one-bedroom apartment. She's poured herself a bowl of Morgan's cereal. There's a swirl of sugar skimming the top of the milk, a trail like a comet. For as long as she's known him, Morgan has always eaten this awful children's cereal. In high school, when she'd go over to his house, he'd shovel it into his mouth by the handful, straight from the box. The crinkle of the bag reminds her of his childhood basement, with the cloud-comfort-able, dog-clawed leather couch; the low ceiling with the wooden beams, which Morgan had to duck starting their junior year; the television, always on while they were doing their homework or talking or covertly having sex, which started senior year. Sugared flakes or rainbow loops all over the floor, crunching beneath Ari's heels when she'd get up to reluctantly walk the ten minutes back to her place, leaving a home to arrive at a house.

Sunday-morning light snakes into the kitchen. Everything about the space already feels different. She pictures the books Morgan will take from their shelf near the front door, the empty spaces like pockmarks; that photograph he snapped from the Weeks Bridge in Boston pulled from the wall behind the couch, the discolored space behind it reminding her that he's gone.

As Ari struggles to keep her eyes open, Morgan lowers himself into the seat across from her, dropping his own bowl to the table, reaching for the milk and cereal.

"Morning," he says, bowing his head. The chocolate puffs tinkle as they hit the bowl. "I think I probably have to go to the library today."

He says it like his accountability matters anymore. He keeps talking as if last night hasn't happened: goes on about his last final on Tuesday before he wraps his MBA; the baseball game he wants to watch later, checking with Ari if he can monopolize the TV at seven. He sucks the milk from the spoon. Crosses his legs, tenses and releases his calf muscles in a nervous figure four.

"You should keep the apartment," he says.

"I can't afford it."

At twenty-eight years old, she makes next to nothing. Tedious copywriting on pharmaceutical accounts for an ad agency, sixty-four thousand dollars a year, which hardly goes far in New York. She'd taken her first job offer so she could provide enough financial stability for Morgan to get through his program. Ari decided it was prudent to make sure one of them had a steady income. She'd figure out her own grad school plans or embrace the instability of a writing career once he was in a solid job. As for Morgan, he is living off stipends and scholarships and student loans; the job he held before business school, operations at his uncle's construction company in Queens, paid a nominal salary. Together, they have enough. Alone, they don't.

"I can help. For a little while, at least," he says, even though he can't.

His spoon drops. He interlaces his hands, wiggles his thumbs. It makes Ari want to laugh, love him.

"I'll find something," she says instead.

First, she'll go to Summer's in Murray Hill. Ari will sleep on her best friend's couch until she figures out what's next, make herself scarce when Luke comes up from Philadelphia. Summer will help her muck through where to live, how to pay for it, how to get by when she's alone at night. Perhaps Summer will push Ari to go far, become exceptional. Perhaps Ari will.

"Where are you going to go?" Ari asks.

"I'm going down to Luke's on Wednesday."

"They know, then."

"Luke knows, yes."

"If Luke knows, Summer knows."

"I guess," Morgan concedes.

Ari's face is probably as blue as the wall behind her. She and Morgan painted it the day after they moved in, living together for the first time. Cross-legged on a two-dollar black plastic drop cloth, they'd drunk beer and eaten a bag of stale pretzels, their arms covered in paint. Water's Edge Blue. She'd laughed at Morgan for choosing an eighties rock playlist they both hated. *It's painting music,* he'd argued. *What the hell is painting music?* Ari had replied. Morgan had leaned in, kissed her.

How long have you planned this? It's the only thing she wants to ask, but she doesn't want the answer. Yet he reads her mind, like always.

"It's not like I've been scheming for a long time. I just . . ."

"Okay," Ari says. She wants to be slashed with Water's Edge Blue. She wants him to kiss her.

"Do you hate me?"

The sugar slick has formed on the top of his cereal, too.

She shakes her head.

"I wouldn't blame you," he says.

"No." The words are leaden. "I can't hate you."

~

"I'm so sorry," Summer says before Ari even says hello. "I'm just so sorry."

Just like she assumed, her best friend has already heard. Ari doesn't reply, just lets her breath pollute the line with static. She loops her Alphabet City neighborhood. She left before Morgan went to the library—couldn't bear to see him leave, even if he'd be coming back, for now. People move with brisk steps; the sky is a criminally bright cerulean, sunbeams blinding. The first Italian ices cart of the year rolls past. She can taste the sweet cherry on her tongue.

"Come to me whenever you need," Summer says, her honeyed lilt.

Ari pictures Summer in her nice apartment, accented in pale pink, dusted often. Her couch is as white as the day she bought it, a blush throw blanket folded neatly across the arm. Everything there is right— peaceful, safe. Even the spines shine on her old med-school textbooks, alphabetized on the shelf below the television.

"Next week, I guess," Ari replies, though the exchange is unnecessary at best. She will go to Summer not only because she doesn't have an alternative but also because she might die anywhere else.

It's amazing how Summer still feels as close to Ari as she did growing up. Their houses, side by side. Windows facing one another, friends waving before they went to sleep, watching the other's lights go off. August nights on Summer's porch, counting stars and pinkie-swearing to be there for each other forever. So much of Summer's light shines for Ari. She's never been so grateful, now that everything's falling apart.

"Did you see it coming?" Ari asks.

"What?"

"Before Luke even told you. Did you see it coming?"

"You were engaged for two years, and you never moved on it. You had to know something wasn't right."

"That's not what I asked."

Summer pauses. "Luke and I saw it. But it was never our place to say anything."

"If it was anyone's place, it was yours."

"I wasn't going to push you one way or the other," Summer says. "I wasn't going to meddle. It's your life, Ar."

"Which way would you have pushed me?"

Summer is quiet, probably chewing at her fingernails—the one bad habit she can't shake.

Maybe Ari did know this was coming. Maybe she and Morgan were a time bomb that took too long to go off. But they'd wanted to spend forever together, hadn't they? Why would he have proposed otherwise, so spontaneously; why would she have said yes? They'd been in Boston when he asked her to marry him. When they'd gotten back to New York the next day, everyone went to dinner together: Ari and Morgan, Summer and Luke, who'd found cover for his residency at the Philadelphia hospital to come up and celebrate. Morgan kept reaching for Ari's hand under the table. They'd all talked about how strange, how amazing it was that they still existed like this: friends who'd taken first-period history together in sixth grade, then couples who'd gone to prom together, now spending their full, real lives with each other. Ari and Morgan were officially engaged. It was just a matter of time before Summer and Luke would follow.

"How are you holding up?" Summer says.

Ari doesn't answer.

Summer exhales forcefully. "If there were ever a time for wine." She laughs, the way she does: pin-straight dyed-red hair swinging; wide, brown-gray eyes blinking under thick-rimmed black glasses.

Ari knows Summer wants to get her out of her apartment, give her time away from the home now inextricably linked with the day that ruined her life. But as much as Summer sympathizes, she doesn't understand Ari only wants to be home. That she has to stay before Morgan leaves, drink him in before her throat goes dry.

～

As Morgan promised, he finds the money to break their lease. He's been slowly packing, taking down little things Ari doesn't notice at first, until there are enough gone that she does. Each time she hears the snap of the tape gun sealing another cardboard box, she disappears into the bathroom, takes a scalding shower, studies herself as the mirror's steam clears. Her brown eyes barely open now; her olive-tinted skin, always blessedly clear, is marred by anxiety blemishes on her chin. She squints, studies the arch of her dark eyebrows. Picks herself apart, pushing up the pointed tip of her nose to see if she'd be more appealing with different features; labors to singe her hair straight, which she hasn't done since high school, to see if maybe it suits her. It doesn't.

Ari has returned to their bed. They sleep next to each other like always, though now they don't touch. As they silently scroll their phones, she wants to run her fingertips across Morgan's strong jaw, angular nose, unbelievably soft hair. Those tense calves. She knows he wants to touch her, too. Inhabit again the electricity of their bodies against each other, the feeling that sex wasn't just pleasure, but also an affirmation of who they were and would always be. But her mouth against his would make everything worse. It'd take them back in time. And the future would lead to the same place.

Wednesday morning, Ari calls in sick to work when she wakes up to three huge duffels by the front door. She drops to the couch again, head in her hands. Isn't she supposed to have processed this by now, made an iota of peace? Morgan touches her damp back with his fingertips. She slips the ring off her finger. Pictures him in a shop in the Diamond District, a sleazy man giving him a fifth of what he paid for it, walking away with a few hundred-dollar bills in his wallet.

"I really am sorry," he says as the jewelry clinks on the tabletop.

He scoops the ring into his hand, sticks it in his pocket. He kisses the top of Ari's head, tilts his temple into hers. Morgan stands, drops his key to the kitchen counter, walks to the door. Pauses. Closes it behind him.

Ari jets to the living-room window. She can see him emerge from their building, boxes on the building's dolly, bags slung over him like a mule. He heaves everything into an idling cab, disappears inside. Doesn't look back.

~

After work the next couple of nights, Summer comes over to help Ari pack. She now has six days to move out, and must vacate anytime the landlord wants to show the place to potential tenants. They're usually couples she passes while she leaves the building to waste time in a coffee shop or on a bench in a pocket park, sweating through her clothes. She wonders if these couples will make it.

She and Summer move through the piles, sitting on the living-room rug Ari will sell tomorrow. Summer puts Ari's favorite album on loop. She hums along, but Ari is silent. Ari will be literally homeless in days, doesn't know how long she'll be sleeping on Summer's couch.

"Ar," Summer says. "Please talk to me. You haven't said a word in, like, a week."

She's not sure what she's supposed to say to Summer, with her perfect relationship and perfect future ahead. She and Luke have stumbled only once, their junior year of college, when she drunkenly kissed a guy in her premed program, in a panic that she and Luke would have to wait until they were almost thirty to start their life together. Luke, in uncharacteristic retaliation, had slept with a girl after a sorority party. Everyone had lost their minds. Morgan ended up taking the train down from Boston to Philadelphia to help Luke shake off his monster, and Ari had spent what felt like every hour on the phone with Summer in Saint Louis, talking her back to earth for weeks, helping her understand that both optimism and dread could live in the same body, and life could still go on.

"I think I'm going to quit my job," Ari says after too long, separating two forks, interlacing their tines again.

"Babe, don't make things . . ."

She looks up at Summer, the empty blue wall behind her. "Worse?"

"Ari."

"It's what you were going to say."

"Not in so many words." Summer puckers her lips, redoes her ponytail, pokes at the split ends. "A part of you had to know it was coming."

"I don't know," Ari says, the words a jumble she doesn't know how to unknot.

"Why didn't you plan anything? Why didn't you look for a dress? Why didn't we ever talk about a bachelorette party?"

It wasn't that Ari didn't want to be someone's wife. What had kept her back was the fear she didn't know what a wife should be, even for Morgan, whom she knew loved her unconditionally. What if he trusted her to be good, and she let him down? What if she screwed it up, landed them in her parents' ending? She'd never talked about her future marriage with the zeal Summer did, and it'd always made Ari feel like something in her was broken. Until she found it, figured out how to fix it, she'd be setting up everyone for certain failure, wouldn't she? And it wasn't all on her, anyway: Morgan, too, seemed to be waiting for the right time. When he wasn't busy with school, probably. He'd been moody, a little down, but Ari chalked it up to exhaustion. Their life would stabilize. They'd return to each other. They had to, didn't they? So she waited.

For everything Ari has been able to tell Summer since they were nine, she never got the guts to say any of this aloud—the more she tried to figure out how she might word it, the more irrational she felt. Why wouldn't she want to marry the man she'd been with for so long? So Summer had pushed her in the first few months after Morgan proposed. She sent an onslaught of gown pictures *for inspiration!!!* Pushed Ari to drive up to the hometown inn where they'd obviously hold the wedding. Ari loved the dresses, the venue, even Summer's gusto. She'd get there eventually. Plus, she and Morgan already felt married, and didn't have the money, anyway. What would rushing do? Why did it need to happen with the force of a scream?

"We didn't want to get married until he graduated," Ari says.

"You're missing the point." Summer sucks in her cheeks. "You didn't go out together anymore. You didn't really talk about anything. You lived around each other."

"That's not true," Ari says, though she can't remember the last substantial conversation she and Morgan had before the breakup.

Once, they were different. Thrilling. They had a love story—one people would envy, and did. She thinks about the beginning, when they were seventeen and reckless, and even more about the years in Boston, their college campuses just a few miles apart. Each decision they'd made felt like the right one. Four years spent tight against Morgan's body in his too-small dorm bed; shifting on cold metal bleachers during his lacrosse games; walking with him along the Charles, even as bitter breezes ripped through. They'd spent every weekend at his teammates' parties, Ari dragging him into repulsive bathrooms to hook up until someone banged on the door. The idea they were free, and they'd decided to spend that freedom together, to meld it into one sense of boundlessness—it was everything. And once they got to New York, they were the couple old ladies looked at as they walked down the street holding hands, seeing their own young love in Ari's smile, Morgan's eyes. They laughed with a nourishing sweetness, at big things and others only they understood. They split overstuffed bodega sandwiches in the city parks while they people-watched. They rode the Staten Island Ferry, just to be out on the water. They walked the length of Manhattan until their heels bled, no destination. Ari would find every dive bar in the city, she declared, and when they'd go to each spot, she compulsively picked the labels off their beer bottles until sticky paper was lodged under her nails. She made him dance with her in the back of those bars, even if no one else was. Amid this glowing life, they both knew in their bones they were different from other couples—ones who didn't understand what it meant to have an encyclopedia of the other's life, a tome they could recite from memory. Ari and Morgan spent hours talking about what their lives would be, and the conclusion was always the same: anything they wanted, as long as they had each other. Why wouldn't they defy the odds, rewire everything she knew about marriage? Why wouldn't they have it all?

Ari lets the forks clatter to the floor. She can't pinpoint when she and Morgan stopped being those people, but Summer is right. They slid away from those days, however incrementally.

Summer stands to drown the emptiness by filling both their water bottles and wineglasses. "Don't quit your job."

When Ari looks around, she can't believe how much they've packed. She can't tell what Morgan took or left behind.

~

The day Ari gets kicked out of the apartment sneaks up on her. Neither of her parents know. She'll tell them eventually. Her father will say he's sorry. Her mother will breathe relief she won't have to spend hours beside him at a wedding reception. Her parents will not call each other, because that would mean facing life together.

Luke drives a rented SUV into a no-parking zone in front of Ari's apartment building, turns on the hazards. Upstairs, he greets her with a tight-lipped something, hugs her. Embracing him feels almost like touching Morgan again. They're all so close, tangled together, from graduation caps in the air, to hours upon hours in the diner, to the night after senior prom on the beach, before the sun came up on their adult lives.

"I wish there were anything I could say," Luke says. He shakes his head, shuts his crystal-blue eyes. As he grabs the back of his neck with both hands, his red-striped shirt shifts up over his belt. His torso is too long, shirts always too short.

Ari is dying to know what Morgan has told him—how he's framed what's happened, spelled out his plans for what comes in the After. Luke has listened compassionately, of course—it's who he is, empathetic as he is tall. Or maybe Morgan has stayed inside himself, instead watching hockey, laughing at stupid things on his phone, piling beer cans in the recycling bin under Luke's sink.

Luke carries Ari's big boxes, two by two, down the stairs of the third-floor walk-up. She only has eight to her name; she's sold that rug, the couch, the coffee table, the kitchen table and chairs, the bed, the lamps, even the dishes. She needs the money, now that she quit her job.

At Summer's apartment, the boxes piled in her living room, Summer says they should all go out to eat. Ari says no, Summer and Luke should enjoy time alone before he goes home tomorrow, since the day has been so heavy and Luke has been so generous, and he's rarely able to come visit lately. Also, because the tacit agreement is that Ari needs to lie low, since Summer has so much going on in the final months of her own residency. Ari plasters on a smile as she urges them out. As the door closes, Luke grabs Summer's hand.

Ari starts to call her mother but realizes her muscle memory has pressed Morgan's name. She gasps and hangs up before the call goes through, but all her breath is balled in her chest.

She gets her mother on the line. "Yes?" she answers.

"Mom." The oxygen is still trapped in Ari's throat, and she chokes out the words. "I need to come home for a while."

Ari struggles her way through the explanation. She doesn't remember much of the past ten days.

Her mother is quiet. "I'm nodding," she finally says.

"Nodding?"

"Just listening."

"Did everyone see it but me?"

"Aria," her mother says, "come home whenever you need."

~

Two hours later, Summer and Luke come back. Ari can tell they've made a pact to drop their smiles at the door.

"It's fine," she says. "I'm fine."

They all watch half a movie, but leave Ari to finish it while they retire into the bedroom. She can picture Summer's legs open on the bed, Luke's body tight to hers. She must want to yell out as he comes inside her, but she can't. Not with Ari on the other side of the door.

MORGAN

Morgan shakes two pills into his palm from an orange plastic tube, splashes water into a used pint glass, downs the tablets in a gulp. He's standing at Luke's kitchen counter. Beside him, Luke drops beige muesli into a bowl, slides the box down the counter. Morgan misses his sweet cereal. He's embarrassed to eat it in front of anyone but Ari.

He hasn't even been at Luke's for two weeks, but it feels like forever. He popped back up to the city to graduate, but he has otherwise stayed shut inside Luke's one-bedroom. He should be browsing apartment listings around New York instead of going for long runs and reading bullshit on the internet. But he's not moving back. Morgan had a good business-development position lined up at a fintech company in the Flatiron, and he'd been planning to start the first week of June. He'd spent hours interviewing for the job, six agonizing rounds. But the second day at Luke's, he'd sent an apologetic email to the woman who was supposed to be his boss, saying he had personal matters preventing him from taking the job, but thank you for the opportunity. He can't stay in New York if the whole point of blowing up his life is to start anew.

Soon, Morgan will go back up to Abbott to see his family, maybe help out at the diner to clear his head. But he's not ready to explain himself, or fall apart in front of his mom. For all the times he hasn't cried when he probably should have, the times Ari insisted he was avoiding his feelings—this time, he cannot hide. Sure, Morgan is the one who left. But he's walking away with gut-deep scars, too.

"What are those?" Luke says, his chin gesturing toward the pills.

Morgan's never taken out the bottle in front of anyone, but this morning he doesn't have the energy to hide.

"Sertraline. Antidepressant."

"When did you start them?"

"A year ago, I guess."

Luke's voice drops. "I didn't know."

"I didn't tell you."

Morgan didn't even tell Ari. He had been embarrassed. Nothing was explicitly out of place—he was in the business school he'd wanted to go to, he was engaged. He'd sheepishly asked Summer if she thought he should see a professional about the sinking feeling, then sat next to her at a Midtown bar while she helped him find a few names to call. Morgan had slumped in his chair, obscured his face with a beer, prayed no one he knew was in a ten-block radius.

That first psychiatrist session, he found himself on the Upper West Side, far from the apartment, sitting across from a woman with turquoise glasses low on her nose, frizzy red hair, and the kindest voice he'd ever heard. It was safe in the small room, and he hadn't felt judged. Yet he'd still been a turtle retracting into his shell. Morgan had felt a thousand times better when the woman said she understood why.

He couldn't bring himself to actually say the heavy D word— *depressed*—and she never made him. He'd walked out with a prescription he'd filled at the second-closest pharmacy to the apartment, instead of their usual drugstore, just in case. In case *what?* In case anyone saw him, in case Ari somehow knew, even with how deft he'd become at tamping down his uneasiness in front of her. He'd kept the bottle in his shoeshine bag, which he otherwise opened only for weddings and interviews. The thought of her knowing how low he was—blaming herself—was horrifying.

Every month for a year, he lied to Ari about where he was going. The gym, studying, seeing one of the guys from the team. Each time, he sank into the couch in that tight office with terra-cotta walls, the leather a color that reminded him of the cognac his grandfather drank. Morgan told the therapist everything, said things he didn't want to. He didn't know if he should get married, he told her, even though Ari was the girl he loved. Couldn't remember ever not loving.

Is it sex? the therapist had asked. Morgan startled. *No.* He'd never worried about sex with Ari, even if he'd slept with only one other person, a girl he'd met on a family trip to Block Island when he was fifteen, done with an urgency just to get it over with, maybe beat Luke to it. But once he found Ari, he hadn't feared never sleeping with anyone else again. He'd loved the smoothness of her inner thighs from the first time he touched them in his basement, and her chest, just too full to hold in his hands. The way she looked when she got on her knees for him. He lost total control of himself. There's never been a second he didn't desire her, even now. From day one, she knew how to make him scream. The way she closed her eyes as he touched her—the light spray of pinpoint sienna freckles on her high cheekbones—indelible.

The therapist sat quietly, staring into Morgan's eyes, a deer in headlights. *I love her,* he made sure to say, because he couldn't find a way to vocalize what he knew in his bones, which was that he was scared, and after two years of being a man who was supposed to get married, he couldn't stop being scared. The woman nodded, as if he'd said it all anyway.

Now Luke stands in his scrubs in front of the open fridge, grabs a peach seltzer and the sandwich he made the night before, stuffs them in the black backpack hanging on a chair at the round kitchen table. He cocks his head as he turns back to Morgan.

"Are you okay?"

The question hits differently this time. Luke, in his unflappable kindness, has asked Morgan each day since the breakup. *Yes,* he has gotten used to saying, or *I think so,* which is generally in the ballpark of truth. One day, he will be able to look back on these years with Ari, the decision he made to end them, in a way that's distant from his brain and body. He will find happiness again, he will go off medication, he will no longer drown in indecision and hesitancy and fear. Usually this hypothesis is enough to force *I'm fine* from his throat. Except today it isn't. He doesn't know why the day is different from any other, why he's finally allowing himself to feel everything he's avoided internalizing, let it leak out in a visible way. But here he is.

"No," he finally says. "I'm not okay."

Luke doesn't expect it, because his head whips toward the clock on the microwave. Morgan can see him tabulating how long he has until he'll be late to the hospital. They both know he doesn't have much time to spare.

"You will be okay, though," Luke replies.

Morgan might pass out.

Once Luke leaves, Morgan takes a moment to gather himself. Stands still with his eyes closed long enough to get numb. From the counter, he swipes Luke's gym card, which he has claimed, since Luke never goes—he's on his feet at the hospital ten hours at a time, and it's not like he's ever had an ounce of body fat. Luke has looked the same for the past decade, a gangly six foot five, more than a head taller than Morgan. On the other hand, Morgan is still struggling with no longer living in the body of an athlete, which he lost the second he walked off the field his last college semester. His arms aren't thick and solid like they were when he always had an attack stick in his hand, and his abs, chest, stomach have all softened with age and alcohol. The pills, too, have made him gain weight. If Ari noticed, she never said anything. She is good like that, knowing how to make another person feel seen and safe and loved.

He dresses: a pair of electric-blue gym shorts and a faded red practice jersey. His number, fifty-five, on the back in white. He throws on a sweatshirt, hangs the hood over his dark hair, too long now. Outside, the Philly street is busy, the sky azure, the breeze clean across his stubbled cheek. He keeps his head down as he weaves through each person heading to a job, a class, a life.

He begins on the rowing machine but quits less than two minutes in. His lower back is a mess from the sleepless nights on his best friend's couch, the hard-backed wooden bar chairs in which he has been drinking, sometimes with Luke and mostly alone. Morgan is embarrassed, hoping no one's seen him give up so quickly. He's not like that. He doesn't just give up. He didn't just give up.

If he could only think about one other thing, for five fucking seconds.

Instead, he gets on the treadmill. Pushes his body faster, farther, harder than he has in years. Even though his knees feel like buckling and sweat is clouding his eyes, he can't stop. He keeps running, past the breaking point, to prove he can. It's only after eight miles, the belt on the treadmill slippery and his lungs spent, that he slams the emergency stop. He sprints to the locker room, pukes in the first shower stall.

~

Morgan makes it twenty-three miles outside Philadelphia before he loses it in the passenger seat of his mom's car. He makes guttural sounds even he's never heard, as the sorrow and anger and terror all rip through. Morgan's mom pulls over on the shoulder of 95, hazards on, and lets her son scream out all the hell.

For as close as they are, Morgan hasn't told his mom much. *Ari and I broke up,* he said on the phone, during an aimless four-mile walk over the Manhattan Bridge the day after it had happened. He stopped in the middle of the walkway, looked out over the choppy, sun-drenched water, kept his voice level—it didn't take much, because every moment felt like a blast with a stun gun. His mom had been silent on the line. *What can I do?* she'd said. Morgan had no idea.

On the side of the highway, he turns awkwardly in his seat, falling all over his mom. He'd called her frantically from the gym bathroom; she'd left the diner immediately, driven the four hours down to Philly without question. Going home for a while, he had texted Luke as he'd shoved his things back in their duffels, his sweat-soaked, ammonia-smelling gym clothes at the top of a bag. Key under the mat.

Morgan's mom pulls back onto the highway, turns off the murmuring music, cradles him in silence.

"It was a feeling," he says quietly. "I don't know how to explain it."

"Try."

He stares out the windshield, into a long string of brake lights. Thinks not of himself and Ari, but of Summer and Luke instead—the way they complement each other, come together as parts to make a whole.

"I felt alone. We'd collapsed into a single person. It wasn't . . ." Morgan stops. "I just had a feeling it wasn't supposed to be like that."

He stumbles over the last part of the sentence because he can't square it entirely. Isn't that what people want, to be so close to someone they meld into one soul? What is wrong with him?

"I hear you," his mom says, but it doesn't mean she understands. Ari is a daughter to her, and she doesn't know what Morgan is supposed to do without her any more than her son does. His mom knows how safe Ari has always kept him, how she always put him first. "You're entitled to feel the way you do. You're entitled to make choices for yourself."

He curls his toes in his socks, still damp from his run. "I declined the New York job."

"Oh. What are you going to do, then?"

"I was thinking I'd stay back home until I know. If that's okay."

"Of course it's okay. But I think you should probably be prepared for people to ask."

Everyone in town knows the Meads. No one knows Morgan without Ari.

"I know," he says. "That's on me."

His mom sighs. "I love you."

Morgan wonders what Ari is doing. Where she is. If he should be there, too.

∼

How's Ari? The question has fallen out of the mouth of the same pharmacist who doled out Morgan's ear-infection medication when he was six, now mortifyingly filling the antidepressant prescription; his high school biology teacher, whom he bumped into at the gas station while filling up his mom's Jeep; and, of course, everyone at the diner. They all say how nice it is to see Morgan in Abbott, inquire what's brought him home. His plan to hide in the back of his family's restaurant hasn't worked. No matter who asks, Morgan insists *Ari is doing great.* Sometimes he swears he sees her skipping rocks on the water when he drives past the beach at night, but he knows he's hallucinating.

He's been here about a week, squirreled away in his old bedroom, now jammed with his mom's sewing stuff. Each night he retires to his small bed, pretending he didn't sneak Ari up here years ago to sleep with her on this mattress. It's been a decade, and the walls are no longer dark green and lined with shelves of lacrosse trophies. Yet there's nothing that can take Morgan out of this home. He loves Abbott, this little Connecticut seaside town, which makes him feel like a schoolgirl. But it's the safest place he can think of, and there is nothing he needs more right now.

His life has to go on, and Luke is right that it will. Morgan left because he wanted to deal himself a different hand, get the latitude to figure out how to be on his own. Get out of a rut, find agency. He envisions meeting other girls down the line, learning what that's like. Teaching himself another woman's laugh, her body.

Ari will find someone, too. She's smarter than she thinks. More nurturing, loyal, beautiful. His life now wouldn't be possible without her: the labor she put in to run their lives so the only thing Morgan had to worry about was school, and the fact she never asked to be acknowledged for any of it; the way she held his head against her chest when he was feeling low for no discernible reason, without him even asking for help, before his depression had a name and a pill to tame it. Just the sound of her laugh alone kept his head constantly above water. Everyone in Morgan's life knows he wouldn't be a quarter of the person he is now without her, and he could throw a dart at any point on their decade-long timeline, always land on a moment where she made him better. He knows he held her back, even if he's not sure from what. Maybe this whole thing is even better for her than it is for him. Maybe there are things she wanted that she never felt she could tell him. Maybe she'll go get them. He hopes she does.

It's just after noon on a Saturday, high sun drilling the back of Morgan's neck. The silver shaft of his high school lacrosse stick is cool in his palm, a sensation he'd know in the dark: the same crisp prick of metal he's felt since he was four. He flicks the hard rubber ball against the brick wall behind the elementary school they all went to together, quick-sticking until his shoulder hurts. He's been here for an hour, listening to two teenagers play basketball. It feels good to have a stick back in his hands, but he doesn't exactly know why he's come. It feels like his body just does things without him.

"Morgo." His sister, Madison, ten years younger and still in high school, is idling in the old, beat-to-shit silver sedan he used to drive. A miracle it still runs. "Aren't you, like, bored?"

She parks, sits on the curb, legs outstretched. Morgan tucks the yellow ball into the head of the stick, drops it to the ground. Feels rough pavement against the backs of his thighs as he slides next to her.

"What are you doing here?" he asks.

"Checking on you."

He cracks his back. "Just screwing around. I'm fine," he says, a phrase he wishes his brain could stop himself from saying. It's so tiring. He's so tired.

Maddie ties back her hair, the same color as his. She's wearing a white tank top, the straps slipping off her shoulders. It makes her look as young as she is. They are so far apart in age that they haven't spent the time together siblings usually do. Still, Morgan feels endeared to her for rolling up in the parking lot, looking for him so he knows someone is. She reaches across his lap, picks up the ball, starts rolling it in her palms. She doesn't play lacrosse, but she's going to college in Michigan on a cross-country scholarship in the fall.

She exhales, adjusts her shirt strap. "Do you regret it?"

Of all the questions people have asked him lately, all the times he's lied through his teeth to answer them, this is the one he hasn't confronted yet. He doesn't know how to reply.

"I'm sorry for asking," she says.

"Don't be."

Morgan plucks the ball from his sister's hands, pops it back into his stick.

"Do you want a ride home?"

He shakes his head. "I'll walk back at some point."

"If you say so." She stands, dusts off her denim shorts. "Girls get over boys," she says, like a seventeen-year-old girl who's seen nothing of the world yet feels so sure of her place in it. "We always find a way."

Morgan bristles but quickly untenses. Maybe the wisdom really should be that simple. Maybe he should stop worrying about Ari, start worrying about himself. Maybe Madison is right. Girls get over boys. They always find a way.

ARI

After a week of sleeping on Summer's couch, Ari meets her mother at the train station. As Ari closes the car door, she can see her mother's hollowed face pulled taut with nerves.

"How was your trip?" she asks, stiff. She clears her throat twice, neglects to put on her blinker as she turns left from the parking lot.

"I have to get my stuff out of Summer's soon," Ari replies. "Her apartment isn't big, and it's in the way."

"Are you staying here, then?"

Ari bites her lip as her mother idles at a red light, slides a cardigan off her pointed shoulders.

They don't speak as they cruise down Seapath, the main street that cuts through Abbott, parallel to the water. Everything always looks the same: the small white colonial houses with low hedges in front, the pharmacy that's older than Ari, the town soccer fields and elementary school where Morgan used to throw a lacrosse ball against a wall for hours. And, of course, the diner. Before Ari knows it, they're at the stop sign beside it, waiting for the car at the hilly part of the intersection to pass. Ari holds her breath. The neon sign glows red in the window: MEAD's. The hours the four of them passed in the corner booth are incalculable. Ari can picture everyone, hovered over a plate of fries Morgan helped himself to from the kitchen as his father shooed him out. Now Ari peers through the window as the car rolls past, squinting to see who's behind the counter. For as long as she stays in Abbott, Ari won't go anywhere near Mead's. She can't imagine herself leaving the house at all, really.

It's incredible how everything is begging her to snap back into her childhood self. Yet she knows the Before version of her life is different from the After. She can't get herself out of the After. That's not how these things work.

They pull into the driveway of their house, white paint flaking from the wooden shingles. Her father used to fix it up, so it's been twelve years since anyone has cared for anything. Ari hasn't seen the rust-red exterior of his own Vermont home in years, but it's probably immaculate because his wife would accept nothing less, and he is proud of his new life, which isn't new yet still feels it. Ari's mother walks slowly up the slate path. She glances back at her daughter with a tight look, unlocks the front door.

"We can talk if you'd like," she says. She wears the same rigid face as before. She's scared of her daughter in this carved-up state. Yet Ari's mother has lived in a similar fragile hell for those twelve years.

Ari shakes her head, offers an empty *thanks* as she takes in her gap-toothed second-grade picture on the wall, long pigtails and a yellow floral dress. She hopes the house will look better this time, but it's still the same mess. Dust over every surface, a mildew smell in the bathroom. There's a red wine stain on the carpet below the coffee table. Ari doesn't have to go into the kitchen to know there's nothing in the fridge besides wine, a pile of greasy dishes teetering in the sink. She never dupes herself into a revisionist history where things were good before her father left, but they've certainly gotten worse since then.

Ari's mother settles into the couch. Ari has an overwhelming desire to run to Morgan's house, bang down the door until his mom answers, collapse in Kathy's long, freckled arms—the ones that saved her so many times from the vacantness of her own home, physically and otherwise. Kathy is the heart in which Ari has confided for years, the savior she has never found in her own life. Some people are good at being mothers; some are not. Even Ari's mother would understand why her own daughter needs Kathy right now. Kathy has also been Ari's mother's lifeline since their family shattered, from late-evening kettles of Earl Grey at the Meads' dining table to sitting beside her in thirty-degree weather, waiting hours for a locksmith when her key snapped in the front door. But Ari will not sprint to Kathy, for every reason.

Instead, she considers the recliner, positioned diagonally toward the television. Lying on the cushion is a paperback, which she pulls into her lap as she sits, bending the cover and thumbing the pages.

"It's brilliant," her mother says as she fumbles with the remote. "The author's only twenty-four."

As the TV turns on, Ari cracks the book. French, the language her mother always reads in. She tosses it to the coffee table, misses. Now all she wants to do is sleep, even though it's still light outside. She hasn't told her mother the details, yet she is exhausted like she's been explaining herself all day, splashing around in her misery. She abandons the recliner, plods upstairs, passes the empty wall where the family photos used to hang.

Ari pushes open her bedroom door, and the candy-apple scent of her high school body spray hits her. She can picture Summer spritzing a pump into the air, sniffing the falling mist, wrinkling her nose. After Summer moved next door, they spent most days together at Summer's. But so many important things still happened in this room. In seventh grade, cross-legged on the floor, Summer declared she had a crush on Luke. Three years later, Ari fessed up to her feelings for Morgan, after relentless nagging from Summer to just admit it. Here, she finally told him she loved him. On this bed, she lost her virginity to him, planned for when Ari's mother was visiting her sister in Iowa, the week after her divorce papers were signed. Every time Ari came home—after school, during college, the years that followed—she walked into her bedroom, let her life wash over her like a warm spring rain.

She heaves her bag onto the bedspread, a navy quilt fraying on two sides. The room is a time capsule. The lilac walls she painted when she was twelve look bizarrely fresh, and movie tickets are still wedged into the frame of the white wicker mirror over her desk. Ari doesn't have to look inside the wooden jewelry box to know it's still filled with the butterfly-stitched lanyards with the glow-in-the-dark string she rushed to claim at the town camp, the tens of neon-plastic beaded bracelets she obsessively made. She hasn't moved her senior yearbook or diploma from the nightstand, the dried corsage from the first homecoming she and Morgan went to as a couple. The tube of cherry lip gloss she was wearing the first time they kissed against the brick wall outside the gym. There's the photo collage, a storyline of childhood highs, arranged in a heart beside her bed.

Now that Ari is back, she rips absolutely everything off the walls. Scraps at her feet, she screams until her throat goes raw.

WELLS

ARI

The East Cambridge office building is new, mostly glass, situated next to a historic brick warehouse, which now hosts a coffee shop. In the elevator to the third floor, Ari checks her face. She's taken a few minutes to swipe black liquid liner across the edge of her eyelids, coat her lashes in mascara, which she never did while at the agency. The June weather has gotten very hot—a sticky Boston humidity—and she does her best to tamp down her frizz halo as the elevator doors fly open.

She opens the glass double doors to the office, checks in on a tablet at the front. Inside, the space is exactly what she expects of a startup. Exposed beams and ductwork nestled into a high ceiling, the industrial feel of a place too cool for Boston, too cool for anywhere. Bright light streams in through tall windows, which overlook a cluster of biotech firms and research labs. Employees are scattered at open-plan desks, headphones on, eyes down; a group drinks coffee together at the kitchen island, while other people are splayed on bright, primary-colored couches, hovering over computers. There's energy here, and she wants to be part of it.

A few glass-enclosed offices line the perimeter, which belong to the men at the top. Ari is here for one of them, interviewing to be an assistant. The job is a far cry from writing sanitized copy about a drug that alleviates IBS with only a small risk of dry mouth or spontaneous combustion, and she needs it to move forward. It's been more than two weeks, and she's still stuck in Abbott with the boxes she refuses to unpack.

A girl with a bleached pixie cut and wide swinging hips, who looks fresh out of undergrad, leads her to a conference room. Ari drums her fingers on the cool glass tabletop, keeps tucking the same strand of hair behind her ear. She hasn't done this in forever. Started anew.

The girl comes back in, introduces herself as Nora. She's the office manager and assistant to the COO; Ari would hold the same position, helping out the CEO. Looking at Nora's fresh face, the apples of her cheeks and the neon-pink hoops in her ears, Ari gets self-conscious of her own age, too old for an entry-level job. Yet Nora bounces right into asking Ari where she lives and went to college, what she likes to do. She gets into the job details: calendar maintenance, travel booking, office logistics, staying on top of the executives about responding to miscella-neous things. Ari knows she can do this, and says so. *It's fun here,* Nora adds with a bright smile, as if Ari isn't clawing for the job already. The girl calls in the CEO.

The first thing Ari notices when he walks in, head down to his phone, is his open stride. He looks up—brown eyes—then tucks his device into his pocket, nods once.

"Wells Cahill," he says, English accent buttery, hand outstretched.

"Aria Bishop."

She slips her small hand into his firm grip. She's both thrilled and embarrassed, the latter a feeling she can't place. His eyes are dark blue, not brown.

"Aria Bishop," he says. "Good."

Wide-eyed, she nods, curls her lips under, feels blood rushing to her cheeks.

Wells sits, crosses his legs. Ari notices the strong curve of his shoul-ders shaping his T-shirt, pulling it taut against him. He runs his fingers through his smoggy brown hair.

"Nora told me you reached out to our recruiter directly. I appreciate you were proactive to get yourself to the top of the pile."

"Worth it to try something different, I guess," she says.

He asks Ari what he should know about her. Her résumé is in front of him on a crisp sheet of paper, but he hasn't picked it up. Instead, he holds her eyes, waiting for her voice. She tells him she's from a Connecticut village of twenty-nine hundred people, that she went to college on the other side of the Charles River. She lived in New York for a while, then didn't.

Wells nods, readjusts in his chair, crosses his legs the other way. "Anything else?"

"I can do this job. That's pretty important."

Wells smiles. "I'm guessing the job will be somewhat boring, in candor. I can try to make it less boring," he says. "We'll see how it all goes."

"I worked in pharma, so."

"This is going to be a proper rocket into space for you, then."

Ari smiles, genuinely. She likes Wells. His energy and humor, his ease, which is exactly what she needs. They've barely been talking for ten minutes, and he hasn't asked Ari what draws her to the company, what makes her qualified. He hasn't seemed to notice she doesn't even live in Boston. Instead, he talks to her like they know each other, always have. Maybe that's what he's looking for. Maybe she's it.

"Come," he says, beckoning her with two fingers in the air.

Ari catches Nora's eyes tracking Ari as Wells leads her into his office. He closes the glass door, tells her to sit. He crosses his legs under the tabletop, switches them once, switches them back. His foot bounces on the floor.

The desk is covered in sticky notes. He catches her inventorying the neon-green squares.

"I know what you're thinking. We literally make software so you don't need these. This is what the inside of my brain looks like. It's terrifying."

"It is." Ari finds herself smiling at her bravery. "And you spelled *market capitalization* wrong."

He leans forward, studies the note she points to. "I'm British. *Zs* are useless to me."

"Look closer." She points at the green-ink script. *Capitolisation.*

He squints, sits back, interlaces his hands behind his head. "I assume you know your job will be making me look good all the time while keeping my dirty secrets."

"I can keep as many secrets as you want." Ari pulls the collar of her black shirt away from her neck. "Why don't you have help already if you're running a company of three hundred people?"

"Five hundred, counting the London office," he says. "It's because I'm pigheaded and don't like to be told I can't do something on my own."

He walks Ari through what he needs. Expenses, which he loathes; calendar keeping, which he's terrible at. He turns his monitor to show his incredibly scattered folder system, which Ari already knows she'll have to blow to shrapnel and piece together again. There's also some personal maintenance, like getting him lunch or making dinner reservations, which he feels guilty asking for, *yet here we are.*

"Also, Leah."

"Leah." Ari nods once.

"My wife. She's great," he says. "I have a habit of leaving my phone everywhere I'm not, so if she needs to get in touch, she'll probably call you to find me." He laughs. "I'm sure you'll meet her soon. And when you do, you can both talk about me behind my back."

"I doubt that," Ari says.

"You'll like her."

She wants to ask Wells how he can be sure. He doesn't know Ari; in more ways than she'd like to admit, she doesn't know herself. She doesn't know who she is now, without Morgan, in a new job. Yet Wells seems so confident in her that she believes him. She will believe anything he says.

He reaches across his desk to shake her hand, but knocks his mug off the edge. It shatters on the floor, and he curses under his breath. Ari drops to her knees, starts scooping the sharp pieces from the puddle of tea on the floor.

"You don't need to do that," he says, cheeks flush.

"Where can I find paper towels?" she replies.

Wells's embarrassment turns to a faint smile. "Follow me," he says.

~

The recruiter calls with an offer the next day, a base salary it would have taken Ari years to earn at the agency. Until she got the call about the job, she'd been scrubbing the house's single bathroom, beating dust out of the curtains, spraying disinfectant in the trash bins. She'd revived the idle vacuum, sucked up months of dirt. It felt like the right thing to do for her mother. The floor of her own space is still covered in the clippings and photos and posters she tore from the wall when she arrived back home. She'd throw them out, but she's not ready to give up on the memories. Anyway, it feels like defeat to treat her childhood bedroom like home again. Sinking into this place would turn her back into the person inextricable from Morgan. She can't be that person anymore.

That's why this next step feels big. Ari is looking forward to getting out of this house. This kitchen with its faded floral wallpaper, which she's always hated. This table, where her father told them he was leaving one crisp spring Sunday morning. Ari had just turned sixteen.

Her mother pushes around peas in the dinner Ari's thrown together, penne with a bland blanket of olive oil, salt, pepper. They stare past each other for a while. Ari studies the toaster's shadow as it climbs the wall. The sun is still out, but the kitchen windows face north, so they get practically no light in the room, even when the sky is blazing bright.

"How do you feel about everything?" Ari's mother asks. She adjusts the T-shirt pooling in her lap.

For the mess she's always been—the pile of bottles in the recycling bin, the license suspensions after the DUIs—her mother was not all bad. No one is. When she laughed, it was contagious, and her singing voice was a swan's. Ari understood there had to be reasons her brilliant dad had married her. Her mom spoke effusively about ballet and French literature, taught Ari meringue cracks if it's taken out of the oven immediately. Showed her how to swim in the ocean and convinced her that if she was strong, the waves wouldn't sweep her under. Ari took these few moments and let herself think there might be a silver lining to her father's absence: her mother would come out the other side of the divorce kinder, with sensitivity and perspective. They'd be closer—like how Ari and her father used to be—even if it took a trauma bond to connect them. When it never happened, Ari felt betrayed, even though it was a long shot to begin with. It's still hard to see past that.

"He seems like he'll be cool to work for," Ari says, trying anyway. Her chest leaps as she pictures Wells across the conference table. What she wants to say is that maybe she is a little optimistic, for the first time since all this happened. But she's so scared to be hopeful, and even more fearful to say it aloud.

"It's a fresh start, Aria."

"Please don't call me Aria."

"It's your name," her mother says, before standing and dropping both their dishes in the sink Ari emptied earlier, restarting the pile with a sharp clatter.

As her mother lowers herself back onto the couch, Ari makes it up to her room on unsteady legs. Pulls out her phone.

Her father's greeting is full and pleasant, like she spoke to him days ago, not months. Like the wedge he put between them is easily removed when he wants it to be. "How are you?"

"I'm moving to Boston. I guess I just thought you should know."

"Well, that's great," her father says. She pictures him in his office in the large Vermont farmhouse, taking in the green foliage out the window over his desk as he leans back in his chair. She has been to his new home only twice. "Did one of you get a job there, then?"

It's like she's forgotten there's anyone left in the world who doesn't know.

"Me." She pulls out the white wicker desk chair she hasn't sat in in years. "Morgan still lives in New York, I think. But I don't actually know."

"What do you mean?" her father says. *In a minute, Cole,* she can hear him whisper to his teenage stepson. He speaks into the phone again. "What's going on, Ari?"

"Morgan and I aren't together anymore."

It's only the second time she's said it aloud.

"Oh. I didn't know."

"Yeah."

"Well, I'm very sorry. I really am."

He doesn't ask his daughter whether she's okay. She has no idea what *okay* even means at this point. Would another person be okay by now? Is Morgan okay? If she spoke to him, would she ask the question or avoid it herself? Does she even want the answer?

"You're welcome up here anytime," her father says. "You'll be so much closer now. We'd love to have you."

Ari hums. He tries to keep talking, buoy her spirits, but she remains a Venus flytrap. She wants to stay on the phone with him, more than anything, but if the point is to move forward, she can't.

"We'll find time to see each other soon, yes?" he says.

"Sure," she replies, the sound of the downstairs television in her other ear.

~

In the pale-purple walls of her room, Ari spends another hour in her bed, struggling through the book from the recliner downstairs, trying to dislodge the French from her mind's vacuum. It's hard to focus when she spends every third second wondering whether Morgan is on his feet already. Whether he'd be proud to know she already has something going, too. She reaches for her phone again.

"Ari, my god," Morgan's mom answers. "My heart skipped to see your name. I'm so happy to hear from you."

Kathy's voice is pure sugar. Ari loves her as much as she loved Morgan, and sitting on the line is reaching for a bulk-size box of salt to rub in her open wound. Yet she can't resist.

"Hi," Ari whispers. "I don't really know why I'm calling."

"You never need a reason to call me," Kathy says, quiet and singularly maternal.

Ari chokes up. Kathy hears it.

"You're going to be okay. You will. It'll all be okay."

Ari wants to ask her how he is, where he is, what he's told her is next.

"I can't say anything that'll make it better, I know. But I love you, and he'll always love you, and whatever decisions you make in the future will be the right ones. You need to trust yourself with your own life as much as everyone trusts you with theirs."

"I love you, too," Ari squeaks.

She already feels so far from Kathy's cocoon, the place in which she has sheltered, transformed. Her eyes are a thousand pounds from the tears weighing them down. She pictures Kathy in Morgan's old bedroom, fingers guiding fabric through a sewing machine with distinct grace as she peers through her reading glasses. Maybe it's Madison's senior-prom dress. She made Ari's, too.

"You know," Kathy says, "I always think about the first time I saw you, when kindergarten started. Your teacher had all the kids circle up, and Morgan sat next to you. She had everyone go around and say their names and their favorite color or toy or something. I kept watching him as you all took your turns, just praying he wouldn't freeze up. He was so small and shy, and I could see his circuits frying the closer it got to him. I can't remember what you said, but you looked at him when it was his turn, and I just saw him unlock. Even back then. You do that, Ari. You've always brought out something buried in people, and it's a gift."

"Carrots," Ari says, swallowing hard. "I said carrots were my favorite food."

"You did, didn't you?" Ari hears a voice near Kathy call out *Mom.* She knows Kathy needs to shake off the memory, go back to her real life. Kathy laughs, but sniffles. "I'm going to go cry a little bit now, okay?"

"Me too," Ari says. "Thank you again."

"Always here," Kathy says. "Always."

Ari hangs up, crumbles. She hasn't cried this hard since the night Morgan broke up with her. She lets herself: a pool gathered on her top sheet, snot smeared on her pillowcase. Chills traveling through her bones, her body so hot she strips all her clothes. She lets herself disintegrate, because this is it, because life is starting again, and she's bigger and better than being someone's past. She has a *gift.* She moves to Boston next week.

~

Ari takes quickly to work. For the past week, on a yellow couch in the communal area, Nora has spent hours walking her through the company's worryingly complicated software: how it organizes information on spreadsheets, turns the entries into charts and boards, sends notifications about assigned tasks. *It's really powerful to optimize workflow, you know?* Nora says, clicking around to sort rows of data, color-code everything. *You'll get used to everything fast,* she keeps assuring Ari.

Working for Wells keeps Ari from stressing. She looks forward to seeing him in the mornings, fetching his specialty coffee from next door, checking in at *half nine* every morning, weaving a narrative about his life from the expenses she's entered twice. The sushi omakase, the natural-wine bar, the train to New York, and the seven-dollar gummy bears he ate in a hotel room. She can picture him at dinner, full glass in hand, splitting with laughter across from a very wealthy man whom he's convinced to invest a large sum of money.

He mostly spends his hours in the meetings she schedules, but finds time to pop out of his office, lean on her desk, ask how she's feeling, what she's doing in the evenings. She doesn't have plans: she

41

hasn't reconnected with anyone from college because she doesn't want to explain why she's back. But, otherwise, in just five days here, she is afloat—maybe even more than she was the last few months with Morgan.

After most of the office has cleared for the summer Friday, Wells emerges, holding the bottle of wine that's been on the corner of his desk. He leans against Ari's empty table, crosses one ankle over the other.

"Weekend plans?" he asks.

It's two o'clock, when the office gets its best sun, beams breaking rainbow against the windows. The golden undertones in his hair catch the light. He crosses his arms, drums his fingers on his biceps.

"My best friend is coming up from New York," Ari replies, hands in her lap.

"Lovely." Wells smiles. He holds out the thin-necked, green-glass bottle with a worn label. "It's been a nice week, I think. You like Chablis?"

"Absolutely." She reaches for the bottle, accidentally grazing his hand.

"My pleasure, Aria. This is a good one. Don't tell Leah I liberated it." He puts one finger to his lips.

"I'm really happy to be here."

"Cheers."

He tells her to go home, crack open the wine. He has to get on a call with his mentor in Palo Alto, the meeting Ari scheduled and sent him the link for no fewer than six times. You're already the functional part of my brain, he'd messaged her earlier.

~

Just after eight, she meets Summer at South Station. They ride the T back to the apartment. Ari has found a month-to-month sublet in Somerville, her block peppered with densely packed multifamily houses and storefronts for rent. The one-bedroom is fully furnished: a scratchy blue couch in the living room, a small table that folds down from the wall. The aging Formica of the kitchen counter reminds her of the well-loved tabletops at the diner. The kitchen drawers are stocked enough that she mostly doesn't need to pick up things from the neighboring dollar store. Every now and then, though, something is missing. She does not have a spatula. She has never considered what she needs or doesn't, because her life with Morgan was so automatic.

"Jesus, Ari," Summer says as she walks through the door and drops her bag. "You have to move. You deserve better."

"Aren't you supposed to be working on your bedside manner?" Ari knows the place is dark and worn in, not in a charming way. It's not that she didn't realize the apartment had flaws, but it's an ice-water bath to hear Summer say it. "I just have to get my sea legs. I'm still figuring stuff out."

"If you don't move in, like, six months, I'm going to burn down this building so you literally can't live here anymore." Summer gathers her white sundress, drops herself onto the pilled couch, resettles the skirt. "Come, my child."

Ari sighs, then sits beside Summer, tilting her head to her best friend's shoulder. Summer wraps Ari in her arms. This week has felt good, working with Wells, having people greet her when she walks through the office door. But now that Ari's skin is against Summer's as they sit in the stark apartment, it's glaring how much has changed. As distracted as she's been with the job, she still misses Morgan violently. With horns blaring and children yelling through the open window, Summer lets her fall apart for as long as she needs. Now and always, she doesn't know what she'd do without her. As much as she loved Morgan, Summer is the real love of her life. Ari knows childhood friends mostly deceive themselves that their lives still intersect in some way. A social media hello for an engagement, a text message for a new baby. But Summer and Ari are a wildfire that keeps spreading, engulfing those empty actions, incinerating them.

"How are you, really?" Summer asks, once Ari can see straight again.

Ari doesn't answer, just goes to her room to change into gray gym shorts and a too-tight purple college T-shirt. Her head is pounding. The thing she is most grateful for is that Summer hasn't asked *Are you okay?* or anything resembling it, those empty and disorienting words. She knows Ari isn't okay yet.

"I only got half my security deposit back from the city apartment," she says, pouring them both glasses of water. "The tiles at the foot of the toilet were stained, so the landlord said he has to replace the floor."

"Men are absolutely gross." Summer reaches for the glass.

"Luke isn't."

"Luke is often repulsive."

Summer loves Luke more than Ari can comprehend.

Ari sips. "How's Morgan?"

Summer places her glass on the table, ringed with years of sweating cups. She shrugs. "He's Morgan."

He's keeping his head down, getting through the days as he does, Summer means: quietly navigating whatever he needs to from dawn to dusk, helped by being strong and broad-shouldered and doe-eyed. He has never broadcast his feelings, telegraphed his intentions. He never needed to, since Ari always knew what he was thinking. Until she very much didn't.

"Have you talked to him?"

"No."

"But Luke must tell you what's going on."

"How about you don't worry about him and take care of yourself instead." Summer downs the rest of the water.

Ari retrieves Wells's wine.

"You didn't have to splurge on my account," Summer says as Ari opens the bottle. "We could drink the boxed stuff for all I care."

"My boss gave it to me for a nice first week, he said. He's either an oenophile or an alcoholic, based on his expenses."

They laugh. And, god, it feels good.

"That's incredibly thoughtful," Summer says. "A good sign."

"I think so."

"What's his deal?"

Ari wants to tell her everything she knows about Wells, which is maybe too much. She's found most of it searching on her phone in the dark while she should be sleeping. Wells is from London; a graduate of Oxford; an MBA from MIT, which is where he met Krish, his cofounder. Ari knows about his wife, Leah, an education PhD who now runs a venture-backed Montessori-toy subscription company. She's blond, small, generally beautiful. There is also their young son, whom she saw on the "About" page of Leah's company website. They live in Cambridge. According to Street View, the house is gray.

"Not totally sure," Ari says, shifting on the pillows.

Summer asks for a photo, and Ari makes a show of taking a while to find one, even though it's already open in a browser tab.

"He's kind of a big deal, I think?" She passes her phone to Summer with Wells's headshot large on the screen.

"Nice to have a hot boss."

Ari shrugs, stifles a smile.

Summer swirls the Chablis in the bottom of her pint glass. "You have a crush."

"No."

"Yes."

"Maybe."

Summer rolls her eyes, toasts Ari, whose blood feels warmer now, from both the alcohol and the admission. It feels good to spend her attention someplace else, on someone else. Gossip about a crush. She considers again telling Summer all about him, but she resists, because Summer's eyes say one thing: *Just don't shit where you eat.*

WELLS

What the fuck, Wells?"

He leans against the wall of the in-law suite, arms crossed. Leah has ordered him downstairs so she can yell at him without waking Rowan. She snatches a white throw pillow from the couch, heaves it at his legs.

"One hundred twenty-five fucking thousand dollars. What is actually wrong with you?"

In one sense, Leah is right. Objectively, he should not have dropped an eighth of a million on a car, at least not without asking his wife. But he did.

After work, Wells had picked up the new hunter-green four-door Porsche at the dealership in Brookline, then without fanfare pulled into the narrow driveway behind Leah's Volvo SUV, just like he would have with the Audi he'd traded in. He'd tossed his keys on the pile of mail at the kitchen counter as usual, poured himself a stein of water and a glass of Napa Sauvignon Blanc, said hi to Irma, plopped himself onto the couch next to his son as she packed up and left. Leah came downstairs from her attic office fifteen minutes later. *We're out of milk for tomorrow morning,* she'd said. *Irma didn't get it?* he replied. *With what time?* she bit back. As always, their nanny had been out all day, chauffeuring Rowan to and from his wall-to-wall activities Leah had programmed. *I'll go,* she huffed, leaving through the mudroom, out the back door. Wells had been on his phone, hadn't even thought to warn her about the car. Thirty seconds later, she appeared at the threshold of the kitchen, dangling his new keys. *Tell me that's a loaner and I'm not losing my goddamn mind.*

Now they are here, in the basement suite, and Leah is probably trying to stop herself from throwing the coffee-table book of Maine lighthouses at his head. Which maybe he deserves.

"What fantasy world do you live in that you didn't even ask me, Wells?" His name, sharp off her tongue.

"It makes no difference to our bottom line."

"You literally see nothing wrong, do you?" she snaps, shaking her head frantically, eyes wide. "You're an egomaniac. You think you're invincible."

"It's not that."

"Oh no. It's just that you don't give a shit."

This is not entirely true. In fact, he gives multiple shits about how his wife feels at any given moment, especially now that he sees how upset she is. He didn't plan for her to get crazy. He didn't think much about it at all.

"I'm sorry," he finally says. "You're right, I should have asked you."

"But you didn't, because you thought I'd say no."

"I suppose so."

Leah grinds the heels of her hands into her eye sockets. Her face is flush; he knows her skin is burning hot to the touch.

But Wells's wife is fine. They are fine. This is who Leah is: strong and volatile and emotional, but ultimately forgiving. Inside, she is plush and vulnerable—vestiges of a girl. And this is who they are together: fiery and elastic and still madly in love.

It's been this way from the first moment—the wine bar in Harvard Square, where Wells met her instead of offering dinner, because it was a setup, and the chances of liking this girl seemed astronomically low. He'd been dating around plenty, didn't need to pin hopes on a random night orchestrated by a mutual friend. Except Leah captured Wells from the first seconds he'd spent with her, a wholly unfamiliar feeling that rattled him. Striking green irises trained on him, and a taut collarbone his eyes couldn't stop running over; loud and obviously brilliant; the filthy mouth of a teenage boy on a twenty-eight-year-old woman. She'd just finished her doctorate, raised an angel round for a toy company she'd been building with a friend on the side. Leah was a woman who knew what she wanted, and it became clear by the time they left to go back to her place that what she wanted was Wells. Two weeks after that first date, she'd asked him not to see anyone else, and bristled when he was smacked by the question. *Why?* she'd almost barked. He didn't actually have a reason to say no to this tiny, well-dressed, intense person, who was already sure of their future together. He'd proposed eight months later.

Wells crosses the basement, sits on the gray couch. Interlaces his fingers, leans forward. "Come," he finally says.

His wife sits beside him. He touches her face. Her skin hot, just like he knew it'd be.

She kisses him, nestles her head into his neck, her honey-blond hair against his skin. "I think you're having a midlife crisis."

"I wanted a car," he replies, his jaw tight. He nudges Leah off his shoulder. "I'm not mulling my mortality."

Wells is turning forty in a month. People turn forty. They turn fifty and sixty, which he will, too. His parents are well into their seventies. Still, he admits, maybe the number is a bit high. He is thriving, successful, nowhere near his peak. He still has all his hair, can ride the Peloton for a half hour without feeling like he's going to die. He has a young child whom he can keep up with, a hot thirty-four-year-old wife whom he still fucks often. All he wanted was a treat.

~

The next day, Wells wakes up bothered, anxious. He hasn't slept well—too hot, too cold, too hot again. Leah is already downstairs with Rowan. The light blanket is mussed, the red silk tank she slept in balled on the sheets. He turns face down into the pillow.

He sheds his shorts, heads to their bathroom. The light streams in, bright and clear, just as Leah planned when they renovated a year earlier. They'd added a window above the new soaker tub, so each morning the eastern sun sweeps across the blue-and-cream porcelain Spanish tile, the crisp white walls. He steps inside the massive shower, water from the gleaming-chrome rainfall head pummeling him. As he soaps his body, he stops at his penis. There's a tuft of white hair he hadn't noticed. How long has it been there? When his wife takes him into her mouth, does she see it? There are faint streaks of silver at his temples, yet this is different.

As the water falls, he studies his face in the shaving mirror. His eyes are tired and ringed in bruise-purple, face covered in graying stubble. Like Leah, he has been pulling long hours and traveling, while fathering a one-year-old. But Wells is not old. This is circumstance, not time. It's why he hired Aria—so he will not be as overextended, so he doesn't have to think about anything that doesn't deserve his attention.

He towels off, dresses in a kelly-green T-shirt and dark jeans. He can hear Rowan crying downstairs, murmurs of Leah talking to Irma. He can't wait to get out of this house. He's agitated at Leah for accusing him of a *midlife crisis*. Does Leah know she has a few little chin hairs, that there's a ridge in her brow forming?

From the car, he texts Aria, asks her to grab him an iced red-eye. When he enters the office, the coffee is next to his keyboard, a stack of brown napkins beside the cup. As he sits, she steals a glance at him, turns back to the pile of receipts he dumped on her yesterday. He watches her through the thick glass of his office. Her long, wavy hair is down for the first time since the interview. He likes it as much now as he did then, imagines his fingers gliding through it, the way it must be thick, wild to the touch. The feeling of wanting to reach out shakes him. Desire hasn't ever made him feel self-conscious, but her eyes do something to him he can't explain. He has never felt it before.

Wells stands from his desk chair, raps on the glass so she turns toward him. *Come,* he gestures. She jumps. He leans against his desk, arms crossed. Coughs, taps his chest to clear his throat.

"Morning," Aria says.

"Morning. You all right?"

"Of course."

The heat is oppressive, but he asks her to walk with him outside.

"Where are we going?" she asks in the lift.

"I'll buy you a coffee."

"You buy me a coffee with the corporate card every day."

"Shush, I'm trying to be charming."

She rolls her eyes as they step out onto the street. Initially, Wells had gotten tight when Krish said he needed admin help. *I'm perfectly capable of managing my own business,* he'd snapped. *No, you're not,* Krish said. Wells had stayed at the office until half nine that night, trying to prove a point, get his affairs under control. At 9:35, before he'd even gotten to his car, he emailed Nora to work with their senior recruiter to post for the job.

As much as it pains him to admit his cofounder was right—he'd never say it, of course—he's glad Aria is here. She's not frantic like Nora, who annoys the piss out of Krish, but she's too good to let go. No, Aria knows what Wells needs, often before he does. He already likes the quiet warmth in her smile that waits for him each morning, always disarming. Little quips that make him laugh as she's reminding him everything he forgot to do the day before, without making him feel like an idiot for losing track. *To err is human,* she's said to him a few times. He always replies the same way: *To forgive divine.*

They loop the office building, past a marketing-automation company that just went public. Wells knows their CEO from the tech-conference circuit.

"So," he asks, "what do you think?"

"Of what?"

"Me."

Aria's eyes go wide. She shakes her head. "I'm not sticking my foot in my mouth when I have to pay my rent."

"Clever."

He stares at the two freckles on her sternum as she gathers her hair into a high mess on top of her head. *Keep it down,* he'd like to say, though that'd be putting his own foot in his mouth.

"The company, then. What do you think of working here?"

"It's really good."

"You still have no idea what we do."

She puckers her lips.

"I won't tell. I don't really know, either." He scoffs. "I really made a fool of myself at your interview, didn't I?"

"You gave me an opening to show you you'd need me." She smiles gently.

"It didn't hurt, no." The sun briefly moves behind the clouds, peeks out again. "What's your story, then?"

Aria stares at her gold-sandaled feet. "Just kind of starting over," she says, voice tiny.

Wells hums. They walk more. He wonders what *starting over* means. He thinks about asking but can't when he sees Aria's shoulders fall.

"I did the same, coming to America," he says. "I was looking for a blank slate, too."

"Why?"

"I overstayed my welcome at a job in London. Right out of uni, I worked as an analyst at an investment bank, got a little too liberal with an expense account. But I also knew some things about my managing director that I shouldn't have, and tried to leverage them to not get fired." He feels a little pang in his side, winces at the tart memory he's spent a good deal of time burying. He can't understand why he's let the words escape—more, why he can't stop them. "At twenty-five, it seemed like strategy. At my age now, it's clearly blackmail. Anyway, there's non-disclosure paperwork around it on both sides, so keep that to yourself. Leah doesn't even know."

"I'd never say a thing," she says. "I just have to ask—why did you tell me?"

"Honestly, Aria, I'm not sure."

Wells feels like he's let out a breath he didn't know he'd been holding. He puts his hand to her back, but it's so brief, he's not sure she notices. It's wildly inappropriate to touch her. But it's hard not to.

"One more thing," he says. "If Leah calls to find me, I'm wall-to-wall today."

"Got it." He likes her tone, her compliance with the lie.

"Cheers, Aria."

They enter the building again, step into the lift.

"Actually, one thing on my end," she says, turning to him in the mirrored walls. "Can you call me Ari?"

"Ari."

The doors open.

Settling back into his desk chair, Wells has no idea what's fallen out of his mouth and why. But, Christ, it shocks him alive to know Ari is keeping one of his secrets.

~

Leah comes home late after dinner with her cofounder, out in the North End. Wells has been starfished in bed for two hours since letting Irma go home, putting Rowan down after three read-throughs of *Goodnight Moon* and a Paddington board book.

"Wells," she calls, gently jostling his arm to wake him. "It's nine. You're not going to be able to fall asleep later." She peels off her oxblood-red shirt, thin lace bra, stares at him until he rights himself.

They descend the stairs together in their pajamas, into the kitchen. He tries to blink away the fog of his weary eyes while she asks him if he even ate dinner. He shakes his head. She opens the freezer, slides a frozen burrito across the countertop, stares at him until he throws it into the microwave.

"I told Molly about the Porsche. She said Jon bought a three-thousand-dollar road bike when he turned forty and basically pretended he was in the Tour de France," Wells's wife says as she opens a bottle of Argentine Malbec, pours them both too-full glasses. "Although I guess that's probably the cost of one of your headlights."

"You had to tell her?" He follows her to the couch, leaves the burrito behind.

"You don't buy a car like that if you don't want people to know."

Leah settles into the couch, runs her fingertips over the gold chain-link necklace Wells bought her when they spent the holidays in London, two years ago. He'd sneaked away to Harrods on Christmas Eve to pick it up with his father, while his mum, sisters, and almost-four-months-pregnant wife cooked at his parents' flat, a few minutes away in South Kensington. Leah has never been a jewelry person, but Wells loved the tiny diamond-speckled knot on the clasp. They'd just told their family they would have a baby soon. They'd be inextricable from each other, forever knotted together. Other than during Rowan's birth, Wells can't remember Leah ever taking it off.

He gnashes his teeth. "How long are you going to lord this over me?"

She sighs, swipes a wisp of hair from her eyes. He can still detect a note of her perfume—bergamot, like the Earl Grey tea he was practically weaned on.

"Men are all the same," she says.

"Are we?"

"Yes." Leah takes a long draw of her wine, grabs the remote, changes the channel to a baking show. "I still love you. You're just a little bit of an asshole."

"I can't believe it took you all this time to realize."

She sighs. "I've been so busy reminding you you're a dick that I forgot to thank you for the flowers. They meant a lot."

"The flowers?"

"Molly and I have been busting our asses, and I appreciate the acknowledgment."

"Right, of course."

"They served as repentance roses, too, so double points."

Leah sits up to kiss him. They stay up for another two hours, finishing the bottle, and she crawls under a cotton throw blanket, resting her head in his lap. As she drifts off, he texts Ari. Roses? She writes back instantly: DTC company of the year in ToyScan awards. You sent macarons from Clement to the whole office, too. Wells's jaw drops. Christ. Thank you, he writes.

His heart beats quickly. Even with Leah's weight against him, he can't stop thinking about Ari, staring at her name on the phone in his palm. He hopes she'll wear her hair down again tomorrow. He can already feel the strands between his fingers.

ARI

It's nearly nine in the evening, and Ari is still at her desk. Partly, she's been organizing flights and hotels for Wells for a trip to Silicon Valley to meet with VCs. Partly, she's avoiding going home, lying on her bed, texting Summer about a stupid reality show with little else to do. Mostly it's because Wells is still here on West Coast calls, and in the three weeks he's employed her, she's only wanted to be in his proximity. But Ari has run out of tasks to make up. She drapes her office sweater back over her chair, plucks her tote from under her desk. Taps his window to wave good night.

He holds up a finger, hangs up the phone, motions her in. "Would you stay? For only a moment, please."

There's no one else in the office, but he asks her to close the door. Ari sits in the chair across from him. He runs three fingertips through his hair. He looks tired. Maybe it's a week of work hanging heavy on him; maybe it's something to which she's not privy. Home, family. He interlaces his hands as he stretches them above his head. Smiles faintly, but lets his lips fall. Clears his throat.

"I don't mean to be forward. Although I suppose I do," he says. His voice softer, more level than usual. "I think we are fond of each other in the same way."

She can't speak.

"Please, you can say no. You have every right to, of course."

Ari feels cleaved open. She considers running to the yellow couch, screaming into a pillow. Her hands are shaking, and she's not sure her nerves won't come out as a pile of vomit at her feet. There's a plea in Wells's eyes, a need she's never seen. The need is her. It changes her on sight. It's now impossible to want anything more than she wants him.

"What would I be saying no to?" she asks, still outside her body.

Wells moves to Ari's side of the desk, reaches to touch her arm. He uses his left hand to blow apart her world with his fingertips, his ring finger wrapped like a golden gift. "I'd prefer you say yes."

~

A half hour later, as the summer night turns navy, Ari climbs into Wells's expensive car, tucked away at the far end of the parking garage, as if he's anticipated their need for privacy. They drive fifteen minutes, a tech podcast murmuring in the background, until they pull into the empty driveway of a large colonial near Harvard Square. A wall of bursting hydrangeas lines the walkway to the red front door, and the house looks freshly painted. They park, and she silently follows him through the back door, down a set of stairs. He leads her into a finished basement: wall-to-wall cream-colored carpet, a large slate-gray couch facing a big TV, a white-tiled kitchenette, a full-size Murphy bed. Wells flips it down.

They say nothing. He takes off her clothes, as if he is peeling back her skin to expose everything. She wonders where his wife is. His child. She's lost herself, too.

As they touch, Ari does not understand what is happening to her sense of time. She feels suspended in eternity, yet it's also slipping away too quickly. His mouth hits her first—his lips on hers, moving to her neck, her collarbone, her chest. His hand slips between her legs, cool fingertips prying her open. Ari feels corporally possessed, literally out of control of her physical self, her mind. His silence is a drug; they have a tacit agreement about the weight of this moment, don't need to say anything more. A month ago, she couldn't imagine herself free of the thoughts of Morgan that have maddened her since May. But look.

It is all so foreign—these hands, these lungs, the entire presence of another person. The only body she knows is Morgan's; the only pressure she has ever felt, his. It's why she gasps as Wells pushes inside her, can't look away from him, especially when he closes his eyes, holds his breath. Even the way he keeps the air back is different from Morgan—this seasoned ease, years of soft bodies pressed against him. There is no comfort of permanence, only the urgency of presence in a fleeting moment. She has never lived like this. She can't believe she ever went without it.

"You don't know how badly I've wanted this," Wells finally whispers, eyelids still shut.

"I do now," Ari says. Her head tips back.

When they are finished, he rolls over, walks to the bathroom. Ari is naked, face up to the ceiling, mouth agape with awe. The room feels humid, smells of sex: sweet, stale, sour. She loses her breath.

Now she's back in the reality of bright overhead lights, Wells's family home. Ari rolls onto her stomach. Realizes what she's done. For all the time she's spent thinking about Wells, she never meant for any of this to happen. Woven into all the novelty that's just washed over her is something painfully familiar. Her father and the life he took from her. Ari is sick. She can't believe what she's done. She can't believe she's done what he's done.

Alone in this bed, she's filled with lust and terror, a pairing that scorches her chest. If she looked in the mirror now, she knows she wouldn't recognize herself. She's not a person who hurts others. No. She props people up, gives them a safe place to confide.

"We absolutely cannot do this again," Ari shout-whispers as Wells returns to the bed. She's scooping for her clothes, the white sheet pulled up to shield her naked body. "I'm not a home-wrecker."

He falls backward to the sheets, penis limp. His legs dangle off the side, and he flops his hands above his head. Takes all the room's air slowly into his lungs, blows it out through pursed lips. He tells her she's right, reaches for his phone.

"Wells," Ari bites, this time louder. "I'm not kidding. This is completely wrong."

She jams her legs into her black underwear and jeans, yanks her shirt overhead so quickly she hears the threads in the collar stretch, the mess of bracelets on her wrist clink. With her body still burning from Wells's touch, mouth bone-dry, she climbs the stairs, puts her ear to the basement door to listen for signs of other life.

"She's in Maine," he calls out, still staring at his phone screen. "You'll have to jiggle the knob if the back door sticks."

His nonchalance infuriates Ari. Hasn't this changed him, the way it's changed her? She pauses before she opens the door, turns back to him. Shakes her head.

He drops his phone against the pillow. "What do you want me to say? You're right, this was a mistake."

She flinches at the idea of being a *mistake*. Even for how destructive her father was, he left something bad. Found something good. What if there's something buried in this mess Ari is meant to find? What if she's wrong about herself? Who actually knows who she is outside of Morgan, what life she's meant to live. There are risks she's never taken, so few moments she's had on her own to even contemplate what she wants for herself. So few decisions she's been truly free to make. Here, stuck with this body and brain, Ari's not asking for so much from the universe—she's just trying desperately to become her own person. To try on life until it fits.

"I don't know that this was a mistake," she says, the cool of the doorknob in her palm.

"No," Wells replies, sitting up. "It wasn't."

~

Ari trudges back to Somerville under flickering streetlights. The breeze is ideal, the summer-evening chill everyone waits for all year. And here she is, walking forty minutes alone in this perfection, with only herself and what she's done. This isn't who she is, she repeats to herself. Yet every time she keeps trying to think it undone, she can't. Being against Wells was a fire she still cannot put out, desire she did not know existed, heat so intense she could vomit lava. It was everything, except a mistake.

~

Ari's phone rings, two o'clock. Summer. She steps away from her desk, slips into an isolation booth to answer. It's been one week, and she still hasn't told Summer about Wells. Keeping it inside has derailed her entire mind, making it nearly impossible to sleep—if she slips into unconsciousness, she'll have to stop thinking about him. But nothing else has happened. It's like Wells and Ari never went to bed, like there was never *Wells and Ari* at all. Maybe she'll ask Summer if she can go down to New York, where she'll confess. Cleanse and force him out of her system.

"Hi," Summer says quietly on the line.

There's a long pause that sits like a stone in Ari's gut.

"Summer? Hello?"

"I have not-great news. Kathy died yesterday."

Ari gasps, feels her stomach drop out of her body. "What? How?" Her voice quaking.

"The intersection right next to the diner—"

"Someone blew the stop sign on Seapath," Ari cuts in.

"Right into the driver's side," Summer whispers. "It's so awful. I just don't even know what else to say."

Ari pictures Morgan's mother's Jeep, crushed like a tin can. She is flush, trembling. She drops to the stool, her legs giving out. Kathy, the mother she loves more than her own. She begins bawling, fumbling with the sleeve of her sweater to wipe her snot.

"I know," Summer says. Ari hears her sniffle.

The hours Ari spent in Morgan's house, talking to Kathy—countless. Kathy's sapphire irises understanding the fear in Ari's eyes each time she ended up at the Meads' house while her mother and father screamed at each other over everything and nothing, as if their daughter wasn't in the room, wouldn't be collateral damage. Kathy's strawberry hair brushing Ari's forehead when she bent down to kiss Ari's cheek, tell her she was safe for now. She can still taste Kathy's homemade macaroni and cheese: the breadcrumb crust, the sharpness of the Vermont cheddar. The look on her face when Ari got into her first-choice college. How Kathy was happier than anyone about the engagement.

Ari exhales, gathers herself. "Did you talk to Morgan?"

"Not yet. Luke went back to Abbott today to be with him, and I'm going home tomorrow. Luke said they don't want to draw things out, so they're going to do a wake at the funeral home on Stone Street at eleven on Thursday, no additional visitation, and a private family burial. Are you going to come in tomorrow night or Thursday morning?"

"Thursday," Ari says, fearful of spending an extra night in Abbott when everything is off its axis.

"I'm sorry, Ari."

After they hang up, she is frozen behind glass, watching the rest of the office go on with their days, the same people they were when they got to work. But she is changed, in the worst way. Twenty minutes later, she wipes the tears from her eyes, picks up her phone to call Morgan. But she doesn't have the courage to hear his voice. In a few days, she'll be ready. Not yet.

I'm so sorry, she writes in a text to him instead. But she erases it. I love you, she tries next. Deletes that, too.

Next, she calls her mother three times, but can't get through. Ari knows what her mother has also lost. Her anchor, her life preserver. Her friend. Perhaps the most remarkable part of Kathy is how she'd loved Ari's mother, even when Ari would spill all the ugliest parts of her home life while crying in Kathy's arms. Kathy knew about her mother's drinking. She'd helped Ari's father with the police when she crashed into the gigantic oak tree outside the library, a quarter mile from the bar she'd frequent. Yet Kathy dug for the best and brought it to the surface. In that way, Ari knows, she and Morgan's mom were alike. *A gift.*

Ari returns to her desk, stares into space.

"What's wrong? You look like shit."

When she refocuses, Wells is standing above her, sipping from his enormous water bottle.

"You can't just tell someone they look like shit."

"Well, in any event, you do."

Ari sighs. "Someone died."

"Oh, I really shouldn't have said that, then." He hums. "Do you need to take time off?"

"Thursday."

"Thursday."

"Are you sure you won't fall apart if I'm gone?"

"Go be there for the people who need you," Wells says.

For the next few minutes, Ari keeps picking up her phone to reach out to Morgan, but can't go through with it. She doesn't know what she'll say to him that could be enough, but she has time to figure it out, test the words in the rearview mirror of a rental car.

At 2:50, she leaves the office without a word. She starts walking, veering down arbitrary streets, until she's totally turned around, unsure which way is home. The only thing that stops her aimless wandering is the sight of a supermarket. For the first time in hours, she knows what to do.

Ari squirrels away in the corner of the produce section. A spritz of water falls to the back of her neck from the sprinklers misting the celery, radishes, carrots. She digs up a six-year-old email—Kathy's name in the sender field, jolting her heart. Looping her arm through a cracked red plastic shopping basket, Ari gathers each ingredient for Kathy's macaroni and cheese, plus a glass casserole dish. She pays. Finds her way home.

The paper bag sits undisturbed on the countertop, all night. It's not like she's locked into her television show, or the book she futilely picked up. She simply can't bring herself to walk to the stove. At eleven thirty, her phone pings with a text from Summer.

This is all so messed up and I can't stop thinking about it. Did you talk to Morgan yet?

Not yet.

ARI COME ON

She places her phone face down on the coffee table, finds a way off the couch.

Well past midnight, she cooks: boils the elbow pasta, stirs the butter-and-cheddar sauce in a skillet until it thickens and bubbles, until her wrist hurts. She sits cross-legged in front of the oven door, watching the crust turn golden. The scent becomes overwhelming—sharp and creamy and familiar to her bones.

~

On Thursday morning, Ari wakes up with numb fingertips, stinging eyes. It feels Sisyphean to drag herself out of bed, feed herself, put on her dress, secure her hair into a tight bun with a thousand black bobby pins. Somehow, she does. Even though Morgan will see her, she doesn't pat concealer under her eyes, line them with a kohl pencil. What is she hiding.

The two-hour drive down to Abbott is excruciating, a prison of space and time. Once the road sign tells her she's passed into Connecticut, tears stream down her face, a leaky tap she can't turn off. Her cheeks are tacky to the touch, peony-pink in the rearview mirror. As she turns off the exit and rolls slowly into town, the sun finds its way out, a flame in the sky. Abbott unfolds before her: the same weathered brick storefronts with gently rippling American flags beside them, the bungalows edging the water. But it's already so much emptier, without Kathy.

It's an hour before the wake, and Ari should go home to her mother, try to be there for her even a fraction of the way Kathy was all those years. Or she could head to Summer's early, since Luke and his parents are certainly there, too. Instead, Ari drives to the funeral home, parks as far as possible from the converted old three-story Tudor house. She waits for the other cars to pull in, carrying the people she's known all her life. She is waiting, of course, for Morgan.

She listens to the shrill cries of birds in the trees shading the lot, the sound of her own breath: heavy, pained. The car feels suffocating, even with the windows open; it's early September, still oppressively hot, especially in her high-necked, long-sleeved wool dress, an insane choice. Ari sniffs her underarms, surprised she doesn't smell ungodly, instead like the powder of her deodorant stick. She chews the inside of her cheek.

Soon, Rick's green truck pulls up. The wheel wells are rusted out, like they've been for years. As much as she's prepared herself, Ari is not actually ready for the moment Morgan emerges from the driver's side of his dad's pickup: a black suit he clearly bought in haste, the pants too tight on his thighs and calves. She has never seen his head droop like that, spine hunch. She ducks so her eyes are just above the window ledge. He waits for Rick to get out of the passenger seat, Maddie from the back. They're a shapeless mass, filing their way through the heavy double front doors.

Ari tips her seat all the way back. She just needs a moment.

By the time she sits up, the parking lot is nearly full. She sees everyone's cars in a row: her mother's, Summer's and Luke's parents', too. They're all inside the funeral home already, nodding at each other and passing around grief like cold hors d'oeuvres. But Summer is not. She stands on the steps, surveying the lot. Ari finally lets herself out of the car, finds her way over, collapses against her waiting best friend. They weep until Summer grabs her hand, leads her inside. When Luke sees her, he sweeps her against his body, too.

There's a thick, black-clad crowd in the navy-walled lobby, just like she expected. Kathy and Rick's family, all of whom Ari nods to as they pass. Each member of Kathy's book club, every person she'd ever served with on a PTA, the liver-spotted pharmacist. The stuffiness of body heat pushes against Ari's cheeks, even as the fan blades spin overhead. No matter where Ari goes, Summer doesn't drop her hand. Ari isn't sure she could move forward without her, anyway.

People begin to file into the main room. There it is: the white chrysanthemum cross beside the slim, dark casket; the family photos of Kathy, many memories that belong to Ari, too. She stops in the doorway. Spots her own mother at a seat in the back row, staring at the front wall, fidgeting with the straps on her purse. Ari tries to catch her eye, but she isn't looking for her daughter. At the front, Rick is talking to Kathy's brothers next to the podium.

And then Morgan. He sits in the aisle seat of the first row, beside his sister. Ari has a clear view of his still and square shoulders, the spot where he's losing a little hair. She knows he's gripping Maddie's hand, can feel the shape of his fingers between her own. Ari's lost her breath, her teeth digging into her lower lip. The pain, nothing compared to his.

"Ari," Summer says, tapping her shoulder. She readjusts the blazer disguising the black party dress underneath. "We have to go sit."

"In a minute," she replies, clinging to the doorframe. "Go and save me a seat."

Standing back, it's overwhelming watching the room fill. Kathy's death is already as real as it will ever be, but the tragedy takes on a human shape as a black hole of bodies emerges. The amplification of death—it's impossible to explain how it sits in her chest. Kathy's brothers sit, and Rick finds himself at the podium.

"I'm here, but I don't know actually what to say," he begins. "I never thought I'd be in this position."

Ari almost blacks out. Summer turns to her, eyes wide to urge Ari into the empty seat. *One second,* she mouths. When she turns back to the front, Morgan's dad looks right at her. Closes his eyes. She shrinks back behind the wall, just peeking beyond the molding, unable to bring herself into the room. She loses herself in her own head, barely hearing Rick—seeing only his dampening eyes, the relinquishment of his strength.

Morgan rises. Ari's cheeks go hot, and she imagines the birds outside have ceased singing. The breeze, she is sure, no longer rustles the leaves. She watches him fumble a creased paper. He picks up his head, gazing into the sea of people who loved his mother. Ari knows, deep in her hollow gut, he is searching for her. She has two choices. The first: dart to the front, stand beside him, calm him like only she can. Ari chooses the other option: sprint out the front doors. For as much as it hurts to be in the same room with Morgan, to lock eyes with him and hear his voice, the reason she runs is not about him. It is because that room is the death of the final good, unchanged piece of Ari's young life, and for as much as she has a new home and a good job, everything is still upside down. She rushes back to the car. Smacks the steering wheel until her palms sting.

As the building slips away, the car jostles on the cracked street, shaking the foil-covered casserole dish in the passenger-seat well. Ari holds her breath as she passes the diner, slowing beside it to see a handwritten sign on the door, shaky red marker in Rick's near-illegible scrawl: Closed in Loving Memory of Kathleen Mead. The neon in the front window is off, parking lot desolate. Everything hurts.

Ari's destination is not far, the home on a street that winds behind the diner, a cul-de-sac with a few cedar-shingled houses. She pulls straight into the driveway, behind the car she spent so many hours in, which now belongs to Maddie. Ari can still smell the smoke on the upholstery, which she and Morgan tried to hide with a nauseatingly pungent pine air freshener, bought in panic at the car wash a town over—how could she have known that a single cigarette, the only she'd ever tried, would sink into the fabric so aggressively? Morgan hadn't even considered a puff, especially as Ari hacked up her lungs. She's sure Kathy figured it out, knew it was her. But Morgan's mom never said a thing.

In the driveway of the Mead home, Ari turns off the car, reaches for the dish. Leads herself around the back, straight to the big garden gnome. She tips it over. Slides out the spare house key.

With a deep breath, she pushes through the door, hinges squealing, and steps into the sunlit kitchen. The refrigerator is beeping, the freezer door open. She gently pushes it closed. On the table, Maddie's navy backpack is surrounded by the chaos of Rick's calculator and invoices. Morgan's lacrosse stick bisects the tabletop. Kathy's tomato pincushion, stuck with needles like a voodoo doll, is ready for its next project. Ari drags her palms across it all, a still life she shouldn't disturb, yet can't resist. Duke bounds into the kitchen, winds up for a huge bark. As soon as he sees Ari, his hackles drop, and he wags so hard his bulky brown body shakes, mastiff jowls quiver. She bends down, smashes her nose into his, tickles his chin. Duke was, is, Kathy's dog.

Ari settles the macaroni and cheese onto the stovetop, scratches a dot of crusted tomato sauce from a burner until it chips away clean. She opens the junk drawer, sifts through a jumble of key chains and coupons and batteries and receipts, extracts a sticky note and pen. *I'm sorry.* She doesn't sign her name, just presses the note to the foil, drops the pen and pad back into the clutter.

Ari looks around the room one more time, kisses Duke's snout, sighs. She doesn't know when she'll be here next—maybe never again. She wants to go through the closets and fold up Kathy's clothes so Maddie doesn't have to, cook months of meals and stuff the freezer until the door won't close. Write all the thank-you notes they'll have to send for the flowers, fruit baskets, trays of lasagna. Instead, she wraps Kathy's pincushion into her palm. Holds it tight to her chest as she finally leads herself out of the house, slips the key back under the gnome.

~

Around nine, Summer calls.

"Are you kidding? Did you actually leave? Am I on drugs?"

"I know," Ari says. "I swear I was going to go in when Morgan spoke, but I just saw him up there, and . . ."

"And *what?* Morgan couldn't even get through his eulogy, Ari. Maddie had to take over."

"What?"

"He couldn't even speak. He needed you."

Ari could puke. If she'd gone inside, he could have spoken. She could have stood beside him, slipped her hand into his.

"After they finished at the cemetery, he unlocked the diner, and we stayed there for a few hours, him and me and Luke," Summer says. "It stung to look at your seat empty. You should have been there."

"Did Morgan know I came at all?"

"Does it matter? He was incredibly hurt."

"Did he say that?"

Summer doesn't reply, because he would never be so explicit. Ari knows he let the weight of the day hang off him, dragged it around like a ball and chain.

"I'm sorry," she says, staring at the pincushion on the nightstand. "I have no idea what the right thing is from one moment to the next."

"I'm not the one you should be apologizing to." Summer stops. "I know you're having a hell of a time, I do, but that was unconscionable."

Ari bites her lip, too hard. "I did something else I shouldn't have," she says, stomach knotting. "I slept with Wells."

"Wait, what? When?"

"About a week ago."

"How did it even happen? How did you sit on this?"

"I'm not sure. It just did. And I didn't say anything because you'd kill me."

She tells Summer everything. The crush that swelled into a desire she's never known, the way Wells reached out to her, how his touch scrambled any sense of logic and morality she once had. The impossibility to write off the moment as a mistake, even under the bright lights, even with what her father did to her family. The fact that she's been splayed on her sheets every night since, fighting with herself to let Wells go, but never punches back hard enough to stop fixating. How she cannot imagine her body without him now. Of course, she knows she shouldn't have done it, just like she knows she shouldn't have left this morning. But since she's been on her own, nothing's been simple. Nothing's been black and white.

"This is the least *you* thing I can imagine," Summer says. She's sitting on her childhood bed with the white mesh canopy, Ari is sure.

"I thought so, too. But I think I'm someone else now."

"But this isn't you."

"How do you know? I've been with one other person my entire life. How do you know what's me and what's not? How am I even supposed to know?"

"I'm not really sure what to say to that."

"Yeah," Ari says. "Neither am I."

~

She is an hour late to work the next day. She oversleeps, fighting to turn off her brain until four in the morning, reaching over to the pincushion constantly. When she walks in, Wells is in his office with the door closed, leaning back in his chair, showing Krish something on his phone. She turns back to yesterday's pile of email, starts looking at venues for the November team offsite.

Krish passes her desk when he leaves Wells's office. He stops, speaks softly. "Sorry to hear. I hope you're okay."

She thanks him, turns back to her computer, feels her organs fail.

"Come in, please, Aria," Wells calls out.

Her pulse quickens at her name on his lips, even if it's the version that has never felt like her—swelling and melodious. It's not the name he used when he was beside her, against the sheets, when he could not have wanted her any closer. *What happened?* she is dying to ask him. *Will it happen again?*

"When was the last time you slept?" he asks, squinting. He glances at her over his monitors, types without looking at the screen. Moves his blue-faced watch farther up his wrist.

"I look like hell, I know." She sighs, thinking of the undereye circles she couldn't make disappear, even after three layers of concealer; the hair she couldn't tame, no matter how she pulled it back. She worries too much skin is spilling over the waistband of her black jeans.

"Did you go to a funeral or a warehouse rave?"

Ari crosses her arms, hides as much of herself as she can. "It's a long story."

"And I have a short attention span." Wells reaches into his bag, slides a pair of keys toward her. "Can you get six copies of each made? Our neighbor's house got broken into. Leah got new locks."

"Did they steal your spare keys?"

"Perhaps? I didn't ask." He starts typing again.

Ari feels trampled by his frigidity. He's been distant all week, but she's chalked it up to how busy he is, how there's no way he could possibly talk about them here. Yet there's something about the staccato of his voice that makes her feel like he's closed the book on them, even if he'd barely cracked it at all.

~

Ari drops Wells's sun-dried-tomato flatbread and sparkling water onto his desk. He twists off the cap, looks like he's going to offer her a sip but thinks better of it.

"Leah's in Minneapolis until Tuesday," he says. "She's a keynote speaker at this women's entrepreneurship conference thing. It's big."

Ari breathes deeply. Hands him the gleaming gold keys. He peers inside the envelope, shakes them around with a jingle.

"Why change the locks if they just break in, anyway?" Ari asks.

"Leah asked me to do it, which means I asked you to do it." He drops the small manila envelope onto his desk. "Did you hear me? Minneapolis until Tuesday."

"I heard you." Ari broods until she gets it. Her jaw goes slack. Summer's voice in her ears: *This isn't you.*

"My son should be asleep by half seven, so you can let yourself in for eight."

"Are we really doing this?" she whispers. The need, acute. When he meets her eyes now, it's like she's emerged in her body for the first time in a week.

Wells pauses. "You're right. I don't know what I'm thinking. We shouldn't."

"I didn't say that."

"We never mention this again, you understand?" He clears his throat, taps his sternum. "Tell Alex to come see me."

~

Five minutes after eight, Wells is reading on the couch, under a table lamp, as Ari descends the basement stairs. She startles to see him in the same clothes he wore to work. He puts down his tablet, peers into the baby monitor on the coffee table.

"You changed," he says, turning off the screen, placing it back down.

He isn't surprised to see her. She was always going to come. He always wanted her to.

"I did," Ari says, unsure how to take the comment.

The moment she got off work, she dashed home: scrubbed herself with every good-smelling thing she owns, shaved every hair below her ears, slipped on a newish black shirtdress. As she locked her apartment door to leave, she knew she was making a horrible decision. But there was no world in which she wasn't going to show up.

Wells hums. Stands. Ari follows him to the bed, where he sits on the edge, reaches out to her. It's slower this time, the way he undresses her, undoes her buttons. Because they are no longer a freak accident, they're a choice. And every move they make together is, too—the way he touches her hair and tips his forehead to hers before he kisses her, hot breath as he pulls back; how his lips trace her breasts, between her legs, so softly; the direct look as he slips himself into her, and the motion with which he pulls her against his chest as he comes. She wants to shriek, possessed. Instead, she concentrates on him deep in her body, feels him let go. It's a force so different from Morgan, she can't make any sense of it—*authority*, the only word that comes to mind, especially in her short-circuiting brain. They have already created something between them that feels real enough to hold and too heavy to blow away. This, she's sure, is what real life feels like. What everyone has told her to find.

Wells scrunches his eyes closed as he peels himself from her sweat-glossed skin, collapses onto his back. She lays her palm on his sternum, entangles her fingers in his chest hair. Morgan's chest was bare. As they breathe, Ari takes in the basement's smell, almost masculine, like citrus and tobacco. She swings herself around, feels the stiff, new carpet against her feet as she heads to the bathroom, sparkling clean and white-tiled like the kitchenette. It's all Leah, Ari is sure. She almost feels like she's touching Wells's wife as she runs her fingers over the neat charcoal-colored grout. She wonders who this basement suite was built for, what Leah thought would happen here.

Ari pees, splashes cool water on her face. Smells the hand soap in her palm, Meyer lemon and mandarin. Perhaps it's Leah's favorite. Wiping her eyes, she examines herself in the mirror. Her hair is ruffled, a tangled puff in the back; her eyes bloodshot, because she is still running on four hours of empty sleep. But although she looks rough, Ari feels beautiful. Worthy. Because Wells thinks so, and she trusts him. She feels desired. Safe.

As she walks back toward him, he reaches for his underwear on the floor. He peers at her over his shoulder.

"You all right?" he asks, no discernible expression on his face.

He pulls on his pants next, both legs at the same time. Zips them, buckles his belt.

"Sure." She's still entirely naked in the warm room. "Yes."

"Good."

He finds his way back over to the side table by the couch, checks the baby monitor again. Ari's heart sinks.

"I'm going to head out," she says. "I'll see you Monday."

He shakes his head. "Here, tomorrow night."

~

"How do you always know when to bring me over?" Ari asks Wells, her head against his biceps.

It's amazing. He has a preternatural ability to know when the house is empty. Ari is responsible for much of the choreography, too. She keeps Leah's full work and social schedule in Wells's calendar, alongside the absurdly packed agenda and care schedule for his son. She and Wells are never here on Fridays, when Leah usually works from home; Mondays and Wednesdays often provide an opening. Still, he seems to have a sixth sense. They both always stutter at any stray noise they hear from bed—but he always knows when to tell her to relax.

It's nine thirty in the morning, and they're penciled in for a breakfast Ari invented. She came straight to the house this morning, a Wednesday. She's lost count of how many times she and Wells have been together now, pressed up against each other in the basement suite with the thermostat too high. September has melted into October, leaves losing their verdancy; the bitter wind that wraps New England until April is coming. But she will stay in his heat. She will not be cold again.

"The schedule is purposely rigid. Leah always tells me where she'll be," Wells says. "She's not a spontaneous person."

She doesn't excite me, is what Ari hears. *You do.*

"You have no cameras or anything?"

Wells shakes his head. "Just the doorbell. She's paranoid people can tap into the feeds."

"It's surprising," Ari says. She readjusts herself on his chest.

"How can it be surprising? You don't know her."

He's right. But, in ways, Ari does. Leah's winter boots are cherry red, and she keeps the clear plastic box overstuffed with their Christmas decorations under the mudroom bench. Ari has pictured Wells's wife reading and drinking coffee on the basement couch. She knows Leah is very smart, because he wouldn't marry a woman who couldn't keep up. She knows the kind of woman he would choose. She is also that woman. There is no better feeling, nothing that makes more Ari certain she belongs in this life.

"How did you meet?"

He brushes a strand of hair from her face. "Blind date," he says calmly, turning to stare at the ceiling tiles. The sheet drapes loosely over his midsection.

This makes perfect sense—that Leah would see Wells, hear his invitation, know on sight he was extraordinary. Ari wonders what it is about her that he needed immediately, permanently.

"She's very pretty."

"Yes," Wells says. "She always has been."

Beyond the hours she's spent looking up Leah online, Ari has stared into the family photos around the room while Wells is in the bathroom. Leah's quarter-size face, centered in a five-by-seven frame, holding her swaddled baby against her chest. Her bright eyes, Granny Smith green, full of love and light and kindness, captured in a professional photo shoot. Her hair is a dirty blond that would look mousy on anyone else. She's thin but not sickly; she has nice breasts. There's a small birthmark on her left cheekbone that looks like a jewel, faded topaz. Ari is glad Wells has someone so good, even as the jealousy hits her like walking on hot coals.

She wants to know how long they've been together, how in love they are.

"Has she always been faithful to you?"

The way Wells's brow furrows, Ari can tell he doesn't expect the question.

He looks toward the wall. "Yes."

"How do you know?"

"How do you know anything?"

What can she say? He's right.

"Have you always been faithful to her?"

"Yes." He turns back to Ari. "Our son is called Rowan. He's a year and a half."

Of course she already knows, yet it hurts to hear him say it aloud. His life with Leah is so real, they've created a new human with a name and a personality and a future. Picturing a baby at Leah's breast, Ari is racked with guilt. She lives in the wake of infidelity every day. It's taken so much from her, and she never imagined she could stand to suck the life from someone else the same way. For the first time, Ari understands the blinders her father had to put on to do what he did to her; she, too, has started to use them.

"You all right?" Wells asks.

"Fine," she says, turning her back to the disgrace. "Do you and Leah still have sex?"

"Yes," he says, like the question isn't surprising.

"Often?"

Which answer does she want? Why does she want to know at all?

"Relatively. Yes."

"Relative to what?"

"To other married couples. To people who are only having sex with each other."

"You're not only having sex with her."

"That's true."

"We're different," Ari says, like she knows.

"That's true, too." Wells kicks the sheet off his legs.

"How?" she asks.

"Leah is a great wife. A great mother."

"What am I?"

"You're you."

"Tell me what that means, though."

As much as she wishes to be flattered, Ari really wants to see herself the way her own eyes can't. If she is here, in his life where she should not be, there must be something to see.

He faintly smiles to himself. "Do you think I'm an egomaniac?"

"No."

"The other night, Leah called me an egomaniac. I can't stop thinking about it."

Ari shakes her head. "I think an egomaniac doesn't care what damage they leave in their wake. Or maybe it's less that they don't care, and more that they're so blind to other people, they don't think they're doing damage at all."

"You don't think that's me?"

"It's not."

"I think more people would agree with Leah than you."

"Let them," she says.

He takes her hand, places it on his warm forehead. With her, he knows he is safer than he's ever been.

WELLS

Wells waves hello to Irma as he drops his keys to the kitchen counter. She's staying late so he and Leah can go to dinner with her cofounder and her husband: a new farm-to-table restaurant with an outdoor patio, warmed by tall heat lamps under the late-October evening sky. He thanks the nanny, tiptoes upstairs quietly so he doesn't wake his son.

In their dark bedroom, Leah is sitting cross-legged atop the mattress, furiously typing on her glowing phone. Her legs are bare, one of his white undershirts draping from her frame.

"Hey," he says. "Aren't we going to be late?"

He flicks on the overhead light. Leah squints as her eyes adjust. She wraps her fist around her phone. Her face is pale.

"We're not going."

Wells cocks his head.

"Jon's been cheating on Molly."

"What? Since when?"

"Like, a full year."

He starts to peel off his jumper, stops. He leans back on the dresser instead, sucks in his cheeks until he realizes it might look strange. "How did she find out?" he asks, willing his heartbeat to slow.

"He was a fucking idiot and brought the girl home with him. Their nanny came back with Heart in the middle of everything. Can you think of anything worse than a three-year-old seeing that?"

Wells scratches his head, feels a familiar weight on his chest. What he's put on the line for Ari has never hit him so hard. The problem bigger than what he's doing with his body is that he's never squarely faced the risk itself. The moments with her—it's like she can make the world stop so he can luxuriate in standing still, no longer worried he's falling behind. When he's next to her, questions run through his mind about who he might have been if he hadn't always been so obsessed with being at the front of the pack. He's happy now, yes. But it doesn't mean there aren't other ways he can be happy, and she's reminded him of that. Ari is, has always been, worth it.

"Who was it?" he asks his wife, skirting eye contact.

"One of his grad students."

"But that's how Jon and Molly—"

"He wasn't fucking married when they got together."

Wells thumbs his wedding ring.

"Anyway, she threw him out like an hour ago."

Leah stands, pulls out a pair of leggings and a thin black tank top. He takes off his shoes, pants. The dark hardwood is cold through his socks.

"I'm going into the fire to try to calm her down," she says. "I need you to call the restaurant and cancel."

Wells nods. Leah fondles her phone.

"Would you ever cheat on me?" she says.

"What?"

"I'm asking."

"I can't believe you even would."

He can't keep his wife's eyes, so he busies himself by peeling off his shirt, picking at a scab on his left hand from where a staple snagged his skin.

She silently pulls on her clothes. "Men are scum," she mutters, leaving the room.

Wells's eyes are burning. He's suddenly cripplingly exhausted. He drags himself into the shower, sits on the bench as freezing water falls.

The force on his chest feels heavier, the entirety of an elephant, a steel beam. He begins to sputter; a sharp pain rips through his ribs. He feels like he's being eaten from the inside out.

He pulls on track pants and the ragged undershirt Leah was wearing, heads downstairs, tells Irma something came up, lets her go home. In the dead-quiet house, he makes his way to his office, closes the door, even though no one is home besides his sleeping son.

As his inbox populates, forty messages cascading down the screen, Ari's name pops to the top. He can't stop himself from picturing her, the last thing on the damned planet he should do. He thinks of her muscular legs hugged in black jeans. The reddish color that backlights her eyes when he gets close enough to see. The strands of her long, dark hair, which he picks off the pillows each time he brings her inside his home, like a *fucking idiot*. He thinks also of the fact that he is still dying to touch her, press inside her, even now. To stop the world.

Ari has overtaken him in a way he did not expect but can't shake. From the moment she walked into his office, she already belonged in his life. He'd been disarmed as he shook her soft hand, what now feels like an eternity ago. He wanted her to like him, immediately—hadn't been so embarrassingly eager since Leah sat across from him in that wine bar. It was a feeling he didn't know he needed so badly to live again until Ari gave it back to him. It's inexplicable. What they are has nothing to do with Leah. It's like he and Ari live in a parallel galaxy. He doesn't want to come back to earth.

Yet for as much as she means to him already, as impossible as it now seems to live without her, he understands he must end it. The hurt on Leah's face, like Jon's affair had been her own—Wells can't even comprehend how much he'd gut his wife if she knew everything. And he needs to release his own heavy pressure, these moments of gasping breath when he internalizes what he's doing. He'll call Aria into his office tomorrow, slip her a too-generous severance check, his signature on the line a tacit agreement they can't work together when they're constantly reminded of the contours of each other's bodies. Maybe he'll come clean to Leah, too. She is the woman, wife, mother he'd die for.

Uneasily, Wells waits hours for Leah to come home. Midnight. He hasn't been sleeping, instead restlessly choreographing the way he'll end things, imagining how Ari's voice will sound when she agrees. He calls to his wife when she crawls into bed beside him, asks how Molly is.

"How do you think, Wells?"

"Jesus, Lee. I'm just asking."

"If you ever cheat on me, I swear to God."

"Who do you take me for?"

Leah says nothing. It's like her life is the broken one. Like, somewhere buried in her subconscious, she knows.

~

The next morning, the moment he sees Ari at her desk, Wells knows he won't do what must be done. Instead, he invents reasons to be near her. Calls her into meetings to take notes he will never review. Walks with her next door to get a flat white, even though he's already wired from the double red-eye, plus three cups of Earl Grey he didn't even realize he'd downed until he saw the tea bags collected on his desk. At the end of the day, they meet eyes through the glass, hold the stare for too long. Christ, does she see him—beyond his bravado and exhausting arrogance and cloying need to own a room—now and from the very beginning.

He comes home to Leah, of course. Feels that gnawing at his organs again.

~

Krish keeps staring at Wells, who is crossing and uncrossing his legs, shifting in his seat at the café. It's half seven, their weekly breakfast before they head into the office, though almost no one else works from the building on Fridays. They like their time in the small, sleek shop a few blocks away, greenery crawling the herringbone-tiled walls. It gives them distance from the distractions of the office, the people who always need attention.

Wells gazes into the egg sandwich he's barely touched.

"Are you eating?" Krish asks, running his thumb along the side of his black beard. "Like, at all?"

"What do you mean? The sandwich is fine. Just tired this morning."

Krish grimaces. "You've looked kind of gaunt lately, to be honest."

This isn't like Krish, who keeps the personal far from the professional. He's unmarried and unbothered by it; only thirty-three, substantially younger than Wells, who is now officially forty, after one red-velvet cupcake and a vehement insistence Leah let the day roll by like any other. They've known each other for years, and Wells understands little more about him than the fact that he has a flat somewhere near Inman Square and an undisclosed number of family members in what Wells thinks is Gujarat but can't be sure. Better than anything, he knows the sound of the special sigh Krish heaves to indicate he's sick of Wells's shit.

"I'm just overwhelmed," Wells replies, even though Krish is not wrong. The salt at his temples has sprinkled elsewhere in his hair, and now that he thinks about it, the shirts that pulled uncomfortably all summer no longer do.

Krish's dark eyebrows furrow, black eyes squint. "Wasn't that the point of hiring Aria? Is she not working out?"

"She's perfect," Wells replies. He bites the sandwich, though it doesn't taste like much, and the yolk drips sticky on his fingers.

He can think only of her full hips, the velvet of her skin, the slick between her open thighs. The hum of pleasure on her lips that lasts all day, well after they're done. It's that feeling, again and again, where Wells is born anew every time he's with her. He doesn't know how four months have gotten lost in secret bedsheets, but he's in deeper with her than ever, even though the transgression festers physically. Every time he pulls down the Murphy bed, he feels sick, down to his bones.

"I'm sleeping with her." Wells doesn't know why he says it, how his voice can sound so controlled. But he must eject it from his body.

Krish speaks quickly. "I think we have to add headcount in UX. The wireframes are still awful, and we have to take Alex off the project."

Wells goes wide-eyed. "Did you hear what I said?"

"Yes," Krish says, pinching his nose bridge and closing his eyes. "Anyway, I think we can support one more seat. I'm just going to do it and find the money later."

"Go ahead," Wells says. "I agree, they're shit."

Krish stands. Wells follows, drops his plate at the counter. They walk back to the office, dead leaves crunching under Krish's boots. He won't meet Wells's eyes. But before they enter the building, Wells feels Krish's hand on his wrist.

"Understand the can of worms you've opened," he says, "because I doubt you do."

~

"Molly," Wells says as he walks through the front door after work. He runs his finger along the slim black remote for his car. "Didn't expect you."

On a stool at the kitchen island, Molly sighs, pushes up the sleeves of her black jumper. Her daughter is in her lap with blue headphones on, playing on a tablet. She sees Wells staring at the game on screen.

"Don't judge me," she says, pupils big. She bats away a springy black curl from her eye. "I give up on everything right now, including good parenting."

"No judgment here."

It's been two days since Molly threw her husband out. Wells doesn't know where Jon is living or what's next for their marriage, but he does know better than to ask the wilted woman in his kitchen. Molly is stunning: six feet tall and slim, with dark skin that always looks touched by dew. He's barely seen her without red lipstick, hardly spotted a single blemish in the years he's known her. Yet that's not the Molly before him now. Seeing her in his home, like this—Wells can't begin to process it.

"I'm sorry about it all," he tells her. "If there's anything we can do, please don't—"

"Heart is staying over tonight so Molly can get some things done in the morning," Leah says, closing the fridge and turning toward her husband. Their nearly eighteen-month-old son is strapped to her chest in a green-striped sling, pink cheeks cherubic. Leah seems irritated Wells has walked into the house, perhaps irritated he's a man at all. What would wind him up before now makes him want to slink away with his tail between his legs.

"Glad we can help," he says, dropping his key to the kitchen table, Porsche logo face down.

Leah checks Heart's eyes are still fixed on the screen before she speaks. "Now's the time for you to say Jon is a piece of shit, Wells."

"Jon's a piece of shit, Molly."

Molly raises the red wine next to her, dumps the rest down her throat. Leah rushes to refill the glass. Molly puts her hands to her cheeks, looks like she might cry. She turns to him.

"Why are men like this?"

"You mean why do they cheat? Women cheat, too."

She pauses, rubs her eyes. "Why do men feel entitled to do whatever they want, and assume there won't be consequences?"

He doesn't say anything.

"I'm asking a serious question. What screwed-up patriarchal calculus is involved here? Do men think they have nothing to lose since there are so many other women out there dying to get married and have babies?"

"Ego," Leah jumps in. She turns to her husband, hands on her hips. Rowan now entirely asleep against her chest.

Wells excuses himself to finish some work, even though it's nearly seven on a Friday night. He'd tell Molly again he's sorry, but the floor isn't really his.

Leah calls for him to wait, gently unwraps Rowan from the sling, hands him to Wells. "He's zonked," she says quietly. "Please put him down."

Wells holds Rowan tight against his chest. His son is warm, cheeks still pink, the same rosy color Leah's skin flushes when she's tired. It's astounding how much his son's face is a facsimile of his own, even this young. His same eyes, brow, nose, lips. He wonders how much Rowan will be like him when he's grown. What Wells will tell him about love when he's old enough to ask. Just a few months ago, he would have held court, gone on for hours about who a man should be for a woman. The resolve he must have, the foundation he must build, the anchor he must drop. He must know her better than anyone, understand who she is and what she needs. Now, if his son posed the question, Wells would blank. Lately, he has come to think maybe it's not just about perfectly seeing someone else. It's also about being seen. He gently zips Rowan into his sleep sack, kisses his forehead, taps on the sound machine.

In his own bedroom, Wells undresses in the closet mirror. Krish is right: he does look thinner than usual. Since Ari happened, he hasn't recognized himself in his thoughts; he's starting to become a stranger in his own body, too.

Leah pops into the bedroom, catches his eye in the mirror behind him. She scans his torso. He's never worried more about what she sees.

"Did you pull down the Murphy bed?" she asks, worrying her necklace between her thumb and forefinger.

He snaps around to face her. "What?"

"In the basement. I'm co-sleeping with Heart down there, and the bed was already down."

"Oh," Wells says. The pressure on his chest again. "I just figured I'd get it set up in case you were."

Leah screws up her face. "I didn't even see you go down there."

He shrugs. "Well, what matters is it's done, right?"

"Right," she says. "Are the sheets clean?"

"I haven't used them since your mum was last here, unless you have."

"No."

"Lee, you seem cross with me tonight."

She drags her palms across her eyes, a little eyeshadow displaced.

"I'm not, I'm sorry. This whole thing with Molly has me beside myself." She shakes her head, touches his arm. "I just don't understand how he could do it. You take a vow, you honor it. If you can't honor it anymore, you respect the person you married enough to tell them in a dignified way."

"Is it that simple?"

Molly's daughter calls for Leah from the hall bathroom.

"Is it not, husband?"

"Of course it is."

Leah raises her eyebrows, shakes her head. After she leaves to fetch Heart, he turns to face the bed he'll sleep in alone tonight. Molly is wrong. Wells knows how much he has to lose. The problem is no matter what he does, he now loses something with any decision. Someone. Struggling with short breaths, he falls to the bed, reaches for his phone. He opens the encrypted messaging app he occasionally uses for sensitive work communication, and with the feeling of Leah's fingertips still on his skin, he writes to Ari that he can't stop thinking of her.

ARI

A ri isn't prepared for the first time Leah comes into the office.
Hey, how are you, great to see you. A chorus of greetings so loud
she pops out her headphones and looks up. There she is: Wells's wife,
emerging on a beautiful autumn afternoon.

Nora rushes to embrace her, tells her it's been too long. She crosses
the floor, raps on the glass of Krish's office, waves. He gives her a
thumbs-up outside the frame of his video call, and Ari can detect a rare
grin on his lips.

Then, as Ari hopes and fears in equal measure, Leah makes her way
directly to her. She's wearing light jeans that cling to her thin legs, a
chunky gray turtleneck sweater that must be cashmere, a leather moto
jacket hanging over it—too light for early November, yet right. She
looks, simply, cool.

"Can I give you a hug?" Leah's voice is gravelly, the opposite of the
songbird chirp Ari imagined. "Is that weird? I just feel like I know you
already."

"Of course," Ari says, opening her arms to the woman Wells sleeps
next to each night. "It's so nice to meet you."

Inside, her gut is a tempest. Acid riling. It's like she expects Leah to
know, to smell her husband on her. Leah's company has spent the past
week and a half moving offices, so she's been home more during the
day, and it's been difficult for Ari and Wells to get time alone. He won't
sleep with her anywhere but his basement, so they're at the mercy of his

family's schedule. He wants her in his home, he tells her when she asks why they never go to Ari's apartment. *No. I want you here,* Wells says each time. *Why? Does the risk get you off?* Ari keeps asking. *The risk is the worst part,* he says, then goes back to kissing her neck.

Leah doesn't flinch, even pressed against Ari's slack body, so close she can feel Leah's warm breath tickling her ear. Once they pull back, her smile is soft—inviting like Wells's, though in a different way. Purer, maybe. Ari doesn't want her to leave. It's insane.

"How's it been so far?" Leah asks.

"It's great. I got lucky."

"Heard you were doing something pretty shitty before this. Am I allowed to say that?"

"You are if it's true. And it is."

Ari feels Leah's phantom arms on her back. She didn't expect Leah's hug to be so strong, especially when she is so conspicuously slight.

"I'm sorry I'm just meeting you for the first time. I've been wanting to tell you that since you got his life on track, he's a man reborn. I'm not even sure how to describe it," Leah says, a sincerity that gives Ari pause.

Ari wants to know what Wells was like before her, how he's so different now that she's here. But part of her thinks she already does. In five months, she has watched Wells's charm offensive dull around her, more each day. He is someone else with the rest of the world: in head-to-toe armor, his own voice a shield. Yet alongside Ari, he gets lost in silky silence, lets himself slow down enough to breathe, listen to someone else exhale, too. *Close your eyes,* he sometimes says when they're not rushing out of bed. She feels his finger trace her jawline, run the Cupid's bow of her lips. *You are something,* he whispers, but never tells her what. This is who Wells truly is, she believes—but she brings it to the surface, just like she did with Morgan. Even Leah sees it, in her own way.

"Anyway," Wells's wife says, green eyes alight, "thank you for putting up with him."

"It's usually not so terrible."

Leah puts her hand on Ari's back, just a moment.

Finally, she heads toward Wells's office, where he's at the window, watching them together. One of his hands is pressed against the glass, right next to a patch of sticky notes he put up earlier in the day with Krish and the new UX designer. Leah walks inside, closes the door. Wells sits at his desk, though she stays standing. Ari can't discern what she's saying—the words, tenor—but he closes his eyes and shakes his head, lips turned under. He crosses his arms at his chest. Ari tries to turn away, but it's futile, and he probably knows she's watching it all. He and Leah shake their heads at each other, exchange short quips Ari can't lip-read. But on her way out of his office, she catches Leah's parting words to her husband: *You're impossible.*

~

Wells is still at his desk at seven, when Ari decides she'll grab a falafel sandwich on her way to the T, see if Summer wants to watch a movie with her over the phone. He hasn't said a word about Leah's visit. She shoves her computer in her bag, swings on her peacoat.

"Aria," he calls, brown-leather bag in hand and a midnight-blue quilted coat draped over his arm. He clears his throat, stifles a cough. "Walk out with me."

Ari's full name raises her hackles. "Sure."

"So," he says, leading her toward the stairs instead of the elevator, "you met Leah."

She eases open the stairwell door, a wail from the hinge. "I met Leah."

"And?"

"And she's great, like you said."

"Usually, yes."

Their footsteps echo in the empty stairwell, Ari's black ankle boots clicking alongside the blunt tap of Wells's white, gum-soled sneakers. She lets her step fall a little harder, just to hear the sound bounce off the walls. The footfall makes her think of Morgan, his impossibly heavy step, the *heel strike* he always lamented when he came back from his runs with his feet throbbing. Miles along the East River with the sunrise, no headphones. Ari couldn't help feeling like he was punishing himself by spending that much time alone with his thoughts, though she never understood what for. Was too afraid to ask, in case the answer might have to do with her. At night, when he'd collapse on the couch, she'd cradle his heels in her palms, dig her thumbs into the thick skin until he fell asleep.

"What was that?" she asks him. "In your office. Why was Leah here?"

He stops at the second-floor landing. Grabs her by the shoulders, pulls her into a hard kiss. His lips are cold, like he's been sucking on ice cubes. He pulls away, restarts his descent before she can shake off her shock.

He motions for her to follow. "She had a doctor's appointment around the corner, swung by." He clears his throat again. "Everything's fine."

She skips a step to catch up. "You fought, though."

"Did we?"

"She said you were impossible."

His eyes go wide, then squint. He doesn't know Ari heard. "She made me an appointment for an annual. You'll have to call and cancel it tomorrow."

"Why?"

"If I want to see a doctor, I'll do it on my own, not because she's holding my hand like a baby."

"She did it because she loves you," Ari says, even as Leah's affection for her husband wrings her own insides like a sponge. "Some people can't help but do things for other people when they love them."

"You do things for me because I pay you."

"No," she replies, the ground floor now under their feet. "It's not because you pay me."

He lets them out of the stairwell, looks back at her. Hums.

"Go," she says. "Leah's waiting."

∼

Ari goes home Thanksgiving morning. When she walks through the front door, her mother is wearing her thin navy bathrobe, checking her pale skin in the mirror above the fireplace. She runs a finger along the bottom of her jaw.

"You look nice," Ari says, closing the door.

"I'm sure."

Both Ari and her mother have known the holidays will be hard. They have always been—never did her parents fight more than when there was a turkey in the oven or a Christmas tree strangled by lights in the corner of the small living room. Shrieking voices and broken plates, her father's anger at fever pitch, every flaw in their chronically awful relationship on display like holiday gifts in a store window. The misery came each year, yet somehow still shocked Ari each time. Now her father spends Thanksgiving in the farmhouse with his stepsons and his wife's extended family. Ari declines the invite every year.

It's the first time in a decade she and her mother will weather the season fully alone. Once her father left, they spent Thanksgiving with Morgan's family; Kathy was there to smother Ari's mother with kindness in that warm kitchen, and Morgan was there to catch Ari, who was still in free fall, even seven months after her dad had abruptly gone. Her aunt and uncle were halfway across the country, which may as well have been halfway across the world—and as much as it hurt to stay in Abbott, it felt wrong to be anywhere else. Even though they owed nothing to Ari and her mother, the Meads had taken them in; back then she and Morgan were only circling each other. This family had sheltered and calmed them. Proved she and her mother were still loved. And then there was Ari and Morgan, and all the Thanksgivings to follow. For a decade, they were family.

With Wells, Ari can steer her mind away from Morgan. But now that she's back in Abbott, it's impossible. Things are different for her and her mother this year—but for him, change is excruciating. It's the first Thanksgiving without Kathy, and Ari doesn't know if the Meads are even in town. Maybe they are with Rick's brother in Hartford, because they can't bear to gather around the hulking, oval-shaped oak dining table, pushing around mashed potatoes while avoiding their own reflections in the glossy tabletop. Ari could have taken Kathy's place. She could have folded cloth napkins into neat rectangles with pockets for silverware, said some words of grace, cooked a tableful of food, filled the house with laughter. It'd mean everything to her, if only to quell the immense regret she has for leaving the funeral. Every day, she's surer and surer Morgan threw the macaroni and cheese across the kitchen, let the dish smash to pieces on the wall. She disappointed him, just as she feared she would if she'd married him.

Ari tosses her coat over the arm of the couch, flicks dust from the corners of her eyes. She carries a shopping bag to the kitchen, full of the food she made last night in the apartment. She turns on the oven to warm the turkey breast. Yet even as she stirs the gravy on the stove, removes the green beans from the microwave, she isn't hungry. It's so hard to be back in this house, where she hasn't returned since the breakup, especially when the air feels like a damp blanket. She only wants to run back to Cambridge, to Wells.

They sit for lunch, a compromise that means she doesn't have to stay the night. They wipe the dust from the kitchen table, stare at each other like strangers. They haven't shared air since the summer. Everything OK? Ari will occasionally text, a check-in every couple of weeks. She has barely solicited more than a Fine, thank you.

Her mother tucks her short brown hair behind her ears. "How is your job?"

Ari's almost startled by the high trill of her voice. "Good."

She's terrified to say more. If her mother knew she was the other woman herself, what's left of their relationship would snap. She'd hear the sharp cries of childhood fights, directed at her.

Her mother rubs her eyes, dark just like her daughter's. Over her shoulder, Ari stares toward the sink, the precarious dish pile towering, tap dripping. That floral wallpaper, which she has the instinct to tear off the walls. Ari pushes a few green beans onto her plate, spears a slice of turkey. She can't help but wonder what Thanksgiving dinner will be like at the Cahills'. If Wells will stuff himself with Leah's cooking, if Rowan will eat scraps on his high chair table as his grandparents dote. How warm they all feel, grateful to be a family, robust and unconditionally loving.

As much as Ari understands how much she could tear down that family, more than anything the image makes her see what her own mom has lost, however flawed it was. She can't believe she didn't see it before; can't believe her own transgressions were what it took to find clarity. Maybe her mother's edges are softer than she gave her credit for. Maybe she can't blame her for finding the bottom of wine bottles, after all.

"How are you?" Ari asks, trying kindness.

"The same," her mother says.

The same means copyediting work, document translation for a Parisian real estate company. She misses teaching French at the community college, but she can't teach from bed.

Her mother looks to the tabletop. "I should probably let you know I'm selling the house."

"You're not serious."

"I am."

"Why?"

"What's the point of staying here?" Ari's mother says quickly, shaking her head. "Your father's gone, I'm not working anymore, Kathy's dead."

"*Oh my god*, Mom."

"Well, tell me otherwise."

It doesn't matter that she's right, or that Ari doesn't even want to come home. The idea of losing her last connection to Abbott shakes her to her core.

"You can't do that."

"I spoke to an agent, and the market is good. She agrees it's the right time."

"What about me?" Ari almost shrieks, shoving her plate aside, almost spilling her water.

"What about you? You have your own life now."

Ari jolts to her feet. She rushes into the bathroom, stoops over the sink, splashes so much water on her face it drips off her chin. In the mirror, she is a shapeless smear. She's been shapeless for so much longer than she realized, especially now that all the molds that kept her together are gone. She won't live like this. With Wells, she's finding something she never could have otherwise.

She returns to the table, eats so she doesn't have to speak.

"I'm doing what's good for me, just like you've done for yourself," her mother says.

"Don't act like you have any idea what makes me happy now," Ari snaps, plunging them back into silence.

She stays at the table for only another fifteen minutes. She heads outside, crosses the yard to Summer's white door, adorned with the autumn wreath of woven branches. Summer opens before Ari even makes it to the porch.

"I saw you walking over."

She hugs Ari tight, invites her into the calm of her parents' home, but Ari declines.

"What's wrong?" Summer stands in black leggings, resettles a pale-pink tank top on her shoulders. "You look like you got hit by a truck."

"My mom's selling the house."

"Oh, wow." Summer puts the corner of her thumbnail in her mouth, which clicks as she tooths it. "I'm really sorry."

As she grabs her coat, Ari stands on the porch stairs, freezing in only her sweater. "Is Morgan in town?"

Summer nods, fiddles with her zipper. "He's opening the diner for us later. You should come."

She and Summer have seen each other only five or six times since Ari moved, and she hasn't seen Luke since she was living on Summer's couch. She'd do anything to spend even an hour with them.

"The car is due back tonight," Ari says instead.

"Bring it back late, then." Summer knows she won't.

"I miss you."

"I miss you."

It doesn't mean the same thing. Summer misses the Before version of her best friend, the one she knew for nineteen years. Who piled them all into her mom's car in high school, drove an hour to get pizza in New Haven on a Friday night. Who flew to Saint Louis during freshman year of college to surprise her best friend because she seemed lonely, even though Ari had no money. Who baked a batch of weed brownies for Luke after he visited everyone in New York last summer, sweets meant to ease the pain of a herniated disk. Who Morgan trusted his life with.

"Morgan would like to see you," Summer says.

Ari could do it. Prove to him—to herself—she's gone forward. But she shakes her head.

Summer sighs, scoops her freshly reddened hair into a high ponytail. Puts her hand to Ari's cheek for an eternal second, turns to go inside.

"Say hi to everyone for me, I guess," Ari says.

Summer says she will.

~

Ari decides she won't go home for Christmas. She briefly considers going to her father's in Vermont, but can't seem to make the phone call. Summer won't be in Abbott, or even New York—she'll be working, as will Luke. Ari spent last Christmas with the Meads; this year, she will spend it in Boston, watching Hallmark movies in ugly pajama pants, alone.

When she tells Wells her plans, he says no. Simply, *no*.

"You'll come to us for dinner," he declares, staring through his office window into a conference room.

The next *no* belongs to Ari. Her reaction cracks like a whip over them both.

"I'm your boss," he says, turning to her, crossing his arms. He stiffens. "You can't really say no."

They both pause. The words cut so deep, she's almost frightened.

"I could not think of a worse idea." But the pushback doesn't feel good, not really.

"Leah would love your company," he says, dropping his arms, refastening his watch.

"Are you kidding right now?"

"Lower your voice." He clears his throat like he's preparing to say more, but doesn't.

"Christmas is for family, not your assistant with no life."

"You very much have a life," Wells says, tapping his foot on the floor, "and I can make the case for it. I can be very convincing."

She doesn't say no. Which they both know means yes.

~

Ari has of course seen the gray colonial before, one of the multimillion-dollar houses of West Cambridge. But as she approaches now, the Cahill home seems far less imposing than usual. The bare branches above cradle it, drawing her eyes to the living-room window, glowing yellow warmth through drawn curtains. Christmas tree lights, twinkling jewel tones. She climbs the steps to the front door for the first time, acutely aware that a family lives here.

She needs to turn around. She is already too lodged in Wells's life, a position she should have never put herself in. How perverse to let him usher her into his home, however careful they might be. She is still grappling with where she belongs, how much space she should take up in the world. But the one place she should not be is here. What would be wrong with sitting in her apartment, in her own good company? Why shouldn't she try to find a last-minute way to Abbott, chip away at her mother's loneliness? The problem, Ari keeps finding, is that her compass is scrambled. She doesn't know what counts as a good decision anymore, what a good decision even means. Now that she understands hopes and plans don't build a reliable future, she just wants to feel alive right now.

Maybe Ari just needs to see Wells with his family in the home they've built. To remind her whom she's hurting and what she could upend. Maybe it's the only way to pull herself out.

She presses the doorbell as diamond-size snowflakes stick to her hair.

Instead of Wells, Leah opens the door, with one hand gloved in a navy pot holder, which she uses to nudge the sleeve of her gray T-shirt up her arm. There's a glaze of perspiration on her upper lip, her hairline.

"Aria, hi. Come on in."

A blast of warm air punches Ari as she enters. She offers the bottle of wine and box of Italian cookies to Leah, who smiles, tells her she shouldn't have.

Slipping off her puffer coat, Ari marvels at the house. It's the exact opposite of the stark, immaculate basement, all whites and grays. Instead, there are worn, dark-wood floorboards under her feet, an enormous navy couch, textured crimson rug below it. There's character in the wainscoting on the walls, gold pendants over the marble island, navy cabinets with brass handles. She stares into a pile of pastel blocks—cubes and arches and triangles—haphazardly pushed against the living-room wall.

"It's a disaster, I know," Leah says. "Our nanny is on vacation, and I'm so used to the mess it's practically invisible to me."

"Oh no," Ari says. She's mortified, making Leah self-conscious of her home, which Ari couldn't find more beautiful. "I'm sorry, I didn't mean—"

Leah waves the sentiment away, her hand still in the oven mitt. "Come."

In the kitchen, she turns on the oven light, crouches, and gazes in. Her shirt shifts up, and a sliver of skin peeks out. Ari doesn't know what to do with her hands—she wants to run her finger across that slip of skin, touch the spot where Leah's acid-wash jeans gap across the small of her back. She wants to feel what Wells touches when he's not with her. Instead, she just pinches the meaty skin by her left thumb.

Leah stands, turns back to Ari, leans on the counter. "Do you cook?"

"I can."

"Need your help, then. I'm behind schedule."

"Of course." Ari smiles.

Leah, it is clear, has no idea the fear and relief Ari is steeping in.

She passes her a knife and a bag of potatoes, instructs her to peel and quarter. Ari begins scrubbing them at the sink as Leah's eyes follow her hands. Leah finally swipes the sweat from her forehead.

"I actually hate cooking," she says. "He wanted a traditional English Christmas dinner this year, and I couldn't say no."

The entire time, Ari has been so fixated on Leah and the way she lives—the red stoneware dish for the roast potatoes, how she mindlessly tucks a strand of her blond hair behind her ear—that she's almost forgotten Wells is supposed to be here.

"Where is he?" she brings herself to ask.

"Schlepping to my dad's house in Newton to steal garlic from their pantry, because all the stores are closed and he didn't buy enough, even though I told him to."

"He's not the best at following directions."

"Of all people, you'd know."

Leah rolls her eyes, then looks at Ari's hands, which haven't been peeling fast enough. She tells her that Rowan is staying over with her dad and stepmother, *so we can be adults for a night, you know?* Ari's struck by how casual Leah is. Ari isn't a threat or a stranger, even though they've met only once, and Ari spends more time with her husband than she does some days.

Ari continues peeling. Strips of dull brown skin flutter into the plastic compost bin she's balancing in her lap. The air is infused with the brine of the turkey, its skin firming, glazing, crackling. Her hand is cramping, but she wants to finish quickly. That's what Leah wants.

"Why didn't you go home for Christmas?" Leah asks.

Ari shrugs. Because home no longer feels like home, she wants to say, and because soon it literally won't be. Because now she's standing in the home that fits her best.

"I was just there for Thanksgiving, so."

Leah cocks her head, hums.

"And my ex will be around," Ari says, like projectile vomit.

"Must have been a bad breakup."

"We were engaged. But didn't get married."

"Jesus. I—"

"If this isn't enough garlic, end me." Wells announces his presence, holding up a plastic bag. "Aria." His voice softens. "Welcome to our home."

"Thank you," she squeaks, drops the last potato to the counter, turns to Leah. "Let me know if you need anything else."

While Leah finishes dinner, Wells and Ari end up in the living room: him, in the big brown-leather chair next to the fireplace; her, on the blue couch with thick, squared-off arms. They stare at each other in a way she worries is sickeningly telling. If Leah were to come out of the kitchen, she'd know.

"What's new?" Wells says.

She shoots him a death glare.

"Your parents aren't bothered you're spending a family holiday with your boss?"

"Didn't ask if they were."

As he stares at her, his eyes soften, lips pull tight. The look shatters her. She could be a wife like Leah. She could be cooking someone's Christmas meal in the kitchen. She could be anywhere else but here.

"Go sit," Leah finally calls from the kitchen island as she pulls a trivet from a drawer.

The dining table is ready with smoked-salmon bites, cranberry relish, a bottle of red wine that looks old and expensive. Leah drops the potatoes, carries out the turkey, then places a bowl of soup on each plate before she sits.

"Leeks," Wells says to Ari, whose nose wrinkles at the word. "Don't make that face."

"I'm not making a face," she nips, flush with embarrassment. Picks up her spoon.

He is the first to eat. He seems immensely satisfied by the food, the company, which makes Ari's stomach turn. She wrestles with whether it's more natural to say anything or nothing. She's also consumed by studying every detail of Leah, down to the tiny gold bobby pin holding back a lock of hair by her right ear, the single chip in her red manicure on her left thumb. It's effortless to picture her on the couch, bare feet propped on the ottoman, book in one hand and glass of wine in the other. Bent over the dining table, having sex with her husband, once Ari leaves.

When she manages to bring her mind back to dinner, Ari is shocked by how normal everything feels. Leah talks about work: supply chain issues hobbling them, a potential partnership with a big-box store Leah *would absolutely die over if it happens, fingers crossed*. She asks Ari about where she's living and how she likes being back in Massachusetts, whether she misses New York. Wells keeps eyeing Ari, but nothing could will her to look over.

"It's funny," Leah says, peering into her near-empty wineglass. "I always wanted to end up in New York after grad school. I hated Boston. Still do, I think. Claustrophobic for a city, which I know is rich coming from someone who grew up in Maine."

"Why have you stayed?" Ari asks.

"I met Molly, then Wells, and all of a sudden my life was here."

"I tried to bring her back to London after we got married," he says, the first time he's been able to get a word in for a while. "It's a real city."

Leah shrugs. "I couldn't leave my family behind. I hated the idea of being alone if something went horribly wrong."

"Like what?" Ari asks.

"Like if I died," he says.

Ari finally looks over at him, but now he's not searching for her eyes. He and Leah finish their wine at the same time.

Leah stands, reaches for Ari's dirty plate.

"Plum pudding next," Wells says.

"I feel like I missed something," Ari says.

His irises look bluer than they ever have. He closes his eyes, as if he doesn't want her to stare so deep into them. "Leah probably needs extra hands, if you'll excuse me."

Ari finds herself alone at the dinner table, Wells and Leah just out of sight in the kitchen. When they return—Wells balancing plates of little brown domes dusted in powdered sugar, and Leah holding mugs of coffee and tea—they seem changed. Whatever is happening is private, desperately human, something Ari understands she shouldn't see, even if she can't piece together what's going on. Only a few minutes later, she declines a coffee refill, instead tells them she'll head out.

"You're always welcome," Leah says, seeing Ari to the door. She looks like she's going to cry.

~

Ari goes to New York for New Year's, because Summer doesn't let her refuse. Luke got the days off, so he's coming up, and they're holding *a little thing* in her apartment. *Morgan's not going to be there,* Summer said when she invited Ari down, even though she hadn't asked. *Doesn't matter to me,* Ari had replied, so transparent and false she shouldn't have even said it.

There are flutes of prosecco dotting Summer's little kitchen peninsula; mozzarella, peach, and prosciutto bites on toothpicks. Ari wonders whether her life with Morgan would have ever looked like this, or if the inertia that ended them would have made it impossible. She wonders what he's doing tonight that he's not here. She wonders who he's kissing at midnight.

Ari finds Summer across the room. She looks ridiculous in a sequined, one-shouldered magenta cocktail dress, standing next to Luke, whose pale-pink button-down is billowing from his rail-thin frame. Ari's wearing the black dress she put on for Kathy's funeral, the wool itchy on her neck. After she scoops a flute of prosecco, downs it in one gulp, Summer clasps her biceps, drags her toward the couch.

"Hey," Summer says to a guy sitting. "This is Ari, who I was telling you about. She's the best of the best."

Ari freezes. She didn't expect to be set up in Summer's crowded living room, on the couch where she slept when she had nowhere else to go.

"Hey," he says, introduces himself. He's black haired, with a strong nose Ari likes very much, and heterochromatic blue-and-brown eyes that knock her off her feet. His solid body reminds her of Morgan's.

Ari feels Summer's hand on her back—she's meant to step forward, introduce herself. Flirt. She should, and must after what she saw between Wells and Leah, a kind of untold intimacy. It's not that Ari is jealous. It's that if Leah ever found out, Ari would cause so much more damage than a divorce. She'd wreck her life. She'd set Leah's son on a miserable path he never asked to walk, that he can now never stray from. Ari knows what that slog is like, the misery of how no amount of hard work can ever beat it. She can't carry that power. Look what happened to her own mother. To herself.

She glances back toward the couch. They smile at each other, and she can't believe how normal she feels in her own body. What if she went home with him tonight? What if they slept together? What if they fell in love, got married, moved to Brooklyn or LA or Paris? *Why not,* she thinks. *Why not me.* Ari extends her hand, feels Summer tap her twice. *Good job.*

They talk and drink, nearly all night. Against all odds, she finds him fascinating. He's Luke's freshman-year roommate, originally from

Toronto and now living in Prospect Heights. He works as a civil engineer for the Department of Environmental Protection. He's an insatiable reader, the same doorstop Russian novels Ari studied in college and revisits over and over. He took two semesters of Russian language so he wouldn't have to read in translation, until the professor pulled him aside and told him he was, *with all due respect, absolutely hopeless.* At midnight, he and Ari kiss.

He asks if she'd like to get a nightcap at his place. She would. In his studio apartment, the laundry is folded neatly on top of a light-wood dresser, and there's an inviting clean scent on the air. Beside his computer monitor, a gold-framed photo of a giddy black dog. An acoustic guitar hanging on the wall. A bottle of Febreze. He's exactly the kind of person Ari should be with. He pours them gin and tonics, and they lie next to each other on his bed, just talking. He tries to kiss her again, but she's not there. Not when her entire being aches for the basement and the Murphy bed and the maddening ecstasy of her time with Wells. Ari doesn't yet know how to live without it.

"I'm going through some stuff. I'm sorry," she says, the digital clock on his nightstand at three thirty.

He nods. "I'm still glad you came over. It was a good night."

~

At brunch the next morning, Summer drinks one-and-a-half-too-many bottomless mimosas, tries to pull the night's details from Ari while Luke is in the bathroom, a tug-of-war rope.

"Why aren't you telling me anything? I had a no-joke crush on him the entire time Luke was at Penn. I might have told him when I was drunk," she says. "What was he like in bed?"

"Nothing happened."

"Nothing? You *stayed over.*"

"Just slept next to each other."

"Why? You kissed, didn't you?"

Ari feigns a smile. She'd made a step in the right direction, but couldn't go any further.

Summer puckers her lips. "What's with the face?"

Ari stirs the celery in her Bloody Maria, exhales out the side of her mouth. "I'm still sleeping with Wells."

"Aria." Summer clicks her tongue.

"I know. I couldn't stop thinking about him, and it seemed wrong to sleep with someone else."

She wants to tell Summer that she beyond understands how incredibly messed up the whole thing is, but she'd also have to explain how impossible it is to cut off. What Ari feels is now beyond a crush. It is necessary, her heart swollen for Wells.

"I need him," she says.

"You don't need anyone. You're better than that."

"It's not that easy." Ari reaches to Summer's cheek, swipes a stray eyelash onto her outstretched finger.

"It's not as hard as you're making it."

Summer closes her eyes to make a wish, blows away the lash. Luke emerges from the bathroom, head in his phone. She sighs at Ari, dabs the corners of her mouth. Ari fiddles with her bracelets in her lap, her fingertips running a tiny chain of rose-gold links, the smooth round of a narrow silver cuff.

"What did I miss?" he says, settling back into his chair.

Summer puts her hand on top of his. "Everything and nothing."

~

The moment Ari leaves Summer's, she texts Wells, using the encrypted app they've shifted to.

What are you doing?

You soon, I hope, he replies. He's in London, with his family.

She tucks her phone back into her bag. Feels like she can breathe for the first time in days.

~

Leah flies to a trade show in Dallas on January 3, the day after the Cahills get back from the UK. Below the entries for Irma's vacation and Rowan's stay with Leah's mom, Wells's calendar shows his wife's flight takes off at one thirty. By three, Ari is at their house.

He lets her in through the back, as usual. He silently studies her for a moment, arms crossed at his chest, then leads her past the basement door.

"Where are we going?" she asks.

He says nothing, just keeps walking until she follows him up the stairs and down a short hall, speckled with family photos. The white-walled bedroom opens up before her, a high king bed with pearly sheets and an emerald-green blanket. Two white nightstands flank the bed, gold articulating lamps mounted above them. It's obvious which side is Leah's: a black tube of Chanel lipstick, cap off; a ring of fabric swatches; a white mug initialed LRC. Wells watches Ari take in the room, his arms still tight to his chest. Her eyes trace the edges of the headboard of the bed in which his wife sleeps, where she probably breastfed their son. Where they've whispered about the plans for how they'll grow old together: a life of substance, promise.

Ari thinks about running, for real this time. Of all the transgressions, she's never imagined herself in his marital bed. Even with everything she and Wells feel for each other, she has never meant to replace Leah, and knows she can't. But when he begins taking off his shirt, it doesn't matter how beyond reason she is. Here, in his bedroom, he is telling Ari how essential she's become. *I need you,* he's said so many times she's lost count. They see together what he is wagering for her. She doesn't see a way forward for herself without his love, either.

~

As Ari leaves the house, her palms are clammy. Heart still racing. The streets are slick, the sidewalks sheeted in ice. Streetlights reflect off frozen pools. She walks her slightly longer route to the train on a side street, so she doesn't risk showing up in the doorbell camera. She pads carefully in her pointed flats, absolutely the wrong shoes. So, when she slips, lands hard, she takes a moment to think how she deserves to fall, before she actually experiences the pain. Then the sensation comes—an incredible lightning shock around her ankle. She screams so loud, the dark street echoes her cry.

She is alone, on her back, shaking. Her body barely touched by the radius of a streetlight. How did she let this happen—how did she choose this life over everything else? How, when all other roads were just as clear for her to walk? Her brain is screaming at her for not answering the questions sooner.

Still quivering, doing everything not to puke, she manages to find her phone. The screen is shattered, tiny shimmering shards radiating from the point of impact. She calls Wells.

"Miss me already?"

She is heaving, choking.

"What's wrong?"

His urgency is her first spoon of medicine. It's only a few minutes before his headlights roll over Ari's pathetic body, until he's kneeling beside her. His forehead is against hers, breath floats above her nose.

"We have to go get help," he says.

"No. Just call an ambulance," Ari ekes out. "I'm not going anywhere with you."

She needs him to rush her into the ER, sprint like the world will burn if she dies. But she barks *no* again, even as the lightning pain burns hotter.

"Don't be an arse," he says.

"You can't risk being seen with me."

"Shut up, Aria."

He lifts her, drags her into the passenger seat of his midlife-crisis car. Ari feels a surge of warm blood, an overpowering tingle. A sensation even stronger than the pain. She is his: Wells's responsibility, his choice.

"Are you okay?" he asks, seated beside her in the waiting room.

This meaningless question Ari has been so afraid of, the same one she's avoided since Morgan—for the first time, it's the right one.

"I think so," she says. She's settled into the pain. If she doesn't move she can stall the horrible feeling as only a fixed stranglehold. "Thank you."

He runs his hand through his hair, holds his breath, opens his mouth. Hesitates.

"Bishop?" a nurse calls.

Wells snaps his mouth closed and jolts to his feet.

He trails behind the nurse as she wheels Ari into a room, then settles into the corner chair while the woman checks her vitals. His eyes meet hers again, uneasy, like there's still something he's straining to say.

Instead, he reaches for his phone, types. It rings.

"Yes. She slipped on the sidewalk outside the office. I just happened to still be upstairs." Pause. "I will. Love you, too."

Ari winces. Wells closes his eyes.

"Leah sends her best."

The nurse sticks Ari with an IV. The curtain flaps as she leaves.

"You can go," she says.

"I won't," he replies. "You know that."

The doctor comes in to set the bone. Wells digs his fingernails into his knees as she screams. A crack, a horror.

~

The other bed in Ari's hospital room is empty for now. She asks when she can have more pills. *Not for a while,* the nurse replies pityingly.

She thinks about Wells driving home once they wheeled her upstairs, walking into his empty house. He'll pour a glass of red wine. Call Leah. Ari wishes she could know how big his story is, if it'll swell to include fabricated details so nuanced it'd be crazy for his wife to question them. Leah will say it's kind he is helping Ari, then tell her husband she loves him, and he will say the same as he slips into the bed where he and Ari were just hours earlier.

She strains for her phone, squints beneath the splintered glass to call her mother. When she gets through, she waits for her mother to ask why she's calling at eleven thirty at night. She doesn't.

"So, I'm in the hospital," Ari says. "I broke my ankle and I need surgery tomorrow."

"How did you do that?"

"I fell outside work," she hears herself say.

"Oh, Aria, that's awful. I hope you're not in too much pain."

"I need help." It's harder than she expects to ask. "I don't have any of my stuff, and I'm alone. Can you come? Just even for the day, tomorrow? I only need a few things from my apartment and it would just be nice if—"

"I can't."

"Literally *why?*"

"It's a lot for me right now." No irony is lost on Ari. "What about that girl from your office?"

"Never mind," she says. She hates herself for even calling.

"Aria, if you can't find someone local, I can—"

But Ari hangs up. She'd rather hire a stranger off an app to go into her apartment and grab her underwear and deodorant, drip water into the snake plant she inherited. It seems a unique pinnacle of misery to be in a hospital without anyone to call, and she knows it's of her own making. Everyone else has people who care, who are terrified to see their loved ones sick or disabled or unwell. Who recognize the people they love are mortal, quake at the very idea. What has Ari done to make sure she has someone like that?

A flake of razor-thin glass from her phone screen pokes into her thumb as she scrolls to call Summer. Her face feels oily, her hair matted with sweat against the back of a flat pillow.

"I was *just* texting you," Summer answers. "Mind reader."

"About what?"

"About a pair of heels that I need you to talk me out of buying."

"You wear Crocs and deliver babies all day."

"When you put it like that." She knows Summer is smiling. "Why are you calling so late?"

"Salutations from an emergency room."

"You're in the ER? What?"

"Actually, not anymore. I'm in the *hospital* hospital."

"What happened?"

"I broke my ankle. There was this huge patch of ice and I was rushing and I just ate it."

Summer asks what the orthopedist said about the break, how it set, whether they've given any details about the surgery, what kind of meds she's on, if the nurses know what they're doing, whether she needs to translate anything. Ari answers all of it with *I'm fine.*

"How did you even get to the ER?"

She pauses. "Wells."

"You were with him."

"I was leaving his place when I fell."

"Oh my god. Is he still there?"

"He left when they admitted me."

"Then who's taking care of you?"

She doesn't respond. Hears typing in the background.

"The earliest train I can get on is six twenty tomorrow morning. I'll find a way to get cover. I can't stay the night, though."

Ari's heart leaps. "No, Sum," though she couldn't mean it less. She needs Summer terribly.

"Spare me. Just text where you are."

"I'll buy you the heels."

"No kidding."

~

Ari could pick out the sound of Summer's footsteps from a mile away. She'd lunge out of bed if she could, throw her arms around Summer's shoulders, and melt against her with all the frustration and disappointment and shock she still feels. She arrives in Ari's room, tote bags dangling from the crook of her arm.

"Don't tell me they haven't taken you in yet? It's almost noon."

Ari shrugs. "They haven't told me anything."

"Have you asked?"

"Not exactly."

Summer lets out an *ugh*, drops the bags to the floor. "I didn't know what you needed, so I brought anything I could think of."

She extracts a new pack of underwear and some hair ties, cleansing wipes, a toothbrush, then places them all carefully on the bedside table. "After surgery, I can run to your place and get anything else. My train is at seven fifteen."

Ari breathes deep. Summer puts a careful hand on her bad leg, stoops to rest her head on Ari's chest.

"I love you," Summer says. "And I hate every reason you're here."

Ari strokes her soft hair. "I do, too."

~

When Ari shakes off the anesthesia fog, Summer is waiting in the chair Ari left her in. She slides her computer into her bag, waits for the nurses to settle Ari back in bed.

"How do you feel?"

"Like I'm on Mars."

"Did they say how it went? How long you'll have to be here?"

"I'm on Mars."

"Right."

Summer texts Luke, tells him Ari is out—high as a kite on morphine, but fine. She says Luke sends his love. It feels strange Morgan doesn't know what happened, isn't here in Summer's stead. While Ari is hazy and opioid-drunk, Summer catches her up on work, her sister and parents, things in the city. "You're not really missing anything," she makes sure to say, though it's not true. Ari wishes she could wiggle her toes.

There's a knock at the door.

"Am I good to come in?" Wells sticks his head into the room, steps in without anyone's permission, a vase of pink roses cradled like a newborn.

"They just let me up, so I figured I'd . . ." He notices Summer, stops talking. "I'm sorry. I didn't know you had someone here." He turns to her. "I'm Wells. I work with Aria."

"I know," she says limply. "I'm Summer. *Aria's* best friend."

"Nice to meet you," he replies, though his voice is devoid of any pep.

He readjusts the flowers, extends them to Ari. She has no idea what they mean. *I'm sorry you're in pain* or *I hope you feel better* or *This is horrifying for both of us* or *Leah told me it'd be nice to bring them* or god knows what else. He stands in dark jeans, his quilted jacket. He shifts nervously, a movement Ari's never seen.

"I'll get going," he says as Ari buries her nose in the roses.

"I heard you helped Ari to the hospital," Summer says. Stale. "Thank you." She blinks slowly, readjusts her thick, black-framed glasses.

"Lucky I was there," he says, more confident. He snaps back into his work self, the public self. "The ice outside the office just gets bloody treacherous."

"The ice outside your front door, too."

He pinches his bottom lip between his thumb and forefinger. "Ari," he says, no longer needing the facade. "You'll come stay with us. It was Leah's idea."

"No," Ari says.

"No," Summer echoes.

"I know," Wells says. "But I don't think you have much of an alternative."

It's clear he realizes Summer knows. They've been so discreet, and the reality that the secret is now bigger than them is showing on his blanched face. Ari feels guilty putting Wells at risk, but what was she going to do. She couldn't hold it from Summer.

"I'll be fine," Ari says, worried for the first time what she looks like. Her dirty hair, green skin, the stinging-hot stress blemish dying to surface. "Right, Summer? I'll be fine."

They watch Summer process the horrible situation that's just compounded. She gnaws a nail. "Actually, you won't be, not for a while. And I can't stay."

Ari lives in a fifth-floor walk-up. She won't be able to go to the bathroom alone, make a sandwich, pick up her toothbrush if she drops it. *Leah* is the only word Ari can eke out.

"It was her idea," Wells says again. He coughs hard.

Ari and Summer can't look away from each other. *What the hell do I do?* Ari's eyes say.

Summer sighs, then asks for her key and a list of what she needs from the apartment. "I can't miss my train," she reminds her. Ari forgets to mention the plant.

~

"You'll have everything you need down here," Leah says after supervising Ari's crab walk down the stairs, two days later.

Ari nods as Wells leans against the wall.

"I'm really grateful, Leah," she says. She is. But wow.

Leah guides her to the U-shaped couch, Ari's walker sliding slowly over that pristine carpet. Wells sits on the other side. He rubs his knees a few times, grabs the back of his neck, shifts. This unnerves Ari, used to seeing him uncannily performing the role of a man who is not cheating on his wife. As much as Wells needs her, he doesn't want Ari here, like this. He would have said no if she had any other option, and if his wife weren't so sweet and reasonable—but Wells, like Ari, doesn't have an alternative.

"Irma and I will bring down meals and whatnot, but just text when you need anything else. Don't worry about bothering me, truly," Leah says.

Why are you doing this? she wants to ask. Yet she's oddly soothed by the idea of Leah's hand lightly pressed into her back as she guides her to bed.

"And you'll call my phone for anything in the middle of the night," Wells adds. "I'll keep the ringer on for once."

"I'm grateful," she says again.

"We know," he replies.

Still, she feels like she's in a dungeon, held prisoner by her own stupidity.

"Obviously, this is paid holiday," he says.

"No."

"Yes."

"Please. I need a distraction."

"Then teach yourself to knit."

"Wells," Leah barks. "If she wants to work, let her. She'll be miserable enough as is."

Ari winces.

"Let me talk to her about it," he says.

Leah ascends the stairs, peeling off her white sweater. "Your doctor is calling in five minutes," she says to her husband. "Make it quick."

He sighs, flops backward to the couch. Stretches his arms above his head, sits back up. "So?"

"*So* what?"

"Here we are."

Ari spins the rose-gold bracelet on her wrist. "I still can't believe we let this happen."

Wells sucks in his cheeks. He reaches out to touch her, but quickly pulls back when he realizes what he's doing. "We didn't let anything happen, Ari. I chose you and you chose me."

His tenderness brings her to her knees.

Wells shakes his head, darts up the stairs when Leah calls for him through the closed door.

Her phone buzzes in her pocket. Happily settled in?

Ari replies to Summer with a photo of herself, sunk into the pillows, looking as gross as she feels. Her hair is a rat's nest on top of her head, eyes bloodshot.

I'm moving in permanently

Not funny in the slightest

On the ceiling, Ari hears quick pitter-pats—Rowan, a maniac toddler in the living room directly above. She pictures the toys stuffed into a corner at Christmas.

I told Luke about Wells, Summer writes next.

Why?

I couldn't keep it to myself anymore. I'm sorry

I will jump off a bridge if it gets back to Morgan

Morgan says get well actually

Oh my god

He doesn't know the rest. I'll keep checking on you

Don't worry

All I do is worry about you since you don't do it yourself.

~

The next week is not as terrible as Ari expects. Irma brings hot lunches, the best home cooking she has tasted since Kathy's; guides her to the cab for her doctor's appointment, at which her bandages shrink.

She doesn't even know when Wells is at the office or upstairs at his desk. She expected to work—argued with him over midnight texts—but she mostly sleeps. The pain pills make her tired. The boredom, too, is killer. Yet against all expectation and logic, Ari likes being here. She is being cared for. People are concerned she's well and getting better. It feels like a giddy privilege. But she also realizes the arrangement is temporary. She has no template for what she should do next.

On the eighth evening, after Rowan's thundering heels cease pounding the ceiling, she hears a soft knock at the basement door.

"It's me," Leah calls down. Now she can just say *it's me*, like a best friend on the phone. A partner. She makes her way over with a bowl of pasta and marinara. "Nothing good tonight. We got lazy."

She sits next to Ari. Her breath smells of wine, tart and crisp. Though she's usually in whatever she's worn to work—dark jeans, a short dress—Leah is instead wearing an oversize white T-shirt, and thin, heathered-flax house pants, which Ari can tell are butter soft.

Leah's eyes track to the television, where Ari is watching a dating show.

"Wells and I met on one of those," she says, pointing at the screen. "A blind date, I mean."

Ari wants to vomit the words, *I know. Wells told me while we were naked and flush in bed.*

"Who set you up?" she says instead.

115

"An old college friend. I don't talk to her anymore. But at least I got Wells out of the deal."

"You seem very happy."

"Sometimes weird stuff works out." Leah cracks her neck, crosses her legs under her. "I'm kind of surprised you're single. Is that okay for me to say? Probably not. I take it back. Sorry."

"It's fine." Ari looks down at her thighs in gym shorts, pulls a blanket into her lap.

"I'd love to introduce you to one of my product engineers. You'd really like him. Super funny and quick on the uptake. A little bit of a lost soul, but nothing you can't straighten out," Leah says. "I'm living proof setups can work."

Ari smiles at the subtle compliment. It'd be such a meaningful step to get out of all this, pay Wells's wife the respect she deserves—herself, too. Ari is a strangling vine around Leah, and she doesn't want to squeeze the life out of her. She can't remember the last time she took a painkiller, but she would like one, or at least a glass of whatever Leah's been drinking.

"I'll think about it," she says.

"You had a bad breakup."

"Yeah."

"How long ago?"

Ari startles. The question is intrusive for a stranger, but Leah isn't a stranger anymore. After all, Ari is living in her home, eating her food, seeing her in pajamas, going to bed with her husband.

"Last May. We got engaged years ago. I don't know what happened," Ari says. "Actually, no. That's not really true."

Leah screws up her face.

"Our best friends started dating around the same time we did. They're still together, and once we got engaged, I think both of us got spooked we'd never be as good as them. Like . . ." Ari trails off. She's never said the words to anyone. But Leah opens her like a spring rosebud. "Maybe we'd always feel deficient. I don't know."

"I can understand that," Leah says, shrugging. "Maybe it was a bullet dodged, who knows."

"Who knows, indeed."

Leah shifts uncomfortably at Ari's frigid response. "Well, I'll leave you to it down here."

Ari asks if she can turn off the overhead lights on her way back upstairs.

~

A few days later, Ari gets her stitches out, one step closer to being herself. She's playing with the Velcro on her new heavy walking boot when Wells and Leah come downstairs with her dinner. He extends a plate of Irma's golden potato pancakes, sprinkled lovingly with sprigs of fresh dill. Leah asks permission to sit. She's clearly nervous from overstepping. Ari says yes, she'd love their company. Seeing Wells again—even with his wife close beside him—is a wave of relief.

He suggests a movie. It's a good idea, everyone agrees. This will be Ari's last night here; gathering feels like a goodbye party, sending off a daughter to college. Together, they do less watching, more commentating, like the most irritating people in a movie theater. The plot is stagnant, much less highbrow than Wells swore it would be. They laugh at the film's sienna tint, its forced pathos.

"Why did you pick this?" Leah sneers, and Wells shrinks into himself.

"Leave me alone, would you? I heard it was good."

Leah grabs Ari's arm with her small hand, an intimate touch meant to say, *We're on the same team.*

Ari thinks again how pretty Leah is. She wishes she had her clear eyes, translucent skin that never needs makeup. She hopes Leah isn't self-conscious about the birthmark on her cheekbone, because it's perfect. Ari has the impulse to run the pad of her pointer finger across it.

Leah was once abstract, but now she's no longer just Wells's wife. She is alive, with her own relationship to Ari. What kind of sociopath ignores another person's humanity? The compassion and respect and water-pure care Leah has shown her? If she physically could run, she would. She has never been so sorry for something she's done; at the same time, she has never been so physically helpless.

Ari feels the couch cushions shift, hears Wells struggle to clear his throat. When she refocuses on the screen, the lead couple is in bed with their friend. The women kiss, tentatively peel off each other's dresses, turn to the man. They fall backward to the mattress. Sheets obscure their movements, their skin—the only time in the past hour the camera angles have been right.

The air is heavy, thick, cricket quiet. Wells readjusts again, the rustle of his jeans against the cushion, soft friction like paws on a scratching post.

He clears his throat. "Funny."

Yes. This all is *funny*, in a terminally sick way. The three-way playing out on the television, but also everything about the past week. They've fused into each other as Ari's presence has normalized. They are vertices of an obtuse triangle. How could anyone have known it'd turn out this way.

"Well, I'm knackered," he says, slapping his hands on his thighs.

"I suppose I should turn in, too. It's late." Leah tightens her short, low ponytail, asks if Ari needs anything before sleep.

She says no, she has everything.

"Happy to hear it," Wells says, standing as he turns off the television.

As he and Leah climb the stairs together, only one fact exists: they are getting into bed, climbing on top of each other, fucking until daylight breaks.

～

Summer arrives in a cab in front of the house around noon. Ari has already shoved her filthy clothes into a bag. She feels guilty she can't strip the bedsheets like a good guest. She finds a notepad and pen, already knowing they're in the top drawer of the chest under the television. *I can't express my gratitude.* It's true.

Summer texts she refuses to go inside the house. Ari knows better than to fight. Having met Wells at the hospital, she is already involved. Her reluctance reminds Ari the past ten days have been objectively unhinged. Instead, Irma helps Ari again, while Rowan naps upstairs.

"Well, that's over with," Summer says as she maneuvers Ari into the car, stuffs her deeply mortifying knee scooter into the trunk.

"It is."

"You didn't . . . while you were there . . ."

"Oh god, no."

She considers telling Summer about the night before, stewing together in that triangle. But she smiles instead, thanks her best friend for coming to the rescue again.

Summer detangles a few strands of hair, fiddles with the zipper on her pink fleece. "What was Leah like?"

"Stunning and too generous. She treated me like family."

"Then please tell me it's over."

"Actually," Ari says as they hit a red light, "it is."

WELLS

From the kitchen, Wells hears Leah hoovering the carpet of the in-law suite. It's just hours after Ari left—a period that felt closer to a year than a week. He downs the rest of his tea, descends the stairs, peers at his wife cleaning by the coffee table.

She startles when she sees him, hand to her heart. "You scared the hell out of me. How long have you been standing there?"

"Just a moment. I came down to see if I could help."

"Sure." She asks him to change the sheets.

Wells retrieves the spares from the chest under the television, begins stripping the bed. He stutters when he spots a small brown spot in the middle of the fitted sheet. It's not from Ari staying over, he knows. It's from a few weeks earlier, when they fucked at the tail end of her period, a streak of sticky blood on the underside of his cock. He'd meant to switch the linens before Ari came to stay—Leah had asked him to, but he'd gotten himself sucked into a text-message argument with Krish—and it wasn't until Ari had gotten into the house that he remembered he hadn't done it. He wonders if she noticed. All along, he's known he shouldn't insist on taking her back here, especially when it's how Molly's husband got caught. But what was the convenience of an empty house the first few times now seems essential. He dips into a different life—one where he's in this home he loves, but he belongs entirely to Ari, and sinks into the path he might have taken were he not obsessed with coming out on top. It's so built into his personality now, there's no turning back from the hubris, except with her.

Leah dumps the full canister of dirt into the bin. "Ari sheds a lot," she says, pulling at the dangling strands. "Is it shitty of me to say I'm glad to have our house back? She's so sweet, but when anyone else is here, it's like—I don't know, you feel it."

"Right."

"What?" Leah's hand goes to her hip. "It's the same thing with our families. It's not particular to her." She taps the canister to free the last clump of detritus, tells Wells to flip up the bed. *As long as you can still manage it.*

He pushes the bed into the wall so hard, she jumps.

"Do you like her?" he asks, his back turned to his wife as he balls up the dirty linens.

"A lot."

It pierces him unexpectedly. "Why?"

"She's kind of a calming presence, and we didn't have to pretend to be the world's best hosts. She just wasn't a burden," Leah says. "I tried to set her up with Evan, but she didn't take the bait."

"Why would you do that?"

"Why would I not?" Leah squints at him, then drags the hoover to the stairs.

"Lee, what are you doing? I'll bring it when I go back up."

"You need to take it easy."

"For fuck's sake, I'm not a bloody child."

She doesn't respond, just keeps bumping the machine on each step as she struggles up the stairs.

Wells settles onto the couch, tries to breathe deeply. Even with everything going on in his own life, all he can do is think of Ari. He's not worried about when they'll be in bed next; he's unsettled not knowing when he'll see her again. He's been on edge every day she's not at her desk, the soothing presence Leah mentioned conspicuously absent. He feels rough around the edges, to the point that even his wife has noticed he's gotten trigger happy with the temper that's subsided the past few months. Without Ari, he feels like he's wasting time. And time is more precious than gold.

Staring at the black television, Wells thinks about the three of them together in front of the film last night. The sex on the screen, the impenetrable silence in the room. He would have buried his own body to know what Ari was thinking. As he and Leah went upstairs, his wife's hand brushed his. His dick was hard, straining against his jeans. But when they'd gotten up to their room, he didn't go to bed with her, even though he knew she wanted to. He ignored her coy eyes, the flutter of her lashes. Instead, he stepped into the shower.

As the scalding water fell, he got himself off thinking about the three of them together. It's the filthiest image he's ever conjured—hands, fingers, lips, tongues running over each other. He wanted all of them, both of them. He wanted Leah and Ari to want each other. For the first time, he couldn't separate them. For a moment, at least, he didn't need to.

~

Driving to see Leah's mum in Maine always feels like the longest two hours of Wells's life. Rowan is a nightmare in the car—no matter how they try to distract him, he whinges in his seat from the time they pull out of their driveway until they walk through the door in Portland. And, like his toddler son, Wells can't sit still, either.

Susan is not his favorite person, if he's being as diplomatic as he was raised to be. He met her two and a half months into his relationship with Leah: a long winter weekend at a Kennebunkport cottage, their first trip. He had relished seeing his girlfriend outside the city, as if being in the place she loved most unlatched her—a calm instead of the intensity, a cruising speed instead of a constant pavement pound. Leah seemed a fuller person: her bright eyes gazing out to the ocean; her hair windswept as they stood beside the lighthouse. They'd spent each of the three nights under a heavy wool blanket, generating a current he'd never felt. He knew then, he loved her.

On their last evening, she asked him whether he would meet her mother. He already knew he would marry this girl. They joined Susan at an upscale seafood restaurant, right on the water. As they took their table, Wells felt a pang. Studying her tight eyes, he disliked her on sight, like a feral dog. He knew she felt the same way. All night, she had been cold, suspect. He understood she was protecting her only daughter, who'd had her heart broken enough by men who couldn't handle her. But Wells was not a man from whom Leah needed protection. On the drive back to the cottage, Leah asked him what he'd thought of her mum, which they'd both known was a tricky, even dangerous, question. Leah was not stupid; she'd been caught in the web of discomfort, too. *She clearly loves you a great deal,* he had said, focused on the road, hands unrelentingly tight on the steering wheel. Leah shrank into her seat.

Driving to Susan's now, Wells reaches for the stereo from the passenger side, but Leah slaps his hand.

"What are you doing?"

"I can't listen to *Daniel Tiger* for another hour. I'll blow my brains out."

"He's finally sleeping. Do not touch a thing."

Wells turns up the heat, then lowers himself into a deep recline, sinking into the tan leather and closing his eyes. He knows it's disrespectful while Leah is idling in car-park traffic, but his head is pounding. They've lost a major account at work, which they're scrambling to renegotiate, and the redesign continues to look terrible. Krish has been in a foul mood for weeks. Ari still working from home has not made Wells's life easier, both functionally and emotionally. He knows he is not exactly relishing each day the way he should. He, too, has been a morose bastard.

Going to Portland is not helping, even though they're only heading up for the Saturday afternoon. Still, he is dreading spending time in Susan's living room. It's punishingly cold when they get out of the car, after forty-five more minutes—late January in Maine, twenty-four degrees with biting wind, gray mounds of crystalline snow at the curbs. He gently unclips a groggy Rowan and pulls up the hood of his coat as he holds his son against the warmth of his chest. They let themselves into the Cape home. Leah's mum greets them at the door. She embraces her daughter, plucks her grandson from Wells's arms. *Nice to see you,* the pleasantry they exchange.

Over Susan's shoulder on the console, Wells can't peel his eyes from Leah's wedding portrait, even though he's seen it a thousand times. His wife in the short-sleeved, oatmeal-colored hand-beaded dress she'd worn to their ceremony in Bar Harbor at an oceanfront inn, then the party at the Barbican Conservatory in London a few weeks later. Her great-grandmother's string of tiny pearls circling her neck. Leah had been maddeningly stunning. During their first look, he had been gob-smacked by an otherworldly beauty he'd never seen of his bride. She was more than human, glowing immortal. He'd felt so goddamn lucky. He still is.

"You okay there?" he hears his wife say.

"Huh?" He snaps back into himself.

"You were staring into space. Are you not feeling well?"

"Oh. I'm fine."

Wells feels like such shit seeing the picture, he's almost angry. He's never stopped loving Leah for a single minute, even the ones he spends with Ari. He still doesn't believe he could love anyone more than his wife. Sometimes he looks at her press her cheek to Rowan's and just hold it there, or touch his own hip in passing as he's standing at the kettle. These moments are extraordinary, and he feels privileged they're his. He hopes she never stops collecting people to love, because the world will miss out.

As they shed their coats, Susan asks if they'd like wine with the lunch she's set out.

"God, yes," Leah says. "There was an accident near Ogunquit. It took us almost three hours."

"Wells?" Susan asks.

"What is it?"

"Sauvignon Blanc."

"New Zealand?"

"Yes."

"I'll pass. It's got that cat-piss taste."

"*Wells,*" Leah snaps.

"What? You know it has those sulfuric compounds I hate."

She and her mother exchange a glance. Susan heads to the open kitchen, fetches the big Greek salad she's made.

Leah lowers her voice to a shout-whisper. "Why are you being such a dick?"

"Why do you think?"

Her face drops.

Wells spends most of the afternoon on his phone, leaving Leah with her mother, who plays with Rowan among the toys she keeps in the corner of the family room. He doesn't want to talk to Susan any more than she wants to talk to him. But he also won't let himself look up from his screen, because he's afraid to meet his wife's eyes, see her body. He knows it's mental, but he keeps thinking he'll see Leah back in her pregnant form, all swollen belly and ballooned feet. Because of her endometriosis, they'd started trying for a baby almost immediately after their wedding, then skipped straight to IVF after eight months without luck. He can't forget the black bruises all over her stomach from the injections—battle scars she'd worn for nearly a year—and the yelp she let out every time he plunged the needle into her body. They still have two embryos on ice, which they've talked about thawing. He knows she wants more children, but now it's so much more complicated.

They stay until twenty past five, when Rowan hits his witching hour. Susan smothers her grandson in kisses, embraces her daughter. *Nice to see you,* the pleasantry Wells and Susan exchange again.

At the car, Wells tucks his son into his seat, right as he begins wailing. "Do you want me to drive?" he yells. Leah sticks her pointer fingers in her ears, shakes her head. They settle in, zip back onto 95, dark road open. She accelerates.

"You were a real a-hole today," she says, reflexively censoring herself for Rowan.

"You're right, I'm sorry."

He pauses, turns to his wife, whom he sees in profile: the gentle slope of her small nose; her slim lips, which she runs beeswax balm over all day. He reaches for her across the cup holder. She briefly stares at his outstretched hand, before slipping her palm into his.

"Leah," he begins, on the deepest inhale. Wells blows out all the air in his lungs, which isn't enough. The admission is on his tongue.

"Hm?"

But he doesn't have the balls to tell her. He never will. He shifts in his seat, pulls his hand back into his lap. "Thanks for driving," he says, reclining the seat once again.

ARI

Ari hasn't been back to the office in three weeks. She's left her apartment for two doctors' appointments. Otherwise, she hasn't seen another soul, including her boss. She's swung back into work as Wells's assistant: video meetings and email and chat, names on a screen. And as much as the isolation exposes the hole he's left behind, this piercing nothing is exactly right. It's where she should have landed herself long ago.

Instead, she's tried to spend the agonizing cabin fever thinking of herself and what's next. She's started flipping job applications to tech companies in New York, now that she has the right experience. Wells, she knows, would give her a glowing reference. Summer is falling all over herself that Ari might come back, sends her listings at all hours. When she's feeling ambitious, Ari clicks through English grad programs at City College, NYU, even Columbia. Maybe Morgan is still in the city. Maybe he's even moved jobs to one of the companies she's applied to. Yet it matters less and less. That she is even able to see a life past Wells, one she built out of desperation—it means everything.

It's nine thirty, a nothing Tuesday, one of those deceptive days when the sun is blinding but the air is a razor blade to the face. She pushes the office door open hard. Nora screams her name across the room, then throws her arms around her, like a lover who's been lost at sea. Ari squeaks out a *hi*, straining over Nora's shoulder to see if Wells is in his office. He is. He catches her eye, motions her in.

"Well, look at you," he says, rolling back his desk chair.

"Almost human," she replies, bowing her head.

"Almost." Wells smiles. "I've got a lot of meetings today."

"I know. I scheduled them."

"You did." He pauses. "Anything else? I need privacy, otherwise."

He holds her eyes for a second too long, then adjusts his monitor to a new angle, head down, as if she is the last person he wants standing there. She trudges to her desk, drops into her chair. Despite all she's been doing, it still hurts. How could it not.

It's like I don't exist, she texts Summer.

Her reply comes three hours later. That's good, remember?

She glances over to him as he interlaces his fingers behind his head, elbows splaying wide, tipping back in his chair while he takes a video call.

Fuck, she texts back. You're right.

~

In the gray of mid-February, Wells messages Ari on chat, asks if she can get him a last-minute pass for a developer conference in San Francisco next week.

Registration has been closed for months and you're not even a dev, she types.

Find a way.

She does. After she gets off the phone with the conference organizers, who accommodate Wells because he is a big deal, she forwards his credentials, adds that his hotel and flight options are lousy, since they've been booked for months. He knocks on the glass, summons her in.

"What are my lousy options?"

He pulls the frayed collar of his rust-orange T-shirt from his neck, hanging too big on him. The Boston winter is still in full force, but his office is boiling from the heater. There's a glaze on his forehead, like it's peak July.

She rubs her hands on her thighs, turning her palms indigo from the dye on her new jeans, a size bigger than the last. She's done a decent enough job of not punishing herself for it; she was on her ass for a month, and is still a little wobbly. Progress. She sucks in her cheeks, clears her lungs on a deep exhale. There's a queen room at the mediocre conference hotel, she tells him, or an unjustifiably expensive suite at the four-star across the street.

He twirls a pen in his hand, always green ink. "Suite."

Her eyes flash wide. "It's almost five hundred dollars a night. Krish is going to breathe fire."

He snorts. "I'll beg for forgiveness."

She sighs. "Also, there's nothing left in business class."

"I'll beg for forgiveness," Wells says again, which means Ari is to book him in first. He slides off the pen cap with his thumb, clicks it back on. Repeats. "How many seats are left?"

"In first? A bunch. Why?"

"Good. Book two."

"Was I supposed to get Krish a pass?"

Wells doesn't answer the question, just tells her to put in the days as vacation. He looks at her with eyes he hasn't for more than a month— soft with permission, desire. A plea.

She freezes, mouth agape. "No, Wells. We finally got ourselves out of all this."

"As you wish, Aria."

"Don't *as you wish* me. I'm serious. No more."

After a sharp glance at him, she settles back in front of her screen. Books the hotel. When it's time to select Wells's plane seat, she stops. There's one vacant row, 3A and 3B both open. She closes her eyes, tries to picture herself in New York with Summer or in bed beside a boyfriend who loves her. In a different job, a classroom. But Ari still can't dream up any world where she's not in the other empty seat.

~

At the airport, nothing feels special. They are colleagues, manager and direct report. They navigate as individuals, queueing one behind the other to print their boarding passes, Wells splitting off to one baggage scanner while Ari goes through another. He gets a sixteen-dollar glass of red wine at the bar near the gate while he sifts through email on his phone; she buys a bag of black licorice from the newsstand, then reads a book by the window overlooking their parked plane. "What kind of American eats black licorice?" he says. He returns to his phone.

They settle into their first-class seats—an absurd comfort—and stay mostly focused on themselves during the flight. Wells keeps trying to reset his poor internet connection so he can work, before he gives up and sits back, paging through downloaded UK newspapers on his tablet. Ari can't focus on her book, instead stares out the window at the expanse of sky. Halfway through the flight, he touches her arm, reminds her not to answer any work email. "Put up your out-of-office," he says. "You're in New York."

But everything changes the moment they step into the marbled lobby of the hotel. Wells taps his foot on the floor, drums his fingers on the counter as they wait for the clerk to finish.

"How many keys will you need?" the woman asks.

He holds up two fingers.

Ari looks over her shoulder at the people pacing through the lobby, groups seated together in circles of large leather chairs on either side of the door. She expects Leah among them, popping up out of nowhere to catch them. But she isn't.

"And yours, Mrs. Cahill."

Ari's head snaps back. The woman holds out the key card.

"Thank you," she says.

Wells smiles to himself in the elevator. "Mrs. Cahill, eh?"

In the mirrors lining the car, they both watch him take Ari's hand, hold it until the doors split open.

The room is spectacular. Ari feels spoiled the second she steps into a wholly unfamiliar, pampered luxury. The suite is bigger than her apartment, open and full of natural light seeping in through the tall windows overlooking the city. She's embarrassed to be so bowled over by a hotel room. But it's not really the suite itself, is it.

"Early dinner?" Wells asks as he drops his bag on the desk.

"This is insane," she says.

As badly as she wants to keep the view, she whips the blackout curtains closed, tugs to cover every last tiny crack of light. She's still terrified they'll get caught.

He laughs under his breath, places his hands on her cheeks, kisses her.

"Why did you change your mind?" she asks.

"What do you mean?"

"You didn't want to be with me anymore. But now you do."

Ari wants him to say that she means everything to him. That he can't live without her. It's simpler than that, though. He just missed her. She is sure, because she just missed him, too.

"I never said that," he whispers. "I want you more than I ever have."

She slips on the black shirtdress she wore the first time he invited her over. As he pulls on his own shirt, she watches his pointed shoulder blades shift. In all the months they've been together, with all the times she's watched him clothe himself, it's the first he's dressing to be with her.

Ari admits it to herself. She's in love with him.

~

They spend two hours at the table. Wells tells her about everything they never had the time and space to talk about, because they were too busy running. He explains growing up in London, his family. His parents are both high-ranking investment bankers, childhood sweethearts, still together after forty-four years. Ari nods. They're all very close, he continues; his two older sisters both still live in London, with their husbands and children. He has three nieces and a nephew. The whole family tries to get together four or five times a year, but he hasn't been back as much as he should, even with the company's office in Islington. The business is growing too fast; it's hard to step away, though it eats his conscience that he doesn't visit often, especially since his mother isn't as healthy as she used to be. He misses her cooking, and their elderly cocker spaniel, Ozzy. He tells her about history and economics at Oxford, meeting Krish in grad school; his guilty pleasure, deep-fried Mars bars; the too-expensive car he loves but knows makes him look like a *tosspot*. He tells her everything he'd tell a first date. That's exactly what it is. It's so good.

"It's all pretty incredible," Ari says.

Wells looks at the table. "You'll do plenty of incredible things, too."

She believes him. The problem is she can't when she's tied herself to him like this.

Even though Wells was the one who wanted to eat, he's barely touched his food. He grabs his stomach, winces. Ari asks if something's wrong. "No," he assures her, short. He cuts a piece of rib eye, sweeps it through the pan jus, his fork turned over, always so proper.

"Sometimes I think about what would have happened if I'd taken another route," he says, a softness that startles her.

"Don't you like your life?"

"Yes. I love my family. I think I've largely built something good," he says. "The past few months, though, I've wondered if I could have been a better person. Done something that mattered."

"You don't think your company matters?"

"In a capitalistic way. But when I got pushed out of that finance job, I thought about going to Australia for a while, backpacking or something. I have no idea what I would have done, and I was twenty-five and stupid, but I was so embarrassed about what had happened in London that I wanted to disappear for a while. I did the opposite. I did whatever would make me big instead. I feel I closed a door of some kind."

"So, quit. What's actually stopping you? You have money."

Wells closes his eyes, a faint smile on his lips.

"What's next for you?" he asks. "You won't stay in this job forever."

You won't stay with me forever is what she hears. *Why not?* she might have said months ago. Now the answer is different.

"Something big."

He sighs. Reaches his hand across the table to grab hers. "It's true."

~

In the room, Wells unbuttons the front of Ari's dress, unhooks her bra, kisses her neck. He is singularly magnetized to her. She's never felt anything so intense, and she's sure she'll never experience a moment like this again. *Something big* is next. But right now she's here with him, and there's nowhere else to look, no one to be afraid of. All the pieces of their life together—that he's brought her here, now—add up to only one thing. He loves her, too.

After they finish, she pulls the sheet up to her throat, careful not to let any of their heat escape. It's unbelievable to watch him get out of the bed and go to the bathroom, like he always does—but this time, there's no haste to hunt down clothes, leave without a trace. She hears him flush, struggle to clear his throat, and she can think only of Morgan's private sounds. Once, she was the only one who'd heard them.

He returns to bed. It's only eight thirty, but they're both jet-lagged. He clicks off his lamp, stretches over her, turns off her light, too. Curls himself around her, body a furnace against hers.

"Wells," she says, shifting him off her, facing up with her hands at her sides like a corpse. He smells like sweat and sex and tea-tree hand soap. "I need to live my life."

The downy white sheets rustle as he readjusts himself to face the ceiling, too. He settles his arm against hers.

"I have cancer, Ari."

"What?" she breathes out.

He doesn't reply.

"No."

"Yes," he says. She turns to him, but he keeps staring up. He gathers his hands at his sternum, that same look of pain from dinner, now rushing out like water from a broken dam. "I wouldn't mess with you, of all people."

The curtains have slivered open, and a beam of city light slices into the room. She sees him face her with eyes she doesn't recognize. Surrendered. Sick. It's a change only she could detect. She wishes he'd shut his eyelids so she wouldn't have to see them. But he doesn't stop looking at her, and she can't bring herself to turn away. She can't cry or shake or seize. She can't even think.

"How long have you known?"

"A little while." He runs his fingers through his hair, stretches his arms above his head until his back arches, cracks. "There wasn't an opportune time to tell you."

"You're going to be fine, though."

In the shadowy room, Wells shakes his head. He blinks slowly. Pulls himself up against the headboard, waits for her to do the same.

"It's stage four lung cancer. I'm biding my time," he says. "Never even smoked."

Ari pauses, searching for words. "What kind of treatment?"

"Only pain management. There's nothing to be done."

"What do you mean *nothing*? There's chemo, there's . . . there has to be *something*."

"We tried. My body can't take it," he says. "It's funny, right? It's like I spent all my energy trying to win everything in life that I don't have anything in the tank when it really counts."

Anger courses through her. Nothing about it is funny. *Save yourself,* she thinks. *Save us all.* She drops her forehead to her hands. The sheet she'd picked up to cover her bare chest falls, but she doesn't replace it. Let him see her. He always has.

"It's probably better to live well than live long, anyway."

He gets out of bed. She hears his hacking cough echo off the bathroom tile, a claw across his lungs.

~

Wells is gone before she even wakes up in the morning. At first she startles to see his side of the bed empty—maybe, mercifully, she's imagined everything. But his bag is still there on the desk, exploding with clothes, and she's certain she'll vomit any minute. She has spent so much of her life saying goodbye.

Ari examines herself in the bathroom mirror. Her body, still naked from last night. It's almost impossible she's wearing the same skin she was before he told her, because she feels so thoroughly stripped. She runs her palms over the small round of her stomach below her belly button, the spot where her thighs kiss. Wonders what she'll do when she doesn't have his hands to hold her anymore. She is not sure she'll ever be able to temper the loss.

Ari dims the lights, prepares a long soak with the hotel's bath salts in the freestanding tub. As she lowers herself into the pink-grapefruit-scented water, she regrets washing him off her. She goes limp, hears the sizzle of the surface, sinks under. When she pops back up, she sees a glow. Wells's phone is on the back of the toilet, screen lit with a call. She ignores it, but the calls don't stop. She towels off, picks up the phone, guesses his passcode: 3009, his anniversary, British date format. She's right. Along with a billion emails are fourteen missed calls from Leah, a stack of texts. Ari dresses quickly, while the phone lights with Leah calling again. She throws it onto the bed, out of sight. If his wife knows—if she's figured them out—Ari will die.

She pictures Leah. Her own mother. It doesn't matter how Ari feels.

Again, a phone buzzes. It's hers. Leah is calling her. She is already falling apart, her gut in her throat.

"Hi, Aria," Leah says. "Is there any chance you've heard from Wells? I can't get in touch with him."

"No, sorry," she says, in disbelief Leah isn't roaring. "I'm in New York while he's away."

"Do you have any idea how to contact the conference or get in touch with him? I'm sorry to ask, but it's an emergency."

"I'll do my best to get to him."

Ari could ask if everything is okay—if Leah is safe—but she doesn't want to know. It's around ten, and she is splayed on the bed, unsure what to do with herself. The moment she closes her eyes, Wells comes back to the room.

"Have you seen my phone?"

She sits upright, hands it to him. "Your wife is looking for you."

His brow furrows as he calls Leah. She wonders whether his heart is also racing, whether he's short of breath—whether it's from the fear or the illness. He keeps eyes with her.

Then Ari watches him crumble.

"When?" he says into the receiver, voice uncharacteristically high, withered. "How? Fuck." He says *fuck* a lot. "I'll leave now and get on standby. I'll see you both soon. I love you so much."

Wells hangs up, drops the phone to the desk. The light in his eyes is out. He sighs, slowly drops to the edge of the bed.

"Rowan has a peanut allergy, and he ate something bad. He almost died."

"Oh god, I'm so—"

"Find me a way home, Aria."

WELLS

It was almost certainly pneumonia, his doctor said at first. Wells and Leah sat beside each other on the edge of a hospital bed, waiting for an antibiotics prescription and discharge papers, three weeks before Christmas. His socks were damp from the snow, and he just wanted to get home. There were strings of lights up around the nurses' station, vinyl snowflakes clinging to the windows. The woman at admissions was wearing a red surgical mask printed with snowmen. A Santa hat.

A couple of hours earlier, as they rode in a taxi to Mass General, he'd felt almost embarrassed about getting sick. He'd passed out while buying gifts on holiday-crushed Newbury Street, flat on his back, in the middle of a shop. He'd come to with his wife standing over him, yelling for a medic. *I'm fine,* he had snipped, making a show of getting himself to his feet. But his head was still light, and he was wheezing, and every time he breathed deeply to gather himself, the sharp pain in his body pulled him back toward the ground.

They knew on December 22. When he'd started to feel even worse, Wells had gotten the imaging done. The word the doctor had used to describe his lungs and bones was *abnormal.* The next thing Wells heard, *biopsy.* Then, not long after, she'd used the one they'd all been afraid of. Sitting forward in her desk chair, her Harvard degrees in dark-wood frames behind her, the doctor said she was sorry. Neither Wells nor Leah knew what to do. They still don't, and they don't have much time left to figure it out.

The plane is over Utah when Wells puts his hand to the window. The cold acrylic feels incredible against his hot palm, the first time anything has felt good in hours. He doesn't know whom he's supposed to be thinking about: Rowan, Leah, Ari. Himself.

Nothing was supposed to happen this way. He had been extremely intentional about when, where, and how he was going to tell Ari. He knew it'd wreck them both, and for him, it'd be the true beginning of the end. She was the last person who upheld, treasured, how alive he was. He waited to get her alone, away from the office and Cambridge and Leah; he'd help her process it, and they'd relish this last time they could be together. Their trip would feel like a sun setting, Wells had thought—a sort of gentle, glowing glide into the horizon. He'd go back to his wife, and his remaining days would play out with his family, exactly as they should. Except now his son is under observation in a pediatric hospital, Leah's sanity is on hold, and Ari is spending the night alone in a king-size hotel bed in a city where she knows no one. And Wells is stuck in a giant metal tube for the next four-plus hours, in the dead of night, unable to fix anything, including himself.

The evening they found out, after they put Rowan to sleep together, Wells and Leah went upstairs to their room. They sat on the edge of the bed, just like they had in hospital, both looking down at his bare feet. His left big toenail was purple from tripping on a toy-easel prototype, moments before they'd left to do that Christmas shopping. He pushed against the bruise, winced. *Stop. Don't hurt yourself,* she had said. He hadn't looked up as he replied. *It doesn't matter anymore, does it?*

Leah had bawled that night. Wells couldn't, or maybe wouldn't. Instead, he held her against his broken body. Every time she quaked, he felt like he was being stabbed. He'd sworn the weight loss, the breathlessness, the ache down to his bones was just from the stress—of getting older, being a father, running a business, falling in love with another woman. He'd never been so wrong, and the only way to face it was not facing it at all. It's why he implored Leah to wait to tell her family, even though the ask was futile; why he didn't instantly pick up the phone to call his parents and sisters; why he only told Krish last Monday. It's why he waited as long as he possibly could to tell Ari. He wanted to be Wells, not a dying man.

Around him, the cabin lights are off. He is exhausted, but he isn't tired. He needs to rest, though, because he'll have to return to real life and take the lead when he gets home. He reclines his plane seat, forgets as much as possible. Yes, we're all dying, he thinks. But he will die soon.

~

Leah has been both catatonic and frantic for the past three days. It's impossible to explain how these states of being can coexist. It destroys him to see her stare vacantly into the distance, especially when he knows her heart is still racing. Wells should have been there.

He has not seen his wife earnestly sleep since he walked through the door, straight off the red-eye. She can't stop holding their son, whom she's pulled from every activity for now. Rowan is okay, if tired. His pink, fair skin—Leah's skin—seems a little paler, though maybe Wells is just imagining it. At night, after they put him down, she sits in the chair in their son's room for an hour, watching him sleep. He can see her shadow on the baby monitor when he's downstairs, trying to find something she will eat.

She has given Irma an impromptu week off since she won't let Rowan out of her sight. Wells has been working from home, though he's mostly forwarding things to Aria, making her handle his affairs. He cannot—will not—think about anything that happened in San Francisco: the dinner with her, at which he felt as young and free and full of possibility as he did the first time he sat across from Leah; the night beside her, warming him brand new. The admission, then the phone call that punched him back to earth.

He texts her the name of Rowan's nurses, asks her to send flowers to the hospital, another bouquet to Leah. They arrive two hours later, white and pink orchids. Perfect.

Leah's mum has been there since before Wells even left California. The help is nice, but he is fully aware Susan is not here for him, even while he is literally dying. Around noon, they're all gathered in the kitchen, Wells and Leah picking at sushi lunch from the Japanese place down the street. Susan retrieves a pouch for Rowan from the fridge—the massive BIG 8 ALLERGEN-FREE seal visible from the moon. She gently hands the snack to Rowan, who trots off with it into the living room. Leah follows.

Wells and Susan stand alone. Prickly silence. This is the kind of unvarnished nothing that constantly envelops them when they are alone together. Soon—perhaps to Susan's joy—they won't have to. He hasn't asked Leah how her mum reacted to the news. Besides a limp hug and an *I'm sorry, Wells*, his mother-in-law hasn't mentioned it again.

Susan studies her nails, gazes out the window overlooking the backyard.

"Wells," she says. She adjusts her glasses, then peers squarely at him. "Follow me downstairs."

She starts walking toward the basement door before he agrees. He is expecting to change a light bulb, take a screwdriver to something. But Susan heads to the hulking chest under the television, opens the drawer.

"Whose is this?"

"What?"

"Whose sweater is this?" She pulls out the tag. "It's too big to be Leah's."

She tries to hand it to him, but he doesn't take it. He doesn't know how long Ari's jumper has been there. Maybe Irma found it as she cleaned, folded it gently, none the wiser. It's horrible, but he wonders if it still smells like Ari's powdery skin.

"How am I supposed to know? Maybe Leah has an oversize jumper. I don't keep an inventory of her fashion choices."

He squeezes his fingers into tight fists. Susan mashes the fabric in her hands. Lines in her forehead appear as she furrows her brow.

"What are you getting at?" Wells snarls, spitting fury. The pressure on his chest is immense.

"It's your assistant's, isn't it?"

"I'm sure," he says, relieved by the logical explanation he was too frenzied to surface himself. "From when she stayed here last month."

Susan shakes her head. "Don't lie more."

"If you have something to say, say it."

"Why would you do this to Leah? Do you think you have some kind of license to do what you want now and not be held accountable for it?"

His heart is beating a thousand miles a minute, stomach filled with boulders, sinking to his feet. He hates Susan. He always has.

"What are you accusing me of?" he yells, until he realizes Leah might hear.

Finally, Susan drops the jumper to the ground, pulling back her hands sharply, as if the fabric is infested. "Why would you do this to her?"

"You're insane."

"Am I? The pretty girl who works for you is suddenly here for your last Christmas with your wife? You're sick with terminal cancer, and you're at the office at all hours, instead of with your family?" Susan shakes her head. "Leah can have tunnel vision, even be naive. Even if your wife doesn't see it, it reeks to me."

From the way she looks at him, pity and malevolence, they both understand Wells hasn't denied it. He cannot bring himself to lie. He's spent almost a year choreographing omission about where he's been, whom he's been with, but saying the words aloud—*That's not true* or *I'm not cheating*—feels physically impossible, even having seen what happened with Molly. Denying Ari's presence in his life is unbearable, even with the cost so high.

"Go fuck yourself," he spits, the only words he can find.

Yet inside, he is shriveled with fear his mother-in-law will tell his wife. That his marriage will end, even before his life does. As he sprints upstairs, it takes everything for him not to slam the basement door, hand shaking. In the main-floor powder room, he hacks so hard he tastes blood in his throat. He cups his hands to shovel water into his mouth, spitting pink in the white vessel sink.

Leah knocks on the door to make sure her dying husband is okay.

~

"I need your help," Wells tells Krish.

It's Thursday, but he's asked his cofounder to the coffee shop. Wells sits with only weak black tea in front of him, untouched. He has no appetite. He hasn't for a while, but it's disappeared entirely since his conversation with Susan on Sunday night. If he puts anything in his body, he'll hurl it back onto the floor.

Krish shakes croissant flakes onto a square white plate. "Go on."

"Aria."

Krish puts up his hands. "I don't want any part of this. Absolutely not."

"You're the only person I've told."

"Lucky me."

"I'm serious," Wells says as a woman passes too close to his chair. He looks around at the flurry of patrons.

"You want my help *how*? What am I supposed to do? This is your mess." Krish shakes his head. "People are starting to wonder. Nora asked me if anything was going on between you two."

Wells curses under his breath. "When?"

"Recently enough." Krish puts down the pastry, wipes his buttery hands on a recycled-paper napkin.

"What did you say to her? Did she say anything to anyone else?" Wells's cofounder is silent. "*Krish*, this is important."

"I told her it was nothing I know about, because you've put me in a position to lie." He shakes his head. "I told you this was a can of worms."

Wells blanks. "Leah can't know."

"Stop sleeping with Aria then." Krish shakes his head. "Get her out of your life, then cross your fingers it goes away when she does."

Ari is woven so tightly into the fabric of his everyday, he's never even courted extracting her. But Krish is right. Krish stands, gets a bag for his croissant at the counter.

At work, Wells slips quietly into his office. He doesn't go to his ten or eleven o'clock meetings, even though Ari knocks on the glass several times to tell him he's not supposed to be at his desk. Instead, he spends the morning getting in touch with every CEO he knows in a three-hundred-mile radius, trying to find a place for Ari. He twists himself in knots trying to explain why she's so great if he is trying to get rid of her—*Internal reasons* or *Please just trust me on this*, the explanations he ad-libs. He's overcome by a sickening urgency: he needs to get this done, and if he doesn't move at sonic speed, he'll lose the courage.

what's going on? you screwed up your entire schedule today, she messages him.

He ignores it, continues to call, plead.

~

It's three o'clock when he leads himself to Ari's desk, asks her to take a walk as he hides his tight fists behind his back. She is fully aware he's been a totally mutant person all morning. Wells is so lightheaded, he would float away if his mother-in-law's slivered eyes didn't keep weighing him down. Susan hasn't told Leah, he assumes, because he is still married. But there is no guarantee she won't rip away what remains at any moment. As soon as Susan left, he'd stuffed Ari's jumper in a neighbor's trash bin.

"I don't want to walk. It's freezing," she says, turning back to her keyboard, as if Wells isn't hovering over her shoulder.

"Then don't forget your scarf."

He lets silence wrap them in the lift, continue for a few blocks past the office. He can't look at her straight on, but she's still the only thing he sees. They're moments from disentangling their lives, and he's as scared as he's ever been. He has so little time left, and he's truly scared to live it without Ari. The promise of her gaze, the unfettered sense of freedom and possibility he feels with her. The way she slows the breathing of his worthless lungs. She puts him first, always. He needs it so much, it's mortifying. For all Leah has given him, he's never been able to show her his weakest parts. It's his fault, not hers. He got himself into a mess of ego, ensnared her in it, and he doesn't know if she'd love any other version of him.

"Are you feeling okay?" Ari says.

She, too, is afraid.

"I don't quite know how to say this," Wells says, his breath like smoke on the sharp air. "I've called a friend—he's going to create a deputy chief of staff role for you. The pay is a third higher."

He's never seen her eyes so wide. Blood drains from her cheeks.

"This isn't happening."

"It has to. You know we don't have a choice."

Her mouth hangs agape.

"I said it was for personal reasons. I told him he wouldn't regret hiring you. It's just the marketing company down the street. It won't be a big change, and you'll have job security once I'm gone."

"Fuck you," she snaps.

"Bloody hell, lower your voice."

"Please, Wells." He can't tell whether she's about to cry or punch him. "Don't do that. We can control ourselves."

"People are talking. Leah's mum knows."

"What? How? Did she tell Leah? Is she going to tell her?"

"We obviously can't control ourselves, Aria."

Before he can say another word, she whips back toward the office. He sits on a rock wall, watches her walk until she disappears back into their building.

By the time he gets upstairs, Ari is gone. His phone vibrates with a text.

I'm showing up tomorrow. Barricade the door if you want. But we both know you won't.

He wants to throw his phone through the glass, into the next galaxy.

ARI

The second her feet hit the cold pavement, Ari calls Summer. She needs to come down for the weekend. She needs to get the hell out of Boston.

On Friday morning she decides not to go into the office. Being near Wells will humiliate her. And after her sleepless night, she can't see through her sagging eyes. In her underwear on the couch, she books a ticket on the worst bus line. The seats will feel scratchy and filthy under her, the fabric putrid from the cigarettes the driver smokes between rides. She'll have to wash her hair just to get the stink out. But she doesn't care about anything, except running away from yesterday.

~

She arrives in the city around nine, bundled tight, and pays for a cab to speed to Summer's building. Her best friend is standing outside, holding a brown bag. More food than they could ever eat from her favorite Chinese place. Ari could cry.

And when she gets into Summer's apartment—the warm, familiar place where she's felt both her highest and lowest—she does. Sputtering, face red as a burn. Between gasps, she tells Summer the story: Rowan, at the hospital, in anaphylactic shock; Leah, hysterical on the phone, after she finally got in touch with her husband; Wells, dropping everything to get home, making Ari book the flight; Ari, alone, mostly of her own making.

She doesn't tell Summer that Wells is sick. She can't say it aloud yet.

"Jesus," Summer says when Ari is finally done vomiting words. She rubs a tear from Ari's cheek with her thumb. "I don't know what to say."

Ari rests her head against Summer's chest, smells the lavender of the color-protecting shampoo she's used for a decade. The first time Summer dyed her hair was two days before she left for college. Luke had already gone. It was the first time she'd be without him, and who knew how long it would last, especially when they both had their sights on medicine next. Summer had panicked, dragged Ari to the drugstore after dinner, bought a box of permanent redhead dye. *Are you sure you want to do this?* Ari had asked, snapping on the gloves in the bathroom Summer shared with her younger sister, Ella. Over the sink, she massaged the sticky orange liquid into Summer's roots, covered every inch of her dirty-blond hair. After all was done, Summer stood in front of the mirror, Ari behind her, in shock. *It's perfect,* Ari had said, fluffing her silky red strands. Ari was leaving for Boston the next day, and that night, they both slept in Summer's bed. It didn't feel like a coincidence that the final day Ari was living on Summer's couch after Morgan, before she went back to Abbott, Summer had wanted to touch up her color. She'd been doing it on her own for ten years, but she'd asked Ari for help. It was like being back in Summer's bathroom that first time, and neither said a word during the process. A couple of hours later, Ari had crawled into Summer's bed again, feeling protected from her own doubt. With the lavender scent in her nose, Ari knew she was deserving of Summer's love, and for the first time in weeks understood, sometime down the line, someone else would love her, too.

On the white couch, Ari listens to her best friend's heartbeat through her pink shirt. She lifts her head, then takes in Summer's face, her full lips pulled to the side. The way she sighs, keeping the breath in her mouth, puffing her cheeks. Summer's eyes fall from Ari's, into her own lap. Ari stares at the chapped skin pilled at the corners of her mouth.

"Do you remember that horrible, creepy cabin we rented in Vermont the summer after sophomore year?" Summer says.

"*You* chose it. We all told you it was probably haunted."

"It wasn't haunted."

"No, it was infested with spiders. Why?"

"I think about it a lot. It was six million degrees out, and I'd just taken my MCAT and was stressed out of my mind. You told me I was annoying and threw me in the lake."

"You were annoying and deserved to be thrown in the lake."

"Beyond the point." Summer snatches a yellow throw pillow into her lap, kneads it. "You told me you wanted to teach literature, like your dad. You said you'd finally figured it out, and you were going to talk to him about grad school and what you had to do next. But you didn't."

"I did talk to him. I took the GRE the next year." But Ari has nowhere to go next. She never followed through. "I was going to. Morgan had too much going on. I just had to get us through to the other side financially first."

"It's not Morgan's fault, Ari."

"I've never blamed him."

"You'd have been such a good teacher. You'd *be* such a good teacher."

"That ship's sailed."

"Not really. The seas are pretty open now. What's stopping you?"

Ari doesn't have a good answer, and she's never stopped wanting it, even if she's told herself it's out of reach at this point. Yes, she knows she has lost some of herself over the years. She was the one who'd found out which burnout at the gas station would sell them alcohol underage and figured out where they could drink it, bought Summer a vibrator when she said she refused to have sex until she was eighteen. After her dad left, Ari held the house parties where fifty teenagers pounded watery beers, took turns spewing their guts into the only toilet. Ari had pushed them all to go to that cabin in the first place, cleared the cellar spiders from Summer's sneakers while she shrieked. But Summer isn't saying Ari has lost herself. It's that she never gave herself the space to find it.

And she needs to now. They both understand she can't do it through Wells. She can't help thinking about Wells's regrets over the paths he hadn't chosen, now ringing so much louder that he no longer has time to start again. But Ari does.

Summer drops the pillow to the floor, kicks it away with her bare foot before she stands. She grabs a pile of magazines from her bookshelf, a piece of printer paper, scissors, glue. Drops it all in Ari's lap.

"We're making you a mini vision board," she says.

"We are?"

She nods, wide-eyed.

Ari thinks the exercise is saccharine, if not a little naive to think a glue stick can solve the future. She's about to protest but pauses. What does she have to lose? She needs to start somewhere, so she reaches for the scissors, flips through the pages, as Summer puts on Ari's favorite record—the same one she played when they were packing up her and Morgan's apartment. Ari thinks it'll be hard to find anything that feels like her in a stack of year-old women's magazines. Yet when she looks up a few minutes later, the paper is entirely covered. A dog she might have, a pile of books she might teach one day, the interior of a well-designed bedroom she could move into, the words *purpose* and *power*. A wedding dress, with a neckline like a Cupid's bow.

Summer studies the paper. "Good," she says, then asks if Ari might want to share her bed.

~

It's Ari's idea to rent a car the next day and drive out to Jones Beach. It's so cold, but her skin is thicker after another winter in Boston. The wind off the water snakes up her nose and nips her earlobes, but she doesn't flinch.

Summer puts up the hood of her hunter-green puffer jacket, slides on her gloves. "Aren't you freezing?" she asks, gesturing at Ari's bare hands.

Ari shakes her head. Under the gray sky, the forward momentum of last night has fallen away. All night, she tossed and turned beside Summer, thinking only of Wells missing from the future she pasted onto that sheet of paper.

"What do you think?" Ari asks. "About all of it."

The tide is high, water so choppy. White foam edges the blue-black waves.

"I don't think you're being honest with yourself about what you're doing. It's hurting you, but beyond that, you could ruin these people's lives." Summer stops walking, kicks the wet sand. The fur on her hood whips in the wind. "Do you expect he's going to leave his wife? Is that what you're waiting for?"

"No," Ari says, shoving away the feeling of being sixteen again. She should tell Summer there isn't even a long game to play anymore. "I just love him."

"What are you even getting out of this? What are you getting from him that you can't get somewhere else?"

How is Ari supposed to answer? Explain that Wells chose *her*? How that makes her feel, with every domino that's fallen in twenty-nine years of being in her own skin? Summer has never been empty and does not know the relief of being full again.

Summer begins walking, hands in her pockets. "What happened to moving back here with me? Why did we stop talking about it?"

"You don't even know if you're going to be here in six months. What if Luke gets a job in, I don't know, Tulsa? You're going to go with him, and then where does that put me?"

"You can build a life, Ari. You don't need me."

"I always need you."

"I always need you, too, but you know that's not what I mean."

Ari feels cold again. They walk until they find a bench, sit side by side.

"Where's Morgan now?" she asks, shoving her stinging hands in her pockets.

"Chicago. He got a good job at a consulting firm there."

"He left New York?"

"The same time you did. He stayed with Luke for a couple weeks, but ended up back home for six months or so."

"Six *months*?"

"His mom died, Ari. He wasn't about to leave his dad alone and, like, jump into a new life with open arms right away. And then he got this offer in Chicago, which I guess he took because he just needed to press reset on the whole year. Luke and I were pretty surprised he'd be willing to move that far, but he seemed really intent on it."

"What about his job in the city? He got that offer in May. Kathy died in September. Shouldn't he have been working there already?"

"He quit before he started."

"I can't believe it. He interviewed for three months."

"He just needed out," Summer says. "Morgan was also a wreck after you guys split. You're not the only one who's had a go of it."

Ari stares out blankly toward the parking lot, tracing the fault lines in the asphalt. It's true, she knows. She just never assumed Morgan might be struggling, too.

"Have you seen him?" she asks.

They start back to the car. Summer is right: it's too cold to be outside.

"A few times. But he's mostly been out in Chicago, working a lot."

"How does he seem?"

"I don't know," Summer says into the wind. "You could ask him."

~

When *Dad* pops up on Ari's caller ID almost the minute she gets back to Boston, she startles. They haven't spoken since she told him she moved.

"Hi," she says tentatively.

"You around tomorrow night?"

"What?"

"I'm coming to Boston for a few days. Tomorrow's the only night I have, but I figured, why not see my daughter?" He pauses. "Unless you're busy."

She wonders if he's even considered the possibility she doesn't want to see him.

"No," she says. "I mean, no, I'm not busy. Is Elisabeth with you?"

"Just you and me. Dinner?"

Ari can't believe he's so sure of his casual ask. What if she says no? That she doesn't want to meet him on his terms, or at all? She has seen her father perhaps ten times in the past ten years. No wonder she didn't call him crying about Morgan—it'd be like handing her very worst news to a perfect stranger. He was dead to Ari and her mother once he told them about his affair with the unusually beautiful, famous writer who'd interviewed him at the Vermont college where he's now a professor in the English department. His wife of twenty years, his sixteen-year-old daughter—they were no longer as important as this woman he'd just met. He'd swiftly decided her family was more desirable than his. At the time, Ari thought he was the only person capable of such hurt. That no one would ever feel the betrayal she did.

"Fine," she says, so desperate for human contact she'd let a serial killer take her to dinner. "Seven thirty."

He tells her he can't wait to see her. She can't get her lips to form the same words.

~

Monday evening, after Ari returns to the office—to no surprise of her boss—she spots her father at a table in the center of the Porter Square restaurant. He looks good. Very good, actually. Along with the smile he flashes, his life choices are also glowing.

She drapes her coat over the back of her chair, adjusts her jeans on her hips so they don't look too tight, pulls down her black V-neck sweater. Her father is also wearing a black sweater, a cable-knit turtleneck. He has a fresh haircut, his dark curls tamed. He looks smart. Contemptibly relaxed and content.

He stands for a hug, but she settles into her chair. He drops into his own seat.

"You look great," he says.

Except she doesn't. Beyond feeling pale in the light of her father, she's gained weight in her thighs and stomach; her pants have started pulling at the button. Her body is rebelling. She doesn't know how to feel beautiful outside Wells, and she's terrified that if she seeks it in the arms of another, she won't find it.

"So, catch me up," her father says.

"I live in Boston now."

He sips the wine he ordered before Ari arrived. "I hoped maybe we'd be able to really talk to each other, with everything you've gone through."

"I'm not doing this now."

She doesn't have the energy to recount the myriad ways she hates her father and also does not. She refuses to mine the hurt and rejection, which remains so raw. After he announced he was leaving, the first thing Ari did was run next door to Summer's. Maybe—probably—she should have stayed with her mother, who was too stunned to even sob as he explained the affair, which had been going on for months. He'd told them about the new life he was starting in Vermont, the job they hadn't even known he'd been going for. Ari had gotten up without a word, slammed the back door. She cried in Summer's bed as she held her, then let Luke and Morgan distract her as much as possible with stupid stories, doing anything to make her smile. Ari still remembers the feeling of Morgan's hand on her sweaty back, soothing her, even though she was disgusting, ugly, dismantled. It was the moment she realized the enormity of her feelings for him, the secret she held close for another year, until they finally kissed.

Despite everything, she can't dislodge the images of her dad as the first parent to volunteer to chaperone the fifth-grade trip to Washington, DC; the dad who held her hand through her flu shots since she was six months old, never told Ari her fear of needles was immature, even though it is. He was the one who knocked gently on her bedroom door after a bad fight between her parents, apologized that she'd had to hear it, even if he never quite tamed the anger when she was home next time. He told her all the time how proud he was of her, and she felt so good that just being herself made him beam. He was the best dad on the planet. He probably still is.

He briefly glances at the menu. "I'm sorry about Morgan."

"Yeah."

"Have you stayed in touch?"

She exhales, gives her order to the waiter. Her father asks for the same thing.

They do not talk about Morgan. They do not talk about anything, really. It's been cold in Vermont, but the snow is beautiful. He's just gone down to Mississippi, finished a new paper on Faulkner; the pressure to publish in academia has gotten worse. They're thinking of getting hens.

"I'm seeing someone," Ari says, unprompted, when it's her turn to kill the silence.

"Oh?" He perks up, like he's relieved his daughter is still functional, or didn't believe it until she told this lie. "That's fantastic to hear. Tell me."

"I met him at work. He's amazing."

She's already in deep, so she lists what she loves about Wells though never mentions his name. He's handsome, brilliant, successful. She has never felt so alive beside someone.

"You deserve it," he says.

As he smiles, wraps squid-ink linguine around his fork, glistening with white wine broth, she wants to tell him what she's been keeping from most of the world. She knows she's gotten into an untenable situation with Wells, especially now, and as much as she hates him for it, her father would understand it all. Maybe he'd tell her how to get herself out, do what he didn't. The path he never took.

Her tears are surging.

"Ari girlie, what's wrong?"

She closes her eyes. She hasn't heard the nickname since he left Abbott.

"Someone I love is dying, and I'm not handling it well." She presses her fingers into the corners of her eyes. She will not cry, not here. Not in front of him.

Her father drops his fork to the plate, the black pasta still wound around the tines. He reaches out to her forearm. She lets him.

"I heard about Kathy, too. I'm sorry about everything. If there's anything I can do, you know I'm here."

Ari jerks her arm back. "But you're not, Dad. You're the literal reason I know how bad it feels to lose someone."

He sits back in his chair, eyes to the table.

Take me home with you, she wants to yell, throw herself on the floor and writhe like a two-year-old. *Get me out of this hell.* She leaves instead.

∼

There she is on the far end of the dry-goods aisle: Leah. The only time Ari has ever come here. Why.

In the specialty market on the outskirts of Harvard Square, Leah is hunched over a bulk bin, pouring dried fruit into a plastic bag. She's struggling to get the twist tie in place; she enters the wrong code into the scale, has to redo the label. Ari could help, but she's frozen on the other side of the aisle, trying to make herself as small as possible. She can't be caught running. She studies a bin of dried kidney beans as if they are the most fascinating thing she's ever seen.

"Aria?" Leah calls. Her basket weighs down the right half of her body, like an unbalanced scale.

"Oh, hi," Ari says, peeling up her eyes. "Didn't see you."

Ari smiles weakly, but puffs herself up when she remembers she has to be perfectly fine in front of Wells's wife. Now it's not only the affair itself; she also can't tip her hand she knows he's sick. By the way nothing's changed at work, she's aware the news isn't out. She wonders if Krish even knows. If Leah knew Wells had told Ari, alarm bells would ring—and they are so lucky they haven't gotten caught already.

Unlike Leah, Ari has picked only three things off the shelves: a nine-dollar jar of house-made salsa verde; an eight-dollar bag of ancient-grain tortilla chips; a pint of artisanal rosewater-pistachio ice cream, the price of which she can't bring herself to check.

Leah goes in for a one-armed hug. Ari holds her breath, basks in the feeling of Leah's chest against hers—proof she still doesn't know what's going on, that she trusts Ari with her own body.

"How are you feeling?" Leah asks, shifting the basket, glancing to Ari's ankle.

"Mostly fine now. Still in the brace, but okay."

She glances into Ari's basket. "Did you just go through a breakup?"

"What?"

"A pint of ice cream and carbs. You just need a box of tissues and a bottle of something pink."

"Oh no." Ari is madly uncomfortable, worries she's just as transparent. "By the way, I'm sorry about what happened to Rowan. I'm glad everything is okay."

"Thank you. I appreciate you helping Wells while you were away. He wouldn't have known how to get his shit together. We're all having a bit of a time right now."

"Of course," Ari says. She thinks of the flowers she sent to Leah, orchids she would have wanted herself. As she opens her mouth to say goodbye, Leah struggles to resettle her basket, purse, and tote. "Could you use a hand?"

"I'm good, thanks," Leah replies, until she tries to maneuver the plastic bag of dried fruit into the basket, and everything tumbles to the floor.

Ari instantly drops to her knees, scoops for the apples, a dented six-pack of nonalcoholic beer. A box of allergen-free cookies. She pops them in her own basket.

"It's no problem," she says before Leah speaks. "My stuff won't be too hard to parse out. Sad-sack food, mine; real adult food, yours."

"You're a saint."

"It's nothing," Ari says, focusing on not throwing up in Leah's organic microgreens.

Leah sighs with her entire chest. "I'm a mess."

"You're not."

She does not look it, at least. Her hair is pulled back into a tight, short ponytail that flatters her face; her cheekbones are kissed with highlighter, shimmering in the overhead fluorescents; her puffer coat is a bright red that would make Ari look like a blimp, even though it's March, and everyone is smothered under layers of down. Still, even though Leah managed to dress and put on makeup, she's not okay. How could she be? Ari can feel her distress in her own body. They share so much more now.

Leah scrunches her nose as they begin walking to the self-checkout. Ari can see the basket is still heavy on her arm, and she'd like to take something else from it. But she's already mortified Leah enough, and seeing Wells's wife disarmed isn't one bit satisfying. Leah is kind. Leah is good. Leah is worth loving. And Leah is in purgatory, waiting for her life to explode.

She starts ringing up the groceries while Ari hands each item to her. Ari stares at Leah's rings as her hands move, the hulking emerald-cut solitaire set in gold. Ari's was also a solitaire, a small round diamond on a rose-gold band. She can't help but wonder how long Leah will wear her rings after Wells dies.

They get to Ari's food at the bottom of the basket. Leah grabs for it.

"On me," she says.

Ari shakes her head; Leah nods. She watches the items cross the scanner. Her rattled despair costs twenty-eight dollars.

~

The next morning, Ari settles into her desk, as she's done for the past two weeks, as if Wells never tried to fire her. Three small succulents sit next to her monitor. She knocks on the glass, pops into his office.

"Plants?"

"Thanks for helping Leah." He doesn't look up from his computer.

On the way home, she buys the box of tissues, the bottle of something pink.

~

He works from home agonizingly often. Ari comes in, anyway, just in case he changes his mind. Even though they've settled back into work, and nothing has happened between them in weeks, his emails have tapered off. Wells schedules his own meetings; enters his own expenses, undoubtedly to his own horror. And when he does come in to the office, mostly for appointments with Krish or the engineers, he barely talks to her. He gets his own coffee and lunch, and if he wants anything from the outside world, he asks Nora. Wells is already out of her grasp. It's the world's worst peek into the future.

Can I come down tomorrow? Ari texts Summer from one of the privacy booths in her office, where she's been hiding since he didn't show up, again.

She sees Summer typing. Stop. Type and stop. Type and stop. Finally: If you want.

If I want?

After thirty agonizing minutes during which she doesn't reply, Ari's phone rings.

"You have a second?" Her voice low, whisper quiet.

"Why are you being weird?"

159

"You can come," she says, slowly. "But I don't know that you'll want to."

"Why not? Is Luke there?"

"Not Luke."

Ari's not stupid. She knows who's there instead.

"Oh my god. Why didn't you tell me?"

"Because I didn't want you to freak out."

"Why is he in the city?"

"Visiting some people."

"Who?"

Summer pauses. "Are you at home?"

"What? No, why? *Why?*"

"He's here with his girlfriend, meeting her parents."

Ari feels like she's left her body.

"How long have they been together?" she asks.

"Maybe a couple months?"

"You've known for that long?"

"I didn't know how to say it without wrecking you."

Summer is right. Ari is wrecked. She imagines her at the Thai restaurant on Thirteenth Street, across from Morgan and his girl-friend. The red curry tofu Ari always ordered, speared on a fork that slides between the woman's lips, soft against her tongue. She is thin, long-legged, exceptional. She went to a college Ari would have never gotten into. Morgan is charmed by the beauty mark between her breasts, how she looks draped in his college practice jersey before bed. He indulges in the way she sings; the way she sighs when he touches her hips. Summer loves her. Kathy would have loved her. Morgan loves her already.

"Have a good time, I guess," Ari whispers. Hangs up before Summer can respond.

~

When Ari gets home, she wants to break every glass in the cabinets, rip the bedsheets to shreds. Instead, she grabs her phone. She doesn't know what a dating-app profile is supposed to look like, but she tries her best. *Favorite book:* Anna Karenina. *Favorite foods: Montreal bagels and New Haven pizza. Quirky fact: I don't have a dominant hand. Looking for: Love, in all its glory and pain.*

~

They meet at a bar in her neighborhood. It's been only three hours since she put up her profile, and he's the first person she matched with. But it's something sweet to overtake the sour taste in her mouth, so she devours it.

He's waiting at the bar when she walks in. His face brightens when he sees her. Light eyes clear, even in the dark room. She smooths out her top, black and tight across her chest. He introduces himself with a handshake. He's as tall as he said he was. She takes the stool next to him, and he asks if he can get her a beer. She'd drink toilet water if it was spiked with something strong.

"Hi," she says, white-knuckling in her lap. She's never really had a first date.

"Hey," he says, as if he's relieved to see her. "Glad you were able to meet me."

Ari can't decide if she's explicitly attracted to him—the blue button-down is stiff, and the way he compulsively touches his sandy hair is distracting. But the room is buzzing around him, and Ari, a stranger, is his only focus. She feels reborn. The feeling was waiting for her the entire time.

~

His name is Soren. He's a biochemical engineer at one of the firms in East Cambridge, a stone's throw from her own office. He's incredibly smart, unusually sweet. In the eleven days they've known each other, he's held the door, pulled out Ari's chair at dinner. A lost chivalry she didn't know she wanted. He constantly asks if she's comfortable, okay with the place he's chosen. Maybe he can help her learn her neighborhood, he's offered, go back to those little taquerias and hole-in-the-wall Chinese places she used to loiter in, to see if they still exist. By the third day, he'd already solidified plans to make good on it.

Most importantly, Soren likes her. He tells her so, unveiled: he likes how she's opened him so quickly, which he's often reticent to do. The second night they spent together, he told her about his younger sister, who'd struggled with mental illness, then took her life when she was a senior in high school. He feels guilty every day he's happy and doing well. He said he'd never mentioned it to anyone but his former long-term girlfriend, but feels like he doesn't have to hold back around Ari—he's not afraid she'll judge him if he's not perfect. She ran her hand through his hair like she used to with Morgan, watched him close his eyes, heave a sigh. *I won't judge you,* she said. He looked over from the other pillow, told her he trusted her implicitly. Leaned forward, kissed her. The more Soren shows up, the more she realizes she's a person worth showing up for. It's quick, but her bed no longer feels like a waterlogged ship. Her heart, either.

The tiny moments they've already begun to accrue make it easier to stop thinking of anyone else. Though it's been more than a month since she last touched Wells, he still takes up an absurd amount of real estate in her head, as impossible to forget as Morgan. But Soren has helped her understand she can make room for someone else to move in. It's time.

It's Friday night, and Ari is cooking at her apartment when Soren lets himself in the unlocked door. She's been home all day; instead of going into the office and hoping Wells will show up, she's worked the bare minimum, cleaned every corner of her place, made time to duck out to the good market where Leah shops.

"What's that smell?" he says, dropping his bag on the kitchen peninsula as if he is home.

"Come see."

He walks up behind her, kisses her neck, glances down to the stove-top. "For me?"

"For you."

The night before, tipsy in the back of a taqueria, Soren told her about paying his own way through college—Harvard, always quick to follow that he feels like an asshole every time he says it—eating boxed macaroni and cheese at least three days a week. *The worst part? It's still my favorite food. I have the palate of an eight-year-old,* he'd said. The first thing Ari had thought about was Kathy's recipe. She'd decided to make it before he'd even finished his burrito. It's what Morgan's mom would have wanted—for Ari to trust her gut, do what's right for herself. The last time they spoke, Kathy said as much.

Soren lowers his nose an inch above the golden crust, inhales.

"It's good, I promise," she says.

Even though everything hurt the last time Ari cooked it, what might have felt devastating somehow feels right. She can rewire her life—in dry mustard powder stirred into cheese sauce, in cheap nights out and kisses stolen on train platforms, in years she'll live beyond Wells. She watches Soren scrape his plate clean twice, undo the top button on his pants. They laugh. She could also cry. She can't wait to clear the dishes, lie next to him on the couch, taste his kiss.

After dinner at the small table, she spoons leftovers into a plastic container, begins scrubbing at the stuck-on halo of breadcrumbs.

"Ar," Soren calls from the couch, where he's queueing the next episode of a true-crime series they've started. "Your phone."

"Is it Summer?"

"Wells," he says, a name that means nothing more to him than *boss*.

"Can you flip it to silent?" She can't believe how automatically the words fall out. She puts down the half-cleaned dish. Dries off her hands, stands by the sink, breathes.

When Soren slips into the bathroom a few minutes later, Ari rushes to her phone to find a text.

Where are you?

She turns off the screen, hears the toilet flush. When Soren comes out, she tells him she wants to walk to Davis Square for ice cream. Ari grabs her bag, stuffs her phone between the couch cushions. He follows her out.

~

The next afternoon, Soren suggests a walk along the Charles, starting near MIT and just wandering. It's early April, and the cold is retreating, the icy air that seems permanent and impossible to shake, like she'll never know what feeling warm is like ever again.

Ari knows walking with him is a good idea. He has lots of good ideas, and she already relishes them. Yet she balks. She's taken the same walk with Morgan dozens of times. Doing it without him feels like handing over history she wants to keep, even though Morgan is now sharing his bed with someone else, flying halfway across the country to meet her parents.

"Come. The day couldn't be more perfect for it," Soren urges on the phone. To be fair, she hasn't been outside yet.

"Okay," she says after a pause, rich with possibility.

The weather actually couldn't be more perfect. The razor-blade breeze is a kind touch to her cheek now. Ari waits for him by the T stop, slips her faux-leather jacket from her shoulders, and drapes it over her arm. After a few minutes, Soren emerges, touches her hip.

He kisses her temple. "Good to go?"

"Let's walk."

He's particularly good-looking today, she thinks as she meets his pale-blue eyes. His hair is slightly disheveled, yet becoming. He wears only a light-gray V-neck that keeps drawing her eyes to his Adam's apple. Dark jeans, dirty white canvas sneakers. The little things have begun to thrill her.

Once they hit the path, see the gentle ripples of the dark water, and spot the crew team gliding past, he reaches for her hand. There's something about the river, the way the sun hits it on a day like this—the light. Morgan would also take her hand, quiet romance. Soren's touch fills Ari with an unmistakable warmth.

"Can I ask you something?" he says. Shyness Ari hasn't heard since their first date.

"Sure."

He holds her hand tight. "What do you want?"

"Like, do I want a relationship?"

"More long term. Do you want to stay in Boston? Do you want to get married and have kids?"

It's practically the only thing they haven't talked about yet. These were never questions she had to ask with Morgan. The answers were always so clear, tacit. They would get married, just like Summer and Luke would; they'd move back here once he wrapped up business school, since Massachusetts was a place they'd grown into together, and Abbott wasn't too far. There would be good jobs for Morgan, lots of school options for Ari. They'd start a family, build a life.

She doesn't remember dropping Soren's hand, but she's no longer holding it.

"I just got out of a relationship," she says, though it'll be a year next month, and if Morgan's moved on already, she also needs to.

"Sure," he replies, like she's given him a meaningful answer. "I did, too."

She can't imagine he lost as much as she did.

"I'm not asking because I'm ready for a huge thing. I'm just . . . I don't know."

"I get it."

They're quiet the rest of the walk. Like he's worried Ari will jet for the first T stop she sees if he opens his mouth. She wants to tell him she desperately wants marriage, a love like Summer and Luke, Wells and Leah. That she even believes Soren could be her person. But looking toward the future isn't always as easy as throwing together a vision board in the cradle of a familiar apartment.

Clouds roll in. Soren asks if Ari wants to head back. She does. At the train, they stop before they tap in. Soren is going inbound, to run an errand; Ari, outbound, to head home. He takes her hand again, leans in. His kiss feels like an apology.

~

Sunday morning, they text. Plan for dinner Tuesday night. The space between now and then is enough for her to let the moment breathe. It's on her to let it go. The question he asked was entirely fair. They don't know each other. They are trying to. This is part of that process: learning someone's vision of the future. She won't let herself squander the opportunity. She has the privilege of that future. If she doesn't hold on to it for dear life, she's learned nothing.

Before she goes to bed, she sends him another message.

Really looking forward

Me too

Ari can do this. Not only because Morgan has a girlfriend, and Wells has a wife, and they've both cleared the space in her life so she can move on. But because she deserves it. She deserves someone.

~

On Monday, Wells asks Ari to stay late.

Once everyone filters out—seven thirty—she raps on the glass, waits for him to motion her in. He points to the chair as he leans back against the desk. *Sit.* He coughs hard, holds his chest. Wells doesn't look sick, just unkempt, past the line of Soren's charming disarray. She can't believe she has gotten herself to a point where she's minimized him in the shape of another man.

"You all right?" he says.

"Yes."

He steals a punctuated glance at her lap, where she's sliding her bracelets up and down her wrist.

"Good," he says. "It's been a while."

"A while for what?" She wants to hear him say it aloud: he misses her. She's worth missing.

"Working late together."

She grimaces.

"Look." He pushes off the desk, takes a lap around it. "Tomorrow, Leah is in Amherst with a friend. Rowan's with her dad."

"What does that have to do with me?"

Ari feels high. Intoxicated with her resolve, her willpower.

Wells sits on the desktop, shins brushing her knees. He looks thinner. She hasn't seen his body since San Francisco. She curls her lips under, stares at anything but the fibers where their jeans touch. There's one computer screen lit in the far corner of the office.

"What are you doing? Someone's still here. Look." She points out the glass. "You said people are talking, so what do you think you're doing right now?"

"Just listen to me," he says. Wells jumps down from the desk, puts some space between them as he looks out to the glow. "Come over. I miss you."

The words hit Ari hard. A hummingbird flutter in her chest.

"I have plans."

"With a man."

"Yes."

"A boyfriend?"

"I don't know. Maybe."

"Good for you." Wells stuffs his computer into his bag, turns off his monitor. "Anything else?" he says, as if they've been discussing work the entire time.

Ari stiffens. She resents him so much. She's almost relieved he'll be dead soon.

She walks out, plucks her bag from her desk chair, takes the stairs so she doesn't have to share the elevator with him.

~

The next day, she tells him she's working from home. He is, too. Quiet house. Nice to take advantage of it, he writes. She doesn't respond. They exchange few words all day. He forwards one email, no context. She watches television until noon, her closed computer beside her on the couch. His jealousy sits like fire inside her, burning devastatingly hot.

All good for tonight? Soren messages, a few minutes after three.

Very good

For too long, Ari stares at the exchange, but they're just meaningless bubbles. It's not Soren. It's not a person. Or maybe whoever is there just isn't as important as she convinced herself.

~

Wells doesn't seem the slightest bit surprised when Ari shows up in the doorway of his home office, shifting her weight back and forth. Her chest molten. He's at his glass-topped desk, covered with pictures of his family, lush plants creeping down the steel-gray wall behind him. He stands, closes his computer. Walks past her, climbs the stairs. She follows.

"I don't think I have much time left," he says, before he removes her shirt in the doorway of the bedroom.

She won't leave. Not to meet Soren. Not for anything in the world.

WELLS

What do you see for yourself in the future?"

The social worker crosses one leg at the knee, tilts her head to the side. Wells hates the way she's holding her pen, between the knuckles of her middle and pointer fingers. She taps it a few times on the yellow legal pad, covered in blue cursive, until she realizes he's staring. She drops the pen against the pad, hides it under her palm.

"I see myself becoming prime minister of Finland and winning the Nobel in physics," he says. "Or maybe I'll open a chip shop in Devon, catch my own fish. Live a quiet coastal life."

"For fuck's sake, Wells," Leah barks from beside him on the couch.

She puts her hand to her lips, embarrassed she's sworn in front of their guest. But she isn't herself. Neither of them is, nor have they been since December. No one knows when to surrender and grieve, or when pretending is better for everyone. They are living in a circus, performing the worst high-wire act, losing their balance, plummeting face-first to the ground, day after day.

It's an April Friday morning, a grassy breeze pushing through the open windows. Rowan is playing in the basement with Irma, keeping the days as ordinary as possible. He's still so young, not even two, but they don't want to risk him understanding. Leah pats her temples with her fingertips, just to busy her hands. Her hair is filthy, and there's a ridge from one of her white hair ties. Lately she looks worse than he does. Or maybe he isn't seeing himself.

"I'm sorry," she says to the social worker.

The woman simpers. She's very kind, and is doing a very hard job—especially since she's trying to guide Wells, of all people, gently into oblivion. But he does not want guidance. He does not want a hospice worker to tell him he's going to find peace, that a golden light will take him to the sky, that he'll see his grandparents again. There is no heaven. Anyway, he's already living in hell.

"I understand," she says. "It's a difficult time."

Wells labors to inhale. "No shit."

"I'd like to see you in the kitchen," Leah says to him, rising from the couch.

"No."

"Fine." She drops back down.

He touches her bare thigh, skin dry and smooth, pulls his hand back into his lap. Rubs his eyes with his sweaty fists. His skin is constantly damp, and he soaks through his shirts every day. When he's in the office, he sits in the wet fabric for too long, hiding it under a sweatshirt until he feels like a drowned animal. He doesn't come in much anymore, but he still can't let anyone notice he's changing clothes three times a day. He doesn't want people to see how frail he is now, how nothing fits anymore.

He turns back to the social worker. "I don't see anything on the other side. You live, then you die. That's it."

She nods once. In his periphery, he sees his wife close her eyes.

"What if you're wrong?" Leah says.

"About God?"

"I mean, maybe." She opens her eyes again, stares into him like she's an abused dog. "There's no way to know."

He leans back to see her, crosses his arms. His wife's body has always been so small, yet Leah has always been enormous. But, each day, he recognizes her less and less. He hates it almost as much as his own deterioration. She gets the chance to live, yet she's choosing to wither alongside him. She doesn't have any idea the opportunity slipping away.

He can't believe they've existed like this for nearly four months now. Sometimes, he just wants it all over with.

"Since when are you religious?" he asks.

"I'm not. Never mind."

Wells stands, slowly, even though there's no way to avoid the pain now. The ache, in his literal bones. He thanks the social worker, leaves Leah behind on the couch.

He traipses upstairs to their bedroom, trying to breathe through the stitch in his side. They all know his wife is actually the one who needs the therapy. She's already in mourning. Wells won't entertain her preemptive grief, but the social worker downstairs will.

Anyway, he thinks as he falls to the green blanket, arms splayed in a T, he already has his own plan. For the rest of his life, the only thing he wants is to touch someone. At all times some part of his body in contact with another person's. He cannot be without Rowan in his lap or close beside him on the couch, this small person who will take his face and his eyes and his hands into a future he will not exist in. This small person whom he will never truly know. And when he and Leah are alone, not in the middle of a counseling session he never agreed to, he cannot unlock his fingers from her hand. He needs her to keep breathing into his neck as she lies against him. He is afraid the second he can't feel her he'll literally turn to ash. Each night, in this bed, he holds her until she sleeps. It's often late—three, four, five in the morning—because they can't stop talking, remembering. He tells her not to cry, because he doesn't want to waste their remaining time with tears. She tells him not to fall asleep, because she's terrified he won't wake up. He doesn't want to close his eyes, either. He's afraid of missing a single thing.

Then there is Ari. He needs her, too. Wells has had a few loves in his life, but none like her. She's the only person who's ever stripped him down to the studs, put him back together better. She expects nothing of him, but somehow pulls everything out of him. The moments she is against him feel eternal, like he is starting his life over each time he's with her. Endless possibility and choice. He needs this kind of eternity, not the one coming for him.

He knows it was wrong to ask her back. She was finally taking care of herself. He knew she'd come. She hasn't mentioned how his body has withered, that his clavicle is breaking from his skin, the pained sound of his breathing, the way he is pale as death. The yelp that comes out of his mouth when he moves sometimes. She hasn't said what they both see, which is that he no longer has any control, even if he still walks through life with his feathers puffed. With Leah, it's impossible to feel like the same person he was before the diagnosis, because she's so laser-focused on his death. With Ari, he's as alive as he ever was.

By the time Leah comes into the bedroom, twenty minutes later, Wells is sitting on the bench in the shower, though the water isn't on.

"Why are you in here?" she asks, face splotchy from tears.

"I don't know."

He is dying to find catharsis, finally, but he can't bear to fall apart in front of his wife. He refuses to let her remember him as weak and tearful; a boy, not a man. He reaches for her hand, holds it between his palms, against his chest. Every moment, he could scream, just to hear his voice alive.

ARI

Everything changes when she goes back to Wells. Overnight, she feels the gravity of the ordinary. She watches him squirrel away into conference rooms with Krish, talking for hours. They're obviously working on succession plans, because what good would it do to begin projects they both know Wells won't be able to see through? The fact that a new CEO will take his spot at the company eats at his pride, just like the cancer is eating at his body.

Even time feels different. She looks at Wells's calendar, stretching into the future as far as she's willing to click. Maybe she's inputting plans for hours he'll never experience. Maybe, with a crooked unreality, he wants her to.

Ari has found herself at the core of an extremely small club of people silently scrambling to claim the rest of his life. More often than she'd like, she thinks of Leah. Alone in her own bed, Ari languishes, awake, certain Leah can't sleep, either. Her husband will die soon. The father of her young son. The powerlessness Ari feels is comparably nonexistent; for all she is going through, Leah is suffering in a way she is not. She wonders whether Leah is already contemplating her life on the other side of Wells, or whether she refuses to reckon with the future. As much as she's gathered about her, Ari doesn't understand her well enough to be sure. Ari is not family or a friend. She is nothing but the other woman.

She wonders how Wells and Leah hold each other at night. If he spoons her to keep himself bigger, if she lays on his chest, committed to listening to his heartbeat for as long as it will go on. If it unnerves her to feel how different his body is when she touches him. His chest hair, now graying like the hair on his head; his rib cage pushing to the surface, little lines of each bone, like scores in his skin.

When Ari is with him, she wants so badly to take care of him, and does. There's no sex anymore, and hasn't been since that day she left Soren behind; the pain is too great, he says, a violence inside him he can't describe. But that's not the point. It's to suspend time, fight life's unstable reality—the one that brought Ari to Wells in the first place. Instead, they lie beside each other, or she pats a cool washcloth on his forehead while he tells her everything he can about his forty years. He wants her to carry it all with her. He wants to live past his life, through her.

This pull: it's why she ignored Soren's calls when she didn't show up to dinner, why she hasn't returned a single text. There's no space for anyone or anything else but Wells, at least not now.

She knocks on the doorframe of his office. "Can I come in?"

He nods. He won't stop working, even though there are so many more important things to do with his time, and he is profoundly exhausted by the long days. He doesn't show the pain, but she can see it, everywhere.

"Are you okay?" she asks.

"Close the door," he snaps. Except it doesn't make Ari start like usual. It's disarmed. It means nothing. He gestures for her to sit, but she shakes her head and keeps standing.

"You're not to say anything here, you understand? You treat me absolutely no differently. I'm not going to let everyone fall all over me."

"You're not planning to say anything, ever? You're just going to not show up to work one day, and that's it, because now you're dead?"

"Shut your fucking mouth."

"Wells."

"Out," he says. "Get out. Go home."

~

He calls at five thirty that evening. Ari has already been crying for three hours.

"I'm sorry," he whispers. He tells her he's pulled over on the street parallel to his home, but can't bring himself to go inside. "Wait. You're crying."

"Of course I'm crying."

"I'm sorry. I panicked. I . . . can't stop panicking." He pauses. "What's your address?"

"What?"

"Where do you live?"

"Why?"

"Because I'm coming over."

He waits, waits, and waits until she whispers it to him.

~

"Can I come in?" he asks, scratching the back of his neck as he fills her doorway. "Please, Ari. Let me in."

"Leah's expecting you," she says, standing in her high school gym shorts and too-tight tank top.

"I told her I'm going for dinner with Krish."

He can do anything he wants now, she understands. He can spend his time exactly as he pleases.

As soon as she lets him in, he breaks down. She's never seen anyone cry this hard. He drops into the seat at the kitchen table, where she usually dines alone, his head in his hands, snot streaming from his nose.

She is frozen—does he want to be touched? Does he just want to cry? What did she even want in the depths of her own despair last year? She can't remember, not because she's so far removed from it, but because she never actually figured it out. She never gave herself the chance to hear her own thoughts.

She places her hand on his shoulder, but as soon as she feels his sweat, she drops her arms around him, her chest against the rivets of his spine. His hair is wet on her cheek. *I love you desperately,* she thinks.

She takes him to her small, unmade bed. The sheets smell acrid from the moldy washing machine in the basement, a tang that never goes away, no matter what detergent she uses or how much the landlord says he cleans the drum. They strip each other's clothes. He curls up against her like a naked newborn, and although the tears have let up, his cheeks are still tacky, eyes infinitely swollen.

"I don't want to die," he whispers.

He won't say it to anyone else. That it's her, purely her, who has given him the chance to be the person he is, not the one he created. Even with Leah, Ari knows he's never split open before. She knows he's worried his wife wouldn't love him if she saw him like this.

"I love you," she says. She'd give him her lungs, her bones, her entire body if he could use it.

"I know." He closes his eyes. "I love you. I don't know how to stop."

The baby hairs on Ari's arms stand, a full-body chill. It's everything she's wanted to hear. While it makes her want to scream out her joy like fireworks, she doesn't. Instead, she is a body at rest, consumed by an incredible fullness, the unmistakable feeling of being whole. She stares at him until his eyes open. But as soon as his gaze finds hers, he breaks down again, shaking, wailing, coughing so hard he spits blood onto those rancid sheets.

～

"I have something to tell you," Summer begins. The next Wednesday, late afternoon. "It's not the easiest thing in the world to say."

Ari envisions her twisting the phone cord around her finger in middle school, back when phones still had cords, and Ari's life made sense.

"Luke and I got engaged."

"Oh, Summer," Ari says. "I'm thrilled for you guys."

She is, both in theory and practice. The news was coming for so long.

"I know it's probably triggering to hear, and I'm sorry."

"There's nothing to apologize for. Stop."

Ari knows Morgan heard first. Luke and Summer must have called together. For Ari, it's just Summer, with a voice three inches tall.

"When did it happen?"

"This morning." They'd had bagels in Central Park, and Luke pulled out the ring on her, midbite. "I had cream cheese all over my face. I'm so gross."

"It's a good story."

"You'll be there for me, right?"

"I'm insulted you even had to ask." Ari tries to infuse a laugh, but the levity doesn't arrive. It's not really funny, especially after everything that happened with Kathy.

Summer sighs.

"Yes. The past is the past," Ari says, even though the past feels more present than it has in a year. "You say jump, I say how high."

Ari forces a smile into her words, but feels bile rising. She can't seize Summer's moment, but the news is boiling sludge in her stomach, creeping its way up and out.

"He has cancer, Summer."

"What are you talking about?"

"Wells. He's dying."

"Since when?"

Ari can't reply.

"Ari."

"December."

"But what did he tell you?" Summer puts aside her own news, dons her doctor hat. "You know cancer isn't a death sentence, right? You can't even conceive of how sophisticated the treatments are now. What's he doing for it? Did he tell you?"

"Summer, he's dying."

Summer is silent.

"I didn't mean to make this about me. I just don't know what I'm supposed to do," Ari says.

Summer makes the squeaking sound that comes when she pulls her mouth to one side. "Nothing. At the end of the day, it has nothing to do with you."

Ari's heart stops.

"You're not his wife or his family. You're his secret. It's better to face it now." She exhales. "I have people to call, so I'm going to go."

"Congratulations. I mean it."

"Bye, Ar."

At 3:21 in the morning, Ari's phone buzzes.

This is the best thing that could possibly happen to you.

She turns back over and resumes staring at the wall.

~

"I need you to do something for me," Wells says.

They're sitting on the stone wall outside the office. Ari sips from her black iced coffee, the first she's had all year. May has landed, spring sun enveloping the city. The cup sweating in her hand, a reminder precious time is passing.

"Tomorrow. There's going to be a piece out about me online. I haven't seen it yet, but the news is in there. I need you to set up an all-hands. I'm going to tell everyone."

She feels sick. "How did I not know about this?"

"Nora coordinated everything. I couldn't let you do it."

She understands. Wells is right. She would be crushed by the finality of it. The idea that he was no longer hiding in her. What exactly going public means.

They walk back to work in complete silence, though all Ari wants to do is talk and talk and talk to him. But when he looks at her, neither can speak. Their life together is over. He slips into his office, draws the shades that are always open. Ari gets to her desk, does as she's told. Nora meets her eyes over her monitor, scrunches her lips. She knows what's coming. Soon, everyone will.

WELLS

He couldn't look at Ari during the staff meeting. He wasn't saying goodbye to his employees. He was saying goodbye to her. She understood. They both know he can't die in her arms. For Leah's sake, and their own, too.

Often, Wells asks himself what he wanted from Ari, long term. He wouldn't have ever left Leah and Rowan, knows he never had a real future with her. He couldn't have kept both Leah and Ari forever, couldn't keep his parallel lives going indefinitely, especially the more they've intersected. He still can't believe they didn't get caught—it almost feels like destiny, as pathetic as the idea sounds. Yet Wells has gone blank each time he's tried to envision a future without one of them. In whatever time he has left, he won't be able to answer the question of where he and Ari would or wouldn't have ended up. He refuses to answer, even if he lived to ninety-nine.

One day, Wells knows, Ari will hate him, like he deserves. She'll see herself as he does: magnetic, gentle, unflinching. Another person will, too, and they will braid their lives into each other, weaving a boundless future. Wells will fade away with time, and in the moments Ari looks back, she'll realize the terrible position he put her in. What an awful person he was, keeping her from the world. Soon he will be a single thread in the long history she'll spool. She's not obligated to remember him at all. Maybe she won't.

These are the kinds of swelling, complicated thoughts he will take to his grave. Many of these things won't ever reach anyone's ears, because Wells is unsure how to express them. In other cases, he will run out of time. Both are terrifying.

He wishes he could verbalize how much he loves his family, and how grateful he is for the life they gave him the opportunity to lead. Krish, for putting up with him at his worst, letting Wells saddle him with his secret. What could he possibly say to Leah that would be enough. And Ari—he'd apologize until his voice went hoarse.

But for as much as he can't express, there are also things he won't say. He knows he owes Leah full-throated honesty, but he can't destroy his wife, not without time to repent and reassure her. Selfishly, he cannot watch her destruction, because it will cause him more pain than he already feels. Wells will die, knowing he is weak willed and pathetic.

Men are scum, Leah had said. He never forgot it.

Still, despite it all—the vile realities he's learned about himself in his last days, the secrets he will bring down with him, the fact that maybe he is ultimately getting what he deserves—he does not want to die. But it doesn't matter what Wells wants anymore, does it.

ARI

Leah is crying in the front row. Not crying, heaving.

The funeral home is the wrong place for all this. It's paneled in dark wood, acrid—even stuffier than the room for Kathy, the feeling of which Ari can't forget. Even with the white orchids everywhere, it smells like death. She can't believe Wells or Leah chose this place. It's so far from who he is. Was.

Wearing the long-sleeved black dress again—too constricting for the humidity blanketing Boston, especially in this interminable rain—Ari sits among her coworkers, blending in, as if she isn't terrified of being merely a mourner like any other. Every minute someone covertly checks their phone, whispers, she wants to lunge at them, wrap her hands around their throat. It takes everything for her not to leap over the chairs, sprint to the front, pull up a seat in the aisle right beside Leah.

She locks her hands in her lap. Stays put.

Two and a half weeks ago, in front of the people in the office and on the screen, Wells took a hard-won breath, shook his head. *Today will be my last day,* he'd said. *I have cancer. I'm about to die.* He and Ari didn't speak the rest of the day, didn't even meet eyes. At five o'clock, she came into his office. He had been waiting for her, she knew. She asked if she could touch him, and he said yes. So they held each other, for a while, his body whittled to nothing. They let go at the same time.

It had to be that way. But, god, does it still live inside Ari, like a bullet lodged.

She fixates on Leah in the funeral home. Her skin has the pale sickness Wells carried with him toward the end.

Wells was exceptional, everyone says from the podium at the front of the room. Dynamic and charming. Impossible to say no to. Ari knows this, maybe better than anyone.

The service ends as it started: murmurs through the room, shared embraces, thousand-yard stares at an urn. She feels a hand on her arm. "Are you okay?" the comms person asks her. Ari nods, picks up her umbrella.

"Aria," Krish calls. He tilts his head, gesturing her toward him. She weaves her way across the room. "Leah is having a few people at the house, and she asked me to see if you'd come."

"Me?"

"Yes." He taps his foot twice, pulls his lips into a lemon pucker. She looks over her shoulder.

"He told you." The smallest voice possible.

Krish nods once, wordlessly.

"When?"

"A while ago."

She can't breathe. "Did you tell Leah?"

"No. It's none of my business."

"But he made it your business."

He scratches his beard. "It will mean a lot to Leah if you come." He holds her eyes too long, loosens his tie.

Ari follows Krish to his car. He doesn't look at her the entire ride, lets them sit in silence. She wishes Krish would say anything: tell Ari she's a horrible person, that she's fired. Stewing is a thousand times worse.

They run in from the rain. Ari expects a swarm of people inside the house, but when they get inside, the gathering is intimate. It's only immediate family and closest friends, all slumped on the couch, leaning against the doorways with clear plastic cups in hand. She steps gingerly into the living room, bouquets on every surface. The flowers alone make her want to break down crying, but she's so wary of making a show. She doesn't belong here. Yet Leah says she does.

Clad in a sleeveless black sheath dress, Leah rises from the chair by the fireplace when she sees Krish and Ari. She hugs Krish, kisses his cheek.

She turns to Ari, stands so close. "Thank you for coming."

Leah drapes her arms around Ari's neck, her head falling to Ari's shoulder. She lets herself go entirely. Her tears soak through Ari's dress, and Ari can feel her racing heartbeat against her own chest.

"If there's anything I can do, Leah," Ari whispers, wrapping her arms around Wells's widow, "don't hesitate for a second."

LEAH

ARI

Clio always barks when the phone vibrates with a call. Ari jumps next to her on the couch, runs her finger between her eyes, down her snout, until the dog sleepily drops against her leg.

She reaches for her phone. Leah's name on the screen. Her heart flips.

"Hi," Leah says, her voice small. "It's Leah Cahill. Hi."

Ari is sure she knows her number is saved. But it's like she has to say her own name, still attached to Wells's, to keep him alive as long as the myopia lets her.

"Hi," Ari replies, dropping a hand to Clio's back.

It's been two months. She has started fostering a deaf, pure-white mutt, whom she takes on long walks around the city; powered through a couple of weeks of barre classes, despite what must be a biological inability to *tuck*; tried to get out more, even just reading at a bar while sipping a beer. She's worked from her apartment since Krish told her Wells was gone. As much as she's kept herself going the past several weeks, even seen some light in the dark forest, it'd still be unbearable to sit near Wells's empty office, hear what people think are sufficient condolences. Even Krish, in his own stone-faced way, knows. He doesn't owe her anything, yet he's found a place for her in content strategy, used his own time to set up transition meetings with the CMO and managing editor. Ari gets on the calls, smiles painfully and agrees with each conversation, but he is well aware she hasn't written a word. In the not-distant future, he told her over video last Friday, she needs to snap back into it. *I know it's hard, but I can't keep paying you if you're not going to work.* He's given her a week to turn it around.

"What's the chance you nanny?" Leah asks, a little breathless on the line.

Her vulnerability upends Ari. The last time she and Wells were alone together, a few weeks before he died, she watched him from her couch as he took out the filter-pitcher in her fridge. Cool water to calm his raw throat. *Are you ever going to tell Leah?* she asked, cracking her knuckles in her lap. He poured himself a glass. *She has enough hell to deal with.* Ari nodded. *Will you take care of her if she needs anything? For me,* he'd asked. Sipped. *Yes,* Ari said. She knew what a risk it'd be, yet somehow it was the easiest question she'd ever answered. Maybe atonement could come in the form of protection.

"Absolutely," Ari says to Leah. She hasn't babysat since she was maybe fifteen, when she stayed with Summer's sister one night. They watched a rom-com together, then Ella went to sleep.

Leah asks if she can come over, as soon as possible. "After all this, Irma just told me she's moving back to Germany in two weeks. I can't do it alone. I physically can't."

"Of course. I'll do anything to help."

"You don't know how much I need to hear that."

~

Two hours later, Ari is at Wells's front door. Her bracelets clank as she knocks.

"I'm so sorry. I look like shit," Leah says, still in the doorframe.

She startles—she's forgotten Leah is so blunt, uninhibited. She likes that about her. It feels intimate, though she is the last person who deserves her trust. But Leah still doesn't know about the affair—that much is clear. In some ways, it's a relief; in others, Ari worries she and Wells burned up with his bones.

Ari shakes her head to say, *No, you don't look like shit*, even though Leah does. Her dirty hair is tangled, swept back into a ponytail that looks like it was secured in the dark. Her shirt is spotted with coffee on her left breast. Mostly, though, it's Leah's face that looks half-human. It's like she can't open her eyes all the way, her skin still blanched.

She leads Ari into the living room, where her two-year-old son is sorting Duplo by color on the floor. It's almost miraculous to be with Wells's child, for real. She knows the sound of Rowan's footsteps better than his face. Beyond the fact he looks startlingly like Wells, he is beautiful. His eyelashes are infinite, not unlike Morgan's, and they make it impossible to look away from the eyes he shared with his father. His fingers are careful, almost elegant, as he methodically lines up the blocks, precisely flush. He drives a wooden truck over the blue pile. Her heart aches for him—the father he's lost, the future he's lost. Ari knows, acutely, the pain.

"I can't imagine what you're going through," she says to Leah, even though looking at Wells's widow is like peering into her own mirror in the days after his death. Ari had barely gotten out of bed for a week. Slept with Kathy's pincushion under her pillow. Kept picking up the phone to call her father, putting it down.

Leah thanks her. "I know it's weird for everyone in the office, too. It must be hard for you."

They talk about Wells. But not like he is dead, instead like he'll burst through the door any second, find it lovely both women are sitting together. Maybe he'll drop his bag and keys on the island and join them, talk about his day, the extremely particular salad Ari brought to his desk. They talk about how charismatic he is, the way he gathers attention in a room. The blind date on which he and Leah met, how she remembers exactly what he ordered: an Italian Ribolla Gialla. It was what Leah had wanted, and she blushed asking for the same thing.

"It wasn't always easy to love him," she says. "But I saw I would before he said two words."

"Of course," Ari replies. "That's so special."

"It was. Anyway." She kills Wells, just like that. "More than anything, I hate this so much for Rowan. He won't remember a thing about his dad. I can't really think of anything more tragic."

Ari stares at her hands, then at Leah's son, who's decided he's done with his blocks, now shoving a book into Leah's lap.

"Not now, baby," she says. His face drops.

Ari wants to reach out to him, read for hours.

Leah picks up her son, settles him into her lap while he opens the board book of opposites from her company, flipping the pages on his own. Ari smiles at him. He looks up, smiles back. Would she have wanted a baby with Wells? A family? Would she have ever actually done what her father did? The fact she's even in a position to ask the questions turns her inside out. Since Morgan, since Wells, she's become someone else—the goal she had when she left New York. But this wasn't who she meant to be. Ari can't undo what she's done, but she needs to find somewhere to start building something new. *Something big.* Make up for the days she's lost in other people, instead of finding them in herself.

Leah tells her about Rowan. His peccadilloes: *his favorite food is frozen corn, he hates books that rhyme, he thinks grape-flavored infant ibuprofen is candy.* Next, his schedule: *swimming, playgroup, library, music class, Mandarin story time, science.* She acknowledges it's excessive, admits she fudged his birthdate on some of the registration forms so they'd let him into the programs for three-year-olds. *Like I'm trying to get him into Harvard before he's five. Wells found this all ridiculous, and there's literally scientific literature that argues against doing it, but here we are.* It's one of the reasons Wells knew he and Ari could be here, alone.

"Rowan basically needs someone to make sure he gets from A to B, eats, generally stays engaged with things. You'll have to actually get in the pool for swim, but otherwise you sort of murmur songs and make sure he doesn't wander off or go face-first into anything. I think it'll be good for him to stay as distracted as possible, and you might have a little fun, too."

Leah hasn't asked once whether Ari is qualified to protect the life of her only child. Ari should tell her she's the last person alive who should be trusted with anything precious to her, especially the only thing that remains of the life she violated.

"I can do all that."

"I know. I trust you."

Ari nods.

"This is sort of embarrassing, but what's the chance I can ask you to do laundry, too?"

It's now a given: Leah will be her employer. It's just like the interview with Wells, where he gave her the position on sight, before she even made a case for herself. *My wife,* he'd said, the first minutes he'd spent with her. *She's great.* Sitting in her living room, Leah hasn't asked why Ari, with a stable job, has agreed to be her full-time nanny. Ari will ghost the company, let her next paycheck be the last, take the burden off Krish.

"Absolutely," she says. "I can cook, too. Anything to help."

"You're a godsend."

She wants Leah to talk about Wells again. All the ways he lived with her, the way he loved her. How she's trying to fill the void. She needs to hear it, because Leah is the only person who can keep him fresh, carry on the feeling of being with him. Keep him from disappearing the way Ari has already experienced enough of throughout her life.

"He adored you," Leah hums. "I understand why."

She isn't sure what that means, but she starts Monday.

~

Ari feels something when her knuckles rap on the front door. A pulse, a current. It's eight in the morning, the first day of her new job: Rowan. She knows how she got here. She can't screw it up.

Leah opens the door, a welcoming, red-tinted smile. She is wearing a crimson T-shirt tucked into dark jeans, tight around the ankles. Even in simple clothes, even touched by death, she looks extraordinary: a beam of early light. A beacon. If he could, Wells would miss her. Ari has shown up in a new black T-shirt, a clean pair of black jeans. Pointed beige flats—the ones she wore when she fell. She hadn't realized.

Rowan is eating toast on the couch, watching *Sesame Street*. He kicks his little legs, doesn't turn around when Ari steps inside. Leah motions her into the kitchen, shows her a gridded printout of his schedule for each day of the week. It's filled margin to margin: when he has activities, when he naps, when and what he eats.

"I know I'm a broken record, but check every food for nuts, and be annoying about it. God forbid, there are two EpiPens in the diaper bag," she says.

Ari's mind whips back to San Francisco: the impossibly short gaps among lying raw in Wells's arms, hearing the words that changed her life, booking his emergency flight home.

She peeks again at the paper, sees she has to get Rowan to library circle by ten. She does the mental math—they'll have to leave in an hour to get to the T, build in enough time to walk from the station. But as she begins to fret over the logistics, Leah slides a set of car keys across the counter. Cheeks red, eyes glossy.

"Wow, I didn't think a stupid thing like this would be so fucking hard," she says.

The keys are for Wells's Porsche.

"Are you sure?" Ari says. It's unreasonable for her to drive it as a nanny, or ever.

"I hate it and I can't bear to get rid of it."

"I'll take good care. I promise."

~

After she tucks Rowan into his seat, settles herself into the driver's side, Ari notices the car still carries Wells in every way. His sunglasses are in the center console, and she can still suck the fresh, oceanic scent of his antiperspirant straight into her lungs. Holding the gearshift is holding his hand. She luxuriates in his ghost for so long Rowan starts whimpering in the back seat.

Leah texts her throughout the day, asks how things are going. Well! she writes from the library, with Rowan's tiny body in her lap; then again at the indoor soft gym, where he toddles up to her with a red puffy cylinder, offers it with a grin. Next, All good here! Having fun! when he is at STEM, deftly putting together a wooden-peg puzzle, also made by Leah's company. What Ari would like to text, but can't, is that she's falling all over herself with gratitude for a place in the Cahill family.

Leah walks through the door just a few minutes after Ari and Rowan get home from the playground, four thirty. She drops her keys on the kitchen island, heaves her tote bag beside them, hexagonal puzzle pieces spilling onto the counter.

"Figured I'd come home early, give you a little break," she says. A light hand to Ari's back.

Ari smiles, then finishes filling a sippy cup with organic whole milk. In truth, a *little break* feels nice—as much fun as she's had, she's not sure why being with a toddler is so draining. They've done both nothing and everything all day.

"Am I going to see you tomorrow, or did he scare you away?"

"I'll be here by eight."

Thank you, Leah mouths, then closes her eyes.

~

Ari has collapsed on her living-room couch, all fifty pounds of Clio draped across her. She's certain she's exhausted like a mother: a deep but satisfying fatigue from watching another human like a hawk, speaking all day to a person who barely speaks back. She loves it.

After three days of her radio silence at the company, the offboarding paperwork from Krish and HR landed in her personal inbox as she rode the T home; her work email no longer loads on her phone. Ari scrolls the exit document, the intellectual-property nondisclosure agreement, with a light beer and bowl of boxed macaroni and cheese on the side table. She doesn't read anything, just signs. Krish leaves a note they'll nuke the hard drive remotely, and she can keep the computer.

Oh my god I'm spent, she texts Summer. But she regrets it immediately. Summer thinks she's been sitting at the desk in front of Wells's empty office all day. She hasn't told her about working for Leah. She wouldn't dare.

Long day? Summer responds an hour later.

Very. She quickly asks if she's hanging in, drowning in work and wedding.

Yes yes and yes

Ari lets herself fall back into the pillows for the rest of the night, reading while Clio yelps with puppy dreams. She is happy. Yet the longer she sits under only the cast of the dim table lamp, the glee of the day trickles away, filled instead by a steady drip of uncertainty. She begins to entirely question entering Leah's life, lunging for Wells's shadow. Forgoing a man like Soren, who was healthy for her, genuinely good. Even passing up Luke's roommate from New Year's, whose name she can't remember now. They're ideas Ari should have reckoned with earlier, certainly before passing the threshold of Leah's front door, renewing her existence in the fig-scented air of their home. She just can't let go of Wells. Not yet.

Ari finds her way to bed at eight forty-five, exhausted from Rowan and herself. Slightly drunk, equally unmoored. She turns over to sleep, heavy lidded. But as she closes her eyes, her hand wanders, as if on its own. Her finger grazes the inside of her thigh, then higher up. Wet, pressure, sweet relief. She's both bound and free at once.

LEAH

How does anyone prepare for their life to change?

This is the question Leah can't stop asking herself, every second. It takes over her brain when she's at her desk, on a work call; when she's at the playground with Rowan, cheering him down the slide; when Molly comes over for dinner because Leah is still too scared to go out into the world alone.

She tried to prepare. She and Wells both did. They wrote the will and established the trust, took his retirement money and moved it into Rowan's 529 for private school and college. They spent every second they could together, took family photos, told each other everything they'd never said. They talked about the memories, the highest highs; opened every rare bottle in the wine closet, even though he wasn't supposed to drink on his pain meds. They held each other as if the world would end tomorrow, because they had to assume it would. They lived as fast as possible, crammed an entire lifetime into each day; they lived as slow as they could, savored every second. But it was not sufficient. Ultimately, there is the Before, and there is the After. No one can do enough in the space between.

Every day, Wells told her it would be okay. It'd made her furious. Because it wouldn't be, for any of them, and he was the person who was coping least. They'd stood in the kitchen, six thirty on Christmas morning, when he had snapped at her about considering home-hospice services, even though he hadn't tried treatment yet. It was the first time they'd fought since the diagnosis; about five months left, now that she remembers. *We need to process this together,* she'd practically screamed, slamming the folder from the hospital on the island. *You need to fucking process this, Wells.* The countertop was strewn with groceries for the dinner she was going to cook that evening—bulbous white onions, leeks, crème fraîche she'd accidentally left out overnight—and she remembers feeling like she was going to pass out from the anger, the fear. *Are you the one dying or am I?* Wells shot back, snatching the folder and throwing it into the trash. She'd glared at him until he plucked it out of the canister, placed it back on the counter. They both knew the answer wasn't binary. He went to grab Rowan from his crib, and as soon as Leah heard him climbing the stairs, she'd gone into the basement and screamed bloody murder into a throw pillow. That night, after they'd spent the day with her family, opening presents and getting piss drunk on mulled wine, Ari had come over for dinner. Leah could have killed Wells for inviting her without asking—it would probably be her last Christmas with her husband. But she was no longer in a position to say no to anything Wells wanted. She still can't believe the act they put on that night: the most extraordinary performance of the ordinary. At least for as long as they could.

It's three in the morning, and Leah cannot sleep again. In the two months since Wells's death, she's tried everything: meditation and bedtime yoga; weighted blankets and a sound machine of waves crashing; gag-inducing teas; CBD tinctures and four strains of indica, baked into cookies, rolled in joints like a teenage dream. Pills of every kind, including one that made her sleepwalk. Nothing's worked. It's the gnawing that she didn't do enough. That maybe, irrationally, his sickness was her fault.

She turns over in bed. Can't force her raccoon eyes closed. She finds herself in the bathroom, flips on the sconces flanking the mirror. The bulbs are too bright, throwing light into every corner. God, did Wells hate these expensive ceramic tiles she insisted on when they renovated. *These make me feel like I'm on mushrooms,* he'd said, squinting at the sample the designer had dropped off. Now they're making her dizzy, too. This time, she's the one who feels like she's hallucinating.

She curls up into a ball on the shower bench. Wells's razor and shaving mirror, his dandruff shampoo and conditioner: she hasn't moved them. For the final week, he couldn't bathe without her—the thing that stripped away his remaining dignity, even more than the around-the-clock morphine drip, the oxygen tube. The smell of his cedarwood soap hasn't yet washed away.

Leah has stopped crying, and she's not sure if she physically can generate another tear. Not after the funeral and the sympathy calls and the thank-you notes for the fatty freezer casseroles and flowers that wept petals onto her living-room floor. No one wanted to see a widow sobbing, yet they all expected her to, and she did. Even though she has quelled the tears, she is so far from moving past shock. She's existing without her feet touching the ground. Leah has to live after Wells, and she is, in the sense that she hasn't stopped moving since he died. She has never spent so much time working, pointlessly talking to fill empty space.

She unfurls, feels the white penny tile beneath her feet as she steps back across the shower. Before she can avoid herself, she catches her reflection in the tall, brass-framed mirror over her side of the white-quartz vanity. She braces herself against the counter, really studies her face, more than she has since she was a teenager with pocked cheeks. Her skin is desert sand, rough to the touch. She's been hiding her pallor behind powdered foundation and rose-colored liquid blush. Hairline veins rip through the whites of her eyes, faded green irises now colored like urine. She has three chin hairs. She never noticed.

In soft red cotton shorts and one of Wells's undershirts, she leads herself down the hall, to Rowan's room. On the right-hand wall, there's a cluster of photos. In the dead center hangs one from Prince Edward Island, just after they'd been married. Two lobsters on the tabletop, empty oyster shells and spent lemon wedges on a bed of crushed ice. The sun is starting to drop, streaking the sky cotton candy and lavender. A Canadian flag whips behind them. Leah, too, is windswept.

She doesn't need the photo to remember each detail, recall the feeling of Wells's hand under the table, wrapped around her thigh. How his fingertips felt when he squeezed it.

She edges open Rowan's door, careful not to let any light creep in. Her son is gently whirring as he sleeps face down in the crib, hands splayed like a murder victim. The sound machine is humming the static of the womb. She curls up in the big navy glider, where she spent so many hours breastfeeding Rowan in the depths of night, sobbing as she wondered whether she'd ever sleep or smile again. Sometimes she startles, swears she sees Wells's actual face on Rowan's tiny body, like a movie mutant. When she breathes again, she realizes it's just her son. Still, the similarity is terrorizing.

Leah gathers her legs under her, leans back in the chair. When she's in this room, well after her son has gone to sleep—lately, often—it's hard to not think of the family life she's lost. Rowan's birthdays, his father placing a chocolate cake in front of him, the smoke of candles rising as he helps his young son blow them out. Wells missed Rowan's second birthday by nine days. There will be no trips to the UK, three generations of Cahill men sitting around the dining table. Rowan's first day of school, his soccer games, his face when he's accepted into his dream college—he won't have a father to turn to for that proud look. Leah will have these visions for the rest of her life, and they will always feel as real as anything. How can she see them so acutely? How can she picture expressions her husband never made, vividly know the shape of her grown son? These moments are what makes Wells's death unbelievable. How deeply wrong, unfair.

Rowan purrs in his sleep, little breaths escaping in rhythm. She hears him adjust; his knees scratch the bedsheet. She'll have to explain to him he's not like the other kids. She'll have to protect him from internalizing it—she can't let him feel even a shred of this.

Leah's mother insists she and her son will recover. But she doesn't know whom to believe anymore, not after the universe betrayed her.

~

Dawn cracks light. Leah opens her eyes when Rowan does, sleepy moans in his crib that ring her maternal alarm clock. She's been in the chair all night. She isn't sure if she's slept, but she's at least turned off her brain enough to drift. She takes her son from bed, changes his diaper, kisses his hair. The sweet, fresh smell of a child. It's 6:55, and she heads downstairs, spoons out yogurt and cuts up a banana for him, turns on WBUR, and hears about a homicide in Back Bay, budget cuts across the elementary schools, terrorism and war. She checks her email at the island.

The front door creaks open, and she shoots to attention, terrified. But it's just Ari, at seven thirty, as always. Leah has loved every minute Ari's been with them—she's needed both a kind voice in the house to talk about what's here instead of what's missing, and another human to offset the reality she is alone. But it's been only two weeks since Ari started, and Leah is still adjusting to a new presence in her house amid all this. Ari's steps are lighter than Irma's, her voice hoarser. Leah can only focus on what's different now: indicators of everything that's changed, so quickly and without her consent.

Ari drops her bag, pulls down the hem of her black shirt, flecked with white dog hair. She's obviously uncomfortable in her own skin, but she shouldn't be. Ari is pretty, in an unusual way Leah can't put her finger on. She's not thin, not heavy, and her frame suits her, as do her bright-brown almond eyes, pale-olive skin. The gentle kink of her hair, which she pulls up and lets down every five minutes.

"Hi there," Ari says as she enters the kitchen.

She walks over to Rowan, nibbling on his fruit, ruffles his hair. Leah doesn't ask her to, but Ari retrieves the rest of the banana, slices it for him. Pours a sippy cup of milk, which Leah neglected. Yesterday, as she and Molly were locking the office at the end of the day, Leah's business partner had asked how she was doing. *Honestly,* Molly had said. Leah had paused, running her finger over the key's jagged peaks. All she could picture was arriving home earlier that week to hear Ari laughing as she rolled a ball across the floor with Rowan. Leah's dinner, a dill-cream salmon, waiting on the stove. *Honestly,* Leah had said, *it's getting better.*

"Good morning." She smiles, grateful to have a reason to, with everything still so raw.

She can't take her eyes from Ari's hands, opening the dishwasher she ran yesterday, her long fingers carefully placing the plates in the cabinet. Wells used to put away the dishes, since Leah can't reach the top shelves.

"I'm sorry," she says, pulling down the pajama shorts she didn't remember to change out of. "I forgot it was clean. I would have done it if—"

"You have enough to worry about," Ari says. As if she can fathom the depths of what Leah is feeling, the weight of loss and vacancy and permanence. As if she already understands how much Leah needs a second pair of hands, another half to her brain.

Leah sighs, covers her face with her palms. "Thank you," she whispers. Exhales.

ARI

In the August heat, Summer is sitting on her parents' porch in a white sundress when Ari rolls into her own driveway. As Ari turns off the car and unbuckles her seat belt, Summer jumps down, over the staircase, like she did when they were children.

"You rented a Porsche to drive two hours?"

"So," Ari stutters through the open window, "it's Wells's."

"I'm sorry?"

She climbs out of the car. "I have a lot to explain."

Ari and Summer crossed paths during her drive-by Thanksgiving, but this is the first time they've earnestly been in Abbott together in—god, how long? It should have been for Kathy, for Morgan. She realizes the last time she and Summer spent real time here, it was the final Christmas before Morgan left. He and Ari had been engaged for a year and a half by then. What she remembers most is Christmas Eve, at Mead's—Ari, Morgan, Summer, and Luke at one in the morning, after Kathy and Rick had closed the kitchen and left, leaving their son to lock up. They all would have stayed forever if they could have.

"Do you want to go in and see your mom?" Summer asks.

Ari glances at the sign on the lawn, the phone number and foundation-caked face of a real estate agent. There's a bag of groceries in the back of the car for her mother, but she isn't ready to bring them inside yet. She shakes her head.

Summer shrugs. "Let's take the absurd car that doesn't belong to you."

"Well, it kind of does."

"I can't even conceive of the explanation you have for this, but I am certain I'm going to hate it."

Summer settles into the passenger seat and glances at the car seat in the rearview mirror. The whole ride down, Ari wrestled with the voice in her head over how to tell Summer about this next chapter. But even after rearranging the words a hundred times, she's still not sure what she'll say. She hasn't even really explained it to herself in a justifiable, sane way.

"Are you excited?" Ari asks as she heads toward the waterside inn Summer is *looking at* for her venue, though everyone knows it's where she'll hold the wedding. Where Ari would have held her own.

"*Aria Claire Bishop*, explain why you are in your dead ex-lover's car."

"Good god, Summer."

Summer crosses her arms at her small breasts. Her dress wrinkles.

Ari takes a deep breath, exhales. "Leah gave it to me. I work for her now. I'm her son's full-time nanny."

"Wells's son, you mean."

"His name is Rowan. He's two."

"I'm trying to figure out if I'm unconscious and having a nightmare."

Ari reaches over and pinches Summer, who yelps, flicks away her hand. "Awake."

She turns onto Seapath, the same intersection next to Mead's where Kathy was killed. Being back home is more unsettling than she expected—she's falsely assumed the space she'd gotten from this place since Thanksgiving would give her honest-to-god distance. Instead, she's finding herself sucked back into Abbott's rhythm, a townie who knows every corner. Her body is bullying her to be a bright-eyed teenager, flush with love, everything ahead. But she is not.

Ari shifts in her seat, wipes a glaze of sweat from her brow. She tells Summer everything she's withheld, afraid of her reaction. She begins with the details from the funeral—the look in Leah's eyes. The depletion. The bloody fury of all things death. She tells Summer about how watching Leah cry broke her open, too. Her sadness about Wells, yes—but this deeper feeling, like open water, where she tried to tread alongside Leah, but they both drowned together.

"You'll never know what Leah is feeling," Summer says.

The words rip through Ari. She takes a breath. "This is just how things happened," she says. Leah called. She wanted Ari around.

Summer reminds her to pull onto the tiny, rocky street for the inn, even though she knows exactly where she's going. Maybe Summer just needs to speak so she doesn't hear the rest of what Ari has to say. They park.

"Why are you doing this?" Summer says, slamming the car door.

The question kicks around before landing a blow to Ari's stomach. "I know it's hard to understand. But it makes sense."

The gravel crunches under their feet, breeze kicking off the water.

"Help me understand how."

"If you'd seen Leah's face at the funeral, you would see it's the right thing."

"Absolutely no *face* or list of reasons could make this the right thing. You almost ruined this woman's life. Why don't you just take the fact that you somehow miraculously didn't get caught and run before it all explodes in everyone's faces?"

She speeds up, and Ari has to jog to catch her.

"Summer. Please."

"*Please* what? People who play stupid games win stupid prizes."

The owner of the venue, whom they've known for years, meets them at the door. He tours them through the indoor and outdoor ceremony spaces. Summer worries it'll be too hot to be outside in the final week of June, but that's not important, Ari says. She reminds Summer that the whole point of this town is being on the water. Summer agrees. The venue holds one hundred forty people, but she and Luke are inviting only sixty. Now that she's back home, Ari wonders if she'd have done the same for her wedding to Morgan. That teenager, eyes glinting, dreaming.

The owner walks them through the hall behind the main party room to show Summer her bridal suite.

She turns to Ari. "It's perfect."

Ari nods. Can think only of the senior prom they'd had there. The wedding that never happened. "I love you," she tells her best friend.

"You're the big reason we made it, Ari. I'm so grateful." Summer breathes in, looks like she's going to cry. "I love you so much."

They hold each other.

After Summer writes the check for the deposit, they begin to drive back toward their houses.

"Actually," Summer says, "go to Mead's."

"Why would I do that?"

"Because that's where we go."

The diner comes into view on Ari's left, looking the same as it ever has: a compact, silver capsule-shaped building, like a magic pill, the red neon sign in the window. It is the most all-American place in the world: the soda fountain, six stools at the counter, apple turnovers beneath a hard plastic dome. The Meads, buzzing about. Everyone except Kathy now. This place is haunted in every way.

Ari turns into the lot, spots Rick's truck back by the dumpster. She swallows, absentmindedly touches the spot where her ring used to be. Recoils when her thumb hits skin, as if it's the first time.

They seat themselves as they always do, a four-person corner booth in the back. Ari has a view of the whole restaurant. When Morgan's dad catches her, his eyes go wide. She waves in return.

Ari and Rick locked eyes at the funeral, before she ran. But she hasn't been around him since the split, now more than a year ago. As he brightens, he quickly dims—what is he supposed to say to Ari, his lost daughter, especially when he has lost a wife, too? Rick slips into the back, emerges with a heaping plate of fries, exactly what she and

Summer want, even at ten thirty in the morning. Summer stands for a hug; Ari follows. Rick wraps her hard into him.

"What are you two doing home?" he asks them.

"Luke and I are getting married at the inn," Summer says. "Came up to make plans."

"Here for Summer."

He grabs ketchup from the neighboring booth, drops it to the table as he places his hand to Ari's shoulder, for just a moment, before he leaves.

Summer plops out a glob of ketchup, the heel of her hand tapping the bottom of the glass bottle. It splatters like drops of coagulated blood.

"I'm exhausted," she says. She bites a fry. It falls out of her mouth, onto the plate. "Careful, they're hot."

"You've got a lot going on," Ari replies.

"No. I mean you're exhausting me." She dredges another fry through ketchup, but doesn't eat it. "Aren't you so tired, too?"

"I'm happy."

"You're out of your mind." Summer scoffs. "Why can't you just build a life that doesn't have anything to do with these people? You *can*, and you *won't*."

"Do you have any idea how to start from scratch?" Ari shoots back. "If Luke left you today, would you have any idea how to live on your own?"

Summer bristles. "I'd figure it out, because I'd have to."

"It's not that simple."

But maybe it is. Ari's made the choices she's made. No one's forced her to do anything.

"Leah will find out one day. What happens after that?"

"She won't. I know how to be careful."

Summer shakes her head. "It's different this time."

She's right. Wells's family is already hanging by a thread. Summer doesn't wait for Ari to reply, just slides right into talking about dress shopping in New York. Ari tells her she wouldn't miss it for the world.

~

Ari loves walking through the door when Leah is in her pajamas. On the days during which she works from home—sometimes Thursdays, often Fridays—Leah is almost always leaning over the kitchen island, propped on her elbows and hovering over her computer, in tiny shorts. Sometimes, Ari can see her nipples pushing at the fabric of her shelf tank, the shape of her breasts. It seems like she is still dressing for Wells—keeping the same routine, for fear of reminding herself. If Ari is right, it's a strange way for grief to be shaped. But everyone molds it their own way.

"Hey," Leah says over her shoulder, a chilly late-November morning.

It's been about five months of nannying Rowan—they've been through all of summer and fall. Now they're heading into the heart of winter. It's become more than some convoluted, solipsistic plan to prop herself up. They are essential to each other's lives, a figure eight. Maybe Ari was the one who craved this most, at first—even more than a pleading, desperate widow. As much as this feeds her, though, they all wear the need. Leah's relief from Ari's care for each detail of her life, love and protection of her vulnerable son—it's something Ari can nearly taste.

She drops her bag on the kitchen table, next to Rowan, who is in his booster seat, poking the blueberries out of a waffle. She kisses him on the head. In the time that's passed, she has latched on to Leah's son as much as he's latched on to her. She feels a singular pride when he bolts off the couch to meet her at the door, drags her by the hand to see a tower of blocks he's made or a peg puzzle he's solved before she can even take off her coat. Leah always stops whatever she's doing, watches it all. Between activities, Ari will sometimes bring Rowan by her apartment to give Clio a short walk; he giggles when she tries to lick his cheek with her sharpshooter tongue. *Love you, dog,* he says now. Marvelous. At the playground, she often pretends he's her son, just to see what it feels like. With Rowan's dark hair, people have mistaken her for his mother more than once. She's never corrected anyone.

"Morning," she greets Leah in the kitchen. "You can head upstairs if you want. I've got everything down here."

Leah glances at her phone screen. "Can I be the worst and ask you to make coffee? Molly has no childcare today and her shithead almost-ex-husband is god knows where, and everything's on fire. I didn't get a chance."

"You're not the worst." Ari walks over to the cabinet to pull out the beans. As she removes the filters, a box of tea bags tumbles to the floor.

Leah slams her computer closed. Readjusts her shorts. "I should throw those out," she says. "I hate tea."

"Me too." Ari thumbs one of the square packets.

"He'd mainline it. There'd be all these used tea bags all over the house, like the minute they were out of his cup, they became invisible. He stained the coffee table and the nightstand and the island," she says, pointing at a faint brown spot on the marble. "I could have killed him."

Ari knows. She'd order Wells boxes of Earl Grey, stick them in his desk drawer. He left the used tea bags on the corner of the desktop until the night cleaner took them away.

"At the end, he sucked on ice cubes. I couldn't get him to eat or drink anything. They told me he wouldn't, but it was so different to see it." Leah shakes her head. "I'm sorry to word vomit on you."

She sits across from Rowan, tears off a piece of his waffle, pops it into her mouth. Ari gently gathers the packets back into the box, tucks the lid closed.

"It's the stupid stuff that hurts, right? The tea bags, or the jar of Branston Pickle that's just going to sit in the back of the fridge forever," she says. "It's just like getting stabbed, again and again."

"I'm so sorry, Leah."

She negotiates with Rowan to eat the rest of the waffle, while Ari finishes brewing coffee. Ari pours a drop of half-and-half into the cup, brings it to her.

"I'm so sorry," she says again, putting her palm to Leah's bare shoulder as her other hand places the mug to the table.

Leah's hand covers Ari's, pressing it to her shoulder. Her palm is hot with worry. "Where your thumb is. Can you push for a second?"

Ari grinds her finger into the muscle just above Leah's shoulder blade, feels a knot jump around as she adds pressure. Leah groans, tips back her head.

"You're so tight back there," Ari says.

"It's where I carry all my stress."

She pushes harder. Leah closes her eyes.

"It hasn't gotten any less surreal."

"I know," Ari says, because she does.

She misses Wells, so much. On one of her floor tiles, there's still a spot of his blood, which she can't bear to scrub away. She misses the feeling of his finger trailing the small of her back, the moments he'd tell her things no one else knew. But, as Leah says, the *stupid stuff*, too. Fetching his lunch and buying the fine-point green pens he used exclusively and the time she had to tell him his fly was down before he walked into a board meeting.

"What can I do?" Ari asks.

"Just be here," Leah says.

She reaches across to Rowan, tickles his tiny palm. Holds Ari's gaze for too long. Ari forgets to exhale.

~

Leah is stuck on calls until after eight, so Ari puts Rowan to bed. She turns on the baby monitor, sees him settling, fingers already in his mouth, bunny tucked under his neck. She adores the big, buoyant personality Leah gushed about, especially his father's cheeky humor, which has developed right alongside his first sentences. He has become a singular source of light in her life.

As much as she thought she could care for Rowan at the beginning, Ari never saw herself in a role beyond *nanny*. Responding to Leah's call felt like exactly what Wells wanted her to do, and of course she jumped.

Now, though, Rowan feels like her responsibility, not her obligation. She understands the loud joy in motherhood; the quiet joy, too. The earthshaking sound of his laughter during belly blows and kiss attacks, or when a repeated word breaks him open. *Zebra, zebra, zebra.* He hides Leah's keys in the fridge or the couch cushions, tugs at Ari's sleeve to show her, and secretly giggles when his mom takes laps around the house, chasing her tail to find them. Once, he hid them in the toilet, to everyone's horror.

As she begins folding the laundry, neatly creasing Leah's pajamas, Ari thinks of how much has changed, *evolved*, since July. It's extraordinary. Spending every day with Wells's son, his wife, caring for them both. It's made Ari more human, too. She loves them, and understands that she, too, is loved. She can't dream of a world where they're not in her life, at least right now. This can't be forever, and she understands that. Ari has her own world to build ahead of her, perhaps one that even looks like this. But she's learning so much about what it means to be a family that she's never known before, not even through the Meads. For all the crazy things Ari has done, it'd be just as crazy to walk away from a life she's always wanted to know, but never could. She is no longer naive enough to think she knows what the future will hold, but she can see this version of herself in whatever ends up happening: someone who can care for others, be a force for good without spending every day steeping in the fear of letting them down. The worries that kept her from marrying Morgan—she's proved them away. She could be a wife if she wanted to. Someday, she will be.

Still, there are evenings on the train home, twilights in front of a television screen beside the dog Rowan has come to love, where it's clear how utterly tangled this all is. Practically, objectively, they couldn't live without each other, even if they wanted to. Without Ari, Leah wouldn't be able to function in her daily life, care for her only child. Without Leah, that space Ari has found unoccupied so many times in her life would be open again. Yet she confronts only the reality that her secret still burns, threatening Leah's livelihood, when she is alone; and now she spends more time with the Cahills than she does with herself. She is carrying Wells's torch, yes—but he never asked her to keep his flame burning like this.

How unbelievable it is that this is the way she's learned how strong she is. The question is what to do with that strength.

She places the soft shorts on top of the rest of the clothes, carries the laundry basket into the bedroom. Usually she leaves it for Leah to put away, but Ari begins placing things into her drawers, hanging the sweaters she never asked her to hand-wash. Those moments on her own, when Ari considers the mess she could make, are loud, yes. But the moments like this are deafening.

~

It's a Sunday in late December, close to Christmas. Rowan is with his grandmother in Portland for a week until the holiday, when Leah will go up and meet them. She wants to spend time with friends she hasn't seen in a while, be selfish. *It's funny,* she faintly laughed to Ari, standing across from her at the kitchen island a few days earlier, *in all this time, I haven't stopped once to grieve.* Ari pulled her lips tight, plucked a seltzer from the fridge, slid it across the counter. Leah sighed, grateful. Said she was going to take an hour-long bubble bath the moment she had the house to herself. Touched Ari's arm, went upstairs to her office.

The day before Leah leaves for Maine, while Ari has the week off, Leah texts her first thing in the morning, asks if she can treat her to lunch.

You probably have plans, but I've been meaning to for months. God knows where the time has gone

I'd love that, Ari replies.
Inside, she's screaming.

Leah takes her to a restaurant at a social club downtown, far too nice for an impromptu lunch. The coffered ceilings above them have hand-carved detail, and they sit in tufted brown-leather chairs, a brass chandelier over their table. The tall windows are framed by heavy cream-colored curtains with gold tassels, the servers dressed in white shirts and black aprons. There will never be another reason for Ari to be in a place like this, so she lets herself sink into the seat, drink in her surroundings. Leah gets sparkling water for the table, tells her to order the most expensive thing on the menu.

"I wish I had the words to tell you how much you've saved my life since everything. I haven't had to worry," Leah says, raising her water glass for a toast. She's in the same gray sweater she wore when Ari met her the first time.

Ari notices little diamond studs in her ears—she's barely seen Leah wear jewelry besides the gold chain-link necklace, which she always tucks under her shirt.

"Rowan is so happy. Honestly, you're the one thing I don't have to worry about. I just . . ." She stops, shakes her head. "I think the world of you."

They clink glasses, sip. Leah squeezes lime into her water. More than anything, Ari is flattered, especially as Leah stares at her with her soft eyes. Wells would have been thrilled. It feels like repentance.

"You've let me live my life and get back to normal. It's so healthy, sometimes I can't even believe it."

"I'm glad," Ari says. "You're amazing. I wish I could do more."

"You don't need to say that."

"I know."

The waiter places twenty-six-dollar tuna Nicoise salads in front of them both. Ari takes the window to ask Leah everything. The person she was before Wells, who she is trying to be after. She is an only child, too; a former all-Maine piccolo player; mostly too bookish to have friends growing up. She worries she's overbearing with Rowan, that he'll grow up hating her. And she wants to be a mother again. *It's complicated, but*

I can be, with Wells. She explains IVF, the frozen embryos, the conflict she keeps turning over—a fear of bringing him back so tangibly, when the reality is just technology and smoke and mirrors. Ari consumes the answers guiltily, as if she's stealing something. She is.

"I've been talking about myself for an hour. You must want to jump out the window."

Ari assures her she does not.

They pick together at a shallow bowl of truffle-honey-and-goat-cheese ice cream Leah orders, taking turns gingerly spooning crescents off the creamy spheres. She's also gotten them both glasses of Chenin Blanc—*Loire Valley*, she specifies. Ari stares at the way she lets her eyelids fall, smelling the wine before she sips.

"How long were you together?" Leah asks.

"What?"

"Sorry. You and your ex."

"Ten years."

"Wow. Are you seeing anyone now?"

"God, no."

"Why such an emphatic no? A million men would fall all over themselves for you."

Ari drinks her wine, peers over Leah's shoulder at a man in a suit, dining alone. "What was it like to be with Wells?"

Leah considers the question, like Ari hasn't intrusively asked it out of the blue. "Complicated."

"Can I ask why?"

Leah breathes out through her nose, places her spoon down.

"He was a deeply insecure person. He never said it out loud, but I know he was terrified of failing. He tried to hide it from everyone, including me." Leah stops, leans back in her chair. "I think he did some stupid things because of it."

"What do you mean?"

She stares at the milky puddle collected at the bottom of the ice-cream bowl, downs the rest of her wine.

"Let's get out of here, yeah?" she says.

She slaps down her heavy credit card to pay, and they walk back to the car. She looks quizzically at Ari, exhales with her entire body.

"Can I tell you something? I haven't told anyone. Not even my mother. It's just—you get me."

Ari is Leah's confidante. Ari keeps Leah's secrets.

They settle into the car. Leah puts her hand on Ari's wrist, tips back her head. "He was sleeping with someone else."

"How do you know?" Ari replies, lightning speed, stomach sick.

Leah removes her hand, shakes her head, starts the car. "I want another drink. Do you want a drink? I have a good bottle at the house. Unless you have plans."

She's angry. She doesn't want to be alone. And Ari needs the answer. "I'd like that."

When they get back to the house, Leah pours them both tall glasses of a red she says she's been saving, though she doesn't know what for.

"Come upstairs," she says, swirling the wine in her glass. The old, dark-wood stairs creak under their feet. A sound that goes to Ari's bones.

In that light-soaked bedroom, Ari feels an incredible mix of pure pleasure and repulsive transgression—something she thought died with Wells. She can feel the texture of the sheets against her back, hear the faint squeak of the bed frame. She can't believe how viscerally each buried detail hits her anew.

Leah pulls out the jewelry box Ari saw the first time he took her upstairs, which she opened one day when he was in the shower. There were a few tangled necklaces, loose earrings, gold bobby pins, replacement buttons—how human. She had pulled out a string of pearls, something she'd never wear herself. Held it up to the mirror and wondered if Wells liked the necklace, if he'd given it to his wife. Where she'd worn it. A gala, a family holiday, their wedding. The shower stopped, and Ari quickly dropped the pearls back inside. She never touched the box again.

Leah opens the silver lid, dips her hand in. "It's not mine."

Ari's bracelet is between her fingers. She can't remember the last time she saw the thin silver cuff; it sometimes slipped from her wrist, and she assumed she lost it on the street. It was just one of many bracelets she's slid on and off, and she hadn't loved it enough to care that it was gone—hadn't even noticed for months. But here it is.

"I know this doesn't sound like a lot to go off of, but once I started paying attention, there were other things, too. Like, the other day, I saw what has to be a menstrual bloodstain on one of the sheets, and I haven't gotten my period since I was pregnant. I've probably washed that sheet a thousand times, but something clicked. There are just all these little breadcrumbs I didn't put together after he died. I've never been so sure of something in my life."

She hands the bracelet to Ari, as if she will feel the betrayal when she holds it.

"I'm so angry," Leah says, though the words sound more like defeat. She bites her red lip. "More than anything, I want him back so I can tell him how much he hurt me."

Ari holds her breath in her chest for a moment. "Do you have any idea who it was?"

Leah shakes her head. "Do you? Maybe in retrospect, if you think about his calendar—does anything strike you?"

"No," she says quietly. "I just booked the meetings. I couldn't have known if he wasn't where he said he was, really."

Leah hums. "I've been thinking about it, and I'm pretty sure it'd be worse if I knew who she was. If I could put a face to all the ways I wasn't enough for him, I'd finally lose it for real."

Ari wishes she could tell Leah that nothing about what happened meant she was deficient. Wells didn't think she was missing anything at all. *He loved you more than you can understand,* she wants to scream. He just loved Ari, too.

She thinks about finding some way to excuse herself. The bathroom, perhaps, where she'll splash water on her face. Regroup. She'll tell Leah she has to go home and feed the dog. Walk through her own door and figure out, in earnest, what is next for her. The problem is Leah's face—the helplessness. As much as it's the right thing to do, Ari can't go because, in his own way, Wells asked her to stay.

Leah looks to his side of the bed. "He was at this weird point in his life. When he hit forty, I think he started worrying he was losing control. I thought it was vanity. You know, the car and doubling down on the investor meetings and that hideous watch he bought. I couldn't stand it, and so I guess I put my head in the sand and just focused on myself. Then, once we found out he was sick, I just didn't have room in my brain for anything else. I still can't believe I missed the signs, especially after what happened to Molly."

"What happened to Molly?"

Ari cocks her head. She knows Molly well now, largely from days she and Leah have circled the dining table debating new website images or reviewing slide decks. Sparring or gossiping. Ari sometimes makes them coffee, lunch. She's always thought Molly sharp and together.

"She's getting divorced because Jon cheated."

The hairs on the back of Ari's neck are on end. "How did she find out?"

"Nanny caught him." Leah sits on the corner of the bed. "I feel like I've just been in this fever dream for a year. The hits keep coming."

She weeps. It's the first time in a long while she's let herself go, Ari is sure. She knows Leah. Now, but from before, too. From being with Wells in her bed, occasionally dipping her fingers into her Korean face cream, watching the books on her nightstand rotate. Ari is still holding the bracelet. She offers it back to Leah, who shakes her head, wipes her nose on her cashmere sleeve. Her eyes look more bile-yellow than green.

"Leah." Ari sits beside her. Can smell the wine on her breath, just like that night she came down to the basement, nearly a year ago. "I don't even know what to say."

She puts her hand on Leah's thigh. Feels like she's breaking through an electric fence, especially as Leah's muscle tenses.

Leah inhales, turns toward Ari with the softest eyes she has ever seen. "I don't know what I'd do without you." She doesn't push Ari's hand off her leg.

Leah falls back to the bed, crosses her hands across her chest like a corpse. Ari lets herself lie down, too, the first time the mattress has cradled her since Wells. They stay beside each other, listening to birds call and respond outside the window, until Leah scoots over and nestles her head into Ari's shoulder. Ari wraps her arms around her, pulls her close. Her body is hot, back of her neck slick. Leah cries quietly until she's asleep against Ari, body fitful with dreams like a puppy.

~

They don't speak again until the new year. Partly, Ari wants to give Leah space. It's her first holiday without Wells, and she can't imagine Leah is even capable of standing, between her husband's absence and the revelation he wasn't faithful. Maybe she's sitting on the floor at the foot of a Christmas tree, opening presents with Rowan, holding back tears until she steps outside into the stinging air, then starts drowning in them. It's what Ari would have done.

More than that, she feels like everything has changed now that Leah knows about Wells. She sees Leah's entire world is made of glass, and has never been so conscious of the stones she holds in her palm. She's fearful she'll trip in this haze, sending one of those stones flying to shatter Leah's world. This whole time, Ari has wished to feel more powerful in her life, but this isn't how she meant for it to happen.

Yet since Leah woke up from her sleep against Ari, sun setting through the bedroom window, Ari has found it impossible to think of anything but her. She saw Leah open her eyes, search for Ari's—clear relief she hadn't left her alone. The thought of moving from the bed never crossed Ari's mind. The close sound of Leah's breathing—one she never imagined she'd hear—rendered her immobile. Ari smelled the faded perfume on Leah's jagged collarbone and found herself overtaken by an inexplicable sense of stunning newness and acute familiarity. For as skeptical as she is about the divine, she's sure their souls linked together. For as skeptical as she is about fate, this was always meant to happen. They have always been bound, and it's Ari's calling right now to make sure Leah's glass life stays intact, glints rainbow when the light hits it.

She's out getting coffee on New Year's Day when Leah finally calls. It's Saturday morning, and the sky is the indefatigable cyan that only happens one day a winter. The sun, blinding.

"We just got home," Leah says on the line, a little unsteady. Rowan yelps in the background. She skips asking how Ari's holidays were. "Are you still good for Monday?"

"Always."

"Thank God."

~

Monday morning, seven thirty on the dot. Rowan runs up to Ari, outstretches his arms, wraps himself around her legs until he runs to the fridge, pulling at the door. He fishes a yogurt pouch from the bottom crisper drawer, pushes it toward her. As she uncaps his snack—her wrists no longer ringed with bracelets—Leah comes bounding down the stairs in a short white shift dress, one heel in her hand, notebook between her teeth.

"I'm a train wreck this morning," she mumbles. She reaches the last step, puts on her shoe, drops the planner into her bag. "And I ran out of fucking milk for him. I can—"

"I got it," Ari says. "It's all fine."

Leah sighs, looks like she's going to either sob or scream. "I'm a mess," she whispers, before she falls straight into Ari's arms. "I have to go. But I'm so happy to see you."

Her heels click against the floor as she crosses the kitchen; her car door opens, closes. Ari is frozen, briefly unsure she can continue the day when all her energy is Leah.

~

At night, Leah is running late, so Ari puts Rowan to bed, asks her upstairs neighbor to squeeze in an extra walk and a bone for Clio, then starts cutting cubes of cheese and dividing portions of veggie straws into reusable snack bags. She takes the liberty of pouring herself a glass of Leah's wine. It's therapeutic, slicing and measuring in this kitchen, just like she did at Christmas dinner with Wells.

It's eight fifteen by the time Leah comes through the door. She looks out of breath, a little disheveled. Her lipstick has faded, lips visibly dry.

"God, I'm sorry," she says, sliding off her coat, depositing it to the barstool. "I could have killed Molly. The check was on the table, but she just kept talking."

Ari walks to the cabinet, pulls down another glass, pours Leah wine, tops off her own.

"Thank you," Leah says, while undoing the side zipper of her dress, letting a sliver of skin peek out from the open flap. Ari almost chokes on the air.

"I know you should go," Leah says, "but maybe you can stay, just a few more minutes."

~

Three weeks later, a woman lets herself into the house, dragging a small black suitcase behind her. She comes in as Ari roves around, plucking piles of pastel wooden blocks from the floor, after putting Rowan down for a nap. It's Leah's mother, Ari realizes. She remembers her face from the funeral, the gathering after.

Leah's mum knows. Ari feels sick.

Dropping her bag in front of the coat closet, she adjusts her red-framed glasses, tucks a strand of bobbed silver hair behind her ear.

"Hi," Ari says tentatively. She sits up, mortified she's been caught crawling on the floor, in front of this woman who knows she's also been on her knees for Leah's dead husband.

"Leah didn't tell you I was coming, did she?"

Ari shakes her head.

"That's so her." She clears her throat. "I'm her mother, Susan."

"Of course." Ari drives down her shoulders. She very much knows who Susan is. One of only four other living people who *know*.

"I'm Ari."

"I know. I've heard all about you."

Ari's eyebrows peak as her stomach drops out. Albeit a relief, she has always found it strange she's never met Leah's mother before. She usually comes down from Portland on weekends, or Leah drives up. It always seemed like reasonable enough logic, but now she wonders if Susan has deliberately stayed away from the house when Ari is there.

Susan still stands by the closet, surveying the room under Ari's tutelage. It looks good, because she's worked hard to give Rowan a beautiful space, give Leah another reason to mark her as essential. When Susan is done scanning, she lands back on Ari.

"I . . . Rowan's sleeping," Ari stutters, though Susan knows her grandson's schedule. She stands, her hands balled behind her back. "Can I make you lunch?"

"Yes," Susan says, still icy. "I'll just drop my bag downstairs."

The in-law suite, of course.

In the kitchen, Ari scans the fridge. It's mostly filled with food for Rowan: his cheese sticks, cold cuts, avocados, sunflower spread, and those overpriced overnight-oats bowls, which Ari should learn to make. She hears Susan over her shoulder: *I'm not picky.* She reaches for a container of fresh potato-leek soup. Heats it in the microwave built into the kitchen island, serves the piping-hot bowl to Leah's mother.

"I've been interested to meet you," Susan says. She picks up her spoon, winces when she takes a scalding bite. As her eyes study Ari, she rolls her shoulders around to settle them in the right place, like struggling through the first moments in an airplane seat. "I know Wells thought highly of you."

Ari stares at the floor, exhales. "Maybe."

It's now, she decides, that she'll pull out bulbous green grapes from the fridge, retrieve a bamboo cutting board, quarter the spheres. She pushes the knife into the fruit flesh, blade gliding through in one precise cleave. As she cuts, she watches Susan try the soup again, this time blowing across the small pool on the spoon before eating.

"Leah misses him a great deal. He loved her very much. They were crazy about each other from day one. I remember her calling me the morning after their first date and telling me she was going to marry him. I laughed and laughed and laughed." Susan shrugs. "She got the last laugh."

This punctures Ari, an unforgiving sharpness. A hard fall from a high place.

"Yes," Ari says. "I know it's hard for her. Him being gone."

"It's a shame Rowan won't know his father," Susan continues, her eyes deadlocked on Ari. "But Leah will meet someone quickly. That's her. I'm sure he'll have a wonderful stepfather in a few years. Someone faithful."

Ari chokes on her own spit. She stutters to force out words, except there's nothing to say. With a cupped hand, she sweeps the grapes into a snack bag. Checks the clock next to the back door. Rowan will sleep for another forty-five minutes.

Susan leans forward onto her elbows, clasps her hands. "You are very important to Leah's life. Which is why I've kept my mouth shut," she says. "You've really gotten yourself into an extraordinary situation."

Ari blanches. Beyond her own life collapsing, the threat of losing Leah guts her. They need each other. Leah has come home earlier and earlier to spend time with her and Rowan, silently asked her to stay later and later with bottles of wine and takeout. Despite Leah's fear of dogs, she's begun to let Ari bring over Clio so she doesn't have to rush home. Then, of course, she collapsed in Ari's arms, a feeling inexplicable.

Susan taps a nail on the countertop. "I can always tell her, though. Just know that."

She rises from the stool, grabs spare napkins from inside the pantry, refills the holder on the kitchen table. Ari has forgotten Leah's mother still knows this house better than she does. Belongs here, when Ari doesn't. At that lunch, Leah told her about her parents: divorced, her father and his second wife a few minutes away in Newton; her mother still in Maine, where Leah grew up and went to college. She and her mom are close, a relationship Ari envies without knowing much about it. Hearing Susan say she is a second away from telling her daughter— it's a new kind of fear that slaps Ari across the face. Reminds her, exactly, the path she has chosen and the others she's forgone.

"Perhaps you should head out early today," Susan says. She plucks a napkin from the stack, dabs the corner of her lip.

"I have stuff to do around here, but thank you."

"I'll look after Rowan."

Ari slips the baby monitor from the back pocket of her jeans, places it on the island, then swipes Susan's bowl for the dishwasher. She takes herself upstairs, collapses onto Leah's pillows.

~

"Ari. Hey. Ari."

She edges open her eyes. It's Leah, halfway across the bedroom. Ari groans, exhausted.

Leah leans against her dresser, clad in jeans and a sweater. Her slight silhouette looks boyish, straight up and down. "How long have you been asleep?" She doesn't ask why Ari is in her bed.

"What time is it?" The blackout shades are pulled, and the only light in the room is Wells's bedside lamp.

"Six thirty. You can go."

Leah plucks two tiny gold hoops from her ears, dropping them to the counter. Ari wishes Leah would fall against the sheets, breathe into her neck for an hour, even if it meant she was crying again.

"Oh god." Ari covers her eyes with her forearm. "I look really irresponsible, don't I?"

Leah clears her throat. "I'm sorry I forgot to tell you my mom was coming. I just assume you know everything in my head all the time." She seems hundreds of miles away.

"What's wrong? Did I do something?"

"No."

"Your mom seems nice," Ari says too buoyantly, swinging her legs around to the edge of the bed, rubbing her eyes.

"She is."

"I'll head out."

Ari isn't sure what she's done, but something is off. She wants to walk so close to Leah they brush arms. Instead, she takes a wide berth, because it's what Leah wants. Ari will do anything Leah wants.

Downstairs, she gathers her bag slowly, draws out a good night to Rowan. Leah comes down the stairs in a white tank top, the flax linen pants. In the corner of her eye, Ari can see her arms crossed as she leans against the banister. She's sucking in her cheeks, faded bronzing powder catching the light. She drops her arms, tucks a short, frizzled strand of hair behind her left ear. Her wedding rings, still glinting.

"I'm just going to head to the bathroom first," Ari says.

In the powder room mirror, she sees Leah follow her in, lips puckered in dissatisfaction.

"Leah, what did I do wrong?"

She watches Leah inhale through her nose, shut her eyes in the reflection. The two Edison bulbs flanking the round mirror drain her pink skin, and she looks like a ghost. Maybe her eyeballs have fallen out from their sockets and into her body; maybe it is hollow on the other side of her eyelids. Maybe the fatigue she's been hiding, the grief she's been muzzling, has seeped out of wherever she's been keeping it, dripped into her bloodstream, and now it's circulating to fill every cell. Maybe it's killing her.

Ari reaches up to touch Leah's shoulder, but Leah puts her hand up to stop her, a supernatural sense of Ari's body.

"Nothing. Please go."

Ari exits the bathroom, leaving Leah behind. When she reemerges in the living room, Susan eyes her carefully.

Five minutes after she leaves the house, standing on the train platform at the tail end of the rush-hour throng, her phone vibrates with a text from Leah, like she hoped it would. She can picture Leah still huddled in the bathroom, sitting on the toilet seat while typing an apology.

When Ari opens it, the message doesn't say what she expects.

My mom will watch Rowan for the next couple days.

LEAH

Leah keeps tapping her chopsticks on the kitchen table. She hasn't touched a single sushi roll, the green salad smothered in ginger dressing. Her mom reaches to her wrist, gently touches it. Leah stops the tapping, exhales.

"You look like you've seen a ghost," her mom says.

Behind her, Leah notices the kitchen hasn't been this clean in years: Rowan's cups and plates are not exploding out of the cabinets, and the stainless-steel fridge hasn't been this bright since they redid the kitchen. It's all Ari. Nearly everything good about her life is Ari.

Leah looks to the ceiling, the floor. Her head lolls to the side. She does feel haunted, by the spirit of a life she counted on, that now will never be. That already looks so much different than she can possibly wrap her head around. Even though she held Wells's hand while he took his last breath, heard the rattle and felt him go cold, she keeps thinking he is still in her orbit. That she'll come home after work and he'll be at the kitchen island eating with his son, or at his desk, feet up on the tabletop as he takes a call. She thinks she'll hear his car pull into the driveway. He'll drop his coat in the mudroom, burst into the house with stories of his day as he pours himself a glass of wine or a neat scotch. But the door never opens, though the Porsche is still parked like he'll drive it to work at any moment, and his clothes are still in the closets, aftershave in the medicine cabinet. She is not ready to give up his ghost.

This is why she startled tonight. Freaked out. Ari didn't do anything to deserve how Leah treated her. But she snapped seeing another person in the bed, asleep on Wells's side, in the very room where he died. It was too much. Sometimes this life is too much.

"I'm fine," Leah finally says.

"You're stuck," her mom replies, guiding a limp soba noodle into her mouth. "But that's not you."

Leah shoves a yellowtail nigiri into her face, an excuse not to talk. The rice is gummy in her teeth, fish slimy as it slips down her throat.

Last night, she lay in bed, fixated on the final time she and Wells went to London together. New Year's, a year ago. They had known about the cancer for only a week. The trip would begin his goodbyes to them, though they didn't know it yet. He'd stared out the window the entire flight, Rowan asleep in his lap. She would have died herself, just to be in his head with him.

Wells's life was ending, but they were just beginning to reckon with it. Yet when he told his family, everyone gathered in the living room of his eldest sister Vivienne's stunning Georgian house in Richmond, it was the first time it really seemed inevitable. They listened to him explain what was happening with a quiet acceptance that floored Leah. She shifted on the toile couch, running her fingers across the nailheads on the arm, impossibly uncomfortable. Didn't anyone want to bleed, break down? Wasn't anyone feeling reality as viscerally as she was? It was the most intensely, emotionally alone she had ever felt, compounded by the fact she'd soon be physically alone, too. She had sprinted into the powder room like she was on fire, run the sink so no one heard her puking her brains out. Vivienne knocked before gently opening the door, crouched next to Leah, who was hunched on the toilet seat, bile burning her throat. She put her hand on Leah's arm. Helped bring her breath back into her body. *What do I do?* Leah had finally said, looking up at Viv. *I don't know,* Wells's sister had whispered. Leah had loved Wells's family, still does. But at that moment, she knew it'd be years before she'd come back to London, even though these people were her son's blood, even though Rowan was half British and belonged here. She couldn't live in Wells's life without him.

The reason she'd spent last night revisiting the memory is because she couldn't find a cable to charge her headphones, and knew Wells always kept one in his nightstand. She'd opened his drawer without even realizing what she was doing. Seeing his things had been a hand around her neck. She slammed the drawer closed, short of breath, but not before she'd seen his Oyster card at the top of the tangled pile. She hadn't felt so alone since her husband died.

"I know this may be hard," her mom says, dabbing broth from her white shirt, "but perhaps you should consider going out with someone. Just to shake yourself out of this. Maybe just one night next to a man could help you feel some forward momentum."

"Jesus Christ, Mom."

"Baby, this can't be the rest of your life. You can't hide." Her mom puts down her spoon, grimaces. "You need to think about it seriously. You need to start rebuilding. It will be good for you."

The legs of Leah's chair screech as she pushes back from the table. She marches to the front door, slams it. She sits on the steps, under the porch light, cradling her knees. Shaking.

She can't explain how it feels to picture herself beside another man, feeling sandpaper stubble against her cheek and calloused hands cupping her breasts. She can't bear the idea of a heavy body atop her, allowing another person to push inside. She has not let go of Wells as her husband, even removed her wedding rings. But she also hasn't forgotten his betrayal, which she still won't speak of to anyone besides Ari. She can't explain to her mother, her friends, even Molly, how it felt to find black bobby pins in the bottom of his bathroom drawer, shortly after she found the bracelet in her jewelry box. They must have been there for a while, but Leah hadn't been looking, until she knew what to look for. She cannot bear to invite another man into her life. To be betrayed again.

No. Leah's mom can think she has the answer, but if Leah can't have her real life back, right now, all she wants is Ari. To be beside her in her home the way Wells was. Ari has made her want to give over each detail of her life her husband knew, to fill the bullet holes in her heart he left behind. Every day, she comes home with the stories she'd tell Wells and the questions she'd ask him, and Ari is always there to hear them. Ari laughs where he would have, never lets Leah doubt that she, too, should be smiling.

Every time she tries to see into the future, pictures her life without Ari, she begins to fall apart. Not only has Ari held together her life and the life of her son, but she's also stretched a bandage across her soul. She's increasingly convinced Ari is here for a *reason*—maybe even a divine one, an idea that would have made Wells cringe. She and Ari are—maybe always have been—connected spirits. She understood that the day she showed her the stupid bracelet, admitted what she hasn't been able to fathom telling anyone else. When she fell against Ari's body, wept, something shifted—her entire intangible being needed Ari, only her. Her pull keeps Leah safe from what Wells did, maybe even safe from herself. She is terrified that if Ari lets her go, she'll be nothing more than a widow shaking under a porch light. She can't believe she pushed her away tonight.

When Leah goes back inside the house, the table is empty. She knocks on the basement door. Her mom's plush voice calls her to come down.

Leah stands at the foot of the stairs, staring with distress at her mom, who sits on the corner of the bed. Leah studies her short silver hair, her face without glasses. Graceful lines in her pink skin, light-green eyes, wise with all she's seen. Her artist's hands have always been delicate, even as they've aged into her sixties. Leah, for the first time, worries she will not live a life as full. If Wells didn't, who's to say she's entitled to do so, either? She bites the inside of her cheek, winces at the flash of pain.

Leah has no idea who or what she is. She fears she'll never know. She sits beside her mother, collapses against her chest, cries so hard she chokes on her own spit. Leah's mom hushes into her daughter's hair, her hot exhale spreading over Leah's itchy scalp.

"I just want you happy," she says.

What Leah can't say: Ari is helping her find happy. Even if she is lost, Ari reminds her that she hasn't died with Wells. Ari makes her feel as though maybe, unbelievably, she will live.

ARI

Ari sits in her apartment, trying to pass the hours so she can get back into Leah's house—Leah's life. She has no idea what she did and is ravaged by fear Leah *knows*. Even Clio understands something's off kilter, hasn't stopped following Ari every time she gets up to pee or fill her water bottle. She lies across Ari's lap like a weighted blanket.

Ari is certain her anxiety can't spike any higher—until her mother calls. The Abbott house has sold, and Ari needs to get her things out in fifty-nine days. She will go to Connecticut immediately, she decides. Rip off the Band-Aid before she can see how deep the wound goes.

She rides the train down, because she doesn't dare ask for Wells's car. Out the window of the cab from the station, the town passes under a steely sky, everything veiled in gray, like an old photograph. The average colonial houses, the main strip of stores, Mead's. Soon, she'll have no reason to return.

The cab pulls up in front of her house. The sign with the ugly real estate agent is gone; the structure already feels invisible. She misses her father. Coming here when she is so fragile and split open was a huge mistake.

She finds her way through the unlocked front door. "Mom?" Her mother is asleep on the couch in the living room, still in her bathrobe at eleven on a Thursday morning. "*Mom*. Wake up."

Her mother scrunches her eyes before she opens them, the lines on her brow rippling waves. The blinds are half-drawn, and the room seems sallow yellow, sickly green.

"I'm home," Ari says.

"I see."

Ari reaches down to grab her mother's hand, help her upright. She whispers thanks, shakes off the sleep.

In the kitchen, Ari pours herself a glass of water. Her mother enters, adjusting the old, stained bathrobe closed across her chest.

"I don't know that I actually expected you to come home when you said you would."

"Why?"

"I know you're furious about the house."

Maybe her mother is right, and Ari's appearance is objectively surprising. She doesn't want to go through her things. Get pulled underground.

Her mother sits at the square kitchen table, clasps her hands. Ari lowers herself into the chair adjacent to her, where her father used to sit.

"Good news for you, about the house," Ari says.

"Yes. They seem like nice people."

It's a young couple with their first baby due in a few months. *Just like you and Dad,* Ari wants to say, but her mother is well aware.

"You haven't told me where you're moving," Ari says.

"I haven't decided entirely."

"How is that possible?" She looks around the house—there are no boxes, no signs of movement, nothing transitional.

"Florida, maybe."

She has no idea how to respond. It's so physically far from her only child; so far in every other respect, too. For a moment, Ari has the urge to ask how she'll find a place in time, pack and get her things to this mysterious new home. *How can I help?* Ari could say. But as her mother sits in the old bathrobe, Ari sees—more clearly than she ever has—that she doesn't want her daughter's help. No matter what Ari tries, she'll never change. But Ari isn't like her. She's better.

She leaves the table, takes herself to her room. Everything hits her, exactly the way she feared: her childhood, the divorce, returning from the city. Morgan, wedged deep in every corner of every memory, filling each hairline crack. A part of her is still moored to him. To Wells. To Leah. They are all buoys in Ari's blue-black sea, and she is holding on to each for dear life in an impossible current.

She begins with the detritus on the floor. Each note passed in class; each photo in which she was smiling because of her friends; each birthday card from the people she once loved, can't stop loving. She ripped them all from the walls when she came back from the city, weak and shattered and possessed with an unfamiliar, despairing rage. Gutted like an unlucky fish. She doesn't even look at them, just shuttles them into a stiff trash bag.

She empties all the clothes still left in the drawers into another bag, destined for the town Goodwill. She doesn't stop to consider there might be something special she'd like to keep. She doesn't fit into any of it anymore, and can't move backward anyway. For a few dollars, a high schooler will own these decade-plus old clothes, out of style; wear her rec soccer T-shirt as an ironic thrift-store find.

Next, her closet. Ari intends to do exactly the same with whatever is left sagging on the thin wire hangers, collected from the only dry cleaner in Abbott. The first thing staring at her is her senior-prom dress, which Kathy made: strapless and seafoam, shimmering to a sickening gold under the town inn's lights.

It was the best night of her life. Skipping out after just an hour, running to the jetties at the beach. The water calm as it lapped the rocks; a rhythm all theirs. Summer, Luke, Morgan, Ari.

She had brought a flask of middling vodka she'd liberated from the mahogany cabinet in the living room. They'd passed it back and forth, their lips surrounding the same cold silver spout. Floodlights from the small seafood shack hit the rocks where they sat. Luke's arm hooked around Summer's shoulders; Ari's head rested in Morgan's lap. The sky had been uncharacteristically clear, stars like glitter. Fireflies glowed around them, tiny beacons blinking in and out. Summer kept catching them, cradling each bug in her palm, then sending them back off into the pure air. Luke had laughed when one refused to leave her hand. It wanted to stay. They all understood.

As the water rolled in and out, Morgan had looked at Ari with this indomitable forever in his eyes. *Let's get married,* he'd whispered. She laughed. He didn't. *I'm serious. One day. Okay?* She buried her face in his damp white button-down. She'd felt embarrassed at how momentous her smile was. Instead, she breathed into his abdomen, smelled too-strong teenage cologne and the musty sweat it hadn't masked. His fingers pushed her hair behind her ear. He wanted to see her, and she felt so seen.

They were going off to college in the same city, which felt like fate and luck and something divine. Morgan already had his Division I lacrosse scholarship in Boston, and Ari had quietly applied to several schools nearby. Neither talked about what it'd be like if they ended up there together. They weren't supposed to plan that way, the guidance counselor had made clear—apply for yourself, go to the right place for you, don't pin your future to young love. But wherever he landed was the right place for her. It'd taken her seventeen years to know that, but now she couldn't unknow it. They'd be glorious together; maybe they'd end up stronger than Summer and Luke, who would have half the country between them. She and Morgan would get married, she thought, as he stared at her on the jetty.

What she remembers most vividly is when they got off the rocks. Ari went first, ran down the beach to the edge of the water, stripped off her dress. She dunked under. Soon all four of them were down to their underwear, swimming. Even Summer had shed her baby-pink spaghetti-strap dress and run into the tide in her beige thong and tube bra. Their hair was soaked, bones cold to the marrow.

They all lay on the sand until one in the morning, pushing the boundaries of when their parents would start worrying. Ari lifted her head, the beach in her hair. Morgan's eyelashes, too, were tangled with sand. He mashed the heels of his hands into his eyes, stretched, and sighed. She held his hand as they walked home, barefoot against rocky asphalt, her gold kitten heels abandoned on the jetty. The four of them peeled off one by one as they passed their houses: first Morgan, next Luke, then Summer and Ari. When she walked in, her mother was sleeping. She'd been moved to wake her, tell her everything. But her mother wouldn't understand, so Ari collapsed on the couch, still buzzed, in her filthy prom dress. Changed from the inside out—a feeling she held on to for ten years.

She can't let the dress go. But she can't keep it, either. After she throws everything else into the black hole, she leaves it behind, hanging in the closet. She's so much stronger, but right now, not enough. Going forward doesn't mean never getting knocked back.

In the living room, Ari tells her mother she's done upstairs. If there's anything else of hers around the house, she says, just toss it. Her mother asks if she dug out any treasures, and Ari just sits on the couch, fixes her eyes on the one o'clock news.

Her mother leans forward, clasps her hands. For as much as Ari is losing, she also understands this marks the end of a bittersweet era for her mom. It isn't that everything here was always bad. Her mom must have been happy with her dad at some point, maybe before Ari came. There was the wedding photo on the bookshelf near the couch, her mother's dress all big-sleeved, her father's mustache bushy like a seventies cop. The frame sometimes shook during their fights, but it was always there. There was the ceremony where her mother was honored as a student favorite at the community college where she taught French. Ari now believes there's something more for her mom, somewhere, if she wants it. There's more for Ari, too.

"Why Florida?" The silence has been uncomfortable, and she's almost grateful she remembers to speak.

"Warm, I guess."

"It's far."

Her mother doesn't reply for a while. "I know. But maybe it'll be good for me."

"I hope so." Ari clears her throat, crosses her legs under her. "I saw Dad."

Her mother blanches. "When?"

"A while ago. I don't know, almost a year?"

"You didn't tell me."

"No."

"How does he look?"

Ari pauses. "Fine enough." She can't tell her mother how he owned the world. She picks a dog hair from her sleeve. "He has chickens."

"Chickens."

Ari shrugs.

"How are you?" her mother finally asks.

"Fine enough." She thinks of Leah. Aches for her.

"Do you like being back in Boston?"

"Actually, yeah. It's been good for me."

"Have you fallen in love yet?"

Ari's tongue pokes at her lower teeth. She isn't sure why this is the place her mother has jumped to immediately. Yet it's appropriate. Because she has fallen back in love with the city. She fell in love with Wells. And, despite how unstable it feels right now, she and Leah and Rowan are a love story, too.

"Yes." It means everything to say it aloud.

Even though she doesn't ask anything more, her mother seems to understand.

∿

The next few hours waiting for her train are heavy. It's a little jail cell, knowing how inflexible time can be. When it's time to leave for the station, her mother grabs the car keys, heads outside. Ari stops, stands in the doorway, facing the house. It is still a home. She can still see her dad's bare feet crossing the carpet, feel his weight shifting the pillows on the living-room couch as he sat next to her for *Jeopardy!* each night. She can see her mother bent at the stove, popping in Ari's favorite baked pasta. The three of them, together at the table, laughing. Ari can't remember what had made that moment happy, but she can feel home spread over her as she lingers on the threshold now. But it fades as quickly as it rolled in. In reality, the house is now drained of everything it once was. It is a blank slate for a new family to relax and cook and laugh in. Ari has gotten better with loss, but no one can really ever outrun it completely.

~

On the train, she closes her eyes for most of the ride, trying to find that liminal state.

Around Providence, her phone leaps.

Can we talk? Leah.

Whenever you want, Ari replies. She tells Leah she'll be in Boston in less than an hour.

Leah asks her if she minds coming straight to the house. **Rowan misses you.**

It's probably true, but Leah's words really mean she's the one aching.

~

"I'm sorry," Leah says. Ari hasn't yet taken off her shoes.

Rowan isn't even home. It's Friday, late afternoon, which means he's wrapping music class. He must be with Susan.

"I freaked out," she continues. "I have no idea what the fuck I'm doing with my life."

"But what have I done wrong?"

"Literally nothing. You've done everything right."

Ari walks to the couch, pulls the crimson blanket off the arm, sits.

"I feel guilty for things working out and for being happy. He hasn't even been gone a year, and I feel like I should still be in mourning or somehow dead, too." She sits beside Ari, pulls half the blanket across her lap. "It's still impossible to wake up to an empty house every day."

"The house isn't empty. I'm here."

Leah looks down. It's obvious Ari is not the same shape as the hole Wells left behind. But don't they both want her to fill it, at least while Leah is still healing? She leans into Ari, tips her head onto her shoulder. Her skin on Ari's, thank god.

LEAH

"Thirty, eh?" Leah says.

She sits sideways in an Adirondack chair, her bare legs draped over the arm. She points her feet, flexes, points again. She paints her nails red, all year round. Clio sniffs her toes, cold nose tickling them.

"Thirty," Ari says, smiling as she watches her dog cozy up to Leah, whose fear of this beautiful beast has disappeared. She adjusts in her own chair, resettles a checked wool blanket across her legs, covering up in the crisp April air.

"If you call yourself old, I'll kill you."

Leah is thirty-six. Sometimes she feels eighteen, one hundred.

They are in Vermont, a small A-frame cabin on Lake Champlain. With the dog curled at their feet, they've spent the past two hours paging through their books in dark-green chairs circling a firepit, the radiant heat humming against Leah's heels as she dangles them by the pale-orange flame. It's their second day of three here, on the trip she arranged as a surprise for Ari's birthday. Rowan is with her dad and stepmother. Ari spends all her energy giving to Leah's family, and Leah wanted to let her step back, be free. She wished to be there to see what Ari is like when her obligations fall away.

Leah also needed Ari to understand how much she means to her. She feels a level of safety with her she wasn't sure she'd find again after Wells. It's not just that she knows things will be done around the house, that Rowan will be fed and watched. It's that she thought she'd spend the rest of her life covered in quills, shooting them at every threat from an unjust world. But Ari let her in, and she dared to do the same. And then life simply did not turn out like that, in the best way. She's never been more grateful to have been wrong.

This morning, neither she nor Ari could sleep through the high morning sun, or their internal clocks, which are eternally tuned to Rowan. They woke up beside each other, as they've gotten used to, when Ari stays over after late nights on the couch with too much wine, or just because neither of them wants her to leave. Leah whispered happy birthday, slipped out of bed, tossed on one of Wells's old fraying sweatshirts over her silk pajamas, made coffee. She came over to the huge leather living-room chair into which Ari had settled, her legs also bare. Ari slipped the mug from Leah's hand. They both watched their fingers brush.

It is still amazing to Leah how her life has shaken out these past few months. It was late December when everything changed between them, the admission about Wells's affair finally cut loose like a balloon. February, when she panicked and Ari brought her back to earth. It's April now, and it feels good just to sink into her life. The guilt of being functional without Wells, *happy*, has thinned with every moment Ari spends beside her on the couch or across from her at a restaurant or kicking a ball with her son. Leah never imagined herself with this kind of love in her life, instead of that of her husband. But the more she repeats this to herself, the more she realizes how meaningless expectations are. People set out plans for themselves; project and assume into the future. Whose life has ever worked out linearly, like a mathematical equation? Whose pieces add up to perfect sums? Leah's do not. Neither do Ari's.

This isn't what I pictured, either, she's sure Ari has been thinking, this morning or for God knows how long. Because it's obvious she did envision a different life at age thirty, even if she doesn't talk about it, and Leah has had to pull the past from her like a rotten tooth. Ari thought she'd be married to her ex, probably living in New York. Maybe even

pregnant, who knows. Leah gets nervous turning it over, wondering if
Ari still longs for that lost future. But maybe Ari also knows conjecture
is irrelevant. Fantastical. Even if she would have been happier with her
former fiancé, or Leah would have been happier with Wells, life hasn't
played out that way. And what can they do about it but be here, in this
cabin, together.

"Summer and Luke sent me a nice message this morning," Ari says.
"My father, too. He was the first one. It's like he knows I'm here."

"What do you mean?" Leah cocks her head, dips her pointer finger
in her third cup of coffee to stir in the milk, licks it clean.

"My father lives in Vermont. Not near here."

"You've never gone up to Vermont as long as I've known you. You
don't see him?"

"We're not close anymore."

Leah isn't surprised. Ari hasn't mentioned her family. She knows her
mother sold her house, moved to Florida. Even with her swift tongue,
Leah has held back asking for anything more. Ari will tell her at some
point, she reasons. Eventually, she won't keep back a thing.

Leah rights herself in her chair, reties the stubby ponytail that rests
at her neck. "You should go see him while we're here."

"I'd rather drown myself in the lake."

"What if I go with you?"

Ari picks up her head. "You would?"

"Why not?" Selfishly, Leah wants to collect this little sliver.

Ari gnashes her teeth. Runs the heels of her hands back and forth
on her thighs. Leah can almost feel the friction on her own skin. She
bites her slim pink lip, lets it slip out from between her teeth.

"Fine. I'll try him. But I doubt he'll be around."

They sink back into their books for another hour, the big dog now
tucked under the blanket in Ari's lap. From the corner of her eye, Leah
sees the outline of Ari's breasts under her purple hoodie, her nipples
hard. It's unzipped low, her two sternum freckles exposed. She thinks
back to when Ari was stranded in their basement, and she tried to set

her up on a date. She sometimes considers proposing the idea again, now that Ari doesn't seem so insecure. Yet Leah is too scared of upsetting the balance of her own life, even if it means keeping Ari from someone else for now.

Finally, Ari picks up her phone. Leah pretends not to listen to the call, but she can hear Ari's dad's bouncy voice, thrilled she's on the line. She speaks to him in clips. *Yeah. Right. Sure. That's fine.* She hangs up, plops her forearm over her eyes.

"We have dinner with them for sevenish."

"Who's them?"

"His wife and her kids." She's still covering her face.

"What am I missing?" Leah says.

"His wife is the woman he left us for."

Leah waits for her to look over, fill the heavy space. Ari explains what's been missing.

"I'm sorry. I wouldn't have guessed." Leah tries to picture what she looked like at sixteen, raw and devastated, but can't. It's not an Ari she's ever known. "We don't have to go. I didn't mean to push you into it."

"I hope you like *braised local lamb*," Ari replies coolly. She pushes the blanket off, takes herself back inside the cabin with Clio at her heels.

~

Ari takes a half hour to get ready, which is about twenty-eight minutes longer than Leah has ever seen her spend on herself. She tries not to watch as Ari redoes her eyeliner twice, changes black shirts three times, puts on a different pair of shoes, only to end up in the flats she started with. Leah wants to ask her if she's okay, but manages to keep her big mouth shut. She can't stop herself from holding Ari's hand as they walk out to the car. Ari lets her.

They drive almost an hour, southeast, the sun behind them. "Turn here," Ari says before the GPS does. The rust-red farmhouse stands amid acres of deep emerald land, evergreens climbing endlessly. Two chocolate labs run free, barking at Leah's SUV while it eases up the dirt driveway. As she parks, she sees a dark-haired, good-looking man emerge from the doorway. He doesn't look like Ari, but from the way she whips her head toward Leah, eyes startlingly wide, it must be her dad.

"I won't leave your side," Leah says.

They walk up to the house. At the front door, he lights. Approaches his daughter, drapes his arms around her while she becomes a limp fish. Next, he shakes Leah's hand.

"Tom," he says.

"Leah," she returns. "A good friend of Ari's."

The house feels warm. A bright white kitchen with butcher-block countertops, exposed wood beams overhead. There are historic New England maps on the wall, miles of built-ins in the living room, packed with books. A cigarette-thin, light-blond woman approaches from the stove with a smile, her movements rigid.

Ari hasn't said a word.

Elisabeth introduces herself to Leah, tells Ari it's good of her to come. She announces the boys are out, so it'll be just the four of them for dinner. Ari, Tom, and Leah sit at the table, skipping the small-talk dance. From her seat, Leah studies Elisabeth pulling a massive pot off the stove, spooning dinner into shallow white bowls. Leah jumps to help her. They place the dishes in front of Ari and her father. Table silent.

"Funny," Tom says as Leah pulls in her chair, picks up her fork. "You two look like you could be sisters." She and Elisabeth, he means. Ari remains silent. "Thanks for coming again," he offers, since there's nothing else to say.

Elisabeth smiles gently, though tentatively. Leah wonders what Ari's mom looks like. If she's not as pretty as Elisabeth.

"It was Leah's idea," Ari says.

Leah is deeply unsettled by her discomfort, and she regrets bringing them all together. Her parents are also divorced, but still friends;

her mom knows her stepmother well, and they're congenial. She can't imagine what it must have been like for Ari, her life blown apart in a single moment. Though, on second thought, she can.

Leah touches Ari's thigh under the table, leaves it there until she sees her shoulders relax.

"So," Tom starts, "how do you know each other?" He shifts his gray polo at his neck, fidgets with a button.

"My boss," Ari says. "Through work."

Leah half smiles.

For the next forty minutes, dinner is largely fine. Tom asks how Ari's birthday has been, says he can't believe his daughter is thirty already. Ari sucks in her cheeks. Leah mostly talks so Ari doesn't have to, gushing nonsense at the same rapid clip she did right after Wells died. She can't stand the sound of her own voice.

They finish, and Ari begins clearing plates to the white apron sink. Elisabeth tells her she'll help, flashing bright teeth.

Don't leave me alone with her, Ari mouths from across the kitchen, pleading.

I'm sorry, Leah mouths back as she feels Tom's hand on her elbow.

He brings her into his office, a cozy, low-ceilinged nook at the back of the house, with hulking wooden bookcases and a worn red-and-navy Oriental rug, its cream tassels tangled. He reaches to the crammed shelves.

"She's got to be twelve or so here," he says, extending a photograph to her.

It's bent, well handled. Ari's sitting on a jetty in a mustard-yellow bathing suit, alongside three other kids. Her wet hair is plastered to her scalp, and Leah can practically hear them laughing.

"Her mother and I didn't give her the best homelife, but she always found a way to be happy."

"Looks like it." Leah squints at a small girl in a pink bikini, a lanky boy in a navy baseball cap. "Are those two Summer and Luke?"

"And Morgan." He points to the other boy, with wide shoulders, strikingly athletic for a child. "I feel bad about what happened. He's a good guy. I'm sorry it didn't work out."

"Oh, *Morgan*," Leah says. His name is different than she expected, and she feels like she's cheated on Ari, stealing what she hasn't offered.

Tom takes back the photo, replaces it on the shelf.

"I wanted to get you alone to ask how she is. You're close, no? Has she been okay?"

"Yes. I really think so."

"Do you know if she's still dating that person from work? She seemed pretty enamored of him."

What person? Leah wants to ask. *When?*

"I don't know," she says. "Ari doesn't talk about her dating life."

"Well, thanks for taking care of her, anyway."

She simpers, clenches her jaw.

She and Ari don't stay much longer. On the drive home, they ignore the night's events so fully, it's as if the dinner never happened. When they get back to the cabin, they light the fireplace and put on a movie. Leah can't stop thinking about the photo. As hypocritical as it is, even with all the time she still spends picturing herself next to Wells, the idea of Ari with anyone else is maddening. She hasn't wanted someone all to herself like this since she met him. She can't forget berating Wells when his eyes went blank after she asked to be together exclusively, so quickly—she still can't believe he didn't run. Sometimes, Leah knows, she's out of her mind.

A couple of hours later, they climb into bed. Ari turns to the wall, but Leah scoots close to her body, wraps herself around her. While she feels the cool breeze from the cracked window, Ari's body is warm against her.

"Who were you dating at the office when you worked for Wells?"

"What?"

"Your dad said you told him about a boyfriend at work."

"Oh," Ari says, breathy. She rolls onto her back. Stares at the beams in the ceiling, squinting, pulling the thin white sheet up to her neck.

"*Oh* what? Did I know him?"

Ari shakes her head, her lips pulled tight. "I lied. I made up someone. I didn't want him to get on my case about dating."

"Dating after Morgan."

She exhales. "After Morgan."

Leah watches to see if Ari starts, now that she knows his name, a detail so private. But she doesn't.

"Your dad showed me a picture of the four of you."

"I'm surprised he still has one."

Leah pushes a few strands of hair from Ari's eyes. She wishes she had known her as a child, seen her explore the world the way Rowan does. She'd thought the same thing of Wells years ago. Told him so the same night she said she loved him, that first time they went away together in Maine.

"He asked how you were," she says. "That's why he pulled me aside."

"And what did you say?" Ari pivots back toward Leah.

"That you were happy. Aren't you?"

Ari sighs. "Thanks to you."

ARI

Ari barely looks back. Not to Morgan, to Wells. Not when she's finally pointing her life in the right direction. She knows with her help, Leah is beginning to see ahead, too. There are things in the rearview they both miss. But those things aren't coming back, so they've both found ways to go forward. Taught each other that it's possible to keep living if they do it beside each other.

Leah, Rowan, and Ari spend the weekends together—at the Museum of Science and running around the arboretum, walking Clio by the Charles while Leah pushes the stroller. Ari and Leah go out to dinner together in Boston almost weekly—call a babysitter each time, the irony. As the weather has gotten nicer, they've lounged at Leah's dad's house in the suburbs, sipping spiked seltzers while Rowan futzes with a toddler scooter in the driveway. They've even gone up to Maine twice. At the beaches, Rowan drives trucks along the sand as they stand barefoot at the tide, cold water cupping their ankles. Susan stays far behind them, and Ari can always feel her eyes. Even with how good things have been, she is still terrified of Leah's mother—understands fully what Susan is capable of. All Ari can do to keep on her side is continue to prove how important she is to Leah, and how—against all odds, logic, decency—she protects her, every day. So far, it is working.

Now that she's stable, Ari can start to envision more for herself. As their walks take them past the city's universities, she begins to wonder if Summer was right. Maybe the *seas are pretty open now*, and she can pick up where she left off with that dream she never took far enough. She's started to poke around English department websites, figure out what she needs to apply for doctorates. She's even emailed her dad some questions. Ari wouldn't leave Boston or the Cahills, but she still hasn't told Leah she's thinking of changing anything.

She also knows she's been extraordinarily lucky to stay under cloak for the past ten months. Starting to gradually peel back by building something for herself seems like the right thing to do, for everyone. As Rowan ages—as his memory sharpens and his relationship with the world becomes concrete—what she did feels heavier and heavier. At the same time, though, she's not yet ready to quit this version of her life especially because she wouldn't have this momentum without it. Soon.

Often, on the way back from going out in the city together, Leah asks if she can see Ari's apartment, just because. *It's weird that I haven't been there, no?* Ari defers, stressing that it's ordinary, and even Clio likes it better at Leah's, where she practically lives now. Mostly, Ari is even more ashamed of the apartment, now that she knows how Leah lives. But inviting her inside also feels impossible, when Ari's loudest memory there is Wells, shaking naked on her sheets. Leah says *okay*, moves on. They always end up back at Leah's—and often, Ari doesn't leave. Instead, she sleeps beside Leah, cooks them spinach and feta omelets when she wakes.

It's Saturday morning, seven thirty, a few days after they return from Vermont. Ari rolls over to check the baby monitor, which she keeps on her side of the bed. Rowan is still sleeping, miraculously. Leah is not. When she sets the monitor back down on the nightstand, resettles into the white sheets, she sees Leah watching her. Leah's hair is stringy. It's so fine that it gets like this when she's gone more than two days without washing it. The brownish undertones come out as the dark blond gets brassy, strands cake together with oil. Ari touches it, laughs as Leah says, "I know."

"He's still sleeping," Ari says.

Leah's eyes scan the air. "I think you should stay here for a while."

"What do you mean?"

"I've thought about it," she says, running her fingers over the chain-link necklace Ari has always thought beautiful. "I think maybe it'd be good if . . ."

"Move in, you mean?"

"Logistically, it makes sense with Rowan's care, and I'm sure he would love to have you around more." Leah rolls onto her back. "I'd love to have you around more."

Ari doesn't know what to say. Leah is right, as she usually is—it would help them all if she could be here first thing in the morning, not worrying about commuting, or riding the T back late at night on the evenings she doesn't stay over. But those nights are becoming fewer and farther between.

"Did I make this so awkward? I always do this. It's like my brain and mouth can't—"

"Stop."

Leah's camisole dips low, and Ari stares at her cleavage. There are a few stretch marks, imperfections she would have never dreamed Leah could possess when she gazed at her from afar. But now these private truths are hers. How did it happen that she's seen Leah's long C-section scar, or know she never puts the cap back on anything tight enough? Why has she watched her shave her legs, or heard the way she wheezes in her sleep when she has a cold? These secrets are Ari's, yes. But they should not be.

She can't agree to move in, even though she wants it so badly she can feel her body temperature rise. Because if she no longer has any-where of her own to hide, what happens if she needs to? She's still holding inside the worst thing she's ever done.

Leah breathes in. "I know there's a reason you won't let me into your apartment."

"Because it's bad." Ari touches the diamond-speckled knot clasp that's fallen to Leah's sternum.

"Then stay here for now."

Leah can't say the word *live*—*live here*. It's too much to acknowledge that Wells's side of the room would no longer belong to him.

"We'd have to for-real adopt Clio. She's still technically a foster."

Leah looks to the dog at the foot of the bed, laughs. "We can for-real adopt Clio."

"Then, yes." Ari can't possibly imagine saying no.

Rowan cries to come out of his crib. She goes into his room, picks him up, holds him against her chest. Settles into the feeling of his downy hair against her neck as he drops his head to her shoulder. She sighs, emptying her lungs, and smiles until her cheeks ache.

~

You in Boston the next few days?

Yes . . . why? Ari texts back to Summer.

She's almost surprised to hear Summer might be looking to see her. They talk less now that Ari can't really tell her about her life with Leah and Rowan. Haven't seen each other in months.

Luke has a fellowship interview at Boston children's

Wait what

We're coming up Thursday night. Just have to figure out where we're staying

Call me

"You could seriously end up here?" Ari says as she picks up the phone. She's dizzy thinking about them all living close together again. Morgan would be gone. But Leah. And whoever else comes next.

"If Luke doesn't blow this interview, it's possible, yes," Summer says. "He's doing the overnight tonight, then driving up to New York tomorrow."

It's Tuesday afternoon now, and Rowan is chasing a soccer ball in a swarm of toddlers, while Ari stands on the sidelines behind a mini orange cone. She waves when he looks back to her, an ear-to-ear smile splitting his face.

"Wow," Ari says. "That's good news."

"Nothing yet. But it could be." Summer clears her throat. "Can we stay with you? Luke can sleep on the couch. I know it'd kind of be a squeeze, but—"

"Sum." Ari bites her lip, too hard. There's an empty space on the line Summer is waiting for her to fill. "I'm actually living at Leah's now."

"Since when? You gave up your apartment?"

"It's just been a couple weeks. It makes sense. You know, with Rowan."

"It does?"

"Yes. It's like an au pair situation." The twentysomething coach blows his whistle. The kids run back toward their adults. Ari takes a pull from Rowan's water bottle, passes it to him. "Anyway, you guys can stay in the basement apartment here."

"Then where are you living?"

"Upstairs," she says. That's enough.

Summer sighs. "As long as it's okay with your landlord."

~

Over a late dinner of seared salmon and farmers' market fiddleheads Ari prepared, Leah hesitates when Ari mentions Summer and Luke. She tops off her wine, finishing the bottle. Swishes the Riesling in the glass.

"Oh."

"Never mind," Ari replies quickly. She's mortified, having wrongly assumed she can invite an outsider in to share their quiet life. This is still Leah's home; Ari is still her guest, her employee. "I shouldn't have offered."

"Well, wait." Leah's head tips to the side. She drops her elbow to the table, cups her chin in her palm. "If you could just take the spare bedroom while they're here."

Ari pokes the tines of her fork against the inside of her cheek. "Yeah."

"It would look weird. I don't think anyone else would get it like we do."

"I understand."

"Aria."

Ari's eyes go wide. For the first time, their bedrock feels threatened. She knows Leah is being sensible—and, in many ways, she doesn't yet want the outside world to touch what they have, either. Still, she doesn't want to feel hidden. The only thing she wants is to live life beside Leah. Build a skyscraper with her into the black beyond.

~

Summer and Luke arrive late Thursday night, after eleven. The Mass Pike was at a dead stop for an hour, Luke apologizes, then hugs Ari with a purely male force she forgot existed. What surprises her most, though, even more than his long-armed embrace, is that she isn't whisked back to Morgan or Wells. She feels more present than ever.

Summer stands on the porch steps, a lavender weekender bag hanging from her shoulder. She looks nervous to be back at Wells's house again. Ari doesn't blame her, exactly—but things couldn't be more different than they were back then.

Clio barks when her friends step through the front door, and she rushes to calm the dog. She asks them to take off their shoes, reminds them Rowan and Leah are sleeping. Summer and Luke steal a tight glance at each other. They all head downstairs.

"Wow, what a space," Luke says. He drops his bag, flips down the Murphy bed, which Clio hops right up onto. Ari pulls fresh sheets from the chest under the television; Summer sucks in her cheeks.

"Leah's husband was from London. His family used to stay here," she says, as if Wells is foreign to Luke, as if he doesn't know Wells's name already, exactly what happened.

"And you're not using it?"

He gently pats Clio to urge her off the bed, then stoops to spread the heather-gray fitted sheet across the mattress. His thin fingers and oversize hands secure the corners with surgical precision.

"Oh," Ari says. "It's just easier for me to be upstairs, so I can hear into Rowan's room."

"Makes sense."

Summer plops her bag on the bed once Luke is done spreading a white woven blanket. She begins pulling out her pajamas. Luke's, too. They're perfect, Ari remembers, in an untouchable way that feels even more imposing as they stand together. She's always known it; she and Morgan always knew it, down to their bones.

It's late, they all agree. Ari will make a big breakfast in the morning. They should sleep in, she says.

"Please thank Leah for us if we miss her before she leaves tomorrow," he says.

Luke pulls his collar away from his neck. Ari can tell he's uncomfortable in the blue T-shirt he's been wearing all day, driving for hours, sitting in traffic in a stuffy car. He wants the navy basketball shorts Summer has pulled out for him; he wants his chest bare, against hers.

"Yes, please do," Summer says, letting down her red ponytail, removing her glasses.

Soon after they split for sleep, Ari hears a knock at the guest-room door. She's in underwear, topless. "One second," she calls out, scooping for her shirt on the floor.

"It's me," Summer calls back, much softer, then pushes open the door.

Ari stands in her underwear as Summer drops to the corner of the bed. Summer looks around for a moment, adjusts her pink pajama pants at her knees.

"Are you having sex with Leah?"

"What?" Ari jolts. "No. Why would you ask me that?"

"Luke had a feeling you might be, and I didn't think the idea was crazy." She shakes her hair from her eyes. "But something's weird that you're not living downstairs. It's like an entire apartment. Don't you want your own space?"

"I told you," Ari says, "if I'm here for Rowan, it doesn't make sense for me to not be right next to his room."

Summer laps the spare bedroom, reaching to the floating shelf for a hand-carved wooden giraffe Wells brought back from a trip to South Africa when he was a child. "Where's all your stuff?"

"Still limping it in from my old place."

"You said you gave it up already."

Ari quietly lowers herself next to Summer. She watches her thighs spread wider her legs hit the sheets, feels her nipples pucker from the cold, scratch against her T-shirt.

"You're living in Leah's room, then."

Ari thinks about denying it, but even the single lie she's told already feels awful. "It's hard to explain."

"Do your best," Summer says. She's looking ahead at the picture on the wall: Leah and Wells's wedding party, a gigantic greenhouse somewhere in London.

Ari tries to line up a grand explanation, starting from the beginning, cataloging everything that led up to laying her head down next to Leah each night, on the sliver of bed where her ex-lover used to sleep. All she says is, "It's just gotten to a point where Leah needs me."

"You mean you need each other."

"I mean, yes."

"That's not an employee doing a good job for their employer. That's straight human codependence."

"I've needed you since we were nine, and we're not *codependent*."

Summer turns to Ari. Pokes her tongue at the inside of her cheek. "Why do I all of a sudden not hear from you for days? Why do I basically know nothing about your life right now? Why haven't you come down to see me in months?"

"Why haven't you come up here?"

Summer shakes her head. "Things are different since you met Leah."

"Things had to be different once Morgan left me after a fucking decade."

"That's not what I mean, and you know it."

"What do you want from me?" Ari barks. "Why are you giving me so much grief when I'm in a better place than I've been in years? Isn't that what you've been pushing me toward?"

Summer stands. "She's going to find out eventually. Then what?" She doesn't wait for an answer, just leaves with a coldness so alien it chills Ari to her very bones.

~

Instead of staying through Saturday morning as planned, Summer and Luke leave Friday afternoon. They take off just an hour after his interview, before Leah even gets home, though Ari's planned a dinner to introduce everyone. Through the front bay window, as the sun is beginning to drop, she watches Luke's car peel from the street. She waves, but no one waves back.

~

Leah is home before Ari and Rowan return from the playground. It's around four, and the May sun is peaked in the sky. The heat has already been oppressive, humidity gathering in the lungs.

"Hey," Leah calls out as Ari ushers Rowan in from the mudroom.

She is perched on one of the three barstools at the kitchen island, her legs crossed under her, computer open. Rowan drops the tattered stuffed rabbit he brought in the car, runs to his mom.

"Hey, little bug," she says, ruffling his hair.

"You're home early," Ari says, like a wife greeting her husband, waiting like a treat.

"Too loud to concentrate in there today."

On the countertop, Leah has spread out tens of fabric samples of gingham and madras in jewel tones. It's taken nearly a year and a half, but her company has finally gotten the retail partnership she was hoping for, and she and Molly have been spending hours at the dining table for the past week, arguing over packaging designs. She reaches to the other side of the island, gestures at the pile of mail Ari usually retrieves.

"You got something," she says.

"Addressed to me?"

Ari's never received mail at this house, like the person on the mortgage. She startles, thinking of her name mixed into the pile of Wells's envelopes and magazines, which still arrive like he will come home any minute to open them. It's still a shock to see his name on those labels, through tiny plastic windows, especially when Leah could update them. She still quietly negotiates with reality to keep him alive. They don't talk about him. But he is everywhere anyway.

Leah extends the heavy envelope, *Aria Claire Bishop* in calligraphy across the front, a heart-printed stamp in the corner. Ari knows what it is. She slips out the invitation, a tall cream cardstock, bordered in blush. *Summer Abigail Kemp and Lucas Wyatt Hallock request the pleasure of your company to celebrate their wedding.* A plucky script.

"What is it?" Leah asks, picking up one piece of a three-dimensional wooden puzzle, shaped like a rocking horse. She presses the pad of her thumb into its tail.

"Summer's wedding invitation."

"Oh, nice. June, you said."

"The last Saturday of the month, yes."

She slips out the menu option card—fish, chicken, or vegetarian pasta—and the RSVP, the *1 guest* already filled in, Summer's handwriting. Ari, her best friend, has not been given even the option of a plus-one for Leah. It feels like a personal siege. She silently gathers the invitation back into the thick, metallic-pink-lined envelope, slides it away.

Leah's eyebrows dip in.

"I'm all good," Ari says.

"Are you? Is it the wedding thing?"

Leah doesn't directly say it—swallowing her wild tongue—but it's clear what she's asking: whether the wedding invitation in Ari's hand wrecks her. Ari doesn't want to prod at the answer, terrified of what she'll unearth. She hasn't dug in months, some of the most immense progress she's made in two years. Still, yes, it feels unequivocally awful. Yes, she'd browsed stationery suites a few times, pictured how *Aria Claire Bishop* would look next to *Morgan James Mead*, but hadn't chosen one. No, she never thought she'd be in a life where she was attending Summer's wedding alone.

"Do you think you'll ever get married again?" Ari asks Leah.

"What?" Leah drops the toy to the countertop.

Behind them, Rowan runs to the fridge, fishes a carton of strawberries from the crisper drawer. He grins back at Ari. His hair is wild, sunflower butter smeared on his right cheek. Leah sharply calls out that he's going to ruin his dinner, which feels like Ari's fault.

"I don't know," Ari says. "I guess I was just wondering."

"Rowan, go have Ari set you up with TV."

Leah does not look at her, instead stares blankly into her computer screen, while the pile of mail addressed to her late husband lingers beside her. She freezes until Ari goes into the living room, firmly out of sight. The air is so thin, the dullest knife could slice it fine.

Leah is not there when Ari comes out of the bathroom before she starts to make Rowan's dinner. She bathes him and puts him to bed on her own.

After Rowan is down, his little chest expanding and falling on the baby monitor, she goes into their room. Leah is on the bed. Sobbing, her entire body quaking. Ari is witnessing a moment she shouldn't— this crumbling, grief, which Leah has been holding inside for nearly a year. This belongs to Leah and Wells; it has nothing to do with Ari. Yet Ari can't look away as Leah chokes on sallow air. Transforms back into a widow. That's what she is. Ari hasn't erased that part of her, no matter how far she's burrowed inside.

Leah's skin is flaming red. Ari burns, too: for Leah, for Wells, for Morgan, for the lives they've each lived, then lost. The ones they never got to live at all.

LEAH

Leah runs away to Maine. Flees. She can't be alone with Ari, Rowan, herself, in the house her husband loved so much. She still doesn't know how she blearily drove the two hours to Portland without crashing into a tree, accidentally or otherwise.

Her dizzy nausea is not really Ari's fault. The question was reasonable. When have they ever held back from each other, when have they ever feared each other? When did Leah become so fragile? Was she always like this? Was it a weakness Wells saw when she didn't, a fault that drove him to another woman?

No, this is an overdue catharsis. Firm footing in a place she has not allowed herself to visit, in part due to her own fear manifesting as stubbornness, but mostly because of Ari. No one has shielded Leah the way Aria Bishop has. Leah had to break at some point, didn't she? Why ask the question. It's fucking crazy it took this long.

It's four in the afternoon, and she collapses on the deep-blue pinstriped couch in her mom's home. She covers her eyes with her hands. She and Rowan have been in Maine for two days; she's planning to drive home tomorrow, Thursday, if she can convince herself to get out of bed. She feels like a broken toy she needs her mother to fix. A child who doesn't want to return to an adult life.

"Breathe, Leah," her mom says, flipping on *Daniel Tiger's Neighborhood* for Rowan, then moving to the kitchen to shake cheddar whales into an orange-silicone snack cup.

She has not explicitly told her mom why she's here. After she broke down, alone in her bedroom at home, Leah decided she'd go to Portland first thing. Ari woke to the sound of her packing before dawn. *What are you doing?* she had called, turning over in bed. *I have to go to my mom's,* Leah said, then shoved her hairbrush and the first three shirts she could find into a bag. Ari shot up straight, sheet in her fist. *Is everything okay?* Leah didn't reply. *Are we okay, Leah?* Another question she couldn't answer.

Leah shifts down to the rug, sits cross-legged, arranges Rowan's tiny dinosaurs in a neat line. Her mom retrieves two stemless wineglasses etched with lobsters, fills each with a generous pour of Long Island rosé.

"I have a little update," she says as she hovers over her grandson at the edge of the couch. "I met someone. He's a carpenter in Kittery."

"Hey, that's great. How long?"

"It's just been a few weeks. But he's very nice and we have fun."

"You deserve the world," Leah says. She smiles, then closes her eyes, breathes out.

Her mom sips. "You still miss him terribly."

"I do," she replies, a mouse-size voice. She swirls the wine, places the glass to the beechwood coffee table.

"It's gotten easier, though," her mom says.

"Has it?"

Leah cracks her back, stares out the backyard slider over her mom's shoulder. Beside her, Rowan is intently paging through *The Very Hungry Caterpillar,* naming each food the caterpillar eats until it's so fat it can't move. "Read to Rowie, Mommy," he keeps saying. She touches his knee.

"I still swear I see him all the time. Like, on the street or at the market. Or when I'm sleeping alone, I wake up startled he's not there."

"*When* you're sleeping alone? Does that mean you're not always sleeping alone?"

"That's not what I mean, Mom."

"But it's good if it is." Susan raises the glass to her lips, but stops.

Leah wants to correct her mom, explain there's no man, won't be for a long time. Ari *is* the person she wants to be sleeping next to. Why seek someone else—open herself again to the hurt Wells caused, the one she still has not told her mother about—when she has everything she needs? She could say she doesn't want to love anyone else when she loves Ari so much it hurts. Leah could list the ways Ari has lifted her, cared for her child, thought of everything to keep her afloat, tempered her incalculable loneliness. Listened to every godforsaken word she's said, never made her feel like she was missing something, the way Wells obviously thought she was. Without Ari, she'd be frenzied and frantic and fighting so hard for an identity that she'd completely lose herself.

If there is anyone who wants Leah to have and do the very things that fill her with life, it's her mom. Leah doesn't say anything, though. Her mom is proud of who she has become, but she wouldn't understand why she wants to live only inside Ari, even when the world is ready for her. Simply, Leah is still not ready for it.

"Ari's living at the house now," Leah says as Rowan drops the book, crawls into her lap. "It made sense."

Her mom studies Rowan's face, contemplates for a few moments. "Are you sure that's a good idea?"

"Why? What are you thinking?" Leah squints as her mother sits in silence. "Mom, what are you not saying?"

With her fingertips, her mom slides the wineglass forward. "You've been through a lot."

Leah lets the wine snake down her throat.

ARI

Luke gets a second interview. Of course he does, because he is Luke, and Luke is good at everything. It's short notice, so he flies from Philadelphia, makes plans to stay with a friend from undergrad. Ari doesn't know whether to take it personally.

After Leah gets home from work, Ari and Luke meet at a pub around the corner from the hospital. He's already there, waiting at the bar in a button-down shirt and paisley tie, nursing a beer, scrolling his phone. He cracks his neck to each side.

"I almost mistook you for a doctor," she says. Drops her bag to a stool.

He looks up, shrugs. "Just a guy in an ugly tie."

The tie is ugly, Ari agrees. Luke stands, tall and thin and clean-shaven. The stiff fabric of his shirt brushes her nose as he embraces her, and he smells of medical sterility. She tips her cheek against his chest, while he pats her back, rests his chin on her head. She doesn't move so he'll keep holding her.

Luke buys her a beer, which she pulls from greedily. She's been floating in and out of her body for four days, since seeing Leah crumble. Ari has slept beside her since she came back from her mom's, but they haven't said much to each other. She doesn't know what Leah is holding out for—whether she is waiting for something from her, or simply waiting for Wells to come back in a grand delusion.

"How did the interview go?"

"It went well, I think. But you never know." He pauses. "How are things?"

Luke sees the pain all over Ari. He knows how she looks when she's stripped bare.

"I don't really know," she says.

"Leah?"

She nods. "I think we had a fight, but I'm not sure."

"Call Summer. Maybe you guys can talk it through."

She heaves a massive sigh. She and her best friend have barely talked in the past few weeks, Ari sending a few just checking you're not dead messages, which Summer replies to with a thumbs-up, often hours later. Summer occasionally sends her reminders about various things she's been assigned to for the wedding, checks Ari's alterations for her cherry-blossom bridesmaid dress will be done on time, that she has the right pair of nude heels.

"I know what you're doing," Ari says, stuffing her puffed-out hair into a messy bun. "Summer's the one who's not talking to me."

"I don't think that's it." Luke trails a finger through the condensation on the glass. "She misses you, Ar. And I know she's jealous of Leah."

Ari drinks. "How's wedding stuff going?"

He slips the tie off his neck, winds the silk into a tight ball before shoving it into his bag. He undoes the top button of his pink shirt, which she knows Summer told him to wear.

"She has a vision. I'm just doing what she says."

They both smile, finally.

Luke tells Ari he's not sold on the pink tie, but the joke's on him for being surprised by it. He shakes his head, laughs under his breath. "I'm sure the groomsmen will love it." Right then Luke drops his smile—she can almost feel him chastising himself for mentioning his side of the wedding party, which obviously includes Morgan.

Ari's voice drops to a whisper. "How is he?"

"I can't really tell, to be honest," Luke says. He finishes his beer. "His job sounds awful. They're sending him all over the Midwest to do evil corporate things, and I think he's miserable. But, you know. It's impossible to tell with him."

"It is."

He rubs fatigue from his eyes. "He asks after you, a lot."

"Why?" she says, squinting. It's the wrong question. Leah's quick mouth is rubbing off on her.

"You know why."

Ari hasn't touched any more of her drink; her stomach feels weak. Sitting here with Luke, she doesn't want to go home to Leah. In all this time, she's forgotten what it feels like to be with someone who knows the way she has grown, who can read her insides. Leah will never be able to. Wells never did.

"I hope you move here," she says.

"We do, too." Luke and Summer, one.

The sun is setting, a glowing orange blanket swaddling the city's tight skyline. Luke has dinner plans with a friend, so they wrap.

"I miss you terribly," she says, gathering her bag.

He scrunches his lips. "It all really will work out," he says, the answer to a question she hasn't asked.

She hugs him with force, begins to leave.

"Ari," he calls to her back. When she turns, he lowers his voice. "I'm sorry about the plus-one."

It was Summer, he means.

∿

Instead of going home—Leah's house—Ari begins walking. Deeper into Boston, the opposite direction. She passes the dorm where she squeezed beside Morgan in his extra-long twin bed, the taqueria that is just as jammed with undergrads as always, where Soren took her back to on their third consecutive night out. Each prick of memory feels worse than the last. It's not that the images are bad—most of them are good, even great. But there's not a single one where she's not beside someone.

She can't recall ever being happy on her own—not in Boston, not anywhere. She came here to start over, like she told Wells during that first walk around the office building. Become someone who could stand on her own, realize herself and her place in the world. Now she does not have a home that's hers, a relationship she can scream about, a career that's flourishing, a child with her blood. All she has belongs to Leah; the rest is burned with Wells, or suppressed inside Morgan. Ari knows there's no one else to blame but herself. She had the chances. She was perfectly capable of walking away or saying no in the first place.

The backs of her feet are raw against her shoes, socks stiff with blood. Yet she doesn't stop walking. What if she course-corrected now, left Leah behind? Of all the decisions she's made and passed up, this would finally be the right one. There's nothing actually keeping her from grabbing Clio's leash and bed, packing her own clothes, gently placing Kathy's pincushion on top, slapping tape across cardboard and putting the boxes in the trunk of a rental car, destination wherever. Ari would be devastated, losing another great love. She'd have to rebuild, but would, like Summer insisted months ago. She'd need to. If she's learned anything, there's no force stronger than *need*.

Her phone buzzes in her pocket.

Where are you? Are you ok? Clio is waiting by the window for you (me too)

It's only then Ari realizes how long she's been wandering—two hours, aimlessly. Miles from the pub, from Leah's, from herself. Despite the overwhelming thoughts knocking around, she doesn't hesitate to reply.

Making my way home.

Someone needs her. And, ultimately, isn't that what everyone wants?

~

Ari is still drifting—toward uncertainty, away from Leah. Not only does she feel like a shell, but the further she leans out, the more she remembers the secret is still there. It will never go away. The reality weighs starkly on her, heavier each time Leah smiles at her, lays her head on a pillow in her lap to watch TV; each time Rowan brings her a watercolor he's made, makes her sit on a kitchen stool to watch an impromptu recital of Mandarin songs.

She has made herself extraordinarily busy. During any spare moment in Rowan's schedule, she takes him to every playground in Boston and Cambridge and Somerville, even Medford, especially when Leah is working from home. The aquarium, the museums, the little park to which she brings a soccer ball and watches him get better and better. She constantly finds Wells's face in his, but the similarity is no longer a threat. Seeing Wells in Rowan thrills her—how amazed he'd be by the light his son has brought into the world. She is addicted to seeing him explore, his eyes widen; yet she's equally obsessed by the relief that washes over her when she's escaped Leah's pull.

Leah has clearly noticed how unavailable Ari's become—the way she now labors over two-hour recipes, compulsively cleans every inch of the house, learns to run. There are also the secret hours she's spending on pulling together writing samples for grad school applications, contacting professors she hasn't spoken to in years for recommendations. Perusing programs outside of Boston, too, just because. *Let's find time for dinner out,* Leah often urges as she sits close to her on the couch. *A night to ourselves.* Ari agrees, but drags her feet.

She's starting to think living with Leah is making this jumble worse. Ari is now resolute on finding a new apartment, to establish her own space that has nothing to do with Leah's voice, Wells's tears, in a neighborhood she never visited with Morgan. There are changes she can make soon, and will. She has to listen to her gut, whose message is becoming clearer every day.

After Rowan goes to bed one night—a week since Ari saw Luke—
Leah asks her if she'd like to go to a benefit gala together the first
Saturday in September. She is on the board of an education charity for
low-income families in Boston, and they're having their annual fund-
raiser, she explains.

"Could be a really fun night out, and maybe we could grab a hotel
room after, just to do something different." She tucks her hair behind
her ears a few times. "Or we could come back here, whatever you want."

"Summer's having her birthday party in New York that weekend,"
Ari says. She doesn't know whether Summer is having a birthday party,
or whether she'd even be invited if she were.

Leah's shoulders drop. She bites her lip, sucks in her cheeks, looks
back down to the dinner Ari's made: cockles and clams with cherry
tomatoes over fresh linguini, garlic aioli. "Well, I'm sure Summer will
be happy to see you. That's good."

They don't speak for the rest of the meal. Leah says she has work
she'd like to get done, and Ari says she'll clean the kitchen.

As Leah pushes in her chair, she turns to Ari. "Did I fuck something up?"

Ari shakes her head. It's not Leah. It's Ari and her mistakes.

Once she hears Leah close her office door, Ari reaches for her phone.

"Oh my god," Summer says. She sounds out of breath. "I'm so
happy to hear from you."

"Really?"

"Really, really, truly."

Ari smiles. "Did I catch you at a bad time?"

"Yes. No. I don't know," Summer breathes into the phone. "I got
out of work an hour late and sprinted across Tribeca for a dress-tailoring
appointment. I'm still dizzy. What's up?"

Ari grabs the sponge, squeezes it in her palm. "Are you on duty
Friday night? Can I come down if not?"

"Oh my goodness, *please*. I'm going to have to drag you to the florist and the printer at some point, but I'd love you to be there with me."

"Good."

"Oh, you know whose RSVP I just got? Jack. I think he'll be happy to see you."

"Who's Jack?"

"Jack, Luke's roommate you kissed last New Year's."

"Right," Ari says. "He was great."

"He still is."

There's silence. Ari puts down the sponge, leans back against the stove, twirls a dish towel. It's hard to look at the kitchen table where she's seen Rowan grow out of his high chair into a booster seat, where they've all sat together in the happy family unit she never had. Where she took Wells's seat to do so.

"I've been thinking a lot about what you said when you were here. You're right about a lot of it," Ari begins. "I'm starting to make some moves. I'm actually working on some grad school applications."

"Aria Claire."

"Yeah. I feel good about it. Nothing would happen until September of next year, but it's a start."

"September of next year?" Summer's voice cracks high. "What are you going to do until then?"

"Ride it out. I haven't told Leah yet. I have time still."

An ambulance blares on Summer's line. "Just tell me what bus you'll be on."

~

On Thursday morning, as they're getting dressed, Leah asks if she can take Ari to dinner later that night. *I have a sitter lined up if you want to go.* Ari replies she does. In all her muck, she misses Leah. She misses the way she feels when they're together, crawling into their plush core.

That evening, she lines her eyes with a slick of liquid black, then picks out something she hasn't worn for a while: the shirtdress she put on for Wells to take off that first time. As she dons it, she worries it won't fit any longer, but she's wrong: the silk slips over her easily, hangs loosely from her frame. She's lost weight, in her haze. She hasn't even been in her body enough to realize.

She makes sure the sitter knows there's dinner if she wants it—Rowan is already down to sleep—then takes the T to the restaurant. Waits by the hostess stand.

"Ari?"

The voice over her shoulder is familiar, but she can't place it. Once she turns, there he is, looking as handsome as he did when she last saw him. Soren. He readjusts his glasses.

"Hi," she ekes out. They're the only ones standing by the door at the small, orange-walled Cambodian restaurant. "What are you doing here?"

"Picking up food."

She realizes they're not far from his apartment, assuming he still lives in the same place. She hasn't seen him in a year.

"How are you?" she asks, unable to stand still under the hammered-copper elephant suspended from the ceiling.

"Fine."

His charmingly unkempt hair is even more charmingly unkempt, and he's switched his clear-plastic glasses to a pair of light, gold wire-framed ones that brighten his face. She'd liked him, so much. It'd been a mistake to choose Wells, but she didn't let herself see it.

"You look good," she says.

Soren quarter smiles. "What happened? You fell off the face of the earth. I thought we were having a really nice time."

"We were. I'm sorry. It was shitty and unfair to you."

"It was incredibly shitty and unfair. I really liked you."

This hurts Ari—the idea someone was attracted to her, as a whole person, with good qualities and a past that didn't matter. That he was not stumbling into her desperately. Soren wanted her there.

"I got scared," she says, an honesty that startles her. The walk along the Charles, the current of his hand in hers—it really was too

272

frightening. Too much like Morgan, too much for her to take in and submit to. Too separate from Wells. She could have gone back to Soren, apologized for not showing up to dinner, made him another macaroni and cheese and delivered it to his door with her tail between her legs. But it didn't happen that way. She was too caught up in what she was going to lose, not what she could have.

"You needed to tell me that. You owed that to me," he says. "You made me feel like a loser."

"I'm sorry. I know."

The woman at the counter calls Soren's name. He steps forward to take his paper bag. He's vegetarian, Ari remembers.

He turns back to her. "Did you even think about how it'd make me feel? I don't really know you, but I didn't think that was you. I guess I misjudged you."

Ari's heart is pounding. She didn't know Soren for long, but she'd never seen him ruffled. She can't believe how much her choices rippled out, that she meant enough to him that he's still harboring anger. Really, though, why should he let her off the hook—why shouldn't she feel terrible about it all? Even if he did excuse her actions, she's learned forgiveness shouldn't give someone a pass to stop internalizing the hurt they've caused, an open door to hurt again.

Just as she prepares to take the responsibility she owed him months ago, Leah steps through the door.

"I'm late, I'm the worst," she chirps across the entrance.

Neither Ari nor Soren says anything.

"Hello?" Leah's eyebrows dip in. She surveys them, still staring at each other. "Am I interrupting?"

"No. I was just leaving," he says. "Good luck, Ari."

Shame drips from her; not only that she's disappointed someone, but that she's also squandered an opportunity to build herself. She doesn't want to be near Leah. Doesn't want anything to do with this life at all.

"Who was that?" Leah asks.

"A guy I went out with for a bit." She thinks of the dating app languishing on her phone, the one she never opened again.

"What happened?"

"I fucked up."

"How?"

"It's impossible to explain."

Leah doesn't reply, instead steps toward the hostess stand, points at a table in the back. She seems bothered. It's like she can't fathom Ari belonging to anyone before her, doesn't want to. If she only knew.

Leah launches into telling Ari about her day, asking about Rowan's, as if nothing is amiss, as if the air in the house hasn't been rigid. They order too much food, drink too much rice wine, come home and put something on television Ari is too distracted to watch. For hours after they go to bed, Ari pleads with herself to sleep. Against her pillow, Leah looks at peace, like she hasn't slept this soundly in a year.

∼

They have been circling the day, but neither will admit it's close until twenty-four hours before.

"My mom is coming in tonight," Leah says. "I know it's last minute, but I think I need her to be here."

From where Ari is standing on the threshold of the bathroom, poking an electric toothbrush at her molars, she watches Leah try to slip on a gauzy black dress, but she can't find her way through the armholes and punches at the fabric until she can finally pull it on. She releases a ripping tiger roar. Ari spits out her toothpaste, walks quietly behind her, fastens the two buttons at the back of her neck.

"I'm sorry in advance," Leah says. Her palms cup her cheeks. "I'm going to have a hard few days. If I do something stupid, don't hold it against me. I'm not of this earth right now."

"Yes," Ari says.

She, too, is going to have a hard few days. Tomorrow, an otherwise nothing Friday in late May, will be a year since Wells died. The pain of his loss has draped over her again. His absence has knit itself into everyday life; as the tapestry has gotten longer, stronger, his thread has become one of many. Except now the fabric is newly snagged: a gaping hole too obvious to ignore.

For as much as Leah is keeping to herself—glaring, a woman doesn't hold back anything—Ari is bursting at the seams, too. Sometimes she wants to scream how much she loved Wells. How Leah is unknowingly tethered to her in their shared grief. As she watches Leah fix a skinny gold watch onto her wrist, her hands shaking, he fills her in a way he hasn't since he last touched her. She can feel her chest tightening with his weight; she can feel her breasts tingle with the ease of his hands; she can feel the pressure of him against her pubic bone. She can smell him, taste him, breathe him. For a dead man, he is excruciatingly alive.

Ari goes to Rowan's room, retrieves him from the crib. Even he looks sad, or at least unlike himself. This toddler, nearly three, sentient in a way he wasn't when his father died, seems wholly aware he is missing part of himself. He doesn't ask for Daddy like he did at the beginning; Ari knows that her presence—calm and steady and loving—is partially responsible for that. She holds Rowan, whispers kind nothings. Feels his skin, the contour of his head in her palm, the gentle wave of his hair. It's amazing how much he's matured since she's been caring for him; more amazing what's happened since she saw that first photo in the basement. How he's grown even further into the spitting image of his father. How he feels like her son.

She helps him down the stairs, makes a whole-grain waffle, pours a cup of milk, settles him on the couch. He sits on her lap, leans back. She wraps him into her, a fresh relief each time.

A few minutes later, Leah comes down, too. "There's a registration slip for the next session of STEM. It's on the kitchen counter," she says.

"It's already filled out and in his bag. You gave it to me last night."

"I did?"

"You did."

Leah is out of her body, her mind. She stands at the bottom of the stairs, scratching her elbow, brushing invisible lint from her ear. Ari brings her a milky coffee from the kitchen, which she accepts without making eye contact. She touches Leah's forearm. Leah flinches.

"Tomorrow, I need time to myself. It's nothing personal," she says. But she seems to realize Ari doesn't have anywhere else to go. She doesn't have friends or another home. "I can get you a hotel room for the night."

"If that's what you want." Rowan calls for Ari to sit. "One second, baby," she returns.

"You understand."

"I do."

Leah rubs her eyes, smears her black liner. Her eyes are deep set, thumbprints in dough. She already looks broken, and there are many hours to go before she gets past tomorrow. She limply gazes at Rowan. Ari can tell she is afraid to touch her son, lest she fall apart—a kiss to his hair is a kiss to Wells's. It feels like the funeral all over again. A weight, unspeakable.

Leah reaches for an umbrella from the hall closet and stuffs it in a tote. Leaves for the office, saddled with bags of the newest prototypes she's had Rowan playing with all week. She never went past the foyer, never got anything to eat. Never drank the coffee, which is now sitting cold on the console by the front door.

Ari walks blankly to the couch. Rowan climbs her like a jungle gym, settles back into her lap, drops his head to her chest. She understands why Leah can't be here tomorrow. She can't face the life she's built with Ari when Wells will be so present.

Ari still needs Leah, though. For all the planning she's doing, the life she can see for herself in the not-so-distant future, the idea of herself without Leah is incomprehensible. Spending the night without her now, of waking up the same way—Ari can't handle it.

An hour later, as Rowan plays with his bright plastic dinosaurs on the floor, proudly exclaiming the names of each—*Spinosaurus, dimetrodon!*—Ari looks up last-minute rooms. She takes Leah's credit card, books the reservation. She will have to face her renewed grief alone, again.

~

Leah's mom lets herself in around four fifteen, just as Ari is heating a kale-quinoa cake for Rowan. She finds them in the kitchen, cups her grandson's cheeks in her palms, then lowers herself into the seat across from him. She reaches to his plate, steals a sliver of the neatly cut-up green patty. He protests, even if he's mostly been picking.

"Aria," Susan says.

Her full name drops from Susan's mouth like an anvil. Ari's unrelenting presence in the Cahill home has never been so stark. Wells is back; she is somehow here, too.

"Tell me how Leah is."

"Not great."

"You're part of that, you know."

"I know."

Sometimes Ari can't believe Susan hasn't said anything. Leah's mom carries a loaded gun; Ari, the bullet that'll pierce her daughter. The only thing keeping Susan from shooting, she understands, is the immense hurt the truth will cause Leah. But Susan always has her finger on the trigger.

After a few moments of silence, Ari asks Susan if Leah has said what she'll do tomorrow.

"She's scattering his ashes." Susan removes her red glasses, cleans them on her shirt.

"Where?"

"The Weeks Bridge. Wells proposed to her there."

277

She's shoved Ari's finger into a socket. It's the same place Morgan proposed. Of all places in the world.

Ari hasn't revisited the moment since she gave back the ring, more than two years ago now. On the bridge that afternoon, a weekend visit to Boston for a friend's wedding, they'd been surrounded by the crispest fall day. Morgan had stopped at the middle, leaned on the edge, pointed out the way the breeze kept sweeping fallen leaves in dramatic whirls. It was unlike him to vocalize simple beauty. That morning, they'd walked the city as they used to. On the bridge, he had slipped his hand in her back pocket, looked into her eyes. *Will you marry me?* he'd said, plain as day. *Are you kidding?* she'd asked. *No.* It just came over him, he said. There was no ring, no celebration planned. *I just couldn't stop myself from saying it.* They were twenty-six. They had no idea what was ahead.

"How did he propose?" she asks, even though it will put them all on that bridge together: Ari, Morgan, Wells, Leah. They are already too knotted in Ari's head, her history.

Susan clears her throat. "It was noon on the dot. He wanted to do it in front of a crowd."

Leah still wears her rings. Ari can feel them when Leah squeezes her hand.

"Well," Ari says, "whatever helps Leah move forward is good."

"Yes."

Susan unbuckles Rowan from the chair, plops him on the floor. He throws his arms around her legs, then Ari's. Runs back to his dinosaurs. Ari asks Leah's mom if she'd mind finishing up with Rowan, then goes upstairs, throws clothes in a backpack. She will leave for the hotel. Anything to get the tart taste of now out of her cotton mouth.

∼

Ari doesn't believe in spirits. Yet the next morning she still fears waking up to a text from Krish, asking her to call him. She buries her phone under her pillow, turns over to sleep again until ten thirty.

She gets up to dress, but first stands in front of the bathroom mirror. She looks at her body, thinks of all it has been through. With Morgan, she began as a child: a pinch of baby fat still on her sides, a figure without hips or breasts, far from the shape of a woman. With Wells, she was full: the molehill of her stomach, round of her chest, thighs to hold. With Leah, she is ribs pushing through, all cheekbones and clavicle. Ari doesn't know which body she belongs in.

She checks out of the hotel late, a slap on the wrist from the sour woman at the desk. It's cloudy, the gray usually reserved for New England winters. The time is eleven fifteen, and Ari knows exactly where she's going.

With a massive coffee and chocolate croissant in hand, she arrives at the Weeks Bridge. Leah will be here at noon. Ari is more than certain. She sits by a tree, makes herself small, waits. Listens to her own breath, stares out to the water in a blank-headed haze.

In the same black dress she wore yesterday, Leah approaches the bridge, five minutes to twelve. She stops, rakes both of her hands through her hair. Her shoulders rise, drop, with a full-bodied breath.

The sky dulls the riverbanks. The rushing Charles bleeds midnight blue. On the bridge, Leah drops her head to the rail. Her body shakes as she holds Wells against her chest. She doesn't want to let him go. This is Leah's grand purgatory: stuck on a bridge, with her husband dead but not yet gone. Ari wants to run to her, tell her she isn't alone. But she can't. She shouldn't be here at all.

As Ari stares at Leah, who can't pull back her sobs, it's clear she can't build her own life in Leah's image, in Wells's, in anyone else's. She can't define herself by what did or didn't happen with Morgan, which she has now been doing for years. It's time to leave this bridge, this city. Find herself, free herself, for the first time.

Oblivious people stroll past as Leah shakes with a chill. She opens the urn, tips the ashes into the river. Most of them tumble straight down, but the wind carries a few across her face, into the afternoon, the ether. She stares into the water. She can't believe she's done it. Neither can Ari.

~

An hour and a half later, Ari squirrels away at a café to pick at a Cobb salad and give Leah the head start home. Leah texts her.

Where are you?

Walking around Harvard Square

Come home

Despite the numbness bordering on regret, Ari does, with a desperate urgency. Again, she is needed. She rushes through the front door, hears a noise. It is Leah, screaming with tears. She sprints up the stairs.

In bed, Leah is quivering, choking on sorrow, gasping like she is drowning in the Charles. She shakes against the sheets in only a black-lace bralette and underwear; her skin is a searing flush. Ari crawls behind her, contorts into a crescent moon, wraps Leah into her. Ari holds Leah while she catches her breath, until the chest-shaking gasps stop rattling her chest. She will hold Leah as long as she lets her.

LEAH

Molly is the effortlessly cool, artsy friend Leah always coveted. Her condo in Jamaica Plain has all the character Leah was afraid to put into her own home: a black herringbone kitchen backsplash, exposed ductwork, chic industrial sandblasted floors. The Saturday-morning light spreads across the concrete, almost glowing, as she lets herself in. She takes off Rowan's shoes, lets him bound into the open living room, where Molly's four-year-old daughter is cooking on a play stove.

"You look like shit," Molly calls from the kitchen, where she's pouring Bloody Mary mix into a generous glass of vodka.

"So do you."

Leah finds her way to the kitchen island, slides herself onto one of the clear acrylic barstools. Molly slips a celery stick into each drink.

They do both look like shit. Molly and Jon have just settled their bitter divorce, which dragged out more than a year; without makeup, the stress craters in her burnt-caramel skin are obvious, the bags under her massive brown eyes dusty purple. Leah presents no better in her stained red leggings and the white T-shirt with a hole in the armpit. Her skin still puffy from crying all night in Ari's arms. She runs her hands through her greasy hair, scratches her inflamed scalp, knocks glasses with Molly. Drinks.

"What's the latest?" Leah asks, desperate not to talk about herself.

Molly shakes her head. "The little whore just got some major fellowship, which I'm sure she also slept her way into."

"How do you know?"

"Because I google her six times a day."

It's been five minutes, but Molly's Bloody is halfway gone. She sinks her teeth into the celery so loud Rowan whips his head around. It's glaring how thoroughly she has purged her ex-husband, how quickly. Leah can still picture the huge photo that used to hang near the front door: Molly and Jon in front of snow-covered mountains in Jackson Hole, easily the best wedding she has been to. But now it's vaporized, as has any indication that a man once lived here, or that Molly was ever married or in love. Leah understands why she did it, but it still seems impossible. Even if she had caught Wells and they broke apart because of it, she can't imagine erasing him like that.

Leah stirs her ice with the celery. "Did you see any red flags before you found out? Was Jon acting weird?"

"Yes and no. I mean, you know this, but things got rough after Heart was born. He'd been distant for a while, but he really wasn't around that whole last year we were together. I should have called him on it, but actually accusing him of cheating made me feel crazy. Maybe I just didn't want to believe it, and if I didn't say it aloud, it couldn't be true." She crushes an ice cube in her teeth. "Do you think Wells ever cheated on you?"

Leah startles. She knows she should vomit out every detail, all the evidence that was right there under her nose. But even in front of Molly, who'd understand more than anyone, she's mortified by anyone beyond Ari knowing she was so inadequate her husband needed to seek someone else's body, maybe even their love; so weak that he thought he could pull it off, and did. Sometimes she wants to go down the hole of finding out who the woman was. She's never let herself. Her resolve is what she's proudest of in this whole twisted thing, a crucial linchpin holding her post-Wells life together. What good would it do to know now? It would stop the world she's worked so hard to get spinning again.

"God knows what he took underground with him," Leah says, biting her lip. Rowan pokes her leg, begging for an applesauce pouch. "Fuck," she mutters, tipping her head backward. "I left the bag in the car."

"I got it." Molly waves her off, rummages for a snack in one of the white, high-gloss cabinets.

"It's like my brain is in a jar at the bottom of the river." Leah sighs, jumps off the barstool, drops her elbows on the counter and lets her forehead fall to her palms. "I'm sorry if I've been useless lately. I know I haven't—"

Molly hushes her. "No work talk."

She feels Molly's hand on her shoulder, lifts up her head.

"How did it go?" Molly is talking about the ashes.

"Briefly thought about jumping off the bridge."

"You'd just have ended up wet and pissed off."

"And thus, I did not." Leah traces her finger through a streak of water on the quartz. "It was one of the worst days of my life."

"I'm so sorry, Lee."

Yesterday morning, she reached to the top of the bedroom closet to grab the cardboard box with Wells's plain black urn inside, which she kept near the plastic bin of his clothes she saved for Rowan. She carried it downstairs, zombified. Just stared into space. Her mom waited for her daughter to speak. But she couldn't. The entire day was lodged in her throat. Tight against her chest, the box felt punishingly heavy, like a whole body was inside. Before she left, she held her son until he wouldn't let her, kissed him so many times he pushed her away.

The approach to the middle of the bridge felt unconquerably long, and Leah could not have felt more exposed, like everyone in the world was watching her under the noon sun. As she remembered every detail of a rarely nervous Wells on one knee, the ring catching the sun as he slipped it onto her finger, the proposal felt like a lifetime ago—it literally was, inconceivable. She'd never imagined her life like this, stooped over a railing, tears staining her face. But as she watched the ashes drop to the water, she felt like an idiot, losing her mind over a husband who hadn't prized her the way she had him, hadn't been faithful. She was embarrassed in front of herself. Who knows what else Wells might have kept from her. Yet every moment she held the urn, she wished she had him back.

"Are you doing anything to take care of yourself?" Molly asks, pulling Leah back to attention.

"Hypocrite," she slings back.

"I'm taking Xanax and getting weekly massages. Botox next week."

Molly pours out a second cocktail, asks whether Leah wants a top-up. She asks for water instead. Downs the entire glass.

"Did I tell you Ari's living at the house now?"

Leah isn't sure why she's said it. It just seems impossible to talk about Wells without Ari in the next breath.

"You didn't," Molly says slowly. "Is that a good thing? I can't tell with your face."

Leah tries to relax her jaw, look normal. Heart is still play-cooking for Rowan, handing him a plate of little wooden eggs, strawberries.

"I think so. I'd be a mess without her."

"Can I throw something out there?"

Molly pauses, then frees dust from the corner of one eye, flicks it off her finger. "Heart, baby," she calls over Leah's shoulder. "Can you get that cup off the couch, please? It's going to leak."

Leah watches lines gather around her mouth as she frowns. The creases weren't there before Jon's infidelity. Leah wonders how she herself has aged in ways she's blind to, if other people notice her degeneration, pity her for it.

"Have you considered, I don't know, blowing everything up and starting from scratch?" Molly asks.

"What do you mean?"

"Moving to a new house, maybe, and not having a person directly connected to Wells living in it?"

"I literally couldn't manage that."

"You could," Molly says. She pours Leah another drink anyway. "I've worried for a while that you're still in Wells's web and you're making it impossible to move on."

"I'm not," Leah insists. She purses her lips.

For all that's good in her life, they are all so spun into each other, Molly is right. Ari will always have started as Wells's assistant, entered Leah's home as a subordinate. She knows Leah's history, has her own role in it. But Ari is Ari. She has become the home Leah needs, since her own is still filled with ghosts.

Leah and Molly direct their gazes to their children, who are happily playing in parallel. Heart, now stamping paint-marker dots onto a piece of pink construction paper; Rowan, arranging animal magnets in a precise line on the easel Molly designed. They are two damaged women, which has never felt so obvious. They are products of miserable circumstances they did not choose, reacting the only way they know how. They are both silently asking themselves, each other, how they are meant to heal. What healing even looks like. Whether every choice they've made, both in the Before and the After, has been wrong. They'll never know. Blind faith was what got them in trouble in the first place, yet they still need to trust that, at each juncture, they'll choose the right path. That is, after all, the only way to live.

ARI

While Rowan is on a playdate, Ari walks Clio to the seamstress, picks up the final alterations of her bridesmaid dress. The chiffon drapes shapelessly on the wire hanger, the halter-neck ties dripping low, like strings of pink wax. *I want to see it on you,* Leah says when she gets home, touching the plastic sheath.

After Leah puts Rowan to sleep, she sits in the white chair in the bedroom, watches Ari unwrap the dress, shimmy it on. She knots the ties behind Ari's neck. Ari smooths out the plain front, adjusts the hem brushing her knees. She turns toward Leah, her hands rigid at her sides.

"It's so good," Leah says.

"Is it?" Ari hasn't looked in the mirror yet, nervous about what version of herself she'll see, if she will still recognize her own hands and eyes and flesh.

"Summer did you a solid. You should see the things I've had to wear."

The wedding is eight days out. The bride is a wreck, creating chaos just so she can restore order. Ari can't bear to hear the word *ranunculus* one more time. When she texted Luke to ask whether they need to hire someone to throw Summer's phone in the East River, he said that for the next week, they're just going to have to let his wife-to-be talk at them like a rabid animal. Ari will take the car and drive down to Abbott on Thursday, with the wedding Saturday; she'll stay with Summer's parents for a night, then take a room at the inn.

Leah tells Ari to stand in front of the closet mirror, then comes up behind her, reties the halter, puts her palms to Ari's bare shoulders. Ari does look pretty, she thinks, especially with Leah standing next to her. The weather hasn't been humid, so for the first time in a while, she has let her hair down. It falls in waves, framing her face the way she's always wanted it to. Her skin is smooth, naturally clear, a berry flush across her cheeks. She likes the way the dress sits on her hips, how the slim tie wraps around her shrunken waist.

"Who's in the wedding party?" Leah asks. Her fingertips are soft on Ari's skin.

"Just Summer's sister and me. The whole thing is very small."

Ari watches herself shift in her chrome-framed reflection, pouts her lips.

"And what about the groomsmen?"

She swallows hard. "Luke's brother. And Morgan."

Leah blinks quickly, the flutter of her eyelashes almost impercep-tible. But Ari sees it.

"Oh. When's the last time you saw him?"

"When he walked out the door," she replies, a little too sharp.

"I'm sorry," Leah says, though Ari doesn't know what for.

She grips Ari's shoulders tighter, lets go. Takes a black dress off a hanger, rehangs it exactly the same way.

"He's in a relationship now, anyway," Ari says, though she's not sure if she's talking to Leah or herself.

"You're safe, too."

~

The afternoon before Ari goes to Abbott, Leah comes home so Ari can run errands around Cambridge. She picks up her beige heels from the shoemaker, who removed the scuffs from the toe tips; afterward, she paces around a beauty store for a new mascara, sniffs perfumes until her nose goes numb. She reaches for a seventy-dollar bottle that smells like citrus and jasmine, sprays the faintest bit on the inside of her wrists, rubs them against her neck.

The light has gone golden by the time she walks back to the house from the train, sky stippled with clouds. There's a hum in her chest. Tonight she and Leah will drink a bottle of orange wine and catch up on a show they've fallen behind on. Leah will lay her head on a pillow in Ari's lap.

Arriving home, she tries to open the back door, but the knob won't turn. She jiggles it, but it's stuck. She goes around to the front, fishes in her bag for her key ring. But Leah pulls open the door before Ari can even get her key into the slot.

"I know," Leah says.

They stand face-to-face, brow to brow. They're nearly the same height when Leah has her boots on. Her eyes are shocked open, a blue vein straining in her neck. She's gritting her teeth behind tight lips, shallow breaths in and out of her nose.

"I can't believe I was so stupid." She hasn't blinked. "I'm not this stupid."

"What?" Ari says.

"You're not stupid, either. Do me the courtesy of acting like it."

She blocks the entrance so Ari can't get into the house, unequivocally her home. Inside, she has drawers with her clothes in them, food in the fridge that no one likes but her. They share a dog.

In the doorway, she peers at the key in Ari's hand. Ari wraps it into her fist. Leah draws her eyes back up, taking in every inch of the woman who betrayed her. The only thing Ari wants to do is reach out and touch her cheek.

Her mouth goes dry. All along, Ari's known what she's holding back and the power she wields. But each time, she has told herself the same thing: she and Leah are so heavy, so real, that even the time with Wells is now obscured by the weight of their life together; the days with him have faded into a past separate from both Ari's and Leah's grief, separate from them entirely. Ari knew she couldn't stay like this forever, but whatever was next for her, whoever she met and whatever life she built, Leah would always play a huge part. She was sure they could stand past Morgan, past Wells, past the world itself. Couldn't they?

"Leah," Ari starts, but she doesn't let her get out another word. "When did it start?"

"I don't—"

"You fucking owe me this."

At Leah's side, Clio is crying for Ari to come inside. Ari closes her eyes. Feels like someone is snapping off each rib, one at a time, pulling apart her rib cage like a wishbone. It's only when she refocuses that she sees the pile at the end of the driveway: cardboard wine-case boxes barely closed, full of everything she owns. This is happening, she thinks, consumed by her own inability to speak. None of this was supposed to go this way. Who would sabotage them?

Ari holds her breath for a moment. "It started about a year before he died."

"The second you started working there."

She exhales. "Almost."

Ari feels her face sagging off her skull. Leah stares at her fist again, clamped even harder around the key. She opens it, and the key tumbles to the ground. *Leave it,* Leah's face reads. *Don't touch a thing.*

"It was just you."

"I can't be sure."

"No, Ari. You were the only one. I would have never believed you had this in you." Leah's voice is so taut. She is still blocking the door—her body, so lithe, is now enormous. It could smother Ari. Kill her. "I feel like I'm dreaming. You're literally sick. Something is broken in your brain." Leah's shouting now. "Is this really my life? Haven't I gone through enough?" She puts her fingers to her temples. "Did you fuck him in my bed?"

Ari doesn't dare speak. Her hands shake—the ones that shouldn't have reached for Leah or Wells. She is sick, she thinks. Something is broken in her brain.

"Look at me," Leah whispers. She puts her hand over her mouth, gasps. Sucks reality into her lungs. "What do I have left? I put everything into you."

Leah has a house where she's been living a life of lies, the same place her husband cheated on her, then died. Grief and horror are lodged in the walls, like the cigarette smoke in Morgan's car. Ari knows Leah can't live another day here. She's given her heart and soul, the air she breathes, to a person who never deserved it. Who lied. She already has to explain to her child that he doesn't have a father; now she'll have to tell him that the only other person who treated him like a son is gone, too. She'll have to calm Clio at night when she cries, waiting for someone who will never come back. She trusted another person to rebuild her life, even as she was still denying and screaming and bargaining and crying and accepting. She trusted, period.

Leah shakes. "Do you have anything to say to me?"

"Nothing would be enough."

"Fucking say something. You sat with this for *years*. I literally can't imagine how sociopathic you have to be to live like that."

"I'm not a sociopath, Leah, I swear. I love you."

It's the first time Ari's said it; it's the last chance she'll get. She is saying it for her own sake, because Leah is so far gone.

"The worst part," Leah says, "is I loved you, too."

She stares over Ari's shoulder. She can't look at her. And Ari realizes, in all this, she never looked at herself, either. Not really. Not enough.

"He loved you so much," she whispers.

"Excuse me?"

"I just thought you should know."

Leah's jaw drops. She's so angry her eyes are tearing. She scoops her son into her arms. This incredibly beautiful small person for whom Ari has cared almost as long as his father did. Rowan calls for Ari, which turns all of her remaining bones to dust.

"Don't you dare talk about my marriage," Leah spits. "You know nothing."

As she slams the door on Ari, Rowan is wailing. It already hurts so badly to say goodbye. But what does Ari's pain matter, when Leah is suffering so much more.

~

Four hours later, in stark silence, Ari death-grips the steering wheel of a rental car. Her boxes are piled in the back seat, obscuring her sight out the rearview mirror. She takes the exit for Abbott. But when she hits the end of the ramp, she doesn't know which way to turn. She doesn't have anywhere to go.

After a deep breath, the pickup truck behind her blaring its horn, Ari continues onto Seapath. She passes the old storefronts and rippling flags, the tiny bungalows and white colonials, the soccer fields and elementary school. She stops the car in front of Mead's. Pummels the steering wheel until her fists throb.

MORGAN, AGAIN

ARI

The problem is the processional. It's the morning of the ceremony, and the planner is arranging the wedding party to practice the walk down the aisle, two by two. Standing beside Summer, Ari sees her best friend's face drop. She now realizes what Ari has seen but couldn't say: Ari and Morgan will walk down the aisle together.

"Oh, wait," Summer calls after the wedding planner, too loud. "Maybe we could switch—"

"It's fine," Ari whispers into her ear. "I'll be a big girl."

Over the planner's shoulder, the wind roughs the sapphire water, and eleven o'clock sunlight glints off the waves like gemstones. The horizon is speckled with thumbprint-size sailboats, masts swaying in the urgent breeze. Above the planner, a florist is masterfully interlacing an arch with eucalyptus and pale-pink ranunculus. Summer will stand below it in six hours, white veil pooling behind her, lace crawling her like a vine.

The planner puts her hands to her hips. Summer says, "Never mind." The woman flashes a toothy smile, tells Ella and Luke's brother to stand shoulder to shoulder, link arms. Ari watches her own toes curl in her sandals. She doesn't wait for the directive to stand beside Morgan, just does it. Still, she can't look at him face on, and hasn't since he arrived fifteen minutes ago, duffel in hand, to get to the rehearsal Summer held until he could be there. Ari feels him hook his arm into hers; in her periphery, he stares to the floor. It means everything and nothing at once, to both of them.

Luke stands at the end of the aisle. The planner tells him to take his hands out of his pockets. He complies, embarrassed. Summer is the love of his life; still, he is nervous. The soft pop instrumental she picked begins to play from a speaker, and Ari watches Ella's shoulders shift as she and Connor walk the aisle, taking their places at the front. Ari and Morgan are next. He flexes his arm, pulls her tighter into him. They walk. She wishes she could see Summer's face behind her, but there's no turning back. Ari is here, with the hair on Morgan's arm tickling her skin, for the first time in twenty-five months.

Yesterday, Summer, Luke, and Ari went to the diner; Morgan's work schedule meant he couldn't come in until the morning of the wedding. Rick lit up when he saw them, calling across the packed restaurant, *I can't believe it's tomorrow!* In that corner booth, Summer told Ari that Morgan was coming alone. *He and his girlfriend broke up a little while ago.* Ari's chest tightened. *Why didn't you tell me?* Almost panting. Summer glanced at Luke, then into the two fries she'd stolen from him, the dime-size dot of ketchup on the plate's rim. *I don't know,* she said, pushing away the food. A few minutes later Rick had cleared their dishes as she thanked him, told him she'd see him tomorrow.

They'd walked back to the inn, joined up with Ella and Connor, all sat in Adirondack chairs on the deck by the firepit as the sky broke tangerine over the darkening water. They said very little, instead let the sunset wash over them until it was time for the rehearsal dinner. Occasionally Summer sighed, squinted into the sky.

No one mentioned Leah. Or Ari's boxes in the garage at Summer's parents', the only place she could go after she aimlessly sped away from Boston. Or that she had to come down early, sleep an extra day in the Kemps' guest room, which faces her childhood home, now freshly painted by the loving father of a newborn. Or that her mother decided not to make the trip from Florida, or that Morgan's arrival was imminent. Or that after the wedding, her dad would pick her up and take her back to Vermont to live with him for an undetermined period of time, because he is the only person on earth who understands what she's done, and Ari needs him. Or that her brain is still soup, which was no secret to anyone as she downed her third glass of Leah's favorite Long Island rosé. She still doesn't know why Susan finally fired the gun.

She thinks about how many hours it took Leah to shove clothes into Wells's giant suitcases, gather all Rowan's things and urge Clio into the back seat, drive one hundred miles an hour to Maine. Or maybe Susan was in the house the whole time, making sure Ari didn't step another foot inside. She wonders if anyone has ever hurt as deeply as Leah is hurting right now. For as well as Ari knows her, she will never be able to understand how much, exactly, she has taken from Leah.

Beside the altar, Ari hears the squawk of seagulls, the rush of treetop breeze, Luke's deep voice. In the corner of her eye, she sees Morgan turn his head toward her. She takes so long deciding whether to meet his eyes that he looks away again.

MORGAN

Morgan feels sweat pooling at the small of his back, the starchy white button-down adhered to his skin. It's from running to the cab to O'Hare before the crack of dawn; then working through the flight, even as his stinging eyes could barely focus on the spreadsheet; then sprinting to the next taxi, speeding the hour from Hartford to Abbott, into the rehearsal. But more than anything, it's from threading his arm through Ari's—the static shock of her bare skin, once again. He didn't expect his bones to go to jelly.

He stands next to Luke and Connor, who are helping each other affix their pink ties in the hotel suite. He still holds his own, limp in his palm, even though the ceremony is soon, and eventually he'll have to get out of his own fucking head to be there for his best friend. Except he can't stop thinking about Ari—how she's ignoring his plea to simply look at him. Maybe they've lost the ability to read each other's minds entirely. He should be in Luke's place, he thinks. He should be the one getting married. Ari would have never chosen pink.

"Mead," Luke calls. "Are you stoned?"

Morgan blinks. "No." He stares at the tie.

"Brings out your eyes," Connor ribs, a chef's kiss on his fingertips.

Morgan could kill him.

It was not supposed to be this hard. He thought he could take today because things have improved. Morgan knows how to answer his own questions, finish his sentences. He's learned that the past may linger, but it doesn't have to be part of every decision for the future. He can cook a little better, kiss a little better. Throughout the past two years, he has healed, in part, like he's tried to. Like his therapist and his mom said he would. He is not off the pills, because he's scared of who he might earnestly be without them—it's been so long since he lived nakedly inside himself. Still, he is better, in many ways.

We have to shake ourselves loose. We need to figure out who we are on our own, he'd said. At least on the surface, he got exactly what he wanted.

Yet even though he promised himself he had no expectations when he left Ari behind, life hasn't worked out like he quietly hoped. His mom is gone, which he still can't even come close to processing. His dad is in pain every day, and Morgan is racked with guilt that he moved so far away, left Abbott at all. The job he hoped would give him a fresh start is misery; he's exhausted, spending anxious days in cornfield-covered towns he never knew existed, instructing sinking companies how to fire people to make more money. He struggled for months through a relationship he isn't sure how he fell into, told a perfectly nice woman with pretty eyes whom he didn't love that he did, until she realized he was faking it. He had sex with too many girls whose names he knew for only an hour, fully aware he was sleeping with them just to feel something. He's stuck with the sound of his footsteps against the empty sidewalks late at night. He goes back home by himself to an apartment he hates, in a neighborhood he hates, in a city he hates.

And he is not rid of Ari. It's clear she's rid of him. He's squeezed Luke like a lemon, found out she's been living with someone, though Luke won't say anything else. Often in the stupid hours of the morning, squirreled away in his apartment loft, Morgan has googled Ari's name, to no avail. Begged details of Summer, who pleads the Fifth every time. He doesn't know a single thing about her boyfriend. *Girls get over boys,* Maddie had said that day he'd been so depressed he couldn't do anything but throw a ball against a wall. Morgan knew it was true. He just wasn't prepared for how it would feel.

But beyond her new-and-improved life, Ari has directly proved her detachment from him through her willingness to hurt. She hadn't been there for his mom, for him. He'd sat dumbstruck in those stiff chairs, his eyes closed nearly the entire funeral, quaking in profound emptiness. Too blank to speak when it was his turn, especially when she wasn't there to listen.

The day of the accident, when his dad had run into the living room to tell Morgan what had happened, the first person he'd thought of was Ari. He didn't hear from her even once, and the longer she didn't reach out, the more destitute—the more furious—he'd become. Maybe he was the asshole for thinking she'd show up. Even after all this time, he's still so angry at her absence, so wounded. Ari is the least selfish person he knows, yet she chose that very moment to think only of herself. He can't fathom it and isn't ready to forgive her—especially because he swore she'd be there. Had a feeling in his gut, as he scanned the faces in the room with searing hope and desperation, that she was. He was wrong.

Yet, for as furious as he's been with her, the time he's lost drinking over it, he also hasn't forgotten she *was* there, even if it wasn't the way he needed. After they'd dragged themselves home from the cemetery, the muffler of his father's truck one mile from exploding, Morgan had found the dish on the stove. It wasn't a random sympathy casserole from a neighbor; he'd known exactly what was under the foil, who it was from, well before he saw the note in Ari's handwriting. Morgan hadn't eaten for days. But at midnight, after sitting at the diner with Luke and Summer for two hours, he'd parked himself in front of *SportsCenter* in the basement, lights off, and ate the entire thing. Literally licked the dish. When he finally went back upstairs at two in the morning, he'd realized his mom's pincushion wasn't on the table. He knew where it'd gone. He had, for the first time since his mom died, absolutely lost his shit.

For as badly as she's scarred him, and for as much time and life and death that's passed since they last spoke, Ari is still there, in every tiny fissure. When he feels so alone, the anger breaks, and Morgan still can't think of anything but her. He catches himself wondering what she'd say about choices he makes or opportunities he passes up. He keeps browser tabs open to send her things she'll find funny, then takes days to close them. One morning he woke up speaking to her aloud, only to realize they hadn't lived together in nineteen months. He'd finished his sentence anyway.

Morgan fears he was wrong about almost everything. He was wrong to think he'd become an independent man making his own adult decisions without Ari to point him in the right direction. He was wrong about his resilience, his ability to settle into a new home and a new job, a new woman with a past he'd never been privy to. More than anything, he worries he overcomplicated what he and Ari were meant to be. Why did love have to look like Summer and Luke, especially when they'd never even lived with each other, known what it was like to settle into real life as a pair? Why did they invalidate, strip what he and Ari had, just by existing? Why were he and Ari so eager to cast themselves in the shape of others—what if they'd stepped back, discovered they were enough? What would his life look like then?

They'd be happy, Morgan is sure. Maybe they'd still be in New York, working at soul-sucking companies. Maybe they'd still be barely scraping by. But they would have done it together.

Increasingly, though, Morgan thinks they'd have taken a different turn. They'd be here, back in Abbott. He would be at the diner, making it run more efficiently, learning everything from his dad to ease him into retirement. Ari would be there, too, behind the counter or in the back office in his mom's chair. They'd have a house off Seapath, a two-bedroom bungalow with creaky floorboards, not far from the water. There'd be a reading nook where Ari would spend Sunday mornings with coffee and a chocolate croissant from the bakery next to the pharmacy, while Morgan got the restaurant ready for the post-church rush. Maybe there'd be a baby: a tiny Mead, with matchstick fingers and pruned skin. Kieran, maybe. Kelsey. Kathleen, if Morgan could stomach it. He and Ari would grow into the people they always wanted to be—both separately and together—and Morgan would laugh as he looked back at the time he wrongly thought they needed to be alone to find themselves and their own happiness.

But that's not his life. And it's not hers. With unsteady hands, he loops the tie around his neck, knots it, as a groomsman should. Luke tips back a few drops of whiskey from a silver flask. Morgan says he has to grab his tie clip in his room. What he actually needs is a moment alone before he witnesses his best friend get married.

ARI

From the bridal suite couch, Ari watches Summer's cosmetician spritz setting spray onto her just-enough makeup. Her hair is still in curlers, freshly highlighted red strands wrapped around wide plastic barrels. In the corner, Ella steams a final crease from the gown. It's dizzyingly elegant: strapless and draping like a column, sixteen tiny mother-of-pearl buttons running down the back. When they slip the dress onto her in a few minutes, she'll look brand-new. Mrs. Summer Hallock, born fresh into life.

Ari adjusts her necklace, falling in a V shape, just above her breasts. It's a thin rose-gold bar Summer gave her as a bridesmaid gift, imprinted with the coordinates of the exact spot between their two houses where they met for the first time, lifetimes ago.

The hairstylist says Summer needs to put on her gown before the curlers can come out. Ella says she'll take her white silk robe, but Summer pauses.

"Ella," she says, "can I have a couple minutes with Ari first? Maybe you can just check on the boys, make sure they're running on time."

Once her sister is gone and the beauticians have their heads in their phones, Summer adjusts a curler. She taps her bare foot on the floor twice. Turns to Ari, clears her throat.

"You know I love you so, so much."

Ari's brow furrows. "Yes."

"I have to get something off my chest." Summer clicks her tongue. "I was the one who told Leah."

There's a sharp ringing in Ari's ears. "What are you talking about?"

"I found her number and called her. That's how she knew."

"That's not true," Ari says before she can think. "It can't be true."

"It is. I told her everything."

Ari feels like she's gone blind. In the black, there's only a vision of Leah, slamming the door. Maybe she should have known it was Summer. Her best friend, who was hours away from donning the wedding dress Ari never did; her best friend, who wanted to save Ari from herself. Maybe if she had had the lucidity of mind, could hear past her heartbeat in her ears, she would have detected it in Summer's breathy *I'm sorry* during the fourth panicked call Ari made, still in the driveway. *What do I do?* she'd said, too stunned to fall apart yet. *I'm sorry,* Summer said again. *I have to go.*

"Why?" Ari demands. "What did I ever do to you?"

"I did it for your sake."

"It was for *your* sake. You get some kind of sick satisfaction out of this," she snaps. "You were so jealous that you were willing to send me back to square one, on the day you start your perfect new life? I finally had momentum, Summer. I was finally figuring it out."

"You weren't."

She needs Summer to fight her, just *react*, but there's nothing. Summer's face tightens as she shifts her weight, then squeezes Ari's hand, dangling at her side. There's no slick of remorse in Summer's palm. She walks slowly to the door, pokes out her head, searches for her sister. Ari wraps her fist around the necklace bar, fingers the engraving. All her pores have closed, and she's locked in her body, this corporal entity comprising nothing but fluid and blood. A body she never really lived in.

Summer doesn't look at her as Ella returns and plucks the hanger with the gown from the hook on the back of the door. "Ari needs a minute," she tells her sister, eyes fixed out the window overlooking the water.

Ari dizzily drags her corpse to her room. She needs to breathe. Gather herself. The ancient floorboards bow under her feet. Her heels tap, echo. There's no one else in the hallway, and the world seems inappropriately calm. The disquiet of the New York apartment, the morning after Morgan broke up with her, washes over her. She can't stand the silence, and when she lets herself into her room, she shrieks into a towel. As her throat goes hoarse, as she hacks up a burning lung, she knows she's not actually lashing out at anyone but herself. Maybe she was just trying to do what was best to rebuild herself, to feel what she thought she should without any example to follow. But she is still wildly culpable for the opportunities she passed up and the path she took instead. She shouldn't have had to ruin another human's existence to realize that. She shouldn't have had to tear apart her own.

Ari rubs her damp eyes, black eyeliner and mascara smearing on her fists. Sweat has gathered underneath her breasts and at the small of her back. She controls her breathing, palms to her cheeks. Cleans her face and reapplies her makeup, doing her best to conceal her red, puffy skin. Even though her head is still filled with static, she needs to go back downstairs, smile and cry for the right reasons. Today is not about her.

She fishes her key from her clutch, locks the door.

"I didn't know you were staying next to me."

Morgan's voice jolts her. It's the first time they've met eyes. Neither looks away.

"I didn't know, either."

He freezes outside his open door. This is not how Ari imagined the moment. At Summer's wedding, she expected to be married to this man, sharing that room. In the thick silence and salt air, she aches for him to speak, but he doesn't owe her anything. She's made her bed.

Ari takes a deep breath. "I'm so incredibly sorry, Morgan. I should have been there for you both. I wasn't. I understand if you can't forgive me."

Morgan bites his thumb. She's startled he still looks so much like himself. Almost plain, expected, even in the light-gray suit that makes him look like the groom. Unlike the one from the funeral, it's tailored impeccably: the jacket buttoned perfectly, shoulders not pulling the way most of his clothes do. She knows he hates the tie, tight on his neck like a noose. Even with how she's sure he's changed, grown past her and gotten better, he's still Morgan. She knows him. God, even with the two lives she's lived since him, he still knows her.

He nods. Looks at the floor for a moment before seeing her again. "You look really beautiful," he says.

"Thank you." She smooths out her bridesmaid dress.

He cracks his back with a subtle arch, steps closer to his room, the door still ajar. "Do you want to come inside?"

Ari begins to move, but stops. Who is ever served a moment like this on a gleaming silver platter? Who is offered a true second chance? Who is given such an explicit choice to become someone, or refuse to become it, just like that? No one will ever know where a decision will lead them: always, the path is jagged; often, there is no turning back. What can anyone do except choose, do the best they possibly can, then hope they are right?

Yet even if Ari can't be sure if a gamble will pay off, she's still learned so much in the past two years. She's spent her life defining herself by what didn't happen; casting herself in the shadow of others, letting them eclipse her light. What if she stepped out now, not because she was forced to, but because she wants to? Because she can? What would it mean to reshape desire like that—for herself? There is so much for her. Stories to write on empty pages, to read in books uncracked. Conversations she hasn't yet had in places she hasn't yet gone. Bodies still to touch and love still up for grabs. The entire world, if she wants it. More than ever, she does.

As Morgan lingers in his dark doorway, golden sun filters through the sole window on the other side of the hallway, a godlike sheen illuminating the floating dust. The beams bisect Ari's body. She fills her lungs. Finally moves into the light.

ACKNOWLEDGMENTS

Every time I pick up a book, I always turn to the acknowledgments first—I've long known it takes a universe before a reader can see a single word. To say it's bizarre that it's my turn is the world's most profound understatement. I am so grateful these people are in my orbit, and even more grateful I get to thank them.

Danya Kukafka is a once-in-a-lifetime agent, friend, and human, whom I would follow off the edge of the earth.

Carmen Johnson saw into the heart of this story, from day one—often before I did—and led me with care, trust, and vision to make this all it could be on the page.

The teams at Trellis Literary Management and Little A made my dreams come true, over and over again. Emily Mahon and Tree Abraham created a cover that floors me like it's the first time, every time. Megan McKeever's careful eyes sharpened this.

Orly Greenberg at UTA had faith from the start. Courtney Saladino and Isabel Sherman at FilmNation gave me a life-changing opportunity.

Caroline Goldstein is my guardian angel. Ryan Boyle is always there for it. Anna Deem knows mics are for both singing *and* swinging. Dr. Jincy Thankachen's eyes were invaluable. Leah Carroll, Caitlin Brennan Donefer, Simon Frantz, Richard Gray, JoJo Lee, Jenny Halper, Hetal Joshi, and Alyssa Martino have taught me, celebrated with me, reality-checked me, and propped me up at various points throughout the past decade-plus of writing and life.

My cohorts at the Yale Writers' Workshop, who were the first to meet Ari and Morgan, set the stage *for craft out the ass* and the *rare magic moments*. Kirsten Bakis is a marvel. Sterling Library is a sanctuary, where many pages were written, painstakingly pulled apart, and stitched into something better.

SH and KM are always in my corner.

Carol O'Connor is my favorite cheerleader. Joann and Paul Turits, I love you. Grandma Bea, I think you know this happened, somehow.

Colin May is my heart. Avery Bones is my soulmate. Brian O'Connor is the one.

ABOUT THE AUTHOR

Photo © 2024 Sylvie Rosokoff

Meredith Turits's writing and interviews have appeared in publications including *Vanity Fair*, *ELLE*, BBC.com, *Electric Literature*, the *Paris Review Daily*, and *Bustle*, where she was a founding editor. She graduated from Tufts University and attended the Yale Writers' Workshop. She lives in Connecticut. For more information, visit www.meredithturits.com.